BISCUITS and GRAVY

**Look for these exciting Western series
from bestselling authors
William W. Johnstone and J.A. Johnstone**

Smoke Jensen: The Last Mountain Man
Preacher: The First Mountain Man
Luke Jensen: Bounty Hunter
Those Jensen Boys!
The Jensen Brand
MacCallister
The Red Ryan Westerns
Perley Gates
Have Brides, Will Travel
Will Tanner: Deputy U.S. Marshal
Shotgun Johnny
The Chuckwagon Trail
The Jackals
The Slash and Pecos Westerns
The Texas Moonshiners
Stoneface Finnegan Westerns
Ben Savage: Saloon Ranger
The Buck Trammel Westerns
The Death and Texas Westerns
The Hunter Buchanon Westerns

WILLIAM W. JOHNSTONE

AND J.A. JOHNSTONE

BISCUITS and GRAVY

A CHUCKWAGON TRAIL WESTERN

PINNACLE BOOKS
Kensington Publishing Corp.
www.kensingtonbooks.com

Chapter 1

Dewey Mackenzie hadn't seen what prompted the slap. But he'd heard the sharp crack of it landing and then, when he looked around, he saw all too plain what was about to happen next—the cocked fist of the hombre who'd been on the receiving end drawing back and getting ready to lash out in response.

Problem was, the target for this intended punch was a young, pretty gal. That was something Mac could hardly allow. Not if he could help it.

He knew better than to stick his nose in other folks' business, especially when it was taking place in a public establishment in a town where he was a freshly arrived stranger. But he also knew there were exceptions to every rule, and a grown man getting ready to slam his fist into a woman, even if she hadn't been such a doggone pretty one, surely fell into that category.

So, before the slapped cowpoke hurled his fist forward, Mac reached out, clamping the man's wrist in a tight grip, and gave the arm a hard yank in the opposite direction.

Not quite six feet in height and still with a trace of boyishness to his clean-shaven features, in spite of being darkened and sharply etched by days in the sun and wind, Mac had a naturally muscular build, made even harder and more solid by the work he'd been doing during all those hours out in the elements. When he grabbed hold of something—or someone—it stayed grabbed hold of until he chose to let go.

The cowpoke—a lanky specimen, average in height and build, thirty or so, with furry reddish sideburns running down either side of his narrow face—was pulled off balance and staggered. Turning half around, he faced Mac with a look of surprise and rage and demanded, "What are you doing?"

Mac met and held the man's glare for two or three tense heartbeats, then shoved his arm down and away before answering, "What I'm doing, mister, is saving you from making a big mistake."

The activity and murmur of voices that had been taking place throughout the rest of the cramped, low-ceilinged, moderately crowded Irish Jig Saloon now ground to a halt. The portly old gent playing a squeeze box over in one corner stopped, too, and his instrument went quiet after gasping out a final sour note. All eyes came to rest on Mac and the man with the furry sideburns. The slap from the barmaid had drawn only minimal interest. But this confrontation, to the eyes of the onlookers, apparently had the makings of something not to be missed.

Furry Sideburns turned the rest of the way around to

face Mac, both of his hands now balling into fists. Lips peeled back to show gritted teeth, he said, "Well, maybe you think you fixed one mistake, you stinking meddler, but I guarantee you made an even bigger one for yourself!"

One of the other two men still seated at the table Furry Sideburns had risen up from said, "Go get him, Jerry Lee!"

Jerry Lee raised his fists and began waving them in small circles, like he thought he was some kind of boxer. "Since you ain't packing no gun, Mr. Nosy, I'm gonna have to teach you a lesson the hard way. And when I'm done, I'll leave enough of you to be able to look up and *still* see me give that snooty gal what she's got coming, too!"

Mac adjusted his weight, hands hanging loose and ready at his sides, and stood waiting. In truth, he *was* packing a gun—an old Smith & Wesson Model 3, .44 caliber, that he kept tucked in the waistband of his trousers rather than in a side holster. A gift from his late father, which, at present, was hidden by the short-waisted jacket he was wearing.

All things considered, that was just as well. While Mac had grown fairly proficient with the gun in recent years, he was never eager to reach for it and this occasion hardly seemed to warrant doing so. At least not yet.

From behind the bar, the elderly apron who was barely tall enough for his scrawny neck and liver-spotted bald head to poke above the level of the hardwood did his best to sound authoritative.

"You gents knock it off. Either that, or take it outside," he hollered. "You know what Farrell will do if he walks in on this!"

Hearing the warning, Jerry Lee snarled, "You keep your beak out of this, Shorty—and to blazes with Farrell!"

And then he charged at Mac.

Mac had been waiting for that. Instead of holding still for the other man's rush, he agilely stepped aside and at the same time swept an empty chair from the unoccupied card table he'd been standing next to directly into the path of the oncoming Jerry Lee. The latter immediately barked his shins on the sturdy chair, resulting in him issuing a painful yelp, and then got his legs tangled up in it as his wild swing at Mac pulled him forward and off balance. Jerry Lee belly-flopped across the toppled chair, taking hard jabs from the sharp wooden edges to his stomach and ribs before rolling off into an awkward sprawl on the sawdust-littered floor.

Some onlookers winced at this painful collapse. A few others chuckled at the ungainliness of it.

Jerry Lee roared in pain and heightened rage as he scrambled to get to his hands and knees so he could then rise to a standing position. But before he could do that, Mac took a hurried step around behind him, braced himself, then leaned over to haul Jerry Lee up to his knees. From there, Mac quickly slipped his left arm under the cowboy's chin, clamping the throat in the crook of his arm.

At the same time, he once again locked Jerry Lee's right wrist in the grip of his own right hand, then wrenched the arm back and up between the struggling cowpoke's shoulder blades.

"All right now, Jerry Lee," Mac rasped with his mouth close to the man's ear, "I think you'd better calm down before somebody gets hurt."

"There's hurtin' to be done, right enough," Jerry Lee managed to squawk out, even with the lock on his throat. "And you're the one gonna be gettin' a hard dose of it!"

"That's the wrong answer, you stubborn galoot," Mac told him. He squeezed the throat tighter and cranked the arm up even higher. "Now you'd best think about changing your mind and doing it quick; otherwise I might decide to start ramming your head against the side of that bar over yonder until you're ready to take a different notion about things."

Jerry Lee tried to issue another angry retort, but this time all that came out was a gurgling sound and some spit bubbles leaking from the corners of his mouth.

"Don't worry, Jerry Lee—we got your back!"

These words, accompanied by the sound of chair legs suddenly scraping on the floor and the clump of boot heels also in hurried movement, caused Mac to look around. Sure enough, the two men who'd been seated at the table with Jerry Lee were shoving to their feet and starting to surge forward.

Mac didn't wait for them to get very far on their intended rescue mission. He immediately hauled Jerry Lee the rest of the way up, whirled him around, and gave him a hard shove that sent him staggering with wind-milling arms straight into his two pals.

One of the would-be rescuers, a plumpish number with a round face, oversized nose, and eyes set too close under shaggy black brows, was directly in the path of the propelled Jerry Lee. He put his hands up, as if to catch his friend, but Jerry Lee's momentum was too much to stop. Round Face was staggered in reverse until the back of his legs hit the edge of the chair seat he'd just vacated, forcing him to suddenly sit down again with Jerry Lee more or less flopping onto his lap.

While this was taking place, the remaining hombre from the table—lean and cat-like, with heavy-lidded eyes, a surly curl to his mouth, and slicked-back black hair complete with another set of thick sideburns—momentarily froze. But then, when he broke into motion once again, it came in a long forward stride with his right hand reaching down to hover claw-like over the black-handled Colt riding in a tie-down holster on his right hip.

Mac swore under his breath. It looked like avoiding gunplay wasn't going to be possible after all.

Yet even as the fingers of his own right hand were getting ready to dive under the flap of his jacket, the pretty barmaid who'd played a part in setting this whole works in motion suddenly stepped forward to help bring it to a halt. She did this by raising the partially poured pitcher of beer she had evidently just delivered to the table and crashing it down on the back of Surly Mouth's head before his fingers had a chance to close on the grips of his Colt.

Chapter 2

Just as Surly Mouth was crumpling to the floor, a dark-haired, middle-aged man dressed in a corduroy jacket worn over a brocade vest came striding purposefully through the Irish Jig's front door. As he pushed apart the batwings and passed between them, his expression was open, amiable. But a single sweep of his eyes, making an appraisal of the scene he was entering into, quickly brought a scowl to his countenance.

"What in blazes is going on here?" he demanded to know.

Then his gaze came to rest on Jerry Lee, struggling to shove up out of Round Face's lap, and beyond that clumsily flailing pair the sprawled form of Surly Mouth. The scowl intensified. "You three chowderheads . . . again. I might have known."

"Now you hold on a doggone minute, Farrell," huffed

Jerry Lee, finally getting untangled from Round Face and standing upright. "You ain't gonna lay this on us, not this time. No, sir. We was the ones *attacked*, and all we was doing was defending ourselves."

"*You* were attacked?" Skepticism rang sharp in Farrell's tone. "By who?"

"By that high-minded wildcat of a barmaid you hired, that's who." Jerry Lee thrust a finger in the direction of the pretty, beer pitcher–wielding blonde standing on the other side of the table. "First, she hauled off and walloped me across the face for no good reason. Then, as you can see, she took that beer pitcher and banged it down on the back of poor Edsel's head! And if that wasn't enough, this slippery stranger"—a jab of his thumb to indicate Mac— "stuck his nose in and nailed me with a sucker punch from behind!"

Farrell listened, the look on his face remaining every bit as skeptical as his tone had been. "A lick of truth in any of that, Becky?" he asked the blonde as soon as Jerry Lee's spiel ended.

Becky thrust out her chin defiantly and answered. "You bet there is. Yes, I slapped that pig Jerry Lee's face. And yes, I also clobbered Edsel with this beer pitcher when he was going for his gun to use on that unarmed stranger. The stranger, by the way, never sucker-punched Jerry Lee. He just grabbed his arm and gave him a shove after Jerry Lee was getting ready to club me with his fist for slapping him. Would you like to know the reason for the slap that started it all?"

"I think I can make a pretty good guess," Farrell said through clenched teeth.

"You can't hold that against a fella," Jerry Lee was

quick to protest. "Any gal who takes a job parading herself around in a saloon is bound to get grabbed a little bit. And don't tell me she don't know it from the start. She not only has to know it, truth to tell she's probably wanting—"

"Shut your dirty mouth!" Farrell cut him off, taking a step forward.

Jerry Lee backpedaled so hurriedly he almost tripped and landed in Round Face's lap again. He held up one hand, palm out. "Now you hold off with that blasted Irish temper of yours, Farrell! That ain't no way to treat steady, paying customers, is it?"

"Whether it is or isn't no longer applies to you three," Farrell told him, his voice strained by the anger he was barely managing to hold in check. "Effective immediately, you are no longer customers here. None of you are welcome in this establishment ever again. Now, collect your change from the table, pick up your friend off the floor, and the lot of you clear out before I take a bung starter from behind the bar and hurry your sorry butts along!"

"You'll be sorry if you try to keep us run out," warned Jerry Lee. "Oscar Harcourt is bound to hear of it, and I can guarantee he won't like it one bit!"

Farrell replied, "You let me worry about that. Tell Oscar to come around any time he wants—I'll be glad to tell him the same thing. In the meantime, clear out of my sight before I lose my patience with you!"

In just a handful of minutes, the three were slinking out the door, Jerry Lee and Round Face dragging their partner with his arms hung over their shoulders. In the doorway, Jerry Lee paused for a moment, casting a bale-

ful glance over his shoulder as if he intended to say something more. But then, facing Farrell's glare, he thought
better of it and went ahead on out.

Once the trio was gone, Farrell turned and again swept
the room with his eyes. Swinging one arm in a broad gesture, he announced, "Show's over, gents. Go on about
your business, nothing more to see here. Especially not
from those three louts . . . who won't be returning, I assure you."

The other patrons scattered around the room returned
obligingly to the conversations, card games, and, in a couple of cases, solitary drinking that had been occupying
them before the ruckus broke out. A nod from Farrell also
started the accordion player squeezing out his music once
more.

With the strains of a lilting Irish tune drifting through
the air, Farrell then turned his attention to Mac, who had
been standing quietly by, watching and listening. Becky,
the pretty blond barmaid, set down her beer pitcher and
drifted over to stand with them.

Farrell's expression was again quite amiable, a touch
of a smile even curving his wide, expressive mouth.
"Now then," he said, his eyes dancing back and forth between Mac and Becky, "are the pair of you done wreak-
ing havoc in my otherwise peaceful establishment, at
least for the balance of the evening?"

Becky's mouth dropped open. "Eamon! You know better than that. I just got done telling you—"

Farrell held up a hand, stopping her. "Of course you
did," he said with a chuckle. "I was just teasing you a bit.
You think I don't know that any trouble involving those
three scoundrels surely wasn't your fault? My only regret

is that you feel the need to be here at all, where exposure to their kind of trash is bound to—"

Now it was Becky who cut him off. "We've been all through that. I need this job, and you know all the reasons why. You agreed to give me the chance and you also know that I've done well at it. I was fully aware from the beginning there would be a certain amount of rough conduct and I'm able to handle most of it without ever causing a scene. But tonight, that sleazy Jerry Lee and his pawing hands . . ."

"You don't have to go into any further detail," Farrell told her. "In fact, if you tell me too much more, I may have to go hunt down that piece of vermin and finish what our new friend here"—a flick of his eyes to Mac—"was luckily on hand to deliver a piece of."

"Number one, I don't want you hunting down Jerry Lee and making things worse," said Becky. Then, bringing her lovely blue eyes also to rest on Mac, she added, "But number two, I certainly am grateful that this stranger *was* on hand to do what he did. Hadn't been for him, I hate to think what Jerry Lee's fist was getting ready to do to me."

Eyes probing into Mac's, Farrell said, "You can certainly add my gratitude to the list. But before going any further, I think it's time to dispense with this 'stranger' business. Will you be so kind as to share your name with us, sir?"

With an easy nod, Mac replied, "It's Mackenzie. Dewey Mackenzie. Most folks just call me Mac."

Farrell promptly extended his hand. "Mac it is, then. I, in turn, am Eamon Farrell. In case you haven't already figured it out, I am the owner and proprietor of our modest surroundings, the Irish Jig Saloon."

As the two men shook, Farrell tilted his head toward Becky, adding, "And this fair princess, to whose rescue you came, is Becky Lewis."

"Pleased to meet the both of you," Mac said, releasing Farrell's hand and pinching his hat to Becky. "Far as that rescue business, no need to make more of it than it was. Mostly, I just happened to be in the right place at the right time. Ain't my way to butt into other folks' affairs, but standing by and letting a man take a punch at a woman . . . well, that ain't my way neither."

"I'd say it sounds like you have some pretty good ways," declared Farrell.

"And I say, again, how very grateful I am that you happened to be in the right place at the right time," said Becky.

Mac felt himself blushing some at her focus on him. Up close, she was even prettier than he'd first realized. Not more than a couple years past twenty, with finely chiseled facial features and those striking blue eyes, all framed by pale gold hair falling loosely to her shoulders. Clad in a simple white blouse and a flaring maroon skirt that reached to midcalf, she was no more than five-two in height, trim but sturdy looking, and very appealingly curved in all the right places.

"Inasmuch as you are present here in a saloon, Mac, I presume you came inclined toward having a drink," Farrell allowed. "That being the case, I'd be honored to buy you one and invite you to join me at one of the tables."

"Sounds good to me," Mac told him. "A cold beer is what I had in mind when I came in."

"You two have a seat," Becky said. "I'll bring a pitcher."

"That's not necessary," Farrell countered. "You need to head for home. It's getting on toward evening and you have a ways to go before darkness settles in."

Becky shook her head. "Nonsense. I've ridden the trail between here and home dozens of times. I could do it with my eyes closed, plus my horse knows the way as well as I do. Besides, before I go I've still got a mess to clean up where I wasted that half-full pitcher of beer on the head of Edsel Purdy."

"All things considered, it was far from wasted," Farrell corrected her. Then, sighing fatalistically, he rolled his eyes over at Mac and said, "But I recognize when an argument is hopeless. Let's have a seat, Mac, and I'll join you in putting away some of that beer after the young lady fetches us a pitcher, as she insists on doing."

Chapter 3

Mac ended up spending an enjoyable two hours in the Irish Jig Saloon. Eamon Farrell proved an entertaining and friendly host, not just to Mac but to all of his patrons—except, as demonstrated, to rowdies like the trio who had bothered Becky.

For an all-too-short a time, after she'd served their pitcher and cleaned up the mess left at the other table, Becky had sat visiting with Mac and Farrell at their table. She was equally friendly and charming and Mac hated to see her leave. But, given the explanation of there being a distance for her to cover in order to make it home before it got too dark, he certainly understood. He found himself wishing for some sort of opening to offer to escort her, but none presented itself without him seeming overly bold.

After Becky had gone, the atmosphere in the Irish Jig

remained very friendly and relaxed. Much of this was due
to the soft, soothing Irish tunes being pumped out by
Feeney, the accordion player. Mac was introduced to a
few of the other patrons, none of whose names he really
remembered other than Feeney and Shorty, the appropri-
ately dubbed sawed-off bartender who'd made an inef-
fective attempt to back down Jerry Lee.

In the course of things, Mac revealed how he was on
the drift, working his way in no particular hurry across
the belly of Montana, aiming eventually to swing southwest for California. He told how, not quite a week ago,
back near Miles City, he'd been on a cattle drive with the
Rafter B outfit up out of Texas and was now once again
on nobody's schedule but his own.

What Mac didn't reveal—the dark secret he carried
deep inside and shared with no one—was the sequence of
events that had taken place going on three years past in
distant New Orleans. Events that had set him on the unlikely course of joining a series of cattle drives as he
drifted . . . or, to be more exact, as he kept on the run.

On the run from the murder frame that cost him the
woman he once thought he loved, made him a fugitive
from lawmen thankfully hampered by jurisdictions while,
most haunting of all, making him a wanted man to the
wide-ranging small army of bounty hunters and paid detectives hired by that scoundrel Pierre Leclerc, the scheming murderer whose actual deeds Mac had gotten blamed
for.

Since Leclerc had parlayed this frame-up into also
winning Mac's former fiancée for himself and, through
her, getting his hands on her family's considerable wealth
and high standing, his obsession to remove Mac as the
only person who could possibly undermine all he had

achieved kept the Frenchman driven to see Mac hunted down and killed.

More than once, even amidst those sprawling cattle drives, Leclerc's hirelings had come too close for comfort. Only luck, Mac's own toughness and survival instincts he'd been forced to develop rapidly along the way, and the aid of some friends willing to not ask too many questions had allowed Mac to keep his hide.

On the recent drive into Montana with the Rafter B outfit, Mac had finally been able to shake the feeling of Leclerc's hired killers always being close, ready to make yet another attempt at nabbing him. For the first time in months he was able to relax somewhat and feel as if he might truly be in the clear. Forging on to California, though, was still what he figured it would take to solidify that feeling once and for all.

As Mac opened up to a limited degree about himself, he in turn got a quick sketch from Farrell about various situations in and around Harcourt City, this place he'd chosen for a night's stopover.

"The name Harcourt . . . ," Mac said, remembering. "Didn't Jerry Lee spout something about an 'Oscar Harcourt' when you were running him and his pals out of here?"

"Indeed he did," Farrell confirmed. "And yes, that would be the same gent our little hamlet is named for. Well, his father, to be completely accurate; he was the one who founded this settlement. A fine, fair, and decent man he was, by all reports. Oscar, his only offspring, is a bit more . . . er, heavy handed, you might say."

"No love lost between you two, I take it?"

"Not one red hair's worth." Farrell's expression soured.

"Fair to say, there's not a great deal of love anywhere around that flows *toward* Oscar—except his own for himself, that is, and the kind of allegiance he demands from the poor souls he has cornered into being beholden to him. Sad to say, there are too many of those."

"And Jerry Lee and his pals are associated with him in some way?"

"Jerry Lee Lawton, Roy Orton, Edsel Purdy." Farrell grunted the names disdainfully. "You know which one was Jerry Lee. Orton was the moon-faced one who ended up with Jerry Lee in his lap. And Edsel is the would-be gunny Becky put to sleep with a beer pitcher for a while. Three lowlifes who would do anything but an honest day's work for money. Which means Oscar Harcourt can buy them cheap to do various odd jobs for him, mostly on the dirty side."

Mac frowned. "So you butting heads with his hired rats ain't likely to improve your own dealings with Harcourt." It wasn't a question.

"Wouldn't have it any other way. The day I do anything that *pleases* Oscar Harcourt, that's the day I'll start worrying," Farrell said with a wide grin.

"Reckon that speaks well enough for you. You're obviously a fella who can take care of himself." Mac took a sip of his beer, then added, "But what about the gal Becky? Any chance those three toads might single her out for some kind of payback?"

Farrell's grin instantly vanished and was replaced by a grimace. "Anything along those lines would be the darkest—and last—day of their miserable lives. And I say that for more than just myself. The Lewises are well liked and respected and have already had more than their share of bad luck. Any harm done to Becky by Harcourt's thugs would be met, I'm sure, by an outcry that would rattle even Oscar and the lofty perch he sees himself seated on."

Mac drank some more beer and then, trying to make it sound like nothing more than casual curiosity, said, "When you say 'the Lewises' . . . does that mean Becky has a husband to help look after her?"

Now a knowing smile came to Farrell's face, recognizing the fact that any red-blooded male who came in contact with lovely Becky—even a stranger just passing through—couldn't help but want to know a little more about her.

"No, unlikely as it may seem," he replied, "no one has yet laid claim to that fine lass. A couple of years back, there was a young cowboy who rode for her father's brand—the Standing L. He and Becky fell very much in love with one another and every indication was that they would get married someday. Then, in the kind of freak accident that sometimes happens in ranch work, a bronc that Tim and some other cowboys were trying to gentle— Tim, that was the name of the young cowboy, Tim Chapple—bucked and kicked with unexpected wildness and struck Tim a vicious blow to the head with one of its rear hooves. The lad was dead before he ever hit the ground."

"That's a mighty tough break," Mac murmured. "The kind of thing you hear about but never figure will really happen."

"A tough break indeed. For Tim . . . and for Becky, too. Needless to say, she was heartbroken. Since then, no other fellow has stirred any feelings in her, and there surely have been many who tried."

Farrell took a moment to tip up his own mug. Lowering it, he went on, "Shortly after the loss of Tim, Becky's mother took ill over the following winter and died before spring. At the start of summer, her father suffered a stroke—actually his own bout of heartbreak, many claimed, over losing his wife of almost thirty years. He lingered a few weeks, never really coming out of it, and then he was gone, too. . . ."

Farrell's voice trailed off into a moment of solemn silence.

"All that, in the space of less than a year," he said as he resumed the tale. "It left Becky and her brother, Marcus, to try and keep the Standing L going on their own. And though they're both hard workers and savvy to the ways of running a ranch, a few more doses of hard luck in the form of a particularly harsh winter and a couple rounds of cattle fever that significantly diminished their herd each time and . . . well, it's been a struggle for them. But they're both stubborn and fiercely bent on seeing it through, no matter what it takes. Becky taking a part-time job here to earn some extra income, serving the lunch-hour rush and on through the afternoon, is one such example."

"You gotta admire folks like that," Mac stated. "And if there's any justice in this old world, you gotta hope that, at least some of the time, their kind will win out in the end."

Farrell sighed. "I certainly go along with the admiring and hoping, Mac. But this old world, as you call it, can be relentlessly tough, especially on certain people it sometimes appears to single out. For them, it seems to dish out wave after wave of hard breaks, while any sign of balance, or justice, if you will, comes far less frequently."

After their conversation took that rather gloomy turn, Mac and Farrell lightened things up by switching to other subjects. A few of the other patrons joined in and Feeney helped by squeezing out some jauntier tunes. A couple he even sang along with, demonstrating a rich tenor voice. One song in particular, something called "Wild Colonial Boy," seemed to be a favorite with the crowd, and several of those present—including Farrell, showing a pretty good voice of his own—joined in.

Mac was truly reluctant to leave such a pleasant gathering. But since his whole reason for stopping at Harcourt City, after many days on the trail, was to restock his supplies and then treat himself to a hot bath and some barbering, a good sit-down meal, and a long night's sleep in a soft bed, he wasn't willing to alter those plans too much. He'd already taken care of the resupplying, the bath and barbering, and a fine meal at a nearby café, and a hotel room complete with soft bed was paid for and waiting.

Now, after deciding that scrubbing and scraping the days and miles of trail dust off his outside ought to be augmented by also rinsing some of the same out of his insides with this stop at the Irish Jig, that additional detail, too, was taken care of. Which left getting some sleep in a soft bed the only thing still unaccomplished, and Mac chose not to let that go begging any longer.

So, bidding a fond farewell to Farrell, Feeney, Shorty, and the others, he took his leave from the saloon and headed for the hotel where he'd earlier secured a room. Outside, the evening air was starting to cool off, although it was still pleasant enough for now. It was full dark, no breeze to speak of.

A handful of well-placed street lamps provided some illumination up and down the town's main street. A block

farther down, on the opposite side, some light and rau-
cous laughter poured out of an establishment that Mac
took for another saloon. Up the street in the direction he
was headed, the hotel building was also well lighted. Otherwise, all of the other businesses on the street were closed
at this hour.

As he walked along, Mac couldn't help noting that the
storefronts all appeared neat and tidy and the range of ser-
vices they offered seemed pretty complete. This matched
his impression upon arriving in the daylight hours. If he
hadn't heard some of the things Farrell reported about the
heavy-handed way Oscar Harcourt ran much of what
took place here in his namesake town, Mac would have
judged it to be a fine example of a young, growing community, probably a good place to live.

At the hotel, there was no clerk present behind the
front desk. This didn't matter to Mac, since he already
had his key, so he proceeded on up the stairs to his room
just two doors down from the landing.

Unlocking and opening the door, he found himself
gazing into a darkened space with dense shadows crowding in on either side. Enough illumination spilled in
around him from the lanterns lining the short, second-
floor hallway, however, for Mac to easily spot the room's
own coal oil lantern, perched on a small, bedside stand.
Leaving the door open long enough to light his way until
he went over and got that lantern going, Mac fished for
some oilskin-wrapped matches in the watch pocket of his
jeans and stepped forward.

A step was all he managed before the first blow
landed. From the shadows off to his left, somebody lashed
out with a heavy, rounded club of some sort and slammed

it against the side of Mac's head just behind the ear. His knees immediately buckled and he took another half step, a faltering one, slightly to his right.

Another somebody was waiting there with a balled fist that drove deep into his stomach. Mac buckled the rest of the way and dropped to his knees as a great gush of spit-laced air spewed out of him. An explosion of pain from his head was pulsing down through his whole body and now he felt as if he'd been broken in half. Mac squeezed his eyes shut tight but behind the closed lids pinwheels of brightly colored light spun and flashed.

A vaguely familiar voice penetrated through the painful murk in his head, saying, "Somebody light that lantern and then close the door. I want to be able to see so we can be sure to do a good job on this meddler!"

Mac felt rage now as he tried to fight back against the pain. He reached out with one hand, groping blindly in an attempt to grab somebody—or at least some *thing* he could maybe use to pull himself back to his feet.

All this accomplished was causing someone to not wait for better lighting. Another blow, coming from the toe of a boot this time, drilled viciously into his ribs and knocked him flat to the floor.

After that, no matter how many lanterns anybody lighted, everything stayed dark as Mac's eyes remained reflexively clamped shut against the repeated jolts of pain that came from a seemingly endless barrage of more kicks and clubbing blows . . . until mere dark became the deeper black of unconsciousness.

Chapter 4

Mac awoke to an awareness of two things. One, he'd finally made it into the soft bed he had been longing for. Two, whatever comfort that might have otherwise provided was lopsidedly offset by the degree of throbbing pain now encasing his body from head to toe.

The words of the man who'd said he wanted to "do a good job" on Mac suddenly rushed to mind, stirring a wave of bitter anger. But even that wasn't enough, Mac realized, to push him past the damage from the subsequent beating. Damage, he could tell, that was going to hold him in check for a while before he could pay somebody back for that "good job."

Slowly, Mac opened his eyes. Bright sunlight stabbed deep into his skull and made him immediately want to close them again. Only the brief glimpse of the people gathered at his bedside made him resist doing so. After he was able to focus his vision clearer still, he could confirm the identities of some who stood looking down at him.

Eamon Farrell was there, his expression appearing torn between concern and anger. Beside him was a man Mac had never seen before, a plump individual of fifty or so with a fleshy pink face and kind eyes peering through the lenses of a pair of spectacles perched near the tip of a long nose that ended in a grape-sized knob.

Next to that man was the sight that had most caused Mac to want to keep his eyes open—Becky Lewis gazing down at him with a look of genuine concern and what he hoped he read as a trace of fondness.

"There now. That's a good sign," said the pink-faced man. "His eyes appear clear and alert."

"Do you hear that, lad?" said Farrell, addressing Mac directly. "Are you *feeling* somewhat alert? Do you understand what's going on here?"

Mac frowned. "This is my hotel room, isn't it? I . . . What time is it?"

"It's shortly past noon. You've been out for that long," Farrell told him. "You remember me, remember being in my saloon last night, don't you? The Irish Jig?"

Mac moved his mouth in what he aimed to be a wry smile. "We didn't put away *that* much beer, Eamon. Of course I remember. But then I came here and . . ."

"You came here and got the stuffing beat out of you . . . in official medical terms, that is," the pink-faced man finished for him.

"Mac, this is Dr. Wheeler," Becky spoke up. "He's been treating the injuries you suffered."

"From the feel of it," said Mac, "I guess I kept you kinda busy, Doc."

"Indeed you did," agreed Wheeler. "Tell me if any of this sounds or feels familiar. Cracked, possibly broken, ribs on both sides; a score and more abrasions and contusions; numerous deep bone bruises, though no additional fractures that I can tell at this time; lacerations requiring a total of sixteen stitches; and last but by no means least, certainly a concussion. Considering the blows you clearly took to the head and face, how you managed to escape either a broken jaw or nose is really quite amazing. Equaled almost by the fact that, after beating you so badly, your assailants didn't even bother to rob you."

"Don't sound so disappointed, Doc," Mac half groaned. "I'm sorry I'm laying here only as busted up as if I'd been rolled over by all four wheels of an ore wagon, and not picked clean of every cent to boot."

"Oh, that's all right," Wheeler replied wistfully. "Like you said, you kept me plenty busy as it was. The lack of you also being robbed adds a puzzlement, a rather intriguing mystery to the whole matter."

"I don't think there's much of a mystery to it," said Farrell, his tone stern. "Just tell us who did this to you, Mac. It had to be more than one attacker. Was it the three lowlifes you tangled with in my saloon last night?"

"Now wait a minute. That's where I come in. I'll do the question asking around here," said a new voice. Another presence in the room, a man Mac hadn't noticed before, moved forward and wedged himself in between Farrell and Wheeler. He was tall and lanky, with a weak chin, and heavy-lidded eyes that nevertheless conveyed a certain intensity.

"My name's Brimball. Miles Brimball," he announced to Mac. "I'm the sheriff here in Harcourt City."

"You'll have to excuse me, Sheriff, if I can't compliment you on running a nice, peaceful town," Mac responded.

Brimball scowled. "Hold on there, mister. I'll have you know things in and around Harcourt City happen to run just fine. One stranger showing up and getting himself in some trouble don't mean the whole bucket is tipped over."

"Getting *himself* in trouble?" echoed Becky. "For crying out loud, Sheriff, you make it sound like Mac did this all on his own. Do you realize how ridiculous that is?"

"Now, Becky, I said no such thing," Brimball protested. "Of course he didn't beat his own self up. But that don't mean he didn't play a part in bringing it on. You and Farrell both told me how he got into that scuffle in the Irish Jig, didn't you? And then, just a couple hours later, this happens to him. All I'm pointing out is that, from the way I have to look at it, the common link is, well, Mr. Mackenzie himself."

"How about the common link of Jerry Lee Lawton, Roy Orton, and Edsel Purdy?" Farrell demanded. "*They* were the cause of the scuffle in my saloon. And Mac, with a little help from Becky, made them look like fools. How hard is it to figure out they were the ones who waited and waylaid him in order to get even? That would also explain why he wasn't robbed. They were interested in payback, but not thievery."

"Can you prove any of that?" Brimball challenged. "Did Mackenzie get a look at who jumped him? Can he identify those three? If you and Miss Lewis will let me do my job, I'm trying to find those things out."

"The answer is no, I didn't see who or even how many men jumped me," Mac said, growing annoyed by the jabbering. "It was dark, I got clubbed the minute I stepped through the door. It was more than one hombre, I can guarantee that. Another thing I can tell you is that, before I got knocked out, one of 'em spoke. It sounded like Jerry Lee."

"*Sounded* like," Brimball was quick to pick up. "But you said you couldn't see for sure, right? It was too dark."

"The dark didn't affect my hearing."

"Maybe not. But how many times did you hear Jerry Lee speak before the trouble in the Irish Jig?" Brimball asked. "You know him from anywhere else before that?"

"Of course not. What are you driving at?" Mac's head was pounding and he didn't care much for the sheriff's tone.

"Yes, what *are* you driving at, Brimball?" Farrell said, a sharp edge to his own voice. "You questioning Mac's word?"

"Now climb down off your high horse, Farrell. You, too, Mackenzie. I'm not questioning anybody's word, not in an accusing way." Brimball scowled. "I'm just pointing out that a fella hearing a voice speak just before he gets worked over and that working over coming right on the heels of another dust-up . . . well, it'd be understandable if the two things got kinda jumbled together in the fella's head. Like maybe thinking a voice he only ever heard say a few words once was part of both times. You see what I'm saying?"

"What I *hear* you saying," Becky responded, anger flaring in her eyes, "is that you're trying awful hard to convince somebody besides yourself that Jerry Lee played no part in Mac's beating. Why is that, Sheriff? Why do you seem more interested in clearing Jerry Lee than finding the truth?"

Brimball's face flushed with a rush of his own anger.
"Now that's a low thing to say, Becky Lewis, and you got
no call for it. It's you and Farrell who don't care about the
truth. You got your minds made up Jerry Lee was part of
this and that's all you want to hear." He cut his eyes to
Wheeler. "Tell 'em, Doc. This concussion thing you said
Mackenzie has . . . it means his brain got kinda scrambled, don't it? Means he ain't necessarily thinking all the
way clear on things, right?"

Wheeler frowned, obviously not wanting to be caught
in the middle of this. Guardedly, he said, "A concussion is
a . . . well, it's a very complex, very unpredictable thing. It
can manifest itself in any number of different ways." He
paused, his increasing discomfort growing more evident.
Then, setting his jaw firmly, he added, "I have to say,
though, that Mr. Mackenzie shows no sign of disorienta-
tion or confusion as a result of his condition."

Brimball's eyes narrowed momentarily, signaling he
didn't appreciate the tacked-on comment. Quickly adopting a more neutral expression, he said, "Well, that's good
to hear. Good for Mackenzie. Too bad he still has more
than his share of other injuries to deal with." The sheriff
shifted his gaze to Farrell and Becky. "Look, I want no
hard feelings. What I want even less is for anybody to
think I won't go full bore after some thug who attacks
and beats a visitor to our town right in their hotel room!
But, by the same token, I can't go rushing off and accusing one of our longstanding citizens of something without making sure I've got sufficient facts."

"Jerry Lee Lawton isn't a citizen," Becky muttered.
"He's a loathsome pig."

"Aye. Trouble is," Farrell said, "he's part of Oscar
Harcourt's personal swine herd. That means, no matter

how much muck he drags out of his pen and leaves smeared around elsewhere, there's always the Harcourt name or money to cover it up."

Brimball winced, almost as if he'd been stricken. When he spoke, it was with his mouth stretched into a grimace.

"All right. You two have had your say. And I've listened to Mackenzie's account. Now here's my say on the matter. Lawton, Orton, and Purdy were shooting dice with the Osgood twins and Ed Poole in the back room of Poole's hardware store from about eight o'clock—that would be shortly after you ran the three men out of your place, Farrell—until near midnight. All six men swore to this, separately, as a result of the questions my deputy, Randall, spent most of the morning asking all around town."

The sheriff paused, as if to let all he'd just said sink in. There was an unmistakable air of smugness about him when he continued, "Now you tell me if all of that isn't enough to pretty convincingly contradict Mr. Mackenzie's identification based on a handful of words he *thinks* he recognized just before getting beaten into several hours of unconsciousness. Would any lawman or right-thinking person of any sort see that as sufficient basis for accusing or harassing somebody in Jerry Lee's position any further? Without something more to go on, I think the answer is pretty clear."

"Aye," said Farrell, with disgust pinching his gaze and dripping off his words. "You always make things pretty clear when it comes to handling any matter involving Harcourt or those who do his bidding."

"Think what you want," Brimball replied in a snarl. "You and your Irish temper and smart mouth are bound to earn you your comeuppance soon enough. In the meantime, particularly when it comes to this business regarding Mackenzie and his beliefs about Jerry Lee, who everybody knows you've got your own personal beef with, I'd advise you to watch your step. I won't stand for any vigilante justice in my town. Like I already made it clear to all of you, unless something else turns up to change things, I consider Jerry Lee and the others cleared of Mackenzie's beating. That had better be understood."

"You've made yourself plenty clear, even to somebody with a cracked skull, Sheriff," spoke up Mac. "Now let me make something clear in return. Whoever did this to me made the mistake of not finishing the job. That means, as soon as I'm able, *I* will be the one with some unfinished business. And no matter how lousy I'm feeling right at the moment, one thing I'm not feeling is inclined to just let things stand as is."

Brimball didn't like hearing this at all. "Now see here, mister. I hope that don't mean you're threatening to—"

"No matter what it means," Dr. Wheeler cut him off, "this has gone on long enough. For mercy's sake, all of you, this man has just woken from experiencing a great deal of trauma. He needs rest and quiet, not to be grilled and argued over like he's the one who did something wrong. No matter what else, he is a victim, my patient, and I demand he receives the treatment I deem proper and necessary."

Brimball and Farrell went quiet, their shoulders sagging somewhat, like students who'd just been reprimanded by a teacher.

After a few tense seconds, Brimball backed away, saying, "Very well. I'm done here anyway, I'll take my leave. I trust everybody's clear on how I see things. I'll check back if anything new turns up."

Chapter 5

Once the sheriff had left the room, Mac heaved a sigh—a careful one because of his damaged ribs—and said, "Thanks for calming things down, Doc. That hombre was starting to put a burr under my saddle."

Wheeler smiled fleetingly. "From what I saw—not really a medical diagnosis, but I believe an accurate one all the same—your remarks toward the end did a pretty good job of irritating our good sheriff in return."

Mac twisted his mouth sourly. "Yeah, that probably wasn't the smartest way for me to play it."

"Nonsense," said Farrell. "It was great to see that phony, puffed-up tin star get his hackles raised and not be able to do a blasted thing about it."

"It was kind of entertaining seeing Brimball so flustered," Becky agreed, though at the same time looking concerned. "But you can't be so sure about him not being able to do something about it. He is the sheriff, after all. I'm sure he can find ways, especially if Mac is planning to stick around for a while. And you didn't say or do very much to improve your own standing with him either, Eamon."

"Let me worry about that," the Irishman stated.

"And as far as me sticking around—" Mac started to say.

"If you listen to me," Wheeler cut him off, "that certainly should be the case. In your condition, you won't be ready to hit the trail again for quite some time. However, neither is that a recommendation for hanging around and getting into further conflict with Brimball or Jerry Lee or any of that lot as part of your recovery."

"Don't worry, Doc," Mac told him. "If necessary, I can be *a* patient and *be* patient, both at the same time. The way I feel right now, I'm willing to ride nothing but this bed for as long as you say, for as long as it takes me to get healed up."

Farrell's brow suddenly puckered. He and Becky exchanged looks. She displayed her own troubled expression.

"What's the matter?" Mac wanted to know.

Farrell cleared his throat. "Well, lad, it's good to hear you're willing to 'ride a bed,' as you put it, until you've done some recovering. The thing is, however, it can't be *this* bed you do it in."

Mac looked confused. "Why not? If those skunks didn't rob me, I've got money. I can pay. Staying here makes it easy for the doc to check on me and such. What's wrong with that?"

"What's wrong," Becky answered, "is that this room, not to mention any other room in the hotel, is no longer available. Not to you, supposedly not to anybody who isn't already booked for an extended stay. The owner, you see, has suddenly announced that any day now he is expecting the arrival of a large group of business associates, possible investors in the growth of our town, and it will require all available space to put them up for their stay here."

"Care to take a guess at who said owner might be?" Farrell asked with a wry smile.

Mac figured out the reason for that expression right away. "Oscar Harcourt," he said. "He doesn't want me in town to make trouble for his three bully boys."

"It was the proprietor of the hotel, allegedly unaware anything had happened during the night, who found you in your battered condition earlier this morning," Becky said, adding more explanation. "He found your door slightly ajar and you lying on the floor. He'd come to inform you about needing to vacate the room and in case you were wanting to stay any longer why that wouldn't be possible. Finding you as he did, he went ahead and got the doctor and sheriff sent for. When the news started spreading through town, Eamon and I heard and came on over, too. That's when we also learned the rest of the details."

"It was all a setup," Mac said, bitter anger rising in him again. "And somebody on the hotel staff was part of it. There was no clerk at the desk when I got here last night. My room was locked, the way I left it, but my attackers were inside waiting for me. That means somebody let them in."

"Scheming varmints all," Farrell bit out through clenched teeth.

Looking suddenly very sad and troubled, Wheeler

said, "I hope you understand that, in my position, I can ill afford speculation on such matters. I nevertheless hope you believe me when I assure you that I pleaded as strongly as I dared that, in your condition, you be allowed to remain in this room for at least a few days. Unfortunately, I got nowhere."

"But not to worry, Mac," Farrell declared. "Becky and I have had time to talk this over and set some things in motion. We think we have a suitable solution. Harcourt can keep his lousy hotel room, and may it rot from lack of use."

"Getting you moved, in your condition, is bound to cause you a lot of discomfort," Becky said. She favored Mac with an encouraging smile. "But once done, we have a place in mind where your comfort will be restored and you won't have to worry about it being interrupted again until you're ready. What we're suggesting is that you come stay with my brother and me out at our ranch, the Standing L, and complete your recovery there."

Jerry Lee Lawton realized he'd been averting his eyes for too long, averting his eyes and not saying anything while he stared down at the toe of the boot he was poking into the plush carpeting that covered the floor of the well-appointed office he'd been summoned to. He lifted his face and met the glare of the man who sat watching him from the opposite side of a broad desk. Watching, and waiting for him to speak.

"Okay," Jerry Lee finally said. Though his expression was remorseful, he nevertheless tried to inject a touch of defiance into his tone. But he could hear that it fell flat, even as he continued on, admitting, "I reckon me and the boys didn't think it through very good. None of us expected that roughing up some no-account drifter would cause folks to get riled the way they did. Heck, I wouldn't've thought anybody'd pay hardly any attention at all."

"Then you thought—for lack of a better word—wrong," said the man behind the desk. "Tell me. Did you find your little exercise satisfying? Was it worth it?"

Jerry Lee frowned, not sure how he was supposed to respond. "At the time, I, uh . . . Yeah, I guess it was satisfying. I mean, it felt good to teach that saddle tramp a lesson for sticking his nose in our business."

"Uh-huh. But as to the rest of my question, was it worth it? In terms of dollars and cents, that is. In case I'm not making myself clear."

Jerry Lee's frown deepened. "I, uh . . . I guess I'm being kinda wool headed, Mr. Harcourt. I don't quite follow the dollars and cents part."

Oscar Harcourt leaned forward and placed his forearms on the highly polished desktop. At forty, he was an imposing figure—his height and sturdy build fully evident, even in a seated position. His brownish blond hair was combed straight back from a long rectangular face dominated by piercing dark eyes glaring out from under a ledge of thick, pale brows and bracketing a nose that was prominent without seeming overly large. His mouth was wide and expressive, capable of forming an engaging smile or twisting into a cruel slash.

It formed into a modified version of the latter now, as Harcourt said, "For a continuation of this discussion, let's keep it to merely dollars, inasmuch as 'cents' may be too easily confused with the other kind . . . the type of 'sense' you and your bumbling cohorts often fail to show a grasp of. So the dollars I'm referring to, then, are those in an amount that will be deducted from the next payday you, Orton, and Purdy are scheduled to receive from me. Said deduction will offset what I had to pay Ed Poole and the Osgood brothers, Harvey and Dolph, in order to purchase their sworn testimony that you three were shooting dice with them at the time when you were, in truth, satisfying your petty grievance against that no-account stranger. So I ask you again: Was it worth it?"

Jerry Lee felt resentful anger surge inside him. All of a sudden, it wasn't hard to not only meet Harcourt's glare but to muster one of his own. He didn't like the idea of losing money that way, and he sure as blazes didn't think it was fair.

But then, almost as quickly as the surge in him had risen, it eased back off again. No matter Harcourt's remarks concerning the sense shown by him and his pals, Jerry Lee was quick to remind himself that they were all smart enough to know which side their bread was buttered on.

Despite his insults and snide remarks, Harcourt was the man with the butter. He paid well for the dirty deeds he required infrequently from Lawton and the others. Better than they almost certainly could make elsewhere—especially if they were forced to resort to something as drastic as honest work, actual labor of some kind for a lot less pay.

All of which made the man's lousy treatment not too bitter a pill to swallow. At least not yet.

Forcing the heat to cool out of his eyes, Jerry Lee said, "No matter how satisfying it was or wasn't, Mr. Harcourt, I hope you'll consider letting us call it a lesson learned. I promise you, me and the boys won't do nothing so fool-hardy no more."

"That's encouraging to hear," Harcourt allowed.

Jerry Lee paused, weighing carefully what he wanted to say next. Then: "One thing, though, Mr. Harcourt . . ."

"Yes? What is it?"

"That business about you having to pay Ed Poole and the Osgoods to speak up on our behalf . . . The thing is, I can't help thinking how many times me, Roy, and Edsel have helped those ingrates out of scrapes they got themselves in. It rankles me, them charging you money to do us some good in return."

"You think they took advantage of me?"

"No, I wouldn't put it that way. You're too sharp for that. Take a heap more savvy than those three lunkheads have got to take advantage of you."

"So what really rankles you is that they cost you money. Meaning, in a sense, it was you and the others they took advantage of, due to the spot of trouble you found yourselves in being something they should have been willing to help with of their own free will."

Jerry Lee scowled. "I wasn't really thinking of it that way, but yeah, hearing you say it like that, it plumb rankles me that those three skunks made money speaking up for us after all the past times we sided with them for no kind of charge."

Harcourt smiled slyly. "Sounds to me like you may have grounds to do some, er, negotiating with Mr. Poole and the Osgoods regarding the money they've been paid for giving you an alibi."

Jerry Lee cocked an eyebrow. "You wouldn't mind? You wouldn't object if me, Roy, and Edsel did some, uh, *negotiating* of our own with those rats?"

"Your personal business dealings are of no concern to me." Harcourt, secretly amused by the thought of the minor conflict he had helped instigate, couldn't help but let his smile linger a moment longer. Too bad he wouldn't be around to see it play out: the two sides huffing and puffing at each other over the paltry amount in question, and then likely settling the issue with a round of rotgut whiskey jointly paid for.

After he put aside that bit of imagined entertainment, his expression turned sober once more as he said, "Just see that none of it spills over into anything that *does* reflect back on me. Settle the affair as you see fit, only make sure not to rile things up all over again. When it's done, stay ready to hear from me. I've got a number of matters hanging fire. When some of them come to fruition, I expect there may be certain contingencies that will require the involvement of you, Orton, and Purdy."

"You can count on us."

"That had better be the case." Harcourt paused, considering something more. Then he said, "But before any of that, there's a more immediate issue I want you and the others to keep an eye on and report your observations back to me."

"Sure thing, boss. Just name it," Jerry Lee said eagerly, relieved that they seemed to have moved past the matter of the ill-advised beating and taking this mention of a new assignment as a good sign that Harcourt didn't harbor any lasting hard feelings.

"According to Marshal Brimball," Harcourt said, "Eamon Farrell of the Irish Jig and that Lewis girl who works part-time for him appear to have taken an unexpectedly strong interest in this Mackenzie that you and the others had your altercation with. I'd arranged for Mackenzie to no longer be welcome at the hotel, thinking that would hasten him on his way so that he'd be of no further bother. But it sounds like the combination of his injuries and the intervention of Farrell and the girl may result in a different outcome. I want you to find out exactly what that is, what they're up to."

Jerry Lee arched one brow. "Want me and the boys to, er, give 'em a hint it might not be such a good idea to stick their noses in where they got no business?"

Harcourt pursed his lips thoughtfully for a moment. Then: "A hint, just a small one, might be in order, yes. But don't get too carried away. . . . One of the matters I've got hanging fire already involves that overly cocky Irishman. Some very direct issues between him and me will soon be coming to a head, regardless."

Chapter 6

It didn't take long for Becky's prediction to reveal itself as being all too accurate. Getting out of the cushy hotel room bed, down the stairs, and up into the back of a buckboard sent from the Standing L ranch proved to be a mighty uncomfortable bit of maneuvering for Mac.

The worst of it came from his busted-up ribs. Even though Doc Wheeler had wrapped them tightly, it didn't take much in the way of movement, or especially a sudden intake of breath, for them to send jolts of misery through his whole body. His legs didn't help much either, being as stiff and battered and bruised as they were from the kicking and stomping they'd received.

Playing a big part in getting the relocation achieved with the least amount of duress possible was the Standing L ranch hand who was requested specifically by Becky to bring the buckboard and help as necessary. He was introduced to Mac as George Arnussen, a towering young giant affectionately dubbed "Ox" due to his hulking size and impressive strength.

The latter was put to use not only when it came to aiding Mac in easing out of bed and haltingly into motion, also with the assistance of Farrell, but even more so when it was time to negotiate the stairs and get in and out of the buckboard. For this, the gentle blond brute physically lifted the patient and then put him down again when and where directed.

Mac found it both disconcerting and a bit embarrassing to be so easily handled in this manner, but at the same time, he felt awed and grateful he was spared the additional pain and effort walking would have required.

Additional arrangements were also provided to make the trip from town to the Standing L as painless as possible. These came in the form of the buckboard driven by Ox arriving with a layer of fresh straw spread over its bed and a pile of thick quilts and pillows on top of that, all in accordance with the instructions Becky had sent via a town youth she paid a dollar to ride out and deliver.

The results cushioned Mac very effectively for the duration of the buckboard ride. His personal gear from the hotel room occupied space beside him, and his saddled paint horse, retrieved from the livery stable where he'd left the critter when he first got to town the previous day, was tethered to the rig and came trotting along behind.

Also trotting along, mounted on a high-stepping steeldust, was Becky herself. Farrell remained in town, needing to tend his saloon business, but he promised it wouldn't be long before he'd be coming around to check on Mac's progress.

Dr. Wheeler made a similar promise, though for him it

was a professional matter, assuring Mac that he would be visiting the ranch the very next day and regularly thereafter in order to assess his patient. For the interim, Wheeler sent along with Mac a small bottle of pain medicine, a concoction of laudanum, to help him rest comfortably for the sake of spurring on his healing.

Mac was naturally very grateful for all this trouble being gone to on his account. He didn't like being beholden to so many people, especially ones he barely even knew. And yet, conditions being what they were, he didn't see where he had much else in the way of options. Furthermore, if he was being totally honest with himself . . . well, any notion of turning down hospitality offered by the lovely Becky had flicked in and out of his thoughts so fast it was like it was never there.

Roy Orton leaned out in his saddle and spat a fat dollop of tobacco juice down into the dust. Straightening up, he worked the wad of chew around in his mouth until he got it where he wanted it, then said, "All I know, Jerry Lee, is that I'm glad you're the one who does most of the direct dealing with Oscar Harcourt. That man plumb confounds me."

"Confounds you how?" Jerry Lee wanted to know.

"Well, like this business right here." Orton waved a hand, indicating their surroundings. "First, the way you told us, he calls you in and chews your hide for how we roughed up that meddling stranger. Then he turns right around and sends us out to hoorah him and that Lewis gal all over again. Now that, to me, is confounding."

Jerry Lee wagged his head. "What's confounded is your way of listening and thinking. So I'll agree with you about it being a good thing that you're not the one who does the direct dealing with Harcourt. Lord, I'd hate to think how off course you might steer us."

Sitting his saddle on the other side of Jerry Lee, Edsel Purdy pulled his handsome face into a long frown. "I hate to say it, 'cause you'll probably snap my head off, too, but I reckon I'm a mite mixed up, same as Roy. It *does* seem like one thing is at odds with the other, Harcourt first being sore at us for going after the stranger and then changing his mind and wanting us to do it all over again."

Jerry Lee heaved an exasperated sigh and wagged his head some more. He and the other two men were reined up alongside the trail north out of Harcourt City, at a spot where the trail cut through a low rise and made a slight eastward twist before continuing on due north again. They were positioned just past the shoulder of the cut so that anyone coming from town wouldn't spot them until rounding the twist in the trail.

"See, there's the difference," Jerry Lee said, wrapping the words in his sigh. "The difference between what I said . . . what I relayed according to what me and Harcourt agreed on . . . and what you two lunkheads heard. The key word was 'hint,' a subtle-like kind of thing, understand? Not 'hoorah,' like rousting a pack of drunks. We just want to *remind* 'em who they're messing with. Make it clear that the stranger and his meddling ways ain't welcome and neither is anybody poking in their noses to encourage him. Do you get what I'm saying? Do you see the difference?"

Orton and Purdy exchanged uncertain glances.

"When that buckboard gets here," said Orton, "reckon the best bet is for you to take the lead and me and Edsel to follow along."

Jerry Lee nodded. "Sounds good. Remember, based on what we saw when they were getting ready to leave town, it will only be Becky Lewis and that big ranch hand they call Ox driving the rig. The way they were coddling the stranger . . . his name is Mackenzie, by the way . . . he's going to be laid out in the back, hardly able to move on his own."

"Gee, I wonder what happened to the poor devil." Orton issued a half-snort, half-nasty chuckle. "Did he have an accident of some sort, a bad fall maybe?"

Purdy smiled a little, but there was a wariness to it. "Sounds like Mackenzie is no worry. But that big ranch hand, that Ox . . . they say he's as strong as one of the critters they call him after. You think we'll have any trouble out of him?"

"I doubt it," Jerry Lee scoffed. "From what I hear, he ain't much smarter than an ox, neither. Sorta retarded. But he can't be so strong or so dumb he'd mess with a .45 slug. That'd be your department, Edsel. I ain't saying to plant one in him, mind you. But if need be, haul out that smoke wagon of yours and keep him in line with it."

Purdy grinned. "Now you're talking language that ain't at all confounding. Not to me."

"Just in time, then. 'Cause I think I hear that buckboard coming," said Jerry Lee. "Remember, let me do the talking. If you have to say or do anything, follow my lead."

Chapter 7

The three horsemen fanned out across the width of the trail, effectively blocking it just beyond the cut. When the buckboard driven by Ox Arnussen and accompanied by Becky Lewis came around the shoulder of the rise half a minute later, Ox was forced to haul back on the reins and bring his pulling team to a halt. For the sake of his cargo, he hadn't been traveling very fast so the rig slowed and stopped easily. Trotting alongside, Becky also reined in. The cloud of dust churning in their wake rolled forward, overtaking the scene and blurring the scowl that formed on Becky's pretty face.

"What's the meaning of this? You're blocking the road," she snapped in a sharp, annoyed tone.

Jerry Lee leaned forward, resting a forearm across the top of his saddle horn and baring his teeth in a taunting grin. "That's sort of the general idea, pretty Miss Becky.

To block the trail. We was afraid that, otherwise, you and your haughty ways might not want to stop and chat with us."

"You're right, I *don't* want to chat with the likes of you," Becky wasted no time replying. "Blocking the road doesn't change that any."

"No, but it's got you held up, don't it?" smirked Jerry Lee. "And even though you say you don't want to, you *are* talking to me."

"Not any more than I have to, I won't be," Becky told him. "But apparently you have something stuck in that craw of yours, Jerry Lee. Spit it out so we can be on our way."

In the back of the buckboard, Mac was slow to come to the realization they had stopped and conversation was taking place. In his weakened condition, the effort of quitting the hotel and getting loaded into the rig, even with all the assistance he had gotten, had proven quite taxing. That, combined with taking a slug of the pain medicine given to him by Doc Wheeler, caused him to doze once they were rolling easily away from the town.

Now, even as he woke, he found that his position in the buckboard, lying on his back and facing toward the rear when he lifted his head to try to look around, left him with no good view of what was going on. But then he heard Becky say the name "Jerry Lee" and everything was as clear as it needed to be.

It was probably a good thing he was still stiff with pain and a bit woozy from the medicine because it kept him from reacting too quickly, too foolishly. It made it easier to will himself to remain motionless, get a better feel for what was occurring and come up with some kind of plan for what, if anything, his part should be.

Becky's voice and Jerry Lee's, responding to her, seemed to be coming from a few yards up in front of the buckboard. Tipping his head and looking straight up, Mac could see Ox's broad back above him, where he was planted on the seat of the buckboard. His mind raced.

If I can't see Becky or Jerry Lee—or Orton or Purdy, who are probably with him—then me being down in the buckboard bed with Ox blocking their view must mean they can't see me, either.

Rolling his head to one side, Mac looked over to where his personal gear was piled on the blankets next to him. Slowly, he slid his hand over and began rummaging through the pile. Luck was with him. Almost immediately, his hand touched and then closed around the grips of his Smith & Wesson revolver, tucked in the folds of a jacket.

Becky and Jerry Lee continued talking.

"Funny you should say that about something bein' stuck in my craw," Jerry Lee responded to her. "Because it's on account of 'sticking' that we're here . . . wanting to discuss folks sticking their noses into places where they got no business."

"You mean like you have no business blocking the road and tying up the time of other folks who have better things to do?" Becky tossed back at him.

"Better things?" Jerry Lee sneered. "I don't hardly call playing nursemaid to a saddle tramp who ain't got the sense to know where he ain't welcome a better thing."

"Who are you to say anybody is welcome or not welcome in these parts?" Becky challenged. "There are plenty of people I can think of who wouldn't consider you or that pair of no-goods you drag around with you very welcome either, if it wasn't for Oscar Harcourt's dirty money stuffed in your pockets. And if you want to talk about tramps, then the lot of you certainly ought to know firsthand—"

"You better hold it right there, sister!" Jerry Lee cut her off. "Girl or no girl, there's a limit to how much I'll take from that sassy tongue of yours. You push me past that limit with any more of your name-calling, I'll show you mighty quick-like what I mean!"

"You're the one who'd better watch your tongue, talking to Miss Becky that way!" Ox spoke up suddenly, his voice surprisingly high pitched coming out of such a large frame. But it carried the hard edge of anger. "Now, enough of whatever this is supposed to be. Clear the road before I whip up this team and bowl you bothersome varmints out of the way!"

"Hey now," came a new voice, its mocking tone leaving no doubt in Mac's mind that it was one of Jerry Lee's pals. "The moron not only can speak but, by grab, he reckons he's some kind of tough hombre!"

To which yet another voice responded, "That just proves how dimwitted he really is. The big dummy thinks he can get away with threatening us like that!" And putting an emphasis on this statement came the unmistakable sound of a six-gun's hammer ratcheting back to full cock.

If he was going to take a hand in this, Mac told himself, then it sounded like it had better be pretty quick. Unable to see any faces from where he lay, he couldn't judge how close to breaking into actual gunplay the situation truly was. But with Becky out there in the middle of it, he couldn't take the risk of waiting too long to find out.

Gripping the Smith & Wesson tight in his right hand, he took a slow, deep breath, gritting his teeth against the pain it caused and more that he knew was soon to come. He braced himself. Then, rolling onto his left shoulder and elbow, he shoved himself up and forward as hard and fast as he could, rising above the sidewall of the buckboard's hauling bed with the revolver fisted at the end of his extended right arm.

The sudden movement sent pain blazing all through his middle and throbbing from a dozen places in his arms and legs. *Push through! Ignore it!* he commanded himself as he blinked away the involuntary watering that threatened to fill his eyes.

Once again Mac was in luck. Half a dozen yards in front of the buckboard, off toward the right edge of the trail—almost directly in front of where Mac rose up and thrust his .44 from under the edge of Ox's seat—Edsel Purdy, the surly gunman of the trio, sat his horse in an insolent pose with a Colt .45 drawn and aimed casually at Ox. Here then, Mac felt confident, was the source of the threatening hammer cock he had heard.

That was all he needed to see. Blinking at the stinging in his eyes before it got too bad, Mac took quick aim and fired. The trusty old S&W Model 3 spat red flame and bucked in his hand, hurling a lead slug straight and true. It slammed into the side of Purdy's Colt, knocking the cylinder loose from the frame, causing one of the cartridges inside the cylinder to discharge simultaneously with the load under the hammer. Purdy yelped as the weapon was torn from his grip, snapping back the finger caught in its trigger guard and folding the digit like a hinge bent the wrong way.

The unexpected, tightly grouped sequence of shots sent horses wheeling and bolting in alarm, including the buckboard's team. When the sturdy animals jumped wildly forward, the buckboard followed suit with a hard jolt that threw Mac backward and sent him sprawling once more onto his blankets and pillows. The subsequent burst of frantic activity that occurred next all took place out of his sight.

For starters, in addition to having his Colt shot out of his hand, Purdy was pitched to the ground when his frightened horse sprang out from under him. The would-be gunny hit hard and then lay there, rocking back and forth and mewling as he hugged his injured hand to his chest.

The only mount that didn't panic out of control was Becky's steeldust. Held in check by a steady hand on its reins and a soothing voice in its ear, the horse merely danced to one side, shifting out of the way as the buckboard lurched into motion.

The nags under Jerry Lee and Orton tried to spin away from the double blast of Purdy's exploding gun and ended up slamming into each other. As their cursing riders tried to bring them under control, Ox made the decision to do just the opposite when it came to the sudden surge of the buckboard team. Even though he had a tight grip on the traces, he made no attempt to haul back on them but rather let the horses go ahead and make their initial forward jump, resulting in a modified version of his earlier threat to bowl the varmints out of the way.

The team's collision with the mounts of Jerry Lee and Orton didn't exactly bowl them over, but it did succeed in crowding them out of the middle of the road. And Ox wasn't through. As the buckboard started to roll past where the two men were struggling to get their animals under control at the edge of the trail, Ox stood up in the driver's box and leaped off full onto them.

The big man spread wide his long, thick arms and swept both toughs out of their saddles, dragging them to the ground with him.

Jerry Lee and Orton each landed in hard sprawls that stunned them and knocked much of their wind out. But Ox, amazingly agile for his size, landed mostly on his feet. Quickly gaining his balance, he spun immediately on the hired thugs, pulling first one and then the other to their feet and then, with a flurry of heavy, melon-fisted blows, proceeded to hammer each into unconsciousness.

The temporarily alarmed buckboard team trotted only about a dozen yards before slowing and stopping. By the time Mac was able to drag himself upright so he could see over the side of the bed again, it was all over. Jerry Lee and Orton each lay in a heap, knocked senseless. On the other side of the trail, Purdy curled into a fetal position, continuing to hug his damaged hand to his chest and whimper over it.

Ox stood in the middle of the road, letting his breathing level off as he sleeved sweat and dust from his face.

Astride her horse, Becky was trotting toward the buckboard, wearing a concerned look. When she saw Mac's face poke up, the concern gave way to a wide, relieved smile.

It was a great smile, Mac thought. Almost great enough to make him forget, at least for a little while, how doggone sore he was.

Chapter 8

It was late afternoon by the time they reached the Lewis ranch. The sun, on its descent above the western horizon, was still bright in a cloudless sky and the buildup of the day's heat, lacking any breeze to disperse it, hadn't yet begun to ease.

Craning his neck to look around from the pile of pillows holding him partially propped up, Mac saw that the Standing L's main house and related outbuildings and corrals all appeared sturdy and well tended. Horses milled inside the corrals, numerous clucking and strutting chickens were in evidence around the buildings, there was a pigpen out toward the back, and clumps of beef cattle could be seen grazing amidst the low, grassy hills that rose and fell in all directions.

As the buckboard rolled closer, two men who'd been involved in repairing an array of tack spread on a temporary workbench set up in the wide, open doorway of the horse barn put aside their work and sauntered over to stand waiting in front of the house. When Ox pulled up and set the brake, they stepped forward to assist with the delivery being made.

Ahead of that, however, Becky leaped down from her saddle. Cheeks still flushed with excitement, eyes wide and gleaming, she related in a rush of words what had occurred back on the trail. After giving all the details, Becky paused briefly to catch her breath and then summed it all up by saying, "You should have seen them. They were wonderful! First Mac, shooting the gun clean out of Edsel Purdy's hand, and then Ox, swooping like an eagle or condor, dragging the other two from their saddles and knocking them cold before they ever knew what hit them! They were like a pair of swashbuckling heroes out of a novel by Alexandre Dumas!"

When she paused again to catch her breath, one of the men favored Mac with a wry smile and said, "That's quite an introduction, mister. Me, I'm Becky's brother, Marcus. I never met a swashbuckler before."

Mac guardedly returned his smile. "Reckon that makes us even. I've never been called one before."

Hopping down from the buckboard seat, Ox addressed Marcus, saying, "What about me? You've known me a long time. You never noticed the swashbuckling side of me either?"

Marcus thumbed back the brim of his hat and eyed the big man up and down. "Let me see. There's a lot to take in. And as I recall, there were also traits of an eagle or a condor mentioned, wasn't there?"

"Go ahead and poke your fun," Becky huffed. "I was there—it wasn't a laughing matter when Purdy pulled out his gun. But the way Mac and Ox reacted . . . well, it was like I said it was!"

Marcus's expression sobered. "You're right, sis. From the sound of it, it *wasn't* no laughing matter and I didn't mean to come across like I was making light of it. And I'm serious when I say to both of you fellas"—his gaze swept over Mac and Ox—"how grateful I am for seeing to it that Becky got away from there unharmed."

"That's better," Becky said with a nod of approval. "Now let's get some more official introductions taken care of. Mac, this is my brother, Marcus . . . and I'd also like you to meet the Standing L's top hand, Ned Baker."

Marcus was tall and trim, half a dozen years older than his sister, with broad shoulders, brown hair, and the same blue eyes as Becky's, set deep between sun- and wind-etched crow's feet in a handsome, lantern-jawed face. Ned Baker, a black man, was some years past the fifty mark, barrel chested and narrow hipped, eyeing the world through alert brown eyes above a gray-flecked walrus mustache, and carrying himself with the rolling gait of someone who'd spent years on horseback.

"And this, gentlemen," Becky concluded, gesturing to Mac, "is the fella you've already heard a good deal about . . . Dewey Mackenzie, who mostly goes by just Mac."

Marcus and Ned stepped to the edge of the buckboard and extended their right hands. Mac shook with each, not at all surprised by the strength in their rough, calloused grips. He made sure they felt the same in his.

"Welcome to the Standing L, Mac," said Marcus. "Except for my sis, you won't find anything particularly pretty or fancy around here. You're looking at the whole outfit. But for as long as it takes you to get healed and back on your feet, we'll do our best to meet your needs."

"I can't tell you how beholden I am for you putting me up like this," Mac replied. "I'll be the least amount of bother I can be, and I'll keep my stay as short as possible. I . . . I don't know how I'll ever repay . . ."

"Hey now. You ain't *re*-paying nothing," Marcus corrected him. "The way you stepped in last evening at the Irish Jig and saved Becky from getting slugged by that skunk Jerry Lee, that was a debt owed to you first. And now you've added to it here again today. No, sir, anything we can do for you ain't nothing but a small step toward squaring that, and don't you be looking at it no other way."

His tone and the look on his face hardening, Marcus then added, "After everything that's took place, though, I'm thinking Jerry Lee and his pack of lowdown partners are the ones who've run up a tab that is well overdue for getting paid."

"Now wait a minute, Marcus," Becky was quick to say. "I wanted to bring Mac out here to help him and to show thanks for him helping me, but you losing your temper and going off half cocked won't do anybody any good. We went through that last night after I told you about Jerry Lee bothering me the first time."

"Yeah, and if I hadn't let you stop me from going into town and cornering Lawton and his two rat pals right then," Marcus pointed out, scowling, "maybe Mac wouldn't be laying here now in the shape he's in and you and Ox wouldn't have got almost shot back on the trail."

"Maybe. But it also could have turned out to be you who ended up lying somewhere in even worse shape," Becky argued. "Those three might be polecats, but that doesn't mean they aren't dangerous, especially when it's always the three of them. And Edsel doesn't wear that tie-down rig just for show. Folks who've seen him work with his gun all say he's fast and accurate. Mac caught him off guard today. But maybe you wouldn't have last night, and you almost certainly won't if you go after him and the others now."

"Your sister's making good sense," Ned said in a low voice that, to Mac's ears, had an almost paternal tone to it.

"What's more," Becky added, "Mac never got a good look at who attacked him in the dark of his room, or even how many there were for sure. Nobody can be truly positive that incident *was* Jerry Lee and the others."

"Bull!" Marcus snorted. "Next you're going to tell me you believe the alibi that Oscar Harcourt bought and paid for to cover his three bully boys for the time Mac was getting beaten up." He pinned Mac with a demanding look. "Tell her, Mac. You don't have any doubts about who jumped you, do you?"

All at once Mac felt very uncomfortable. From suddenly finding himself in the middle of this argument, and also from fresh waves of pain throbbing in his head as well as all through his middle. Fighting not to show a grimace, he responded neutrally to Marcus, saying, "It's true I can't think of anybody else who had reason to jump me . . . but it's also true, like your sister said, that I never really got a look at who it was. Best thing for right now, my opinion, is to step back and let it simmer for a while. But don't anybody make the mistake of thinking I mean to just forget about it. I got some things to chew over while I'm healing, that's all. And no matter what happened to me, that don't change the business from back on the trail or what happened in the Irish Jig last night. But a little patience, not being in too big a rush to call in Jerry Lee's marker, might still be the best thing for right now."

Marcus held his eyes for a long moment, probing deep to try to read clearly what was behind the words. Whatever he thought he saw there caused him to finally give a faint nod and reply, "Okay. Fair enough. Maybe letting things simmer some ain't a bad idea. Reckon you got as much call as anybody, Mac, to say if and when those three get confronted."

"The thing that's called for now," announced Ox abruptly, crowding in between Marcus and Ned, "is to get Mr. Mackenzie out of the sun and out of this rig and in to wherever Miss Becky wants him put. He's starting to look a mite frazzled and Doc Wheeler said the best thing for him was quiet and rest . . . which all this squabbling, especially after what happened on the trail, don't hardly amount to."

Mac suppressed a smile. He realized Ox's statement meant he was about to be picked up again, but he didn't mind. He *was* feeling frazzled and the prospect of being transferred to a real bed as opposed to that of the buckboard—no matter how gussied up it was—sounded pretty darn good. Nor did a nip of Doc Wheeler's pain medicine, as soon as the throng around him had thinned out some, strike him as a bad idea either. . . .

Chapter 9

Mac's first night at the Standing L ended up with him experiencing one of the deepest, most refreshing stretches of sleep he could remember ever having. After failing to convince the Lewises he would be fine on a cot out in the bunkhouse with Ox and Ned, he was put up instead in a spare bedroom of the main house. There, on a wide, impossibly soft bed covered with fresh-smelling sheets and layered even more with thick blankets and fluffy pillows, he burrowed in and told himself what a blasted fool he'd been for having argued in favor of a bunkhouse cot over this.

For the duration of the evening and night he never left the big bed, except to tend to some private necessities. Becky insisted on bringing supper to his room—a bowl of thick, delicious beef stew; cornbread layered with creamy butter; a tall glass of cold buttermilk—and sat visiting with him while he ate. No meal ever tasted better and no dinner companion ever made dining more of a pleasure.

Helped along by two or three gulps of Dr. Wheeler's laudanum concoction, Mac dozed much of the time, even before full night descended. In addition to Becky peeking in frequently, Marcus Lewis and Ox both came by to see how he was doing and to visit briefly. Whenever he was awake, Mac felt a great sense of appreciation and comfort.

But the bitterness he also felt toward those responsible for leaving him in the battered condition that required such kindness and caring was never far from his thoughts, either. Even in his deepest slumber, there came flashes of shadowy figures hovering over him, of the initial pain streaking through him, and the accompanying sounds of their feet and fists landing repeatedly.

Yes, Mac was very aware of the debt he owed to those now aiding him, one he might never be able to repay.

But at the same time he never forgot there was another debt—the one owed to those who'd left him beaten and broken—and that one he *would* be paying off, as soon as possible.

In the days that followed, Mac grew increasingly more ambulatory with less and less overall discomfort. His bruises faded, his lacerations closed up nicely, and the stiffness and soreness in his legs was soon gone. The headaches and brief touches of dizziness from his concussion stopped early on. The most bothersome and most lingering disruption to getting around freely were the busted ribs that restrained him from reaching or bending over or any sudden movement that might cause more than an easy, measured intake of breath.

After the first morning's breakfast, which he woke to once again being brought to his room before he could voice any objection, he insisted that no further such extra trouble be gone to on his account. He took his meals from then on out at the kitchen table with the others. This involved some slow, painful hobbling the first few times, but each trip got a little easier.

Although Ox and Ned had their own sleeping quarters in the bunkhouse, they took their meals in the main house. These gatherings gave Mac the chance to get better acquainted with them, as well as Marcus and Becky. There was a genuine camaraderie in the group and they all helped to make Mac feel comfortable and welcome, even if only temporarily.

Dr. Wheeler came to call every other day, rewrapping Mac's ribs each time and proclaiming his overall condition to be progressing very well. When he offered to bring a refill of the pain medicine on his next visit, Mac told him not to bother, he could manage without it.

One afternoon, after completing her shift at the Irish Jig, Becky returned home accompanied by Eamon Farrell, who stayed for supper and beyond, regaling all with his easygoing manner and tales of different encounters he'd experienced on his journey from Ireland to the American West.

By the third day, Mac was feeling well enough and familiar enough with the routine of things to start finding ways to pitch in and be of some help. This began with him preparing lunch for himself, Marcus, Ox, and Ned. Becky was always on hand to make breakfast and supper but, with her being gone in the middle of the day to work in town at the Irish Jig, that left her brother and the cowboys to fend for themselves as far as the noon meal. Although Becky tried to set them up with something they could easily fix, they usually resorted to just sandwiches or sometimes only beef jerky and coffee.

Given Mac's experience as a chuckwagon cook on the trail drives he'd been part of, he quickly demonstrated the skill to put together something considerably better and more nourishing. He whipped up a batch of his biscuits and gravy, a meal usually thought of as breakfast fare, but as far as Mac was concerned, it could be eaten for any meal. Everyone agreed, with great enthusiasm. And when he went ahead and baked an apple pie to be served as dessert following supper one evening, his spot sharing cooking duties with Becky was solidified.

It was this development that led to Marcus bringing up a matter that hadn't been discussed any time prior in Mac's presence. One day after lunch, after Ox and Ned had gone back out to tend to whatever tasks were on tap for the rest of the day, Marcus lingered at the kitchen table over an extra cup of coffee.

"It's something I've been kicking around for a while now," he explained as Mac went about clearing the table. "Becky and the fellas have some awareness of it, but mostly I've been planning and calculating and doing some mapping on my own. What I got in mind would be a bit of a risk, to be sure . . . but if it succeeds, it could put the Standing L back on its feet and give us some strong momentum going forward."

"That first night at the Irish Jig, Eamon Farrell filled me in on some things in general around Harcourt City," Mac responded. "He mentioned how you and Becky have been hit with a string of tough breaks out here."

Marcus nodded. "Yeah. Hate to admit it, but there was a time or two when it came close to grinding me down. But Becky wouldn't hear of it, wouldn't let me give up. Told me we had to find a way to make a go of it if for no other reason than to honor our folks, who'd put so much into making it something to leave in our hands."

"Anybody who takes time to look past only how pretty your sister is . . . which ain't easy to do, hope you don't mind me saying . . . would quick enough see that she's got a bright mind and plenty of grit, too," Mac commented, couching the words with a cautious smile.

Marcus grunted. "You don't have to tell me that. About the having grit part, I mean. Though I ain't blind to the pretty part, neither, even though she doesn't seem to have much interest in anybody paying any attention to that anymore. Not like she should, not to none of the fellas who keep noticing all the same. Leastways, none since . . ."

When he let the words trail off, Mac said, "Yeah, Eamon told me how one of those tough breaks was her intended accidentally losing his life."

"Sounds like Eamon spent quite a bit of time filling you in about us," Marcus remarked, cocking one eyebrow.

"It was after that ruckus with Jerry Lee and his pals bothering Becky. Naturally she came up in what we talked about," Mac told him. "Eamon is a talker. About all sorts of things, in case you never noticed. And the fact there were two or three pitchers of beer involved certainly didn't slow him down any."

"No, I'm sure it didn't." Marcus managed a brief grin. "But Eamon's okay, I know he wouldn't have spoken disrespectfully of Becky. Him giving Becky that part-time work at the Irish Jig has helped us money-wise, that's for sure, and I think he did it as much out of kindness as actually *needing* a barmaid. That, and I'm pretty sure he's another fella who's sweet on my sister, even though he's never made any kind of move or come right out and said it in so many words yet."

Mac was caught quite off guard when he heard this. Neither anything Eamon had ever said nor any of the times he'd been around Eamon and Becky together had given him any hint that what Marcus was speculating might be true.

On the other hand, it would be perfectly understandable for Eamon or any other man who came in regular contact with Becky to grow infatuated with her. Mac didn't have to look any closer than himself for proof of that. His time here at the Standing L, frequently in Becky's presence, had kept his heart and imagination spinning a lot more than he—a drifter, a man on the run—had any business allowing them to. What was more, the thought of good-looking, gregarious, affable Eamon Farrell possibly having his cap set for Becky was enough to suddenly send a pang of jealousy worming through Mac.

Before he could reflect on that any further, Marcus went on talking. "Well, one thing I know Eamon couldn't have told you about is what I'm about to bring up now. You see, what I've been considering, Mac, is a cattle drive."

This got Mac's full attention. "A cattle drive?" he repeated.

"That's right. We've got a little more than two hundred head rounded up and gathered in close on good graze. Prime beef, ready for market. Trouble is, beef prices all around are pretty flat right now, with no sign of 'em going up anytime soon." Marcus's expression was sober. "For that drive you were on recently around Miles City, you said the rancher had his price set in advance, right? That was smart of him, probably got him the best payday any cattleman's likely to see for a while."

"You look into taking your beef to Miles City?"

"Uh-huh. It wouldn't gain me much, especially considering the distance we'd have to push 'em." Marcus took a drink of his coffee. "It ain't like we'd necessarily *lose* money selling at current prices closer around, mind you . . . but after expenses and all, it'd be a mighty short step above breaking even. In other words, we'd be left still scraping to get by, just like we have been for too long now. Scraping by and being only one more turn of bad luck away from not having anything to even scrape."

Mac wasn't sure what he was supposed to say to that, so he just kept quiet.

"I hope I don't sound like a greedy person, like I'm angling to be some kind of cattle baron or some such. Neither me nor Becky have those kind of ambitions," Marcus said. "All I want is to get the Standing L back on solid footing financially, the way Ma and Pa had it headed when they were alive. If we can get it there and keep it on an even keel for a few years, why, then there'd be plenty for Becky and me to stay here and each raise families and be right comfortable for the rest of our days."

"Doesn't sound to me like too much to ask for. Not at all."

"This cattle drive I've got in mind could take us a long way toward reaching that goal, Mac." Marcus regarded him intently. "Recently, there's been a gold strike up to the northwest, place called Rattlesnake Creek. You heard anything about it?"

"No. Can't say I have."

"Not too many have. Not yet. But word is spreading fast and reports are coming back that it's a big one. Schemers and dreamers of every stripe, all with visions of gold dancing in their eyes, like you'd imagine, are starting to flock in that direction."

There was fresh excitement starting to glint in Marcus's eyes and for a second Mac thought he was getting ready to say something foolish, like he was thinking it might be worthwhile to join those gold seekers. But then Mac remembered the repeated mentions of a cattle drive, the thing that had brought their conversation to this point, and he suddenly had a different idea about what Marcus was *really* leading up to.

"You're thinking," he said, "that a pack of hungry prospectors suddenly jammed together a long way from home, with gold dust starting to line their pockets, would be willing to pay top dollar for some fresh beefsteak to put in their bellies."

"That's exactly what I'm thinking," Marcus confirmed, a wide smile further displaying his excitement. "You see any reason to figure otherwise?"

"Nope. Can't say I do," Mac answered. "Matter of fact, I'd go so far as to say it sounds like about the safest bet I ever heard anybody figuring to lay down."

Now the curve went out of Marcus's smile. "Yeah. The prospectors wanting the beef and being willing to pay big for it, that's sure enough a safe bet. But pushing my herd the three hundred–plus miles to offer it up to 'em . . . that's the gamble that has been causing me to drag my feet when it comes to getting started."

Mac frowned. "Why? Surely Becky must recognize

what a good opportunity it represents. And you can count on Ox and Ned sticking with you, can't you?"

"Right on all counts. But four hands . . . and that's counting Becky, who can ride and rope as good as anybody around . . . pushing two hundred cows that far over country we're not familiar with . . . you gotta see, don't you, how that's quite an undertaking to bite into."

"You can't hire a couple of short-timers? Two more men would give you enough of a crew."

Marcus made a sour face. "We ain't exactly in the best of shape for affording more help. Especially not anybody worth beans. The decent hands are already hired on to other outfits, except for the blamed fools who lit out for the gold strike."

Marcus fidgeted with his coffee cup, rolling it back and forth between his palms.

"There's something else giving me pause, too. You see, all of us here—me, Becky, Ned, Ox—we're ranch hands. We know how to work cattle on our own spread, move 'em back and forth between pastures and the like, but ain't a one of us ever participated in an actual cattle drive." He looked intently at Mac and added with the clearest meaning in the world, "Like you have."

Chapter 10

"You can't be serious! Mac is in no condition to start out on a three hundred–mile cattle drive. He hasn't recovered enough from that awful beating he got from Harcourt's thugs. You expect him to hold up to a month of eight- or ten-hour days in a saddle?"

This reaction from Becky, after hearing the plan her brother and Mac had spent the afternoon hatching, wasn't exactly unexpected. The intensity of her reaction, however, was a bit stronger than they'd counted on. Not even waiting to spring it on her until she'd been comforted by a suppertime meal of chicken and dumplings, prepared by Mac, had calmed her to the point they were hoping for.

"I'll be the first to admit," Mac replied agreeably, "that I'm not exactly ready for that much time straddling a hurricane deck. But the same thing from the seat of a chuckwagon . . . now that, I figure, would be a different story.

And since it'd take a few more days before everything could be pulled together and we'd be ready to roll, I'd be that much further along in my healing."

Becky shot a look over at her brother. "You have it all very well rehearsed, don't you?"

"We spent some time *discussing* it, yeah, if that's what you mean," Marcus allowed.

Now Becky's eyes went to Ox and Ned. "And I suppose you two are in on it as well?"

Ned held up his hands, palms out, but couldn't quite hold back a faint smile. "Hey. We're just hired hands around here."

"Oh, bull!" Becky huffed. "You've been part of this ranch for almost as long as I can remember, Ned Baker. I know how much store my brother, and our father before him, put in your opinion. And rightfully so. Which means I don't believe for a minute that he put this plan together without running at least some of it by you."

"Okay, Miss Becky," Ned said tolerantly, his little smile still in place. "You know we been talking about this notion of Marcus's for a while now. I think it's a good one, and I recall you saying the same."

"But even though we talked about it and I agreed it was tempting as far as the payoff it could bring, we all also recognized the problems that would come with actually attempting it," Becky reminded him.

"But with Mac agreeing to come on board," Marcus interjected, "those problems don't seem nearly as big. He has experience driving cattle over a long distance and he has experience grubbing a chuckwagon."

"Are you forgetting who's been doing the cooking around here for quite a spell now?"

"Of course not. And you're an excellent cook," Marcus said. "But there's a difference between kitchen cooking and grubbing for a trail drive. For one thing, the chuckwagon rolls ahead of the herd, out there alone for considerable stretches every day, in order to have food ready and waiting at each meal stop. I wouldn't feel comfortable having you that far out ahead on your own, not considering some of the wild country we'd be passing through."

"I know how to take care of myself," Becky insisted stubbornly. But at the same time a trace of concern tightened her eyes momentarily at the description of what would be called for.

"I never said you didn't. But that still don't mean I'd want to put it to the test," Marcus responded. "And another thing to think about, considering how shorthanded we are, is that we really couldn't afford anybody to scout ahead to mark trail and make sure we regularly got the herd to water. Mac tells me he's had some experience at that, too, pulling double duty from the seat of his chuckwagon during a few stretches of trouble when his outfit's regular scout had to fill in elsewhere."

Eyeing Mac under a sharply arched brow, Becky said, "I guess you're an even more remarkable man than I realized, Mac. Are you sure you even need the rest of us at all to push the herd to Rattlesnake Creek?"

"Becky! That was rude and uncalled for!" Marcus said.

Becky immediately flushed a bright pink and the heat went out of her eyes, replaced by a deeply remorseful softness. "Yes. Yes, of course it was. I . . . I'm sorry, Mac. Please forgive me. It's just that we've been talking about this drive for days now, and it would mean so much if we could pull it off. But it seemed too good to be true, like an impossible dream that I refused to allow myself to ever really believe in."

"But with Mac agreeing to help, it can happen!" Marcus said, the same excitement flashing in his eyes that Mac had first seen earlier in the day. "It still won't be a picnic, it'll be tough as all get-out. But here's how I picture it: With Mac going ahead in the chuckwagon, handling the grub and marking trail, that leaves the four of us to work the herd. Ned can ride drag with the remuda, I'll be on point, you and Ox can wrangle the cattle from either side. I've been poring over a couple of maps I was able to get my hands on. Looks like there'll be some broken land and a few mountainous areas we'll need to weave around. But finding water shouldn't be too hard this time of year, and neither will good graze."

Looking on, Mac could feel the excitement pouring out of Marcus and he could see it building on the faces and in the eyes of the others.

"Like I said, it ain't gonna be easy," Marcus continued, "but it has the makings of being well worth the effort. A lot of the other spreads around have already sold their beef at the going rates. That don't mean there ain't some who couldn't still put together a herd as big or bigger than ours, though. As far as I know, nobody else in this area has hit on this same idea. But if any of them do, then it stands to reason that whoever gets their cows to Rattlesnake Creek first is going to get the best price. That means if we're gonna do this, then we need to make up our minds and get to it, pronto."

Nobody said anything for several seconds. Marcus's eyes traveled around the table, from face to face.

Until Becky said, "Do we even have a chuckwagon?"

Marcus smiled guardedly. "There's that old rig out in the machine shed. Mac and I looked it over earlier today. He reckons it could be fixed up good enough to do the job. I can take care of that while Ned and Ox are rounding up the herd and gathering 'em in close. Mac has started writing up a list of the supplies we'll need. . . ."

"From the sound of it," Becky observed somewhat tartly, "I'd say those 'discussions' that apparently have been going on all day had somebody feeling awfully darn sure of himself."

Marcus replied soberly, "Only because I knew my little sister was smart enough to be won over once she heard all the details laid out proper-like."

"What about everything we'd be leaving behind?" Becky asked. "The house, the pigs and chickens . . . That can't all go completely untended for a couple months or so."

"Old man Hooper over at the Circle H," Ox spoke up for the first time, "has been going stir-crazy ever since they had to cut off his foot on account of that spider bite he got last fall. So now his wife and sons won't let him do hardly anything around the ranch no more, despite him being able to hop about pretty handily on a crutch and one foot. I'd be willing to bet anything that he'd jump . . . well, hop, I guess I should say . . . at the chance to come over regular-like to check the house and tend the animals, just for something to do."

Marcus spread his hands. "See? One more detail taken care of."

Becky appeared to be wavering. But then she said, "That still leaves something else, though."

"Now what?" Marcus said, some annoyance starting to show.

Becky smiled. "The little matter of . . . how soon can we get this doggone cattle drive under way?"

Chapter 11

"He caught me off guard," said young George Bradley, scowling. "I mean, he said Mac's name so slick and easy, making like they were old friends or something. And then, after he got me talking . . . well, only then did I realize he was pumping me for information, asking me more than he was telling me. And by that time I might have already said too much."

"So what did you tell him? What did you actually reveal?" prodded his brother Henry. That the two were brothers was evident in their resemblance to one another, the clean-cut good looks and almost identical eyes, the sun- and wind-burned faces. Henry, half a dozen years older, in his middle twenties, had paler hair and a milder, more easygoing air; George was somewhat slighter in build, his hair a darker chestnut, and fairly vibrated with a penchant to get overly excited about things. Both wore standard cowboy garb, well-broke-in boots and pants, each sporting crisp new shirts.

George's scowl deepened at his brother's question. "Well, I . . . I don't know that I *revealed* anything. Other than how Mac had been riding with us, that is. But the way Blassingame—that was the name he introduced himself by—brought it up, he already seemed to know that much."

"He *seemed* to know. So, in other words, what you did by responding was to confirm it for him," pointed out Henry.

"Take it easy," advised Roman, the oldest of the three Bradley brothers. Taller, thirty, lean yet corded with a ropey musculature, same handsome facial features under a darker complexion from longer exposure to the elements. Like his brothers, he wore standard cowboy duds with a crisp new shirt. "It ain't like there's a whole lot that George, or any of us, *can* reveal about Mac. Other than that he rode with us for a while as our chuckwagon cook and played a part in fighting off the bloody tactics of Van Horne and his army of gunslingers when they tried to steal our herd."

Roman paused and turned to the fourth man seated with him and his brothers at the hotel dining room table, the empty plates of a just finished lunch and steaming cups of postmeal coffee arrayed before them.

"Ain't that right, Malloy? We've been open about everything right down the line to the authorities here in Miles City. Described the whole works, in detail, regarding the gun battle out by Buffalo Kill Gap and Van Horne's shady dealings—reaching clear back to Bellow County— that brought it all to a head. And you wired your Ranger bosses down there in Texas with the bare bones of it, too, telling 'em how we'll be returning to give 'em the whole story, with you backing us up in order to straighten out any remaining questions once we get there. Whatever this Denver detective is sniffing around about, I don't see how it can come back on us or the Rafter B. Do you?"

"No," Garfield Malloy agreed readily enough. He was the oldest of the four, late thirties, a fullness to his deeply tanned face that gave it a boyish quality . . . until you got to the penetrating, seen-it-all-before brown eyes set between deep, sharply pointed crow's feet. The unmistakable star-within-a-circle Texas Ranger's badge riding shiny and proud on his panel-front shirt further erased any sense of boyishness and caused many a covert glance from other diners in the busy eating establishment at this hour of the day.

Continuing, Malloy said, "But based on what George has told us, I don't think the Rafter B or any of that business with Caleb Van Horne is what's at issue here. This detective fella was asking strictly about Mac. Isn't that what you said, George?"

All eyes swung back to the youngest Bradley brother.

"Yeah. That's how it started out," replied George. "He came up to me when I was standing at the bar, said he heard I'd arrived in town with the Rafter B outfit. Then he said he'd also heard how an old pal of his, Dewey Mackenzie, was part of our crew but he hadn't seen him anywhere around and wondered if I knew where he'd gotten to."

"But Mac rode off before we ever made it to town. And none of us ever mentioned him after we got here. Had no call to," said Henry.

George's scowl faded into a glum expression. "Yeah, that's what I remembered after it was too late. After I'd already said as much, that, yeah, Mac *had* been riding with us, but he'd drifted off on his own before we got all the way here. Next thing I knew, Blassingame turned a little pushy and he was waving his detective badge under my nose and telling me how he'd been on Mac's trail for a long time and it wouldn't go good for me if I was holding out on him."

"So how did you leave it?" Roman wanted to know. "Did he say what it was that had him so interested in Mac?"

"No. After I clammed up on him, he did the same to me. I told him the Mac Mackenzie I knew never did anything to deserve a bloodhound on his trail. Then I repeated how I didn't know where Mac had headed off to but, even if I did, I said I wouldn't tell the likes of him anyway. When I said that, Blassingame sort of huffed away and that was the end of it."

Roman and Henry both smiled, showing pride in their little brother's spunk.

But Malloy's expression remained sober as he said, "Reckon that's all well and good as far as it goes. I repeat that I don't see how any of it changes anything as far as your family or getting the Rafter B business squared away once we're back home. But let's face it. I think we all came to know, especially with some of the things he did and said toward the last, following how it ended with Van Horne, that Mac had something in his past. Something that, at best, was bothering him, or, at worst, he was running away from. Because we knew and accepted him for what he was to us, we chose to let him ride off and deal with it how he saw fit, not question him or even think about it too hard. Well, I'm guessing this Blassingame represents whatever that past was. And just like

Mac seemed to sense, it's still trying to catch up with him."

Henry's brow puckered. "Well, that's too bad. Even if a fella makes a mistake early on, he ought not to have to run from it forever. Especially if he's straightened himself out and proved to be the kind of man we all saw Mac to be."

Malloy's expression darkened even more and his eyes appeared to gaze off at something far away. "I'm afraid that ain't how it works. As a Texas Ranger, there's been more than once when I had to haul in some hombre who'd taken on all the trappings of a good and proper life . . . but there were papers on him that made it my job to see he got took back to face the music for some past bad deed. I did what I had to do and learned not to think about it too hard. You wear a badge, that's the only way. You start thinking too much, you might start hesitating in your duty. You hesitate at the wrong moment . . . well, both your thinkin' and doin' days can get over with in a hurry, permanent-like."

Roman frowned. "So what are you saying? You sorry you let Mac ride away like he done?"

"Not saying that at all. I didn't *know* any reason to try and stop him. Without that, I didn't have to think or hesitate one whisker about letting him go. And I'm fine with having it that way."

"So what are we going to do about this Blassingame character if he keeps nosing around?" asked Henry.

"Not a thing," Malloy told him. "None of us has anything more to tell him. No more than what George already did. A fella named Mac Mackenzie rode with the Rafter B outfit for a while, then took his leave before making it all the way here to Miles City. He was on the drift when he showed up, made a heck of a good trail cook for the time he stayed with the outfit, then decided to drift on again. Simple as that."

"But shouldn't we do something to help Mac somehow? At least try to warn him?" asked George.

"How?" countered Roman. "It's been more than a week since he took his leave from us. We only know he was headed in the general direction of California. But having any idea how far he's made it by now or knowing any way to get hold of him . . . we got nothing."

"Roman's right," said Malloy. "Seeing how the herd is sold, our business with the local law here is squared away, and your pa and Sparky Whitlock are healed up good enough to start on the trip for home, that's what we need to stay focused on."

Roman nodded. "The stonemason making those markers for the graves of Shad and Nolan says they'll be ready this afternoon. That's the final thing we've been waiting for. Means we can go ahead and leave tomorrow."

"Keep in mind, too," added Malloy, "there's still going to be plenty to do once we reach Bellow County. Namely, making sure we're able to convince the necessary people there about Van Horne's corruption and his scheme against your pa in order to be certain the Rafter B gets reclaimed by your family, its rightful owners. We let ourselves get too distracted by this trouble of Mac's, we might draw unwanted attention that could slow all that down and we might even let something slip that will do Mac more harm than good."

"I'm not sure what that would be, the part about doing Mac any harm," allowed Henry. "But I reckon getting home and getting our lives put back together there should be our main priority."

George didn't look fully convinced. "It still kinda seems like we're . . . well, sort of abandoning Mac. But I reckon you're right, all of you. We don't know where he is, we got no way of getting in touch with him." He paused, heaved a sigh. "That pretty much leaves it as nothing we can do."

"I'll tell you a couple of things we *do* need to do, though," said Roman. "We need to talk to Pa and Sparky and let them know this has come up. There's a chance that Blassingame hombre might look one of them up, so we should have them prepared. And we should also make sure Pa's in agreement with rolling out tomorrow."

"What about Colleen?" asked Henry. "We need to fill her in, too. Right?"

Roman's brows pinched at the mention of the fourth Bradley sibling, their sister. "I guess so. But a part of me wishes we could avoid it."

"Why? Ain't it just as important she's also prepared, in case she runs into Blassingame?" Henry asked.

"That's just it. I hate the thought of her running into that blasted detective and finding out what he's up to. It's bound to upset her. I'd rather she didn't know." Roman cut a wary look in the direction of Malloy. "Not to touch a sore spot or anything, Ranger, . . . we've all seen how you and Colleen have took to making cow eyes at one another . . . but before you came along, there were signs of her and Mac striking a few sparks. That don't mean nothing now, except I can't help thinking how it would trouble her to find out he was in some kind of trouble that had bloodhounds on his tail."

"I understand," said Malloy. "I'd rather not see her upset either. But since there's the chance she might hear something before we leave town, don't you think it's best if she hears it up front, from one of us? Knowing Colleen, I suspect she'd be more upset if she found out we were pampering her by trying to hold out on her."

A corner of Roman's mouth tugged back wryly. "Appears you've gotten to know some things about our sister pretty quickly."

Happening, at that moment, to glance out the dining room's wide front window near where their table was situated, George spotted something out on the sun-washed early afternoon street that caused him to sit up straighter in his chair and stare with increased interest.

Sitting next to him, noting his reaction, Henry said, "What's the matter? What are you looking at?"

Bringing his attention back to those seated around the table with him, George announced, with a concerned look on his face, "Well, you can quit worrying about keeping or not keeping the matter of the detective from Colleen. She's coming down the boardwalk outside with Marshal Everett and two other men . . . one of 'em being none other than Blassingame."

Chapter 12

Upon entering the hotel dining room, Todd Everett, the town marshal of Miles City, and accompanied by Colleen and two other men, strode directly to the table occupied by Malloy and the Bradley brothers. "It's convenient finding all of you together. I was hoping that might be the case," he declared. "Since George is with you, I'm guessing he's already informed you of this matter that's now been brought to my attention. When we encountered Miss Colleen on the way over here, I requested she come along so we can cover things as quickly and concisely as possible."

"To me, it sounded more a demand than a request," Colleen was quick to add, tossing her mane of chestnut hair and displaying a frown on her pretty face that indicated she didn't much care for the treatment by any term.

"But now that we're here, I'll admit curiosity has got the better of me and I'd like to know what the devil is going on. Maybe you can start, Marshal, by identifying who this pair is"—a toss of her head to indicate the men who had entered with her and the marshal—"and what about us is any concern of theirs."

In deference to Colleen being among the new arrivals, the four men at the table had all risen. Their number having suddenly doubled, helped along by Colleen's voice also rising somewhat sharply in volume, drew no small amount of attention from others in the room.

Glancing around, Malloy said, "I suspect we're all in agreement about getting this business over with quickly and concisely, Marshal, but certainly there must be a better place to conduct it than here in the midst of a crowd."

"Would you rather march this procession back to my office?" Everett asked gruffly.

Malloy's gaze fell on a set of closed glass doors covered by filmy curtains on the far side of the room. He'd noted these on previous visits to this main, albeit modest-sized dining area and determined that the doors opened to a larger banquet hall used for special occasions. Tipping his head in their direction now, he said to Everett, "You have a badge, I have a badge. Don't you think that's enough to gain us entry into the banquet hall for the sake of a little privacy to discuss this matter?"

The marshal considered the question and the closed doors barely a second before turning to start in that direction and saying over his shoulder, "Follow me, then."

A handful of moments later, the eight people were reconvened in the banquet hall with the doors closed again behind them, shutting off the chatter and nosiness of all in the first room. Once Malloy held out a chair for Colleen to take a seat, most of the others perched, too, on chairs pulled up to the long tables currently lacking any settings. Only Everett and one of the strangers who'd arrived with him remained standing.

Everett, a tall, trim, hard-looking slab of a man with a neatly trimmed mustache and streaks of gray at his temples, restarted the discussion he had come here to have. "For the sake of all of you except George . . . who, from what I understand, has already met one of them . . . let me introduce to you Mr. Quinn Blassingame." The marshal swept a hand toward the stranger who also remained standing and then, with a second gesture, added, "And his partner, Mr. Ray Muncie."

Blassingame was another tall number, equaling Everett's six-plus feet in height, dressed in a corduroy jacket and high-quality trail clothes. He had craggy facial features, borderline homely, and a boldness about the way he held and carried himself that, combined with the cut of his clothes and the intelligence in his pale blue eyes, made a lasting impression on people. By contrast, Muncie, average appearing in every way, was one of the most unmemorable individuals anyone might ever meet.

"These two gents," the marshal went on, "are operatives for the High Grade Detective Agency out of Denver, Colorado. They approached me a little while ago with an inquiry they claim involves the Rafter B and the cattle drive you folks recently delivered here. I'm in no position to pass judgment on their claims, other than I know the High Grade Agency to have a pretty solid reputation. Plus, the nature of their inquiry is one that would naturally cause any lawman to perk up and pay attention."

"The subject of our inquiry," Blassingame spoke up, edging a half step forward, "is a man by the name of Dewey Mackenzie—'Mac', he generally calls himself. We have information that such a person was traveling with your outfit up until just before you reached your buyer here in Miles City."

"Who says? Where did you get such information?" Colleen immediately challenged.

Blassingame smiled thinly. "Well. It was partly confirmed by a conversation I had a short time ago with that young man seated right over there." He pointed. "I believe he's your brother George, is he not?"

Colleen first looked surprised and then shot a disapproving look toward George. The young man reddened and found a spot on the floor to frown down at.

"Do you dispute that confirmation?" Blassingame prodded Colleen.

"No, I suppose not," Colleen said grudgingly.

"In addition," Blassingame continued, "my partners and I also encountered three men on the trail south a few days ago—three cowboys on their way back to Texas. They admitted to having ridden for one Caleb Van Horne, a name I believe you all are also familiar with. After some, er, coaxing, they told a tale of disputed cattle claims over the herd your crew drove up from Texas and how it all ended in a bloody conflict near a spot not far from here called Buffalo Kill Gap. The good marshal has since told me the whole story surrounding that, how you seem to have been in the right, with the backing of Texas Ranger Malloy, when it came to fighting and winning that conflict. Since that's been settled to the satisfaction of Marshal Everett, it's none of my concern . . . except for the fact that those three ex–Van Horne cowboys revealed to us how they happened to have all heard the name 'Mac Mackenzie' as someone who was part of your outfit."

Now it was Roman who threw out a challenge. "How could they know that? And why would anybody believe anything they said? They were riding for that corrupt, thieving Van Horne!"

"Which they freely admitted," Blassingame allowed with a nod. "But they were hired on merely as cowboys, they explained. After they'd been on the trail with him for a while, supposedly to help drive the cattle Van Horne was out to reclaim because he swore they were rightfully his, the cowboys started getting suspicious about some of the talk they overheard and especially because of the small army of gunslingers that made up the rest of the crew. When the big gun battle at Buffalo Kill Gap broke out, they took off for the tall and uncut grass, but not before they had heard the names of everyone in the Rafter B outfit, including Mackenzie's, mentioned and cursed many times over."

"And how much coaxing did it take to remind them of that?" Roman's question dripped acid.

Blassingame gave an indifferent shrug. "Believe what you want. They admitted to everything else, why lie about a name that meant nothing to them?"

"How about because they knew it's what you wanted to hear?" suggested Malloy.

"What purpose would it serve us to pressure anybody into giving us a false lead?" Blassingame countered.

"Besides," interjected Muncie, almost lazily, "those three cowboys weren't the first to attach the name Mackenzie to the Rafter B outfit. There was a town farther back, a ways to the north and west of Cheyenne, where some of your outfit paid a visit. Town by the name of Torrence. They recalled the Rafter B real good . . . especially three hombres who got in a ruckus there. One of 'em they not only remembered being called 'Mac,' but they were double certain it was him who matched our handbill."

"You have a handbill?" Malloy echoed.

George scowled at Blassingame. "You never said nothing to me about no handbill."

"You ended the conversation I was trying to have with you rather abruptly, if you recall. Never gave me the chance," Blassingame reminded him.

"It's the handbill," said Marshal Everett, "that I was referring to when I said Blassingame's inquiry was enough to cause any lawman to perk up and pay attention." He jerked his chin at the detective. "Go ahead and show 'em."

"Mac? Our Mac? A murderer?" Norris Bradley, patriarch of the Bradley family and the Rafter B, huffed disdainfully at such a notion.

"An *accused* murderer," his daughter was quick to amend his words. "It's the law of the land, don't forget, that everyone is presumed innocent until proven guilty."

"The only proof I need is the time I spent with the man and who and what I saw him to be," Bradley said with conviction. "If Mac killed anybody, then they durned well had it coming."

"It's all well and good for those of us who got to know him to maintain our faith in him," said Gar Malloy solemnly. "But none of that changes the fact that Mac is a wanted man with what appears to be some very powerful forces bent on going after him. He may be technically innocent until proven guilty, like Colleen says, but as long as he's on the run from a proper court of law, the question of his innocence will stand as a big question in the minds of many."

"So are you saying you think it's wrong for Mac to be on the run from those ridiculous charges?" Bradley demanded.

Malloy shook his head. "I don't know what's stacked against him. Must be some reason for Mac to think he doesn't have much chance in a New Orleans court. According to those detectives, his alleged victim was a man of considerable prominence. That's backed up by the size of the reward being offered for him on that Wanted poster they showed us . . . those powerful forces I mentioned."

"Prominence and big money don't always add up to everything being on the up-and-up," Roman Bradley muttered. "Our dealings with Caleb Van Horne and the corruption surrounding him were proof of that."

This discussion was taking place in Norris Bradley's hotel suite following the meeting that had occurred a couple hours earlier down in the banquet hall. Present in the suite were Bradley, his daughter and sons, and Malloy. Sparky Whitlock, a Rafter B cowboy who, like Bradley, had been wounded in the gun battle at Buffalo Kill Gap, had also been summoned to join them.

"So what's the upshot of the whole sorry mess, as far as where *we* stand?" Bradley said, balling his fists and pressing them down on the heavily padded armrests of the easy chair in which he sat. "How did you leave things with the marshal and those detectives?"

"For our part of it," Roman answered, "things ain't really no different than they were before that bloodhound Blassingame showed up. The marshal had already accepted our account of the business with Van Horne. I think it boiled down to him not being ready to switch gears and suddenly believe we were knowingly harboring a wanted murderer in our midst. Same for having any clear idea of where Mac might have headed off for. Still, truth to tell, I think Everett's got to the point where he's more than a little anxious to be rid of us."

Bradley grunted. "In his place, I don't reckon I could blame him."

"Just remember," said Colleen, casting a fond look in Malloy's direction that assuaged any concerns he might have had about any of this stirring dormant feelings in her for Mac over him, "having a Texas Ranger on our side has carried a lot of weight as far as gaining us the benefit of any doubts."

"Yeah, we're all grateful for how helpful Malloy has been, and how we'll need him to speak up for us when we get back home," allowed Henry. "But I don't think anything he had to say earlier carried much weight with that stone-faced Blassingame. I'm afraid Mac is in for a hard time of it with that stubborn rascal on his tail."

"I don't disagree," said Roman. "But all of that is out of our hands. Blassingame is no threat to us, not without any kind of buy-in from Everett and especially not with us heading back to Texas."

"Is that what we're fixing to do? How soon?" asked Sparky.

"I talked to the stonemason again just a little while ago. The markers for Shad and Nolan are ready," Roman replied. He brought his gaze to rest on his father. "As soon as Pa gives the word, we can hit the trail. Speaking for myself, I say the sooner the better."

The elder Bradley was quiet for a long moment, considering. Then, sighing, he said, "Roman's right. There's nothing more to keep us here, and plenty yet to face once we get home. We'll head out at first light tomorrow."

The others went quiet for a minute, too. Until George finally said, "I guess that's the way it has to be. But I still can't help feeling we ought to try and do . . . something, I don't know what . . . to try and help Mac."

"There is something we can do," Colleen said softly, her gaze drifting out the window toward where the afternoon sun was descending in the west. "We can pray for him."

Two miles south of town, Quinn Blassingame sat his horse in the shade of a tall, reddish rock column that jutted up from the surrounding grassy terrain dotted here and there by other such outcrops. Beside him, Muncie sat his own saddle in a casual slouch. Reined up before the two men was a third operative for the High Grade Agency, a man kept on the payroll for his renowned tracking skills. His name was Albert Running Horse, a half-breed Arapaho, middle thirties, lean and wiry, with a sunken-cheeked, pock-marked face and a cleanly shaven head under a slouch black hat with a colorfully beaded band around the base of its crown.

"So we had no trouble finding the Bradleys," Blassingame was saying, summing up a report to Running Horse as the latter tended to steer shy of towns as much as possible due to his lineage sometimes drawing unwanted attention. "But they turned out to be of little help. We got 'em to admit knowing Mackenzie and to the fact he was riding with their outfit, but they held fast to a claim that he left before they reached Miles City and they had no clear idea where he was headed or how far he might have gotten. Couldn't crowd no more out of 'em and the local marshal wouldn't go along with letting us try, so that was pretty much the end of it."

Running Horse grunted. "You're right. Don't help much."

"Other than determining that Mackenzie was here, close, only about a week ago," said Blassingame. "No, it ain't much . . . but it's something. Means we're nearer rather than farther."

"But if we don't know which way he went or where he might be now," said Muncie sourly, "that 'farther' could be stretching out in a hurry."

Running Horse rubbed his chin, then said, "Might be I could shed a little light on where our man is headed."

"How so?" Blassingame wanted to know.

"Those fellas we first ran into on the outskirts of town yesterday, the ones who told us about the big gun battle the Rafter B bunch got into before going on to Miles City . . . remember them?" He barely paused, continuing on without waiting for an answer. "They also told how a couple of Rafter B riders got killed in that fight and how the others buried 'em out here on the prairie. So, while you two was in town, I had time to scour the area plenty good, looking for any sign that might tell us something worthwhile."

"And you turned up something?"

"Didn't necessarily know it at the time but, yeah, based on what you got told by those in town, maybe."

Running Horse twisted partway around in his saddle and pointed. "Back yonder I found those two fresh graves. Circling all around wide, studying the ground close, I saw where a handful of riders and a wagon went on into town from where they was dug. Then, a while later, a bigger bunch of riders came back and brought in the cattle. They made sure to swing out clear of the graves. But apart from all of that, I found sign of a lone rider. Best I can tell, I judge his trail to have been left between the graves being dug and the cattle being took in, striking out strictly on his own, away from the town or the path of the others."

Blassingame was suddenly sitting up straighter in his saddle, eyes boring intently into Running Horse. "You're saying it could have been Mackenzie?"

The half-breed shrugged. "You tell me. Sounds like it fits what those Rafter B folks in town told you, don't it? And like I said, it also fits time-wise."

"Which way did that lone rider head out?" Muncie asked.

Running Horse jerked his chin. "That way. West."

"That fits, too. A general track north and to the west is how Mackenzie has been angling ever since he left Louisiana," Blassingame noted. His eyes bored even harder into Running Horse. "You think you can continue following that lone rider's trail after this long?"

"You kidding?" Muncie said, not trying to hide his excitement. "Running Horse can track a sugar cube through a snowstorm!"

A rare smile touched Running Horse's mouth. "I don't know about that. But this grassland, for as far as I can see, is patchy and bare in enough places. If it stays that way and the weather holds . . . yeah, I reckon I can stick with his trail."

"That's good enough for me. Better than anything else we've got," declared Blassingame. He swung his eyes to the west, where the sun was hanging low in a pale blue sky. Thinking out loud, he said, "Muncie and I loaded up on supplies while we were in town. And we've still got a good three hours of daylight left. Gentlemen, let's ride!"

Chapter 13

The minute he pushed through the batwings of the Irish Jig Saloon, Mac knew something was wrong. For starters, there was tension hanging heavy in the air. He could feel it. His eyes swept the room, looking for Eamon Farrell, and came to rest on him seated at a table in the far corner.

The three men sitting with Eamon, business types in well-cut suit jackets and string ties, Mac didn't recognize. But the three additional hombres hovering over the seated men, he recognized all too well: Jerry Lee Lawton, Roy Orton, and Edsel Purdy.

It was the final day before the Standing L outfit was planning to start its cattle drive north to Rattlesnake Creek. Mac and Ox Arnussen had come to town to purchase the last of the supplies needed to finish stocking the makeshift chuckwagon the old hauling rig had been converted into. Marcus, Becky, and Ned Baker remained behind at the ranch to take care of final preparations and make sure there was enough feed for the pigs and chickens while Cy Hooper took care of things during their absence. The herd had been rounded up and brought in close, grazing lazily now, fattening up and resting, even though they didn't realize it, for the trip ahead.

With their purchases completed and the buckboard loaded, Ox had expressed a desire to make a stop at the local barber before heading back. Mac wanted to say good-bye to Eamon, so they'd agreed that Ox would come by and pick him up at the saloon when his barbering was done.

All of which left Mac in a good mood, lighthearted and anxious to get started on the drive, feeling well along on the road to being fully healed from his recent beating and looking forward to enjoying a couple of beers with Eamon—until he saw who the Irishman was presently in the company of.

For a moment, Mac worried he was witnessing a betrayal, a sign that his friend had for some reason backtracked on allowing the three thugs into his establishment. But a closer examination of Eamon's face, the barely controlled anger showing there—maybe even borderline rage—quickly told a different story. Something was indeed wrong. Something was *forcing* Eamon to put up with having those three gathered about him.

As these thoughts tumbled through Mac's mind, he paused only a few steps inside the saloon, unsure how to proceed. Upon deciding to make the trip into town with Ox, for the sake of helping to make sure all the provisions on his list were available and to choose adequate substitutes in case they weren't, Mac had wondered about the possibility of running into Jerry Lee and his pals. Immediately following his beating, he'd intended *purposely* to look those boys up again in order to deliver some payback. Had, in fact, vowed as much.

But enough time had passed for his hunger to have diminished some. The encounter on the trail out to the Standing L that first day and the hurt he'd been able to return then with Ox's help went a ways toward that.

Other circumstances had changed, too. While he wasn't a hundred percent healed from the injuries he'd suffered the last time he was in town, Mac figured he was in good enough shape to deliver another dose of getting even if that was in the cards.

But at what cost? His ribs remained tender enough so that only one or two blows slipping through could do serious damage all over again. And what of Sheriff Brimball, so obviously under Oscar Harcourt's thumb? What action might he take against Mac, an outsider, if he went ahead and cut loose with handing out payback to Harcourt's three hired thugs?

Considering these possibilities when faced with making the trip to town, Mac still had decided to go ahead with it. He convinced himself that the likelihood of running into the three toughs during a brief afternoon stop at the general store or a quick good-bye drink with Eamon— at the Irish Jig, where the men were barred—was too small to worry about.

Only now, here they were.

Thinking about how much Marcus and Becky were counting on him for their cattle drive—what a setback it would be to the undertaking if he got reinjured and couldn't participate, or tossed behind bars for who knew how long on some trumped-up charge meant to satisfy Harcourt—

is what held Mac in check. A big ego wasn't part of his makeup, but facts were facts. Without him, the Standing L cattle drive would be stalled. Indefinitely.

Turning and walking back out the door of the Irish Jig, risking the appearance of having it look like he was doing so to avoid facing Jerry Lee and the other two, went hard against Mac's grain. Yet that's what he was about to do, out of consideration for the greater good of all concerned.

A heartbeat before he spun on his heel, Eamon called out and stopped him.

"Mackie boy! Quit standing there blocking the doorway, lad. Come on over and join our little party."

Locking gazes with the Irishman, Mac saw beneath the pinched brows and above the clenched jaw a twinkle of deviltry suddenly form in his eyes. He didn't know exactly what it meant, but it was all he needed to abandon any thought of leaving and to accept the invitation to stick around and find out.

In the middle of the afternoon, between the lunch crowd and the evening drinkers yet to start dribbling in, there was only a handful of other customers in the Jig. Accordion-playing Feeney was nowhere to be seen and the bald dome of Shorty, the bartender, was barely visible behind the mahogany as he busied himself back there with some menial task. Becky, who would normally still be present, had quit her barmaid duties in order to start making preparations for the drive.

As he approached their table, the three men seated with Eamon watched Mac with measured interest. The three toughs standing behind them eyed him sneeringly but with no outward sign of aggression. It gave Mac a measure of satisfaction to note that the first and second fingers of Edsel Purdy's right hand were splinted together and wrapped stiff and straight in a bandage. But he noted, too, that the surly gunhand now wore a new Colt .45 holstered on his right hip in a cross-draw rig so he could pull it with his left. Mac had heard of gunmen who were equally skilled at shooting with either hand; apparently Purdy was—or *thought* he was—of that ilk.

"I was hoping you'd stop by before hitting the trail," Eamon greeted, flashing a crooked grin as he relaxed back in his chair. "If you didn't show, I was going to ride out to the ranch this evening and say my good-byes. But now, you not only saved me the trouble, but by coming around as you have, you get the opportunity to meet some of the most prominent men in the community you're leaving behind."

No one except Eamon appeared particularly pleased at the prospect of such a meeting, but he proceeded anyway. "Mac, this portly gent on my left is Keith Moorehead, president of the Harcourt City Bank and Trust. To my right, just as his shifty eyes suggest, is our city attorney, Malcolm Croft. And on the other side of him is none other than Harcourt City's very own Oscar Harcourt. . . . Gentlemen, in return I give you Mr. Mac Mackenzie, from parts unknown on his way to places yet to be determined."

None of the businessmen made any move to rise and no hands were extended by either them or Mac. The deviltry dancing in Eamon's eyes twinkled brighter. Gesturing indifferently, he added, "And as for the three mongrels standing behind Harcourt, I expect you remember them well enough from your previous visit to town."

This drew an indignant scowl from the plump, grayhaired banker, Moorehead. "Here now," he huffed, the cottony blobs of brow above his heavily pouched eyes pulling closer together. "We're in the midst of a serious business transaction, Farrell. I hardly think this is an appropriate time for interruptions or caustic comments."

"And I take offense to that remark about shifty eyes!" declared Croft, the attorney, a middle-aged number sporting a pair of wire-rimmed glasses perched near the end of a long, bony nose that jutted like a spear tip out from his narrow, pale face.

The twinkle in Eamon's eyes abruptly turned into a hard glint. "*You* take offense, you say? That's rich, considering how offensive this whole sham of a so-called 'business transaction' is!"

The Irishman turned his gaze back to Mac, who had again come to a halt and stood waiting to see what was going to happen next.

"Take a good look, Mac, you're witnessing robbery masquerading as what some at this table want to pretend is legitimate business. But it's robbery sure enough, conducted by words on paper put down by the point of a pencil rather than at the point of a gun or knife." To emphasize what he was saying, Eamon seized up a handful of loose papers from the tabletop and then slammed them back down before adding, "And I, for one, would find more honor in facing steel or lead over this kind of cowardly theft."

"You keep runnin' your mouth—" Jerry Lee started to say, but was cut short by a quick, chopping gesture from Harcourt.

"You're being unnecessarily insulting and totally wrong in your assessment," insisted Croft, glaring at Eamon. "What's being presented to you here is not uncommon and certainly not illegal."

Eamon continued to address Mac, saying, "What I've

been 'presented' with, you see, is news that my note with Moorehead's bank has been taken over by Harcourt. In other words, except for what little I can claim as my own from the monthly payments I've made to the bank, Harcourt now owns the balance of the Irish Jig."

"It's not uncommon for the deed of a property or business holding to be transferred from one investor to another," Moorehead said rather stiffly.

"And when a new investor, or owner, if you will, takes over," Croft sniffed with an officious air, "said person or persons has every right to set new terms for the property or business involved to continue being paid off by someone currently occupying it."

Mac had heard enough to add it up the rest of the way. "Let me guess," he said to Eamon, "the new terms being offered are not very agreeable to you."

"It's not just the terms I find disagreeable," Eamon replied, his mouth twisting sourly. "It's also the pompous twit behind them. I'd sooner see the Irish Jig burnt to the ground than share the running of it with the likes of Oscar Harcourt."

Now, finally, Harcourt spoke. As he did, Mac for the first time took a moment to focus on him, to give a quick assessment of this big wheel around which the whole town and most everybody in it—with one of the notable exceptions being Eamon Farrell—seemed to rotate.

He wasn't what Mac would have expected, not pampered or soft looking in the manner of Moorehead and Croft. He looked to be only about forty or so, trim and powerfully built under his finely cut attire. And in addition to the physical kind, Mac was promptly and keenly aware of another kind of power about the man—an aura, a confidence and self-assuredness that was invisible to the eye but could very much be felt in his presence.

In a calm, well-modulated tone, Harcourt said, "If I were you, Farrell—which is, of course, a ridiculous concept in and of itself—I would choose my words much more carefully. In addition to a possible slander charge for your abusive public claims and references, there are now five witnesses—six, counting Mackenzie, though he's of little consequence one way or the other—who just heard you threaten to burn down this establishment rather than accept the fact of my ownership."

Eamon turned his head almost casually and glared at Harcourt with eyes as hard and dark as two chips of coal. "Mister," he said quietly, "if I ever *truly* threaten you, you will know it and you won't have time to spout no fancy words when it's coming straight at you."

"I think that's quite enough," exclaimed lawyer Croft, sliding his chair back suddenly, as if being caught in the line of the glares being exchanged between Eamon and Harcourt placed him in some kind of jeopardy. "If we can't conclude this matter civilly, without it turning into a . . . a . . . Well, perhaps the presence of Marshal Brimball is required."

"Nonsense," Harcourt said, snapping out the word. "No matter how much Farrell may dislike it, this piece of business is clear cut and finished. Brimball can't add or detract anything, not at this time. My terms for Farrell continuing as proprietor of the Irish Jig are spelled out clearly." He tapped a forefinger down on the sheaf of papers Eamon had brandished earlier. "He has twenty-four hours to accept them and proceed accordingly . . . or to gather up his personal belongings and vacate the premises. If he resists further at that point, *then* I certainly will not hesitate to call in the marshal!"

Eamon shoved to his feet. "I don't *need* twenty-four hours. I don't need twenty-four seconds. You can take those terms, Harcourt, and shove them so far up your—"

This time Jerry Lee reacted too fast for Harcourt to stop him, even if he'd wanted to. As soon as Eamon shot to a standing position, Jerry Lee was in motion, too. Taking a lunging step forward and at an angle from where he stood behind Harcourt, he twisted his long torso and lashed out with his right fist, shouting, "Nobody talks to the boss that way!"

The combination of his shout and the blow landing effectively cut short what Eamon had been trying to say and the force of the punch sent the feisty Irishman staggering wildly.

In practically the same instant, without conscious thought or decision, Mac rushed forward, reaching to grip the edge of the table in both hands, then continuing to drive ahead with all his weight, ramming the table as hard as he could into everyone around and behind it!

Chapter 14

All of a sudden, the saloon's quiet, midafternoon lull was tossed on its ear and turned into a scene of scrambling, toppling bodies; flying fists; curses and yelps of alarm; and sheets of loose paper kicked high into the air, then left to flutter down over everything like over-sized snowflakes.

Banker Moorehead and lawyer Croft were immediately and unceremoniously dumped from their chairs. Sprawling onto the floor, both found themselves scurrying and crawling in undignified desperation to get clear of the shifting bodies and stomping feet that surrounded them. A purple-faced Moorehead uttered protests of outrage between puffing to try to catch his breath, while Croft merely whimpered and sniveled for fear of getting crushed.

Oscar Harcourt, too, was spilled from his chair. But he proved agile enough to twist away just before the table was driven into him, so that he ended up only dropping briefly to one knee and then regaining his footing almost immediately. This maneuver placed him off to one side, largely removed from the action that ensued around the center of the hurtling table.

With Harcourt dodging off to one side and Moorehead and Croft ending up on the floor underneath, it was the three thugs—Jerry Lee, Orton, and Purdy—who took the main force of the ramming table, which was more or less what Mac had intended. By catching them on their feet but off guard, he was able to shove them back against the wall and hold them pinned there, at least momentarily. Long enough, he was counting on, for Eamon to recover from getting sucker punched and rejoin the fray for the sake of helping balance the odds.

Because the punch hadn't knocked him off his feet, Eamon jumped back into the mix every bit as quickly as Mac hoped, and every bit as aggressively. He didn't waste a second zeroing in on Jerry Lee, going after him with a snarling curse as he leaped over a corner of the table to get his hands on him. With the table pressed against him, Jerry Lee could neither flee nor duck. All he could do was throw his arms up and try to protect himself from the human missile sailing in his direction.

As his lunge sent him onto and sliding across the tabletop, Eamon thrust his reaching hands through Jerry Lee's attempted defense. One hand landed a punch half on the chin, half to the throat. With the other, Eamon grabbed Jerry Lee's shirtfront and yanked savagely, pulling the man to him.

The weight of both men now struggling on its top,

combined with Mac shoving from one side and Orton and Purdy trying to shove back from the other, was too much for the abused table. It collapsed, partially down onto the unfortunate Moorehead and Croft, who hadn't yet managed to crawl all the way clear.

With the table cracking and splintering loudly and the two men underneath wailing even louder, the two combatants, Eamon and Jerry Lee, now entangled in a knot of gouging fingers and pounding fists and kicking feet, toppled off one end of the wreckage and went rolling across the floor. This abruptly left Mac on his own to face the two remaining hired thugs, no longer at a disadvantage by being pinned in place. What was more, the varmint who kept them on his payroll was just a few feet off to one side.

In spite of being outnumbered, part of Mac felt the urge to follow Eamon's lead and charge across the wrecked table to go after Orton and Purdy with his fists, even at risk to his lingering injuries—which, to his surprise, weren't hurting nearly as bad as he would have expected. Still, a more sensible part of his brain was telling him to play it safe and go for his gun, no matter if this hadn't yet escalated to a shooting situation.

His indecision was settled when Purdy made the first move toward gunplay, his left hand starting to slip somewhat tentatively over to the cross-draw rig on his opposite hip. There was nothing tentative about Mac's reaction. In a blur of motion, the Model 3 was out of his waistband and aimed straight at Purdy.

Through clenched teeth, Mac said, "Go ahead, Lefty, slide that paw another quarter inch. But if you do and you ever intend to shoot a gun again, you'd better be able to draw with your feet and pull a trigger with your toes, because this time I'll turn that second hand into a stump instead of stopping at just crippling a finger."

Purdy's face went white and his hand dropped loosely to his side.

A moment later there was the solid-sounding thud of fist against meat and bone, and out of the corner of his eye, Mac saw Jerry Lee hit the deck and remain there in a battered lump. The saloon went quiet again, except for the soft flutter of a final sheet of paper drifting down and settling on the collapsed tabletop. From underneath, there came a single whimpered sob from Croft.

Eamon stepped up beside Mac. His hair was standing on end, a trickle of blood ran from one corner of his mouth, and he was breathing a little hard.

"I think," he said, "my business transaction has concluded."

From where he stood, looking on with ice-cold eyes, Oscar Harcourt said, "I can assure you that the likelihood of you *ever* conducting any kind of business in my town has concluded, Farrell. If you know what's good for you, you'll head out on that cattle drive with the fool standing beside you and neither of you will ever look back."

"Uh-oh, Mackie boy," said Eamon, "I think we just got kicked out of town. Can you bear it?"

Mac replied dryly, "I was hoping to have a cold beer before I left. Otherwise, I was sort of figuring on kicking myself out anyway."

"I'm afraid that cold beer will have to wait. But as for the rest of it . . . aye, I'm thinking that getting shed of Harcourt City has a very appealing ring." Eamon cocked his head to one side. "Do you think the Lewis cattle drive to Rattlesnake Creek has room for one more hand?"

"You know anything about cattle?"

"I know which end the hay and grain goes in and which end it, er, comes back out."

Mac grinned. "That means you know which end to point in the direction we want to go. Sounds like a pretty good start to me. I expect the Standing L will be able to use you."

"The lot of you deserve one another!" Harcourt sneered.

"That reminds me," said Eamon, taking a step around Mac. "Since this place is still mine for another twenty-four hours, I feel duty bound to do a final bit of tidying up before I take my leave."

Harcourt appeared puzzled as the Irishman strode purposely toward him. Then, when it was too late, he suddenly looked startled and attempted to raise his hands protectively. But the right cross Eamon uncorked slammed through easily and the punch landed solidly on the hinge of the powerful man's jaw, dropping him like a sack of wet sand wrapped in expensive clothes.

With their body language and with rage flaring in their eyes, Orton and Purdy showed the urge to want to try to defend their employer. But the urge wasn't strong enough for them to make a move while under the muzzle of Mac's Smith & Wesson.

As Eamon was turning back from slugging Harcourt, the batwings popped open and a freshly barbered Ox came through the front door. A quick scan of the scene caused his mouth to drop open. He asked, "What the heck is going on?"

"Eamon just signed the Irish Jig over to a new owner," Mac calmly said over his shoulder. "He's going to be riding for the Standing L brand."

Chapter 15

Oscar Harcourt sat once again behind the spacious desk in his private office. Outside, the darkness of full night had descended. A single lantern, its wick adjusted low, sat burning near one corner of the desk. This cast the desk in a soft glow, left the rest of the room edged in murky shadow.

Harcourt's rectangular face was also etched in shadow and the bruise along his left jawline stood out like a smudge on his otherwise clean, sharply cut features. A bottle of top-quality brandy stood at his elbow, and in his hands, rolling it slowly back and forth between the palms, he held a glass of the amber liquid. His expression was brooding and, when he spoke, his tone was unmistakably bitter and the words came in almost a flat monotone.

"Only you made any move in my defense. Your action

was perhaps too hasty and not, in the end, terribly effective . . . but it was nevertheless properly intentioned."

These statements were being addressed to Jerry Lee Lawton, who stood before the desk in partial murkiness. Jerry Lee's face also bore marks and bruises from the afternoon's conflict. He stood fidgeting a bit, as he usually did when summoned here, and wondered what Harcourt was leading up to.

He didn't have to wait long. In the same bitter monotone, Harcourt continued, "Those other two buffoons, on the other hand, stood as useless as dead branches on a tree, while that brazen Irishman walked right up and hammered me to the floor. *That*, I cannot condone! Therefore, I'm looking to you, on my behalf, to make them aware they are no longer in my employ and I no longer want to see their stupid, useless faces anywhere around me. Be sure they understand that. Any attempt by them to seek me out directly, begging for some kind of second chance, will be met by even harsher treatment."

Jerry Lee hung his head. He hated hearing this. He'd been thick with Orton and Purdy for a lot of years. The three of them had been through some hard times together, long before the lucrative jobs they'd all enjoyed since signing on with Harcourt.

Now not only had he been tasked with giving them the news about no longer having a job with Harcourt, but he was also under orders to make his own break with them. He could, of course, stick up for the pair, try to convince Harcourt they deserved some better consideration, maybe even threaten to quit himself if he was no longer sided by his two longtime pals.

But a second after that thought crossed his mind, he

knew, number one, such a threat to Harcourt would never work and, number two, he didn't have enough guts to even make the attempt. How far was a fella's loyalty to his pards expected to go?

"After you've gotten rid of those idiots," Harcourt went on, "I want you to immediately seek out some replacements. You know the type and I imagine you know where to find them. For the first job I'll be sending you on, I suggest recruiting more than just two. I'd say four, perhaps even five. And best make sure that at least some of them know a bit about wrangling cattle."

"Cattle, sir?" Jerry Lee arched an eyebrow. "What sort of job do you have in mind?"

Harcourt took a drink of his brandy. "I should think that would be obvious. I'm sending you after the Standing L herd that's being driven to Rattlesnake Creek."

"You mean you want us to rustle that herd?"

"Nothing quite so crude or blatant," Harcourt responded. "Oh, make no mistake, I intend to acquire those cattle, to be sure. But I will do so in a manner not quite so . . . well, I haven't worked out all the details yet. And that's where you and the new men you find are going to come in. I want you to ensure I have the time to get those details ironed out and ready for when that herd reaches Rattlesnake Creek. We'll let the Lewises and those two troublemakers they've aligned themselves with, Farrell and Mackenzie, do all the hard work, and then I'll make my move."

"You're planning for that to happen all the way up there at Rattlesnake Creek?"

"Didn't I make that clear?" Harcourt scowled. "If everything goes reasonably well for them, I calculate it should take the Standing L outfit a little short of a month to complete their drive. I want you and your crew to buy me an additional ten days to two weeks to ensure I'm able to make the necessary arrangements I want to have ready for when they arrive at their destination."

Jerry Lee nodded. "Okay. I think I'm starting to get the picture. You want me and the boys I put together to follow along on the trail and find ways to fix it so things *don't* go so well for the drive. Spook the cattle, foul up some water holes maybe, block a pass or two they figure on going through so they have to swing wider around . . . anything to slow 'em down, cause 'em to take longer to get to the finish."

"Exactly. Don't harm the cattle, I plan on making a tidy profit off them once I take over the herd." Harcourt rolled the glass of brandy between his palms some more. "While I disapprove of the people he surrounds himself with, I have to hand it to Marcus Lewis that his plan to push his cattle to the beef-hungry gold strike region where he can sell them at a highly inflated price is quite clever. I hate to admit I didn't think of it first. But now that it's set in motion"—a corner of Harcourt's mouth twisted up slyly—"I'll still insinuate myself. A bit late, perhaps, but not too late to turn it to my advantage."

His mouth pulled once more into a straight, tight line and Harcourt lifted one hand from the brandy glass and touched it absently to the bruise on his cheek before adding coldly, "And when I again face the likes of Eamon Farrell and that meddler Mackenzie, this time I'll be ready to have my advantage over them as well!"

Forty-five minutes later, in the one-room cabin they shared near the east edge of town, Jerry Lee, Orton, and

Purdy sat around a bare wooden table in the kitchen area at one end of the shack. A half-empty bottle of cheap whiskey, three dented tin cups, and a pair of fat, partly melted candles occupied the top of the table. Faintly pulsing illumination from the candles played over the shadowy faces of the men. All three wore glum expressions.

"Well, it's a lousy deal, that's all I got to say," lamented Orton, head hung low over the whiskey fumes rising from his cup. "After all the dirty jobs we've done for him, Harcourt chops his hand down and brings it to a screeching halt."

Beside him, Edsel Purdy joined in. "What was we supposed to do with that .44 of Mackenzie's stuck in our faces? The way it was shoved in his waistband under his jacket flap, I never knew the sneaky polecat even *had* a gun."

"You're carrying around a pretty strong reminder that he knows how to shoot," Jerry Lee said, jerking his chin toward Purdy's bandaged hand. "I'm surprised you gave him any chance to get the drop on you."

Purdy scowled. "That's just the trouble. If I'd still had my good right hand, I could have outdrawn that meddler three times over, even if he'd gone for his gun first. But with only this"—he thrust up his left hand—"I'm pretty good and getting better, but still not equal to my right."

"He's getting there, though," Orton was quick to add. "He practices every day. I watch. He's improving every time."

"I know, I know. I've seen it, too. But unfortunately," Jerry Lee said with a sigh, "you wasn't ready when you needed to be. Not when you could have convinced Harcourt. And now he's made up his mind against both of you, and I don't know what to do!"

Moon-faced Orton looked even more forlorn. "Hell, Jerry Lee, don't you think he'll eventually cool down? And then, when he does, you'll be able to get him to change his mind about giving us another chance?"

Jerry Lee took a drink of his whiskey. "I don't know. Once his mind is made up, he's a mighty stubborn cuss. And Farrell laid hands on him, marked him . . . while you two just stood there, the way he sees it."

"With a blasted gun pointed at us, near point-blank range!" Purdy wailed. "If me and Roy had made a move and got our heads blowed off, how would that have done Harcourt any good? Can't he see that?"

"Not the way he's looking at it. Not right now, anyway. And as for me trying to get him to reconsider in case he *should* cool down some," said Jerry Lee, "I won't be around to do any talking to him at all, on account of I'll be gone chasing that blasted cattle herd for the next five or six weeks."

"Well, it's a lousy deal, that's all I got to say," muttered Orton.

Purdy cut him a sour glance. "If that's all you got to say, then why do you keep saying it over and over? Repeating it every five minutes ain't gonna change nothing."

"Knock it off," Jerry Lee grumbled. "You two going at each other's throats ain't gonna change nothing either. And it for sure ain't gonna help."

Orton and Purdy stayed quiet, avoiding looking at each other.

"But," said Jerry Lee, "I got an idea that might give us the best chance of working through this problem."

Two hopeful gazes swung to him.

Jerry Lee went on, "It'll involve me sticking my neck

out some, but I'm willing to take the risk. And I can't make no promises it will work out in the end. But if you want to keep having a job for at least the next six weeks and take the gamble with me it might be a way to bring you back in favor with Harcourt, then I'll lay out what I got in mind."

"Let's hear it," Orton was quick to say.

"I'm listening. You ain't ever steered us wrong up to now, Jerry Lee," Purdy said solemnly.

After another drink of whiskey, Jerry Lee lowered his cup and said, "It's pretty simple, really. I'm proposing you two go ahead and ride with me and a couple other fellas I got in mind to bring in. We'll all follow and harass that Standing L herd. We'll be gone away from Harcourt City, so ol' Oscar can't be butt stung because he won't have no way of knowing we're still sticking together. For myself, I'll feel a darn sight better knowing I got my two pards I can count on for those weeks out in the wild, and you rascals will share in the pay Harcourt is shelling out for the group he wants me to put together. In the end, if we get the herd to Rattlesnake Creek and he's had the time he needs to put together his big scheme and it all comes off as a success . . . well, what better circumstances to hit him up for reconsidering about you two?"

"I like the sound of it!" exclaimed Orton. "You can count me in."

"Same here," agreed Purdy. He looked thoughtful for a minute, then added, "Look at it this way. Even if Harcourt don't want to give us a second chance, that would leave us up there in the middle of a gold strike with grubstake money in our pockets. Shoot, we might end up richer and better off that way!"

Jerry Lee arched a brow. "Go ahead and dream if you want. Me, I'll take the bird in the hand . . . and that's staying on Harcourt's payroll. But before we worry about any of that, we've got to get the cattle drive business out of the way and all make it to Rattlesnake Creek. The first step toward that is for you two to clear out of Harcourt's sight while I take care of some other matters. I'll need time to gather provisions and find a couple more men to ride with us. So, until I'm ready, here's the way we'll work it. . . ."

Chapter 16

The cattle drive streamed away from the Standing L ranch headquarters at first light on a Wednesday morning. Mac rolled out ahead of the rest, rocking back and forth on the seat of the chuckwagon, fingering the traces of the four-up pulling team of horses. In the past, he'd worked with mules and had actually developed a bit of a preference for the jugheads. But the Lewises had no mules among their stock, so these hayburners would have to do. The animals made a good set, though, strong and responsive, giving Mac no reason to anticipate any problem.

The morning was clear, brisk for late summer, but warmed rapidly as the sun climbed in the cloudless sky. Mac felt good, loose, shed of almost all the soreness that had been pounded into him some days past. His ribs were still somewhat tender, but not even the strain he'd put on them yesterday with his bout of table-shoving had left them feeling any worse.

He was glad to be under way with the drive. On reflection, he recognized he was also glad for the chance to have been part of getting a few licks in against Harcourt and his thugs—a measure of payback, although a lesser one than he'd contemplated at one time—before pulling out. He didn't figure on returning this way once the cattle were delivered to Rattlesnake Creek, so he'd have to be content with leaving it at that.

Eamon Farrell returning from town with Mac and Ox had been a surprise to Marcus and Becky. Even more so was hearing the reasons why, coupled with his request to join the drive. Eamon was accepted without hesitation, no matter that when it came to working cattle the Irishman admittedly was as green as the grass the critters fed on.

Any reservation about taking him on was removed when he proclaimed to one and all, "I'm a good horseman, a quick learner, and you can count on me to stay the course, no matter how hard it gets."

"That's good enough for me. You've long since proven yourself a solid, dependable friend, Eamon," Marcus had responded soberly. Then, the soberness giving way to a lopsided grin, he added, "In no time at all, we'll turn you into a solid, dependable cowboy."

And so it went. Over the course of only a couple of days, Eamon was pulling his weight when it came to working the herd—keeping the cattle moving, keeping them in line, alternately cooing and cussing them like an old hand. Getting accustomed to long hours in a saddle took its toll on him, but it never caused him to shirk or complain except for a bit of involuntary groaning when he tried to maneuver into a comfortable position at mealtimes or, even more so, when it came to crawling out of his bedroll at daybreak.

But he was hardly the first cowboy who'd ever done some groaning on a long drive, as proven by looking no further than the others in the Standing L outfit whose normal day-to-day activities around the ranch didn't make them fully conditioned for extended saddle time either.

Luckily, Mac had thought to stock some liniment for muscle strain and aches among their supplies. In the early going, he was passing it around liberally, including some that got smeared on his own backside. Especially first thing in the morning and last thing at night, the camp fairly reeked of the nose-stinging medicinal smell. Some of the horses even balked a bit at the sharp odor when approached to be saddled up.

Other than that, the first three days went very well. They averaged fifteen, close to sixteen miles a stretch. The weather held, still and plenty warm, without getting too punishingly hot. And the terrain they passed over was an easy expanse of rolling, grassy hills broken only occasionally and briefly by a rocky section.

Everybody knew they wouldn't have such favorable conditions the whole way, but it was especially good to have them now at the beginning, while crew and cattle were getting broken in to the routine they would be living for days and weeks to come.

The camaraderie of the group, something Mac was already familiar with and felt a part of due to his days spent healing at the ranch, remained unchanged once on the trail. And Eamon's addition to the mix in an ongoing capacity only added to it. Everybody looked forward to hearing his tales of the various things he'd experienced in his travels, spun at night camp and told with the entertaining touch he had for making them all the more enjoyable.

Another added attraction, something that came at the Irishman's personal expense yet a matter he handled with self-deprecating good humor, was his struggle to master the throwing of a lasso. What started as private practice sessions he began conducting each evening after supper, off on one side of the camp's perimeter, became a sort of group activity after the others took notice and gathered to watch and offer advice and instructions. When none of this resulted in Eamon being able to drop his loop with any repeatable success, the sessions, though still taken seriously by all concerned, became a source of light-hearted fun and a bit of friendly ribbing.

What made the kidding around acceptable, because lassoing was a useful and important skill for the job at hand, was the fact that everyone involved knew it was just a matter of time before Eamon's determination would not only win out, but might very well drive him to become the best doggone roper in the outfit.

Another area where Eamon's determination was of note to a particular member of the outfit, namely Mac, was his interest in Becky. Mac hadn't forgotten Marcus's comment that time about the Irishman being attracted to his sister. And although Mac hadn't seen any sign of such an attraction initially, that had changed: he could see it now. Nothing overt, nothing improper, but it was definitely there. The way Eamon looked at Becky at unguarded moments, the spark in his eye when she was speaking directly to him. Yeah, he was for sure smitten.

Whether Becky had any similar feelings or even noticed the ones in Eamon, Mac couldn't tell. But there was no mistaking his for her.

And who could blame him? Mac certainly recognized the impulse. He, too, was smitten with Becky, practically from that first moment when he'd seen her about to be punched by Jerry Lee. And spending so much time in her presence since then had certainly done nothing to diminish what he saw in her.

The slight pang of jealousy he felt at the thought of Eamon possibly winning her was pointless. For one thing, he liked the Irishman too much to feel any ill will toward him. And for Becky's sake, he could only hope that one day she *would* put down her guard and accept having a good man like Eamon at her side.

As far as fancying himself as that man, Mac knew such a thing was even more pointless. Him being a wanted man, a fugitive running from a murder charge, what right did he have thinking he had anything to offer a decent woman?

But that didn't prevent him from still having feelings and hopes. . . .

From behind a jagged, sun-bleached spine of rocks running along the crest of a hogback about a quarter mile to the southwest, five men looked out on the Standing L cattle herd where it was bedded down at the close of its fourth day's push.

The sun had dropped behind the western horizon, leaving everything in the pale gray half-light that lingers for a time between day and full dark. A chill breeze was blowing out of the north, and overhead, the sky seemed undecided as to whether it would take on a cloud cover or yield to an eventual wash of star- and moonlight.

"Well, gents, there it is," said Jerry Lee, leaning slightly forward with his forearms resting on the rocks that still retained a bit of the day's heat, before the breeze had come up. "Take a good look. There's what we'll be dogging for the next five or so weeks."

To his left, Floyd Sleet, also leaning against the rocks and gazing out through eyes that seemed perpetually half squinted, as if he was always on the verge of being mad about something, muttered, "Better to be dogging those mangy, plodding slabs of beef on the hoof than having to be part of pushing 'em along."

"I don't disagree," allowed Jerry Lee. "But remember, if Harcourt gives the word, we *might* get the call to do some wrangling near the end of the trip, when we're close to Rattlesnake Creek."

Sleet twisted his mouth sourly. "If it has to be, it has to be, I guess. Ain't like we all haven't done it before. Comes to it as part of this, though, I just hope it don't amount to much."

Sleet, along with 'Bama Wilkes, positioned on the other side of him, constituted the additional men Jerry Lee had recruited for this latest Harcourt job he was taking the lead on. He'd done work with both Sleet and Wilkes in the past, though it had been quite a spell back. Still, he knew them to be cut from the kind of rawhide he needed, and hearing they were currently working as cat house bouncers in nearby Bantaville, he had a hunch they'd be up for a break from that, especially when they heard the kind of money Harcourt was willing to pay.

Sleet was a tall, thick-bodied man, somewhat brutish in appearance. He moved with surprising grace for a big man, smooth, almost catlike at times. And Jerry Lee had witnessed firsthand how, in the face of danger, those movements were controlled by icy, steel steady nerves.

'Bama Wilkes contrasted physically, being lean and wiry, a couple inches shorter. But his movements, too, were smooth and assured, and behind the wiry man's shifty, calculating eyes, Jerry Lee knew there was another set of steady-in-the-face-of-danger nerves he could count on.

To Jerry Lee's right, Roy Orton said, "So now that we've caught up with 'em, what have you got in mind as far as the first bit of devilment you aim for us to serve up?"

"You sound a mite anxious, Roy," Jerry Lee said, turning a cocked eye to the moon-faced man. "You get bored with just kicking back and waiting out here in all this fresh air and emptiness?"

A sheepish grin tugged at Orton's mouth. "Yeah, I guess I did at that. Reckon I've got settled too deep into town living after all the months we been working for Harcourt mostly in and around the settlement. Getting these old bones back suited to a bedroll on the hard ground and squatting over a campfire at mealtime ain't coming so easy."

After Jerry Lee had struck the deal with Orton and Purdy to be part of harassing the Standing L herd, against Harcourt's wishes, they'd ridden on ahead, away from town to ensure they stayed out of Harcourt's sight, and waited out on the prairie at a predetermined spot for Jerry Lee to show up with necessary provisions and the additional men. That had taken place yesterday. Now, today, after an intervening day and a half of following the herd's trail, they had caught up.

In response to Orton's lamentations about getting used to living out in the open again, Edsel Purdy rolled his eyes and said, "Boy oh boy, ain't that the truth. I been having to listen to him this whole while, Jerry Lee, moaning and groaning like an old grandpaw with practically every move he makes."

"Well, excuse me all to Hades," Orton snapped back. "And I been having to watch you pull out that .45 of yours, spinning around and practicing your left-hand draw, about five hundred times a day. You think that ain't been nerve wracking? Folks are born to trouble, or so the Good Book says, so get used to it."

"That's right. And you both had better get used to it, so knock off the bellyaching," growled Jerry Lee. "Roy, the ground between here and Rattlesnake Creek ain't gonna get any softer and campfire meals are all that's on the menu for the foreseeable future. And Edsel, you'd *better* get the hang of that left-hand draw because in case you have to face Mackenzie again and you hope to make a good impression on Harcourt if you do . . . well, you ain't gonna get but one chance."

Everybody was quiet for several moments. Jerry Lee continued to frown in the direction of Orton and Purdy. They averted their eyes and glared out at the lumpy black mass of the Standing L cattle and the flickering campfire and shifting shapes that milled about the associated chuckwagon.

And then, his mouth spreading in a wide grin that signaled he was hoping to lighten things up, Wilkes leaned out away from the rocks and called over to Orton and Purdy, "Hey, fellas. You want to talk about making a dubious trade when it comes to taking on this job? You know what me and Sleet was doing when this silver-tongued rascal Jerry Lee showed up and lured us away with the promise of a big payday? We was bouncing in a cat house over in Bantaville. Madam Fifi's. You probably know the place, right? Pay wasn't much, but the fringe benefits . . . ooh-la-la!"

"So why'd you leave, if it was such a sweet deal?" asked Orton.

Wilkes' expression puckered with exaggerated dismay. "One reason and one reason only, friend . . . my health. I needed a rest. Those girls, each one of 'em had it so bad for me. They plumb wouldn't leave me alone."

Orton looked like he suspected he was being put on, yet was uncertain how to react.

Sleet reacted for him, saying, "The thing you need to learn right quick about Wilkes here is that the stories he tells ain't *completely* hogwash. So when he says he had to get away from Fifi's for his health, that much is true. But what was threatening said health wasn't so much a matter of the gals wearing him out. No, it was more like Fifi's husband suspecting that the lovely Fifi was paying part of 'Bama's salary with warm personal favors instead of just cold cash."

"So what about you?" asked Purdy. "Did you leave, too, out of loyalty to Wilkes?"

Sleet waved that off with a pass of one hand. "Shoot, no. If he's dumb enough to get caught poaching apples out of the wrong orchard, that's his tough luck. Trouble was, I fell for the temptation of going after some of the low-hanging fruit in that same orchard."

Everybody had a good chuckle over that.

Until Orton said, "Well, Jerry Lee, it sounds like you might at least be in for a change of pace. You're always complaining how the snoring of me and Edsel keeps you awake at night. Now it could be that our snores are gonna be offset by a lot of restless tossing and turning and lonely murmurs of 'Fifi, Fifi' in the wee hours."

"Too many nights of that might be enough to make me go volunteer for punching cattle instead," grunted Jerry Lee. "But unless or until it comes to that, we'd better start thinking about the job at hand, like Roy brought up to begin with. Come on. Let's drop back a ways, set up our own night camp and take on some grub. Then, before we turn in, I'll share with you some ideas I got for how we're gonna start pestering those cow pushers over yonder."

Chapter 17

*F*ive days coming to a close and everything so far has gone without a hitch.

That was the thought that kept running through Mac's mind as he and the chuckwagon crested a blunt, grassy hill and began rolling down a gentle slope on the other side.

His eyes swept over the broad, shallow hollow that spread out ahead. Off to the right, a ribbon of sparkling water wound through a fringe of trees. To the left, the slope rolled back some and left a sort of flattened shoulder that would make a good spot to park the wagon for night camp. Between the creek and the shoulder, plenty of grass for the herd to graze and bed down until morning.

This was one more thing falling neatly into place. *Five*

*days coming to a close and everything so far has gone
without a hitch.*

That thought and the lack of problems behind it, Mac
reminded himself, should have been comforting. And it
was. Up to a point. Trouble was, Mac had spent too much
time in the company of leathery old veterans who, almost
to a man, voiced some version of the belief that the most
comfortable circumstances were when life ran in the middle—not going wrong too much of the time, but not always
going right too much of the time, either. The unstated im-
plication being: A stretch of everything going smooth for
too long meant that a bad turn was surely due.

Mac talked to his team and worked the traces, swinging the course of the wagon over toward the shoulder of
the slope where he would set the brake, unharness the animals, and begin preparations to have supper ready for
the rest of the crew when they came along with the herd
in another hour or so. Although any clear sign of the sun
had been obscured behind a soot gray cloud cover all day,
a discernible glow that nevertheless marked the fiery orb
was faded almost completely behind the western horizon
now.

When it dropped completely, twilight would be short
and full dark would set in earlier than usual. Mac hoped
the chill wind that had been present along with the cloud
cover all day would abate with the sunset, as such breezes
often did. On the other hand, he reflected with a wry grin,
maybe he should accept that the cloudy, windy day was
what he'd been looking for as a balance to everything
being too ideal.

Once the wagon was parked and braked securely, Mac
left the horses standing in their traces for a short time

while he built a stone fire ring and then turned to gather fuel in order to get his cooking fire started. While the initial flames were building into a suitable blaze, he would finish tending to the horses.

Along one edge of the shoulder Mac had chosen for night camp, there was a small stand of trees with a tangle of underbrush twisted around their trunks at ground level. It was from this tangle that Mac meant to pull the fuel he sought.

"Come take whatever you want," drawled a voice out of the underbrush. "Plenty of good burnin' material in here to go around."

Those words gave Mac a start. He stopped short in his tracks and his hand moved automatically to hover near the Smith & Wesson in his belt.

"Whoa there. No need to haul out any hardware, pard," protested the voice. "If I meant you any harm, I wouldn't hardly call out to warn you I'm in here, would I?"

The statement sounded reasonable enough and was made calmly enough so that Mac relaxed a little. But not so much that he moved his hand away from his gun.

"What reason have you got to hide, then?" he replied. "Step on out and show yourself."

A moment later, with some rustling and crunching of brush, a man emerged from the trees. He was middle aged, wiry in build, dressed in common trail garb that had seen some wear. A Frontier Colt was holstered on his right hip and slung over his shoulder was a saddle.

"I wasn't so much hidin' as gettin' myself nested in out of that chilly wind," he explained as he came forward, leaning somewhat wearily under the weight of the saddle. "Been walkin' most of the day with that raw air bitin' my face. Walkin' and hopin' I'd run into somebody or some place that might offer some shelter."

"I take it, then, you're not from around here?"

"That's a fact," the man conceded. "Hail from Nebraska of late, but I've done my share of driftin' before then. On the drift again now, as a matter of fact. Or leastways I was. There's a gold strike up north, in case you ain't heard. Place called Rattlesnake Creek. Soon as I got wind of that, a fierce itch rose up in me to go try my luck there."

"From what I've heard, you're not alone," Mac said.

"No, I expect not. But just because I got knocked sideways a little, that don't mean I'm givin' up," the man said determinedly. "You showin' up like you done proves I got every reason to still have hope. With evenin' comin' on and not havin' no better prospect at the time, I decided the brushy growth under these trees looked like a good spot to settle for the night. I tucked myself in and stretched out to rest for a spell before buildin' a fire. Guess I dozed off. The creak and rattle of your wagon and team woke me. When I first looked out, I thought for a minute I musta been dreamin'."

"I ain't no dream," Mac allowed. "But you ain't explained yet how you came to end up on shank's mare. What happened to your horse?"

"Biggest rattler I ever saw flashed out from behind a rock and pumped a load of poison into the critter quicker than an eyeblink," came the answer. "I killed the snake. But it was too late, he'd already done for my horse."

"Hard way to go, for man or beast, either one," Mac muttered.

"Is for a fact. But I plan to get the ultimate revenge on

that serpent. For me and my horse, too. You see," the man smirked, "I carved that rattler up and cut myself a couple thick slabs off him that I got saved in the saddlebag on my shoulder. I figure on *eatin'* that varmint for my supper tonight!"

Mac's eyebrows pinched together. He'd heard of folks eating snake meat before, but it wasn't something he ever figured on trying for himself.

"You go right ahead, if that's to your liking," he said to the stranger now. "But if you'd rather, I'll be whipping up some other vittles here"—he jabbed a thumb to indicate his chuckwagon—"that you're welcome to share with me and my outfit instead."

The stranger's eyebrows lifted. "Yeah, I see you got yourself a chuckwagon there. You must have a cattle herd comin' along behind, eh?"

"Uh-huh. The Standing L brand from back Harcourt City way."

"Me just passin' through these parts and all, I can't say that means anything to me. I'm sure it's a fine outfit, though, and I would be obliged and powerful grateful to break bread with y'all. I don't mind snake meat, I've et my share, but I'd be a fool to pass up your cookin' for it."

Mac grinned. "You haven't had my cooking yet. It might not be such a good trade for you."

"Aw, I doubt that. That rig of yours, I can tell, be-speaks of turnin' out some mighty fine grub. And beyond that, since you must be travelin' with a remuda, I'm hopin' I can arrange with whoever's ramroddin' your out-fit to buy myself a replacement mount. I can pay, I got grubstake money."

"Our ramrod's a fair and decent sort. I'm sure you can work out something with him."

"Man, that would be great. Looks like this day is gonna end up not so bad after all. Now, since I wasted so much of your time, is there anything I can do to help you finish gettin' set up?"

Mac pointed. "Yeah, go ahead and unload your gear over by the fire ring. Then, if you want, you can give me a hand scrounging up some kindling and good, dry wood for a cooking fire."

"Oh, yeah. There's plenty in that underbrush. We can have a whole pile of it in no time. My name's Jones, by the way. Joshua Jones. Folks call me Josh."

"I'm Mackenzie. Go mostly by Mac."

Neither man made any move to shake hands.

Minutes later, they were foraging through the brush, pulling out handfuls of twigs for kindling and also selecting thicker branches for a longer-lasting burn. It felt like they were going to need plenty of fuel tonight, Mac thought to himself, because the chill wind showed no sign of diminishing with the sunset like he'd hoped. If anything, it felt like it might even be picking up a little and was now carrying a hint of dampness, possibly rain.

As he considered this, idly wondering if a cold rain qualified as enough of a bad turn to balance out the trend of everything going too smooth, something stirred close behind Mac and a branch snapped sharply. Not from the wind. Straightening partway out of his stooped position, he started to look around. Then another branch—a thicker, heavier one—made an even louder sound . . . as it came crashing down on the back of his head.

A sudden gust of wind whirled across the shoulder of the slope and rattled through the brush all around Mac. But he neither heard nor felt it as he pitched unconscious to the ground.

Chapter 18

Mac slowly, painfully came to.

A relentless ache throbbed in the back of his head and down through his neck. He felt cold, wet. When he opened his eyes it was to a gloominess only slightly brighter than if he'd kept them closed. Not full darkness, but close to it.

Off to one side, light flickered. A small fire was burning. Made visible by the pulsing illumination it threw, three faces hovered close over him.

"Looks like he's coming around," said Eamon Farrell's voice.

"Thank God." That was Becky, her tone sounding relieved, a little breathless.

Mac couldn't make out their shadowy features all that clearly, but he had no doubt who it was.

"Wha . . . where . . . ?" he started to say, but he let the

words trail off in a sudden rush of recollection pouring over him.

He recalled everything then. Or most of it. Up to the point where he and the drifter calling himself Joshua Jones had been gathering fuel for a fire and Mac had started to turn at the sound of movement directly behind him. Then blackness . . . becoming the pain of now emerging out of it.

Mac dug his elbows into the ground, meaning to push to a sitting position. A hand placed gently yet firmly on his chest held him in place.

"Take it easy, Mac. No need to be in too big a hurry," said Marcus Lewis, the third face floating murkily over him. "You took another bad whack on the noggin, best not to rush coming out of it."

Mac settled back on the wet ground, frowning, closing his eyes again. Slowly, he lifted a hand and turned his face to one side so his fingers could cautiously probe the back of his head. Since he was soaked already by the cold, drizzling rain that had begun to fall, he couldn't tell for sure if any of the dampness back there was from bleeding. He didn't think so, there didn't seem to be any gash or break in the skin under his hair.

Eamon confirmed this a moment later, saying, "No, they didn't bust you open. Apparently your head is hard and thick from the outside layer clear on through."

"That's not the way it feels to me," Mac countered. "From my side, it feels like I've got a crack running through my skull all the way down to my neck. But no matter what, I can tell you one thing for certain . . . and that's that I'm getting mighty tired of people bashing me over the head!"

Nobody said anything for a few seconds until Marcus

asked, "So what happened? Did you get any kind of look at who came up on you?"

With his eyes kept shut, biting out the words quickly, tersely, Mac related the appearance of the alleged Joshua Jones and the story he'd spun. Summing it up, Mac said, "Much as I hate to admit it, the skunk fooled me right down the line. He had an easy southern drawl, an aw-shucks way about him, and his story sounded reasonable. I never saw him as a threat."

"Well, he sure turned out to be one," responded Becky. "To you . . . and to all of us."

Mac continued to keep his eyes shut, not wanting to face Becky. He felt like he'd let her and everybody else down. Dreading the answer, he asked, "What did he do? Rob a bunch of supplies from the chuckwagon?"

The reply came from Eamon. "You could say that. He robbed the whole blinkin' rig!"

Now Mac's eyes shot open and he snapped to a sitting position. The pain this caused to jolt through his head and neck was no worse than that resulting from Eamon's revelation. "What?"

Marcus nodded in the flickering half-light. "You heard right. The whole works is gone. The chuckwagon, the horses, everything."

"For a while, we feared you had gone missing, too," said Becky, her eyes still showing concern as they swept over Mac's face.

"The sun was gone by the time we got to this spot," Marcus explained further. "We saw the hollow, the good grass, the stream . . . it was clearly a spot you would have chosen to make night camp, bed down the herd. But there was no sign of you. So we went ahead and settled the cattle in, knowing it was too late to take them across the stream tonight, even if you'd taken the wagon on over, for some reason, to check something on the other side. The only thing we could hope was that you hadn't run into some kind of serious trouble and would eventually be showing back up."

"When it started to rain," Becky said, taking up the sequence of events, "I brought some slickers and bedrolls up here to this higher spot, meaning to try and rig up some kind of shelter in these trees for when the men came in from getting the cattle settled. First, I saw the fire ring you'd laid out. Then I looked around until I spotted your hat lying on the grass . . . and then I found you."

"I'm glad for that," Mac allowed, rubbing the back of his head. "But, boy, do I feel like a fool for letting my guard down and getting caught like I did. And for letting the chuckwagon get stolen. The whole blamed chuckwagon! I never heard of anything like that." His brow creased as he dragged his gaze across the faces looking down on him. "Any of you got an idea what would make a varmint pull a stunt like that?"

"We've been puzzling on it, same as you," replied Marcus. "First thing that comes to mind is that there likely was more than one culprit involved, not just the hombre you talked to."

"Either that," Eamon added wryly, "or he was one hungry fellow, planning to eat his way through a whole wagonload of food and supplies."

The creases in Mac's forehead deepened. "If there was more than one man in on it, it could mean a gang of rustlers planning to hit the herd."

"We thought of that, too. Ned and Ox are out slow-circling the cattle now, keeping a sharp lookout," Marcus told him.

"But if it's rustlers," Becky said, "wouldn't it be kind of dumb for them to give us what amounts to a warning by first stealing our chuckwagon and letting us know they're out there?"

"Thieves and owlhoots, in general, ain't a particularly brainy lot," said Mac. "But Becky makes a fair point. Now that I think it through, taking the wagon and *then* making a play for the herd wouldn't make a whole lot of sense, no matter how dumb they are. Anybody who succeeded in taking our cattle away from us would almost certainly get the chuckwagon in the bargain."

"What kind of motive does that leave then?" said Eamon.

Mac massaged the back of his head some more. "I don't know. Only thing I can figure is maybe a pack of lowlifes who set out for the gold fields without being properly supplied. The wider the news spreads about that Rattlesnake Creek strike, the more desperate characters it's gonna bring, swarming like bugs to a honeyed biscuit. Plenty of 'em will be starting with nothing and won't be the least bit queasy about doing whatever it takes along the way, as long as there's a chance to claw their fingers into some gold. If a pack like that happened to spot our wagon full of supplies . . . well, like I said, I don't think they'd be queasy about helping themselves."

"I think Mac's on to something," said Eamon. "It's an explanation that makes as much sense as any. Certainly as a possibility. I spent some time in the vicinity of a gold strike once and I can vouch firsthand for the kind of ruffians it brings forth. Aye, there's nothing too low for them to stoop to."

"Well, whoever it was, they at least didn't get our funds for finishing the drive," Marcus said. He slapped his waist, where a money belt was secured under his shirt. "Nobody's going to get this unless they take it off my dead body."

"Don't say such a dreadful thing! Don't even think it," scolded Becky.

"All I'm saying is that as long as we've still got our cattle we can buy more supplies," Marcus said. "According to the maps, there are some towns fairly close by where we ought to be able to get what we need. It might take nearly our last cent and we might have to scrape by a little leaner than how Mac had us set up to start with, but we ain't gonna let this stop us!"

"I'm all for that—not letting this stop us," Mac agreed. "But I wouldn't be so quick to give up on our chuckwagon, on trying to get it back. Whoever took it can't have gotten far, not in the dark and the rain. And unless this storm cuts loose a lot harder than it is now, we should still have a good chance to track wagon wheel marks come first light."

"I like the sound of that," Eamon was quick to say. "We need to show some dirty so-and-sos how wrong they were if they thought we were easy pickings!"

Marcus frowned. "Trust me, that sounds mighty tempting to me, too. But if there's a big enough pack of scavengers backing the one Mac saw, we can't afford to lose one of ours in some fight to reclaim the wagon. And leaving the herd unprotected to go after 'em . . . Maybe that's what this whole thing is about after all, to distract us, pull some of us out, so they can go ahead and hit the herd like they maybe had in mind all along."

Mac matched Marcus's frown. "We can spend all night hashing it out if you want. In the end, it's your herd, yours and Becky's, so it's your call. But come morning, I hope you'll at least consider letting a couple of men . . . me and Eamon, say . . . take a ride after that wagon to see what we can find."

"I say the same," Eamon urged.

"But Mac, if anyone *did* go out on such a venture," said Becky, gazing at him with deep concern in her eyes, "it certainly ought not be you. You still haven't fully healed from your last injuries, and now you just got—"

Mac cut her off. "Miss Becky, the biggest hurt I'm feeling right now is knowing I let my guard down and made it easy for that weasel to come up from behind and brain me. The best way for me to heal from that is to go after the son of a . . . well, to catch up with whoever clouted me and took our supplies. And with all due respect, that's *my* call to make."

Three miles from where the Standing L outfit was huddled in the meager shelter provided by the cluster of trees, trying to come to grips with the loss they'd suffered, Jerry Lee Lawton and the others he had gathered to work in the interests of Oscar Harcourt were far more comfortably situated under a wide tarp extending out from the stolen chuckwagon.

Scattered recklessly, wastefully all about them, some items cast out in the rain, was much of the contents from the wagon. The drop-down table at the rear of the rig was folded down and propped flat, the five men crowded around it. The tabletop was strewn with unscrewed jars of canned goods, gouged-open airtights, and a scattering of leftover but still fluffy and tasty biscuits. Bacon was sizzling in an oversized frying pan placed alongside a bubbling coffeepot on the edge of a fire burning near the end of the protective canvas above.

"Those Standing L cow pushers was sure set up to eat good, you gotta hand 'em that," Roy Orton crowed, sticking his fingers into an open can of peaches and spearing a juicy slice that he crammed in his mouth.

"Yeah, they *was* set up that way," agreed Edsel Purdy. "But I wonder what they're having for supper tonight?"

"I can make a good guess," Floyd Sleet said as he scooped a gob of strawberry preserves onto a piece of biscuit. "If any of 'em was lucky enough to maybe have a chunk of beef jerky stuffed in his saddlebag, I reckon right about now they're divvying that up and passing it around. And to wash it down? Plenty of nice fresh rainwater!"

A round of derisive laughter followed that.

"If that's the case, then it's all the more noble of 'em to make that kind of sacrifice while providin' us with all these good eats and plenty of hot coffee to warm our innards," exclaimed 'Bama Wilkes. Then, holding high one of several bottles of whiskey also found in the wagon, he added, "Not to mention this here extra precaution against the cold and damp!"

As Wilkes put the bottle to his mouth and took a long pull, Jerry Lee scowled and said, "Just remember not to get carried away with that stuff. You did a good job, 'Bama, smooth-talking that meddlesome Mackenzie and putting him off guard so's you could lay a tree branch across his skull. But it ain't time for too much celebrating. Not yet. This job is a long way from over. Pulling this stunt with their chuckwagon will slow that drive a couple days, maybe three. But that's just a start."

"What've you got in mind for pestering 'em next, Jerry Lee?" asked Purdy.

"I'll let you know when it's time. No hurry, not for a while. We'll let 'em lick their wounds over this for a bit, start to relax, thinking whatever was behind this spot of trouble is past . . . then we'll give 'em another taste."

"Well, whatever comes next, it's a shame I won't get to play as big a part in it. I'll have to hang back some on account of that Mackenzie fella would be bound to recognize me if he laid eyes on me again." So stating, Wilkes started to raise the whiskey bottle again but catching sight of Jerry Lee's glare out of the corner of his eye made him lower it. Then his mouth stretched into a crooked grin. "But I sure had fun this time. Did I mention how I told that ranny my name was Joshua—Josh for short? 'Cause I was joshin' him the whole time! Get it?"

"Yeah, we get it. You told us often enough," Orton said wearily.

"I don't care. It's derned funny, no matter how often I hear it," declared Sleet. "'Josh' on account of you was joshing him—that's a good one, 'Bama!"

"Yeah, I guess it was. So have a laugh, enjoy it," said Jerry Lee. "But you'd all better finish up this celebrating before much longer. We're gonna want to clear out of here early in the morning, in case any of that Standing L crew comes nosing around. Ain't the right time for no kind of confrontation with 'em, not just yet. Now somebody pull that bacon off the fire and get it up here before it's too burnt. I want some meat to go with these biscuits before they're all gone."

Chapter 19

Having finally won their argument for going after the stolen wagon, Mac and Eamon rode out at first light of the new day. Under a clear sky and a rising sun that quickly erased the cold and damp of the long night, they had little trouble following the wheel ruts of the wagon. It was well short of noon when they came in sight of what they were pursuing—what was left of it.

It was still a welcome sight, though, and when they rolled back into the Standing L camp with it, some hours later, those waiting there viewed it the same. But they also were quick to spot the damage that had been done. Even at a distance, as Mac and Eamon ascended the slope toward the flattened crest and the grove of trees that had provided the previous night's meager shelter, the others couldn't miss the rig's battered appearance. Part of its canvas cover was torn away, revealing the storage area to be missing most of its contents. Also, the team was missing. In its place, Mac's and Eamon's saddle horses were strapped into makeshift harnessing and doing their best to drag their burden jerkily along.

When the wagon was brought to a halt near the fire ring, at almost the exact spot Mac had parked it upon first arriving yesterday, Marcus and Becky were quick to gather close. Ned and Ox, spotting the arrival from down where they'd been minding the cattle, rode up to join in, too.

"There was no fight, no skirmish of any kind to get it back. The thieves were long gone by the time we found the wagon," Mac reported bitterly. "But as you can see, the yellow skunks took a pretty costly toll on things before they lit out."

"Meaning, sorry to say," added Eamon, "they gave us no chance for the satisfaction of planting some lead in their scurvy hides."

"Nor, thankfully, any chance for them to do the same to you," Becky was quick to point out.

"No sign of the team, eh? They didn't shoot 'em down, did they?" asked Ned, his worried expression signaling his deep fondness for horses in general and the missing animals in particular.

Mac shook his head. "My guess is they used at least a couple of 'em for pack animals to tote the added supplies they took on. Any got turned loose, there's a chance they might find their way back here. But with all this open grassland and a stream running through it, I wouldn't count on seeing 'em again."

"No, I expect not," agreed Ned, a disappointed sag to his shoulders. "Long as they're unharmed, that's the main thing."

"Means we'll have to choose some replacements out of the remuda and break them in," said Ox. "That's gonna take some work."

Ned nodded. "Too true. So, since we've got a fair chunk of afternoon left, we may as well make our picks and get started."

By now, Mac and Eamon had climbed down from the retrieved wagon and were standing on the ground beside it, along with the others.

"Hold on a minute, Ned," Mac said. "Before you start picking new horses, you'd better take a closer look at what you've got here. When those varmints released the old team, they weren't any too careful about how they freed them from the rigging. Some of it they unbuckled proper, but other parts they just cut it loose. Me and Eamon managed to cobble it back together good enough to hitch up our saddle mounts. But to hold a four-horse team again, especially a new one you'll be breaking in, is going to take some serious mending."

Ned and Ox moved to where the saddle mounts, commandeered into duty they didn't much care for, stood fidgeting and blowing. Ned spoke soothingly to the animals as he began examining the rigging that held them in place.

"Aw, look at this," groaned Ox. "So much of this fine gear hacked up for no good reason except plain orneriness. Any low-down cuss who'd do something like this deserves to have their hides peeled with one of these cut straps."

Ned's jaw muscles bunched visibly. "Before the war, boy, I seen many a decent man get his hide whipped raw. Ain't something to be wished for, nor something you really ever want to see. But the scoundrels who took our wagon and did this . . . maybe there's some who *are* deserving of such."

Frowning as he listened and looked on, Marcus said, "What do you think, Ned? Can you make the necessary repairs?"

Still examining, Ned murmured, "Expect so. Looks like most of the buckles and clips are still here. And I got some mending gear in my saddlebags. Gonna take time. Rest of today and some of tomorrow, I'm guessing, to get it back right. But yeah, with Ox's help, we can do it."

"Do what you have to," Marcus told him. "Let the rest of us know if we can do anything to help."

Ox's expression turned from forlorn to hopeful. "Does that offer include something to eat? Is there any kind of food fixings left in that wagon? My belly's getting so empty it thinks maybe my throat has been cut."

This got an agreeable laugh out of all the others.

Marcus said, "I can't match empty bellies with somebody your size, Ox, but I sure understand where you're coming from. And if I have to go much longer without a cup of coffee, I'm warning one and all that I will become a very disagreeable hombre to be around."

"You can both relax," said Eamon. "Even though those scoundrels went to the trouble of scattering and tearing apart most of what they didn't haul off, me and Mac salvaged everything we could scrape or scoop out of the grass. There's some coffee beans, thankfully, and various other odds and ends that Mac, given his wizardry with simple ingredients, will be able to whip into something edible, I'm sure."

"I'm hungry enough to settle for something *halfway* edible," said Ox.

"With expectations that low, I can't lose," Mac replied

with a wry grin. "If somebody wants to fetch some dry wood and finally put to use this fire ring I laid out yesterday, I'll scrounge through what Eamon and I were able to salvage and see what I can turn it into."

After a meal that lived up to expectations from Mac, washed down with two big pots of coffee, the camp settled into planning the balance of the day. Ned and Ox laid out the harness rigging on the ground near the wagon and began methodically working through the necessary fixes; Marcus spread open his maps and studied on where was the closest town they might resupply without veering too far off course; Mac concentrated on re-sorting and rearranging what goods were left and what essentials needed to be replaced; and Eamon took a rifle and a fresh horse and went in search of some game, hoping to bag something in order to provide meat for supper.

For a time, Becky lingered close to Mac. She helped with some of the sorting he was doing, made small talk. Even though the others weren't very far off, Mac saw it as having a piece of time almost alone with Becky. He welcomed that about as much as Ox had welcomed finally getting something to eat. Ever since the drive had left the Standing L ranch—what with him riding out ahead with the chuckwagon and then being busy with the meal at each stop while Becky was weary from long hours in the saddle—there had been precious little chance for just the two of them to converse much at all.

While Mac knew he had no right to harbor feelings for any decent woman, given his status as a drifter on the run from a murder charge—albeit a trumped-up one—he nevertheless continued to find himself drawn to Becky.

Even realizing there could be no future for them, he couldn't deny that at least part of the reason he'd agreed to join Marcus's drive had been to spend more time around her. Crazy as it was, that's what it boiled down to all the same.

Even crazier was the fact that Mac had struggled with a very similar quandary on the drive he'd recently taken part in with the Rafter B outfit. For a time, he and Colleen Bradley, the very fetching daughter of rancher Norris Bradley, had had a bit of a romance going. It ended with the appearance of a young Texas Ranger named Malloy who stole away Colleen's heart, which Mac was able to accept as a far better conclusion, certainly for Colleen.

You'd think, you lunkhead, you'd be smarter than to jump right back into the same kind of thing all over again, Mac scolded himself now. But with Becky right there on her knees in the wagon bed with him, shoulder to shoulder as they rummaged through what the scavengers had left behind, it wasn't easy to think straight. Especially not when she'd once called him her swashbuckling hero.

On the other hand, maybe it would be Eamon who stepped in to play the role of Ranger Malloy this time around. There was no doubting his interest in Becky and it wasn't like she was exactly cool and reserved to him either. Exchanges between them often gave Mac a twinge of jealousy, no matter how much he genuinely liked the Irishman.

The two of them had never spoken of their mutual interest in Becky, even though Mac was sure Eamon recognized it the same as he did. But each also saw that getting the cattle to their destination was the main thing to focus on for now. Matters of the heart could wait to be settled until later.

But that didn't mean, Mac told himself, that a few stolen moments with Becky along the way—like now—couldn't still be enjoyed if and when they occurred.

"I'm sorry if I seemed overly crabby about you wanting to go after this wagon," she was saying as they continued to sort and rearrange what had been retrieved. "I didn't mean to add to the problem, but I feared the thought of you and Eamon possibly catching up with the thieves and getting into a confrontation with them, no matter how many there might have been."

"Getting a crack at them was something we were kinda hoping for," Mac told her.

"I know you were. That didn't do anything to help ease my fears," replied Becky. "And then, too, I was worried about the fresh injury you'd suffered, another bad blow to the head."

Mac flashed a reassuring grin. "Apparently my head can stand a lot of walloping."

"Maybe. But then again, maybe your eagerness to go out and face more danger might be a sign that what's between your ears isn't working totally right. For one thing, after that latest whack that left you knocked out again last night, I'd think your head would still be pounding with pain."

"When I first woke up this morning, that was definitely the case," Mac admitted. "But I was so mad about our wagon getting stole and me being the one who got suckered into letting it happen that I just didn't care. Finding the wagon, at least that much, helped me start to come around. By now I don't hardly notice it no more. And having you close by and worrying about me, well, I guess that's pretty good medicine, too."

Those were the boldest and most direct words Mac

had ever spoken to express his feelings for her. They seemed to tumble out as if of their own volition and he immediately worried what her reaction would be.

To his relief, she beamed a dazzling smile at him and said, "That's sweet. But if you stop and think about it, it's largely because of me that you've gotten into these recent scrapes. First, that run-in with Jerry Lee, then the beating in the hotel room, then the incident on the trail to the ranch . . . and now what happened last night."

"How have you got anything to do with what happened last night?" Mac wanted to know.

"It all stems from the same thing, don't you see? If you hadn't been out at our ranch recuperating, Marcus wouldn't have had the chance to talk you into joining this drive and you'd never have been here for that scavenger to ambush you the way he did."

Mac wagged his head. "That's awful convoluted reasoning for me to try and follow. Maybe you're right, maybe I do still have some pieces rattling around loose."

"Well, don't think on it too hard. If you do and you end up coming to your senses, you may decide to hightail away from us for your own good." Becky paused, her eyes gazing deeply into Mac's from a distance of mere inches, before adding, "And I surely would hate to see that, Mac."

Suddenly there was a lump about the size of Nebraska in Mac's throat. He fought to swallow it down, but still didn't have words to replace it. For a wild instant he had the urge to grab the beautiful girl before him and pull her lips to his.

But before he acted on that impulse, Becky abruptly broke eye contact and glanced down at something on the floor of the wagon bed.

"Well, look here," she exclaimed, reaching down and seizing what she had inadvertently pressed her knee onto. She held it up, revealing an intact bar of soap. "I guess it comes as no surprise that a pack of dirty, thieving scoundrels wouldn't be interested in anything like this. But it certainly speaks to me!"

"A bar of soap speaks to you?" Mac echoed in bewilderment.

"Yes. It's calling for me to make use of it," Becky explained. "It's a nice warm afternoon and there's still plenty of sunlight left. There's bound to be a suitable spot upstream from where the herd has been watering. I'm going to take a bath!"

Mac frowned. "Didn't you get drenched enough last night?"

"That's not the same thing, silly, and you know it. I've been so tired each time we stop for night camp that I've settled for just washing out of a bucket. But now I've got plenty of time, a warm sun, a clear stream, and a brand new bar of soap." Becky stood up in the wagon and gave a little laugh. "This gal is going to indulge herself with a nice, long, sudsy soak!"

Chapter 20

The first warning Becky got was when the horse she'd left tied to a clump of brush on the south bank of the stream began fidgeting. Even then she didn't pay much heed, thinking the animal was probably just expressing its annoyance at being singled out this way while the rest of the remuda was still roaming free back where there was better grass.

As for Becky herself, she was feeling far from annoyed as she stretched out in a pocket of very faintly eddying water just outside the gentle current that flowed down the middle of the stream. A layer of foam from the soap lather she had worked up rode on the surface, slowly circling Becky until portions of it got caught by the main current and swept away.

Although the water was rather chilly, especially after last night's rain, it felt very relaxing once her body acclimated to it. Becky was thoroughly enjoying this soothing immersion, the pleasant soap scent in her nostrils, and the warmth of the sun on her face and shoulders.

It wasn't until a horse from somewhere nearby responded to her critter's fidgeting with its own challenging snort that Becky realized she might not be as alone as she'd believed herself to be. Instinctively dropping down deeper into the sudsy water, so that it covered her to within an inch of her chin, she looked around furtively.

It only took a moment to spot the last thing she expected—or wanted—to see.

On the opposite bank, diagonally across from her only marginally secluded bathing spot, two men sat their horses, gazing openly at her. The stillness of their mounts and the postures of the men, both having the appearance of ranch hands, gave the impression they had been there, looking on, for some time.

The younger of the two, tall and lean, not very far into his twenties, was hunched forward with one arm resting on his pommel. A wide, leering smile split the bottom half of a roguishly handsome face that looked to be no stranger to bold expressions.

Becky felt an embarrassed warmth flood over her cheeks. But then, quickly, it became a hot flush of anger. Crossing her arms over her breasts, even though they were fully submerged, she called to the horsemen, "Whoever you are, put your eyeballs back in your heads and ride on away from here. Go back to wherever you belong!"

The young one's taunting smile stretched even wider. "Now, darlin', you are asking some purely impossible things. First off, ain't no red-blooded male in the territory who'd be willing to tear his eyes off you, not with the show you're putting on. And as for me and Otis going where we belong, well, we're already there. You see, this whole stretch through here belongs to my old man. That'd be Hiram Walters, of the Bar W. And me? I happen to be his son, Tobe. So the thing is, we're at home. But you, plopped down taking a bath in the middle of our property, you're sort of trespassing."

"The water in a stream or river can't be claimed by anybody," Becky argued, scowling. "Boats travel waterways all the time with no never mind to the property or even the territories or states on the banks to either side."

Smirking now, Tobe Walters looked over at his companion and said, "She sounds almost like a lawyer or some such, don't she, Otis? I guess it sort of fits, though, if you stop and think about it. I mean, it's true that any lawyer I ever saw was decked out in a suit . . . but I never saw one in just a birthday suit before!"

Tobe threw back his head and brayed with laughter at his observation. Otis, a heavyset specimen about five years older, with close-set eyes and a perpetually hangdog expression, looked uncertain about finding any humor in the situation.

"I don't know about no lawyer stuff, Tobe. But we've had ourselves a good peek and a little bit of a laugh. Maybe we oughta just ride on and leave the gal alone now."

"Ride on?" Tobe echoed, looking aghast. "Are you loco? The best part of the show is yet to come. Sooner or later, Little Miss Lawyer is gonna have to climb *out* of her bath and go for those clothes she left hanging on that tree branch yonder. That's the part of the show I don't intend to miss."

"If you think I'm getting out of here with you perched

over there gawking, you're out of your mind!" Becky exclaimed.

"Aw, come on," Tobe lamented. "You can't stay in there
too long or you'll prune up something fierce. Be a shame
to do that to such a fine, smooth body as we've already
been treated a look at. And you can't stay in there after
the sun goes down or you'll freeze."

"I'd rather freeze—or even drown—than give you the
satisfaction of seeing me come out in front of you,"
Becky said through clenched teeth.

"Now that's plumb reckless talk. Before I let anything
like that happen, I'd be duty bound to jump in and save
you," Tobe told her. Then, canting his head to one side
and regarding her with a challenging glint in his eye, he
added, "Then again, maybe that's what you want. Maybe
I could join you and scrub your back for you. Maybe we
could get to be real good friends."

"You *are* out of your mind!" Becky said. But for the
first time she felt a faint tingle of fear run through her.
Fear that this awkward, embarrassing moment might
have the potential for turning into something worse. She
tossed a quick glance over her shoulder, back toward the
camp, wishing she hadn't wandered so far upstream in
search of what she thought was a suitably private spot.

"Tobe," said Otis, starting to look worried. "I think
we've had enough fun with this. I don't think your pa
would like us pushing it any farther. We need to be getting back, anyway."

"Shut up, Otis!" Tobe snapped. "What the hell's wrong
with you? Especially you, looking the way you do. How
many chances you think you're ever going to get at a filly
as prime as this one? And you want to turn around and
run away?"

"Don't listen to him, Otis," Becky urged. "You're thinking right, he's the one who's thinking wrong and twisted. The people I'm traveling with—my brother and a dozen cowboys, some of them former gunmen—are in a camp just a short way past these trees behind me. If I cry out, they'll come running. With guns blazing!"

"That's a lie!" Tobe scoffed. "She knows it and so do you, Otis. Stop and think. We saw the herd she's traveling with, spread out on the flat across the bottom of that wide hollow past those trees. Her camp is up on the slope, clear the other side of that hollow. Even if they heard her yell, they wouldn't know exactly where it came from. And before they could figure out where, and get here, we'd have all the time we needed."

Otis's worried look turned into one of increased alarm. "Needed for what, Tobe? You don't mean . . ."

"Why the hell not?" Tobe demanded. "She's asking for it, ain't she? Splashing around naked out here in front of God and everybody! What does she expect! Shoot, she's probably hoping one of those cowboys from her own outfit will find their way over here and have the guts to give her what she's asking for. Why should we hold back and leave all the fun to them? They'll still be traveling with her after they move on from here. They can have their turn some other time."

"Those are dirty lies! You're nothing but a filthy-mouthed pig!" Becky responded furiously.

Tobe's eyes narrowed and his mouth became a grim slash. It was clear his thoughts were moving toward something more than just getting a free peep show, almost as if his spiel to Otis had had the effect of encouraging himself to do more.

"Say what you will," he grated, his gaze burning into

Becky. "But any woman who looks like you needs what only a real man can give her. If you ain't getting that from any of those boys in your outfit, then it's high time somebody saw to your needs proper. And I'm just the hombre who can get the job done."

Tobe gigged his mount forward. As Otis watched, his mouth gaped open and he said, "Tobe? What are you doing?"

"If you don't know," Tobe said over his shoulder, "then watch and maybe you'll learn something. But keep an eye peeled in case anybody unexpected shows up."

A moment later, Tobe urged his horse over the lip of the north bank and into the stream. Less than fifteen yards away, on the other side of the leisurely flowing ribbon of water, Becky watched with growing alarm. As before, however, it didn't take long for her emotion to turn to anger.

"Stay away, I'm warning you!" she called.

Leaning forward over his horse's neck, slipping his feet out of their stirrups and extending them back to keep them mostly out of the water as his mount surged toward the deeper middle of the stream, Tobe smiled. "You know you don't mean that, darlin'. In just a few minutes, you're gonna be begging me to press as close as a man can get to a woman."

Becky gave him one more warning. "Stop now. Turn back, or I'll kill you if I have to. I swear it!"

Tobe laughed in her face, even as water splashed up in his. "How? You gonna beat me to death with your bar of soap?"

That's what drove Becky to do the second to the last thing she wanted to do—expose herself for the visual pleasure of this oncoming pig. But the *very* last thing she would do was let him get his hands on her and have his way once he did. She knew she likely couldn't overpower him physically in order to prevent that. But with the right weapon in her hands, it could be a different story.

And that weapon was the Winchester Yellowboy rifle that Mac had insisted she take along once she'd stated her intent to roam a ways from camp for the sake of finding the privacy she wanted for her bath. "In that case," he'd said, handing her the Yellowboy, "take this on the chance you stumble on a snake or diseased skunk or some such. You never know."

So she'd brought the rifle. It was up on the bank, just a few feet away, leaning against the sapling from whose branches her clothing hung. The latter, as luck would have it, served to hide the weapon from Tobe's vantage point. And as long as she didn't hesitate any longer, Becky had enough time to hoist herself up onto the bank and seize the rifle. The only thing inhibiting her was stupid modesty, the thought of rising up and exposing herself to make that grab.

If you wait any longer, you fool, her mind screamed, *he's going to end up seeing you naked anyway, seeing you and doing a lot worse, because you won't be able to stop him!*

That, finally, was what it took. With a defiant cry, Becky thrust up from the modest crouch she'd dropped into upon first realizing she was being watched. Water cascaded from her glistening wet form as she turned and lunged for the bank, grabbing for long stems of grass to help pull herself up.

Three-quarters of the way across the stream, Tobe hooted gleefully at the sight.

"Oh, yeah, darlin'!" he called. "Scooch up there on that nice, soft grass and I'll be joining you there pronto!"

Seconds later, the glee left Tobe's expression as he saw Becky reach through the clothes hanging from the sapling branches and then whirl back to face him with the Yellowboy leveled at her bare hip, aiming straight his way.

"Holy hell!" he exclaimed, jerking back in his saddle. "She's got a gun, Otis! Cover me!"

Tobe continued throwing himself backward, letting go of the reins and pitching off his horse on the side farthest from Becky just as she triggered a round from the rifle. The slug sizzled through the air less than a foot above the now empty saddle, right about where Tobe's brisket would have been if he'd stayed put. Instead, he hit the water in a flailing dive, throwing up a high splash that swallowed the curse he was trying to spit out and turned it into a gurgling sputter.

On the other side of the stream, trying to respond to Tobe's command to cover him, Otis drew his sidearm, a long-barreled Remington, and waved it around as if uncertain what to do with it. The sight of a nude Becky now standing up on the other bank wasn't doing much to help him think clearly.

But Becky, spotting Otis's movement out of the corner of her eye, didn't have any trouble deciding what to do. Levering a fresh round into the Yellowboy, she spun toward Otis and fired in his direction. The shot was high and wide, but was close enough to make Otis decide he should return fire.

So he did, but hurriedly and sloppily, his shot also going high, rattling through the leaves of the sapling above where Becky's clothes hung. Before he could even think about correcting his aim, Otis's horse, spooked by the sudden burst of gunfire, wheeled unexpectedly and dumped the heavyset man into the dust.

With both of her tormentors unsaddled and posing no immediate threat, Becky edged back to gain some cover behind the sapling and the underbrush close around it. A sense of modesty, even in this tense moment, made her reach out and grab a handful of clothing to pull along with her.

Fumbling to select something she could quickly drape over herself almost caused Becky to end up on the receiving end of a bullet. As she was momentarily distracted with the tangle of garments, Tobe suddenly broke to the surface out in the stream. He came up partially behind his horse, still spitting water and curses, and immediately raised one arm with a Colt pistol already drawn and gripped in the fist. Pushing water off his face with his free hand, he wasted no time locking a fierce gaze on Becky and then swinging the Colt in line with his glare.

"You tried to kill me, you little witch!" he yelled—and began pulling the trigger.

Chapter 21

Tobe's first trigger pull clicked futilely on a water-logged cartridge, buying Becky a second to react by ducking lower and farther around behind the sapling. However, the wad of clothing she'd grabbed now entangled one arm for an equally precious second, slowing her from being able to get her rifle raised again in order to return fire.

As she struggled with that, an enraged Tobe kept cocking and squeezing the trigger of his Colt as he sloshed frantically through shallower water toward the bank. On his third try, the hammer finally fell on a cartridge dry enough to fire and the slug it hurled ripped away bark and wood chips mere inches from Becky's face.

As Becky jerked back from the near miss just as she at last got the Yellowboy's muzzle raised, her bare feet slipped on a patch of grass and dirt made slick by all the water pouring off her body. This resulted in her feet skidding out from under her even as the rifle roared and licked a tongue of red flame. Unfortunately, the bullet sent sizzling from that flame was wildly off target.

Seeing Becky topple back and realizing her shot hadn't come anywhere close to him made Tobe all the angrier and bolder. As he clambered up onto the south bank, reaching and clawing with his free hand while keeping the Colt thrust at arm's length out in front of him, he hollered across the way, "Get ready to pour it on, Otis! Help me out here in case I have any more misfires!"

When he heard the sharp crack of a gun just a moment later, Tobe thought that fool Otis was responding too soon. But even before the thought finished flashing through his mind, he realized that wasn't the case at all. He knew someone else was shooting instead—and the impact and fiery pain of a bullet tearing through his shoulder and spinning him around, threatening to knock him back into the water, told him that their target was *him*!

On the opposite bank, Otis saw Tobe go down, his feet and legs flopping back into the edge of the stream. The heavyset man was struggling not only to get back to his own feet but was also groping desperately for the revolver that had been jarred from his grasp when the horse dumped him. At the sight of Tobe getting shot, he froze in disbelief and horror. "Tobe!" he gasped hoarsely.

Before he could shake himself loose from his stunned inaction, Otis spotted the source of the bullet that had taken down Tobe. A lone rider was coming hard around the downstream bend of the south bank, one arm extended out ahead of him with a short-barreled pistol gripped in his fist.

Galloping closer to where Tobe lay half in, half out of the water, the rider kept his pistol trained on the fallen man. Then, seeming satisfied there was no longer any threat posed there, he abruptly wheeled his horse a quarter turn and swung the pistol until it was aiming over at Otis.

The distance was stretching the range and accuracy for a handgun, especially a short-barreled model, but the potential was enough to discourage Otis from attempting anything. Still on his knees, he suddenly regained enough mobility to throw up his hands and announce loudly, "Don't shoot! I won't make no trouble!"

Pinning the heavy man with a fierce scowl, the rider growled, "You'd better not. Keep those hands high until I say otherwise."

From the underbrush clumped around the bullet-riddled sapling, Becky called out, "Take it easy on him, Eamon! He was trying to reason with the other one, the one you put a bullet in."

"Well, he didn't seem to be doing a very good job of it," Eamon countered. "I heard the things this scurvy lout was saying and threatening to do to you. Are you all right?"

"Other than being mortified and skinned up a little, I'm fine," Becky's voice floated back. "But you stay right where you are. Don't you dare come any closer until I've had a chance to make myself presentable!"

It wasn't long before the others from the Standing L camp, rushing in response to all the shouting and shooting, arrived on the scene. Time enough, however, for Becky to have gotten dressed and for Otis, under the steady muzzle of Eamon's pistol, to have crossed over from the other side of the stream. Once the Irishman had searched him to make sure he was clean of any weapons, he was allowed to lower his hands and put them to use helping to pull the wounded Tobe back up onto dry ground. That task had just been completed when the rest of the outfit showed up.

"Becky! Eamon! What happened?" a somewhat breathless Marcus was quick to demand.

Gesturing with the pistol still in his hand, Eamon answered, "These two hombres, especially this one"—making an added jab toward where Tobe lay—"tried to intrude on Becky's bath. They had something a lot less innocent than scrubbing her back in mind. And when she objected too strongly, the one on the ground got even nastier. Becky was doing her best to put a bullet in him, but I showed up and beat her to it."

Mac took a long stride over to Becky and placed his hands somewhat tentatively on her shoulders. "Are you okay?"

She managed a brave smile. "Thanks to Eamon, yes. I'd feel a lot better, though, if I had succeeded in putting a bullet in that foul-mouthed pig! I guess the next time you lend me a rifle, you'd better include some shooting lessons."

"There ain't gonna *be* no next time for you needing to be lent a gun," said Marcus, who had also moved closer to his sister. "Because you ain't gonna be wandering off by yourself no danged more, bath or no bath!"

"Speaking of shooting lessons," said Mac, turning to Eamon, "that was some mighty handy work with that Baby Russian you pack."

Eamon grimaced. "Tell me about it. I've only fired this thing a couple times before, never at a distance greater than the width of a barroom and certainly never from horseback. I guess the old saying about better to be lucky than good is sometimes true."

"Call it luck or skill or whatever you want," declared Marcus, "I'm just powerful glad you showed up with it, Eamon."

"I was returning from my hunting venture," the Irishman explained, "when I heard the ruckus over this way. Thankfully, I was in time to intervene before things got too far out of hand."

Mac jerked his chin toward where Eamon's horse stood a short distance away. "Judging by the carcass of that young antelope draped behind your saddle, it looks like your hunt was successful, too."

Eamon smiled. "Aye. That was a rifle shot, and for it I will immodestly claim skill and accuracy."

"Well, whatever you want to chalk your handgun shot up to," spoke up Ned, from where he knelt beside the wounded, moaning Tobe, "you did a pretty good number on this varmint. He ain't dead, but he's busted up plenty and losing a lot of blood."

"How bad?" asked Marcus, frowning.

"If the bleeding gets stopped and there ain't no sizable chunks of lead left in him, he ought to make it okay," said Ned. "Don't know how much use that arm's gonna be, though."

"Please. Do everything you can," Otis said in an earnest tone.

"Is there a doctor anywhere close by?"

"Town of Keylock. About twenty miles."

Ned wagged his head. "He'll bleed to death long before a sawbones can make it from that far. And he ain't in no shape to be hauled there, neither."

His frown deepening, Marcus said, "I know the skunk probably ain't worth it, but I've seen you patch up bullet holes before, Ned. Is there anything you can do for him?"

The old cowboy's dark face was an unreadable mask for a long count. Then, heaving a sigh, he said, "Reckon we can't just stand by and watch the life leak out of him. Let me first pack that bullet hole, slow the bleeding. Then, if Ox will give me a hand getting him up to the camp, I got some stuff in my gear I can work on him with. Try to do more, if I can."

"Anything you can do to help," Otis urged. "Please."

Ned scowled at him. "I'll do what I can. If your friend lives he's gonna need to see a doctor soon as possible."

Otis looked around anxiously at Eamon, who still had his gun drawn. "Can I go get help? A doctor? Tobe's pa?"

Eamon glanced at Becky, then back again. "Maybe you ought to be asking the lady you and your pal were tormenting what she thinks. Up to me, wouldn't either one of you rate much consideration."

Otis shifted his pleading gaze.

For a long moment, Becky met his look with a glare. Then, relenting, she said, "Ned's right, of course. We can't just let a man, not even a lowlife, die without doing what we can. I guess you should go get the nearest help available."

"Excuse me for horning in, but not so fast," said Mac. He planted his own glare on Otis. "What's the story on you two rannies? Why are you out this way, and who does this 'Tobe' belong to? You said something about getting help from his pa?"

"It's like he—Tobe, that is—already told the lady," Otis answered. "His pa is Hiram Walters, boss of the Bar W, one of the biggest spreads around. His range runs for about as far as you can see all on the other side of the creek. Me and Tobe was out this way on a sweep, looking to round up strays, when we spotted . . . er, that is . . . well, when we happened to come upon the lady."

"So you decided to first sneak up close for a long peek at what you had no business seeing, and then try to do even more, didn't you?" Becky accused, her anger flaring again.

Otis's expression crumpled pathetically. "I'm sorry about that, ma'am. Truly I am. Tobe has always been high spirited around the ladies and usually they don't . . . But I tried to discourage him where you was concerned. You heard me do that."

Becky set her jaw grudgingly. "Yes, I have to admit that much."

Mac kept his eyes on Otis. "Tell me more about old man Walters, Tobe's pa. What does he think about his son's 'high-spirited' ways? Does he put up with 'em? How's he likely to react to his boy getting shot, even if he had it coming?"

Now a dark cloud settled over Otis's expression. "How do you expect any man would react to his son getting shot? No, Boss Hiram ain't gonna like it much. Not even if . . . Well, he won't like it."

"That's what I figured," said Mac, his own expression grim. He turned to Marcus and Eamon. "You see the picture, don't you? We could be in a fine fix if the big, he-bull rancher of the whole territory gets a hump in his back over us shooting his kid."

"What are you saying? I shouldn't have shot him?" responded a frowning Eamon.

Mac waved off that notion. "Any of the rest of us would have done the same, situation being what it was. All I'm pointing out is that we'd better be ready to face some backlash when word of what happened gets carried away from here."

"Well then, that's what we'll have to do. Face it," stated Marcus. "We've done nothing wrong. Even if we wanted to, we can't very well run, not with a herd of cattle and a broken-down wagon."

Mac nodded. "Okay. Just so we all understand it might turn ugly."

"It turned ugly," Marcus growled menacingly, "when that high-spirited varmint charged across the stream meaning to get at my sister."

Chapter 22

Twilight had faded into full dark when they showed up. Ten riders. A black mass of men and horses plowing through the stream, churning a foam of water that glistened silver in the early starlight. Angling across the mouth of the hollow they came, skirting the herd of cattle grazing there, then surging up the slope to where those in the Standing L camp waited.

Flames crackled within the fire ring, throwing a pulsing oval of illumination over the campsite. A tall pot of coffee rested on the coals to one side of the fire, fat cuts of roasting antelope hung from a spit on the other side. On the perimeter of the firelight, his back resting against one wheel of the chuckwagon, knees drawn up in front of him, a cup of coffee between his palms, sat Marcus Lewis. Off to one side of him, stretched out parallel to the wagon bed on a cushion of blankets, lay the still form of

Tobe Walters. The other members of the Standing L crew hung back at either end of the wagon, in the shadows just out of reach of the light.

The riders reined up a few yards back from the crest of the slope, also remaining mostly in shadow. A tall, broad-shouldered figure sitting his saddle at the front of the pack called out, "Hello, the camp."

"Hello back," Marcus returned, not rising. "If you're Bar W, we've been expecting you. Come ahead on."

The lead rider nudged his horse forward until illumination from the fire played across the broad, weathered, scowling face of a thick-built man in his early fifties. He said, "You're damn right we're Bar W. I'm Hiram Walters. Both the spread and the brand are mine."

Marcus rose unhurriedly to his feet. "My name's Marcus Lewis. The Standing L brand on those cattle down in the basin belongs to me. Me and my sister."

"You know blasted well I don't care about your brand or your cattle. I'm here about my boy," declared Walters. His gaze left Marcus and dropped to the form lying on the blankets. The hardness suddenly left his eyes and in a somewhat hushed voice he asked, "Is he dead?"

Marcus shook his head. "No. All things considered, he's in pretty good shape. I have a man in my outfit who's had some experience patching up bullet wounds."

Walters's eyes hardened again. "The same man who put the bullet in him to begin with?"

"No," Marcus told him. "But would it matter if it was? The point is, we went to the trouble of taking care of your son. More trouble, some might say, than he rated."

"That's a hell of a thing to say to a man about his son!" Walters exclaimed. "Especially coming from the gaggle of no-accounts who pumped him full of lead."

His face reddening even through the orange-gold tint of the fire, Marcus said, "My sister isn't a 'no-account,' mister. If that term applies to anybody, it's your son and the abusive way he went after her. Consider it his good fortune, and yours, that it wasn't me who pulled the trigger on him. I'd've shot to kill!"

"In that case," replied Walters, his own face darkening, "the killing wouldn't have stopped there. And no amount of accusation or conversation would have mattered. What's more, if anything happens to my son, even now, that is still very much in the realm of possibility."

"If you're really so worried about your boy," came Ned's voice out of the shadows, "then have you got a doctor on the way? I told your other man that somebody had better see to that."

"The doctor's coming," reported Otis, from where he sat a horse a short ways behind Walters, just within the fringe of shadows.

"Yes, yes. I've sent for the doctor out of Keylock and even supplied men to lead him here in all haste," confirmed Walters. His eyes came to rest again on the prone form of his son and a softness returned to them. It remained even when he glanced over to Marcus. "Can I come forward to see my boy?"

Marcus nodded. "Come ahead. Alone."

Walters dismounted somewhat ponderously and advanced slowly, his gaze locked all the while on his son. As he bent to one knee beside him, Marcus said, "He's still kinda out of it. Luckily we had some who-hit-John on hand to pour in him as a pain duller against the digging it took to go after the bullet in his shoulder. Ned got it out, though. And the bleeding stopped, too."

Walters reached out and gently laid a hand on Tobe's

forehead. In a low voice, barely audible even to Marcus, who was just a few feet away, he said, "We lost his mother when he was just six years old. He's always been a handful and I . . . I know I didn't always handle him right. Sometimes too strict, sometimes too loose . . . We could never seem to connect eye to eye, though I keep believing that day will come. Until it does, I'm not ready to give up on him. And surely not to lose him."

Marcus cleared his throat and said, "I don't think there's any danger of that. Not right now, anyway. But that doctor showing up would sure help."

Walters pushed back to his feet, his expression turning flinty again. "In the meantime, I'd like to have some words with the individual who shot my boy. And your sister, too—the girl who's to blame for it all."

"I don't care much for that word *blame*, mister," Marcus snapped in reply. "My sister was minding her own business, bothering nobody. The blame for what happened starts and ends with your two men showing up and not respecting her privacy."

"That's not the way I heard it," Walters said.

"It's the way it was told to me," countered Marcus. "And it's the way I believe, mainly because I trust those who told me and also because of what I saw at the scene where it happened."

"Then let the ones who have such a convincing tale to tell say it to me. To my face," Walters insisted. "If they're so innocent and so in the right, why are they hiding behind you and lurking back in the shadows like cowards with something to hide?"

"Maybe it has something to do with you charging up here with fire in your eye and a handful of heavily armed men backing you up. Ever think of that?" Marcus said. "And just to be clear, the rest of my outfit back in those shadows ain't exactly lurking without being pretty well armed, too."

"Is that a threat?"

"It's a statement of how things are. You choose to take it for anything else, that's on you."

Walters's chest swelled and he glowered fiercely for a long count. Then, exhaling a ragged breath, he said, "You might be interested to know that, in addition to the doctor, I've also sent for our local sheriff. I'll give you some friendly advice and let you know that he doesn't take kindly to threats, especially not from free-grazing drifters who pass through here and stir up nothing but trouble."

Marcus gave a measured nod. "Thoughtful of you to call him in. I'd welcome the chance to jaw with him some. You see, when it comes to nothing but trouble, that pretty much describes what me and my outfit have experienced ever since arriving in these parts. We've had members of our party ambushed, robbed, accosted, and shot at. . . . Yeah, I'd plumb like the chance to give a piece of my mind to anybody wearing a badge around here and let 'em know what a sorry job I think they're doing when it comes to keeping the peace."

Walters was so caught off guard by this response that his mouth gaped open but no words came out.

Into this slice of silence, Eamon Farrell stepped out of the shadows. Holding a Henry repeating rifle at his side, barrel angled downward, he announced, "If you've got something to say to me, Walters, I'm the fella who put that slug in your son's shoulder."

Walters went rigid. His mouth clapped shut tight and

his eyes blazed bright. The riders fanned out behind him also went rigid in their saddles and, even in the murkiness, half a dozen hands could be seen brushing close to holstered six-guns.

At the same time, Mac eased into sight and halted two paces behind Eamon. This left him standing right at the head of the prone Tobe Walters. Mac's Smith & Wesson was in plain sight, held down at his side just as Eamon was holding his rifle—only the muzzle of Mac's gun hovered directly over the unconscious man's face.

"Just so we all understand each other, gents," he said in a low, toneless voice, "I'm real sorry it wasn't me who got the chance to plant some lead into this ill-mannered varmint to begin with. So now, if I hear the slightest click that might mean a hammer being cocked somewhere out there in the dark, or if I see a single twitch that might mean one of you rannies is reaching for hardware . . . no matter what happens next, I won't pass up another chance."

The rage that had been distorting Walters's face, aimed at Eamon, was instantly replaced by a look of confusion as his eyes cut to Mac. It took only a fraction of a second for whatever he saw there to produce a horrified expression. Wheeling to face his men, waving his arms frantically, Walters shouted, "He means it! None of you try anything. Just hold fast, don't move!"

Slowly, his breath coming in anxious puffs, the Bar W boss turned again to Eamon. But his eyes kept darting to Mac, who stood motionless and blank faced, his pistol hanging steady above Tobe.

"You wanted to talk to me face-to-face," Eamon prodded. "Shall we get on with it?"

Walters's eyes came to rest on him. But then, before he

could say anything, a shout from one of his men farther back in the pack rang out.

"Hey, boss! There's a buggy and some riders headed this way from the direction of town. Must be Hank and Buster bringin' the doc and the sheriff!"

Exhaling another ragged sigh, Walters muttered, "Thank God."

Chapter 23

The doctor—introduced as one Abner Cunningham, a spindly gent of thirty or so exhibiting prematurely thinning hair and quick, birdlike movements—leaned back on his heels after a thorough examination of Tobe and announced to all gathered close around, "From everything I can see, someone did a first-rate job of treating this wound and deserves to be highly commended."

"Commended?" echoed Hiram Walters, hovering close. "Commend one of the very intruders responsible for causing the wound in the first place? That's preposterous!"

Rising to his feet and facing the cattle boss with no sign of intimidation, the doctor said, "The cause of the injury is not my affair. I was addressing the treatment, and I stand by what I said. Your son is lucky someone was close at hand to so effectively stop the bleeding and help minimize the risk of infection by promptly removing the bullet. Had it been otherwise, my arrival here very likely would have been too late."

"That changes nothing," declared Walters. He turned to the short, stocky, gray-mustached man who had arrived with the doctor. The star pinned to the front of his shirt identified him as the local lawman.

Walters said, "I reckon the boys filled you in on the bare bones when they fetched you from town, Rafe. Now you can see the result for yourself. I demand some arrests be made. Assault and attempted murder, for starters."

The sheriff appeared to give this demand some unhurried consideration. Then he said, "Just like that, eh? I understand you being rightfully upset, Hiram, what with Tobe shot and all. But let's not be so quick to shove the cart ahead of the mule. All I've heard is what your boys came tearing in to tell me. Seems like there's more to the whole story."

"What more is there that matters? My son has been shot, maybe crippled for life in one arm. And there stands the admitted gunman!" Walters thrust a finger at Eamon. "What's more, there's a girl—the temptress who brought it all on—hiding back in the shadows somewhere who also took a shot at Tobe and tried to kill him. You don't see bullet holes in any of them, do you?"

The sheriff turned to Eamon, who had been standing by silent and unmoving. He said, "My name's Rafe Tevis, son. I'm sheriff hereabouts and I'd like to hear your—"

"I think it's time somebody heard what *I* have to say!" These words, cutting off the sheriff in midsentence, came from Becky as she suddenly stepped out of the shadows at one end of the wagon. "I'm getting tired of being talked about in the third person and particularly tired of being referred to in slanderous ways by this blowhard!"

She cast a venomous look in Walters's direction before she marched over to stand directly in front of the lawman.

"My name is Rebecca Lewis and it's true I was taking a bath in the nearby stream. I chose a secluded spot well away from any reasonable expectation of being seen. If that makes me a 'temptress,' then Mr. Walters and I have very different ideas on what that term means. It might be interesting to hear what he calls a lecherous piece of slime like his son, who sneaks up and watches a woman at such a private moment and then works himself into a state of believing she would welcome him to join her, even if he has to *force her* to see it his way!"

"That's a lie! Tobe has known women all over this territory and never needed to force a one of 'em," insisted Walters. "Look at her, not only ain't there no bullet holes in her, there ain't a mark of any kind on her. Where's the sign of him trying to force her?"

Eamon was through being quiet. "That's because I got to him before he could reach her. Haven't you been listening to anything, you pompous fool? Your son got shot on this side of that creek down there because he'd already charged across it. And by that point he was no longer wanting to just get his hands on Becky, he was shooting at her! Here, this is proof."

The Irishman pulled Tobe's Colt from where he had stuffed it in his belt earlier, and now pushed it into Sheriff Tevis's hands.

"If they're honest, I'd say a number of men in the Bar W crew can identify that as the wounded man's gun. You'll find the cylinder is halfway rotated from two misfires because the rounds got wet from being dunked in the stream, and then a spent cartridge that *did* go off. I can show you damage from that slug down there in the tree behind which Becky was hiding for her life."

"But the girl was shooting, too! She had a rifle, she was the one who shot first," insisted Walters. "Tell them, Otis. You saw it firsthand. Tell the sheriff how it happened."

"Yes, I fired the first shot," Becky admitted, intervening before Otis could say anything. "But I did so because your son was already on his way across the stream, spouting all the vile things he said he intended to do to me. My shot went over his head and he took to the water. When he came back up, he came shooting . . . or trying to. If his gun hadn't misfired, he would have killed me. The fat one took a shot, too, but he proved to have even worse aim than me. And if his horse hadn't spooked and dumped him from the saddle, I believe he would have kept trying."

By now Tevis's face was set in a hard scowl. "How about it, Otis? Did you and Tobe both take shots at this girl?"

Still mounted on his horse and positioned on the edge of the firelight with the other Bar W riders, Otis suddenly looked confused and a little desperate.

"Sheriff, I . . . It all happened so fast. . . . Tobe and the girl were yelling at each other, and then Tobe was spurring his horse out into the water . . . and all of a sudden they both were shooting and—"

"Yes or no, Otis. Did you shoot at the girl, too?"

Otis squirmed in his saddle, looking like he wished he could melt into the shadows and disappear.

Tevis held out his hand. "Let me see that big Remington popper you pack around."

Otis couldn't meet his eyes. "I . . . I guess I lost it. . . ."

It was Marcus who stepped forward and filled the sheriff's hand with what he was asking for. "We picked it up from where he dropped it on the other side of the stream. You'll find one shot fired."

As Tevis was starting to examine the Remington, Walters reached out, grabbed him by the shoulder, and jerked him around so that they were face-to-face.

"What the hell are you doing, Rafe? Why all this pussyfooting around? My boy has been shot and the culprits are right in front of you. Arrest them, damn you!"

The sheriff knocked Walters's hand away with a hard backhand swat. "Don't you ever grab me like that, Hiram! Not ever again."

"Then do your job!"

"I am! I'm doing it my way—the right way—not just the way that pleases you." Tevis's eyes blazed. "I'm sorry Tobe got shot, Hiram. Sorry for you. But he's come close too many times in the past for it not to have eventually caught up with him if he didn't change his ways. Well, by the sound of it, he didn't and it did. You're both lucky it wasn't permanent-like."

"So you're going to do *nothing* about it?"

"I didn't say that. I don't know yet what I'm going to do. I'm trying to get the full story so I can—"

"It don't matter no more! It's too late!" Walters leaned in closer to the somewhat shorter sheriff, his face a mask of rage, droplets of spit flying with his words. "I'll have your badge for this. You're done!"

"Not yet, I ain't," Tevis countered defiantly. "Now back up and act like you got a lick of sense, or I'll turn this into something you definitely don't want."

"What's that supposed to mean?" sneered Walters. "You

and that tin star you refuse to enforce have already made a mockery of this crime against my son."

"If you insist on going there, Hiram," Tevis said in a flat voice, "we can really talk about crimes that have been a mockery of the law. You said a little bit ago how Tobe has had his way with women all over the territory but never had to force any of them. Only that's not true and you and me both know it, don't we? Too many of those times that's exactly what he did—forced himself on women. And then got away with it because your money paid them off, got them to drop charges and clam up."

"Opportunistic sluts, every one!" Walters claimed. "They led him on and then cried rape precisely so they could wangle an easy payoff for their conniving ways."

"I treated some of those women after Tobe got done with them," spoke up Dr. Cunningham in an icy tone. "Even if they were silent later, their injuries spoke volumes to me as far as the truth of their ordeal. No woman brings on that kind of treatment willingly."

"Shut up, you pill-pushing little pipsqueak!" Walters snarled. "You made your money each and every time, didn't you? So you got no complaint."

"And no complaint—at least no legal one—is what I think you've got here, Hiram," stated Tevis. "Based on what I've heard and what I know of Tobe's background, I think the actions taken against him and Otis were reasonable self-defense. On the other hand, if these folks"—he swept his hand to indicate Eamon, Becky, and Marcus—"want to press some charges, then that'd be something I might have to take more seriously."

Walters inhaled and exhaled loudly through his nose, glaring at the sheriff the whole time.

"You're crowding me awful hard, Rafe. I didn't set out

for it to come to this, but counting the two men who brought in you and the doc, I got an even dozen Bar W riders backing me here. Before I'll stand by and see this pack of interlopers and liars get off unpunished for what they did to my flesh and blood, I may have to take matters in my own hands."

"That's crazy talk, Hiram," replied Tevis, a trace of unsteadiness in his voice. "What are you going to do—gun down me and the doc, too? Are you really prepared to push this that far?"

A long moment, heavy with tension, ticked slowly by.

Until Mac, where he'd remained, motionless and all but forgotten in the flurry of increasingly heated exchanges, hovering close to the prone Tobe, once again drew attention to himself by speaking for the first time since the arrival of the sheriff and the doctor. Quietly, shifting his body ever so slightly to make certain the Smith & Wesson in his hand and the way it dangled less than a foot from Tobe's head was very evident to all, he said, "Remember me, Walters, and what I said I'd do if any of your boys reached for hardware? That holds truer now than ever. So you'd better think real good about the sheriff's question: Are you willing to push this that far?"

Walters's eyes widened and the look on his face shifted back and forth between horror and rage. "You'd really do that?" he husked. "You'd kill an unarmed, unconscious man?"

"No, I'll only be pulling the trigger," Mac replied tonelessly. "You give the wrong answer, you'll be the one killing him . . . and probably a lot of others, too."

Chapter 24

It was the middle of the day when Quinn Blassingame came riding up to the campsite two miles east of Harcourt City. He reined in his horse, alighted from the saddle. Leaving the animal ground-hitched to graze and cool, he strode over to where Muncie and Running Horse were seated before a campfire over which a pair of dressed-out sage hens were roasting on a spit.

Snatching up the tin cup he'd left on a stone beside the fire earlier that morning, Blassingame tapped it upside down against his thigh a couple times, to clear out any dust or bugs that might have occupied it while he was away, then poured some coffee from the pot bubbling on the edge of the coals. Drawing the cup to his mouth, he blew a cooling breath down onto its contents before taking a sip. Then, eyeing the sage hens that were looking brown and crisp and ready for eating, he said, "Looks like I'm just in time for lunch. Who bagged the fresh meat?"

Muncie jabbed a finger. "Running Horse. He went out and snared 'em. Never fired a shot."

"Best way for a bird. Snare 'em, twist their neck. A bullet can ruin too much good meat," Running Horse said.

"No arguing that what's hanging there on the spit looks and smells mighty tasty," Blassingame said.

"Only one problem," said Muncie.

"What's that?"

"I see just two birds succulatin' there. That calculates out as one for me and one for Running Horse." Muncie's eyebrows lifted. "We reckoned you'd go ahead and take your lunch at a café or some such while you was in town."

"Then I guess you calculated wrong," Blassingame informed him. "Would've been plumb rude of me to eat a stove-cooked meal in town while you two were out here making do over a campfire."

"You and me eat a lot of meals in towns while Running Horse is making do over a campfire," Muncie pointed out.

"That's different. It's his preference. He don't like towns and he don't like town cooking."

"Burnt meat, vegetables boiled to mush, overused grease—what's to like?" grunted Running Horse.

"I've got to admit, your trail cooking measures up awful good to a lot of kitchen-prepared meals I can think of," said Blassingame.

"Go ahead. Flattery might get him to share part of his bird with you. But I've got my mouth all set for a whole hen," declared Muncie, "and my belly ain't going to settle for no less than that."

"How about a swift kick in the pants to help you change your mind?"

Muncie lifted his eyebrows again, then gave a little grin. "Well, since you asked so politely . . ."

"The hens are ready," Running Horse announced, leaning forward to lift the crossbar off the spit. Then, deftly using a knife, he pushed first one bird and then the other onto a tin plate. "If you two roosters are ready to eat instead of just clucking about it, there's plenty here to go around."

For the next several minutes, the men enjoyed tender, juicy slices of meat that Running Horse carved and distributed. To go with it, he passed around a jar of canned stewed tomatoes from which each man scooped a portion for himself.

Halfway through the meal, Muncie addressed Blassingame, saying, "Okay. So we know you didn't spend your time in town at a café. How about your visit to the telegraph office? Did you hear back from Leclerc? Did he respond to the wire you sent yesterday letting him know we'd tracked Mackenzie this far and that he'd headed out on another cattle drive?"

"Indeed he did," Blassingame answered. "Naturally, he wants us to continue after the man and to make sure he doesn't make another unexpected detour away from this current drive. But here's a new wrinkle: He wants us to keep track of Mackenzie but, as long as we're able to do that, not to make any attempt to apprehend him. Not until Leclerc has a chance to catch up and join in on it personally."

Muncie stopped chewing. "Are you serious?"

"I wouldn't joke about something like that," said Blassingame. "Apparently this crazy Frenchman's hate for

Mackenzie is nearly as big as his bank account. He figures the time it will take the cattle drive to reach Rattlesnake Creek will allow him to make it up here and be part of Mackenzie's capture."

"What's he gonna do? Fly like a bird?"

Blassingame shrugged. "I don't know for sure, but he seems to think he can do it. By railroad and stagecoach, I guess, maybe by water. If I'm not mistaken, I believe I heard somewhere that steamboats have made it up the Missouri River as far as Great Falls. That's not too far north of the gold strike at Rattlesnake Creek and that's where he wants one of us to meet him and then guide him the rest of the way so he can be on hand for taking Mackenzie."

Muncie went back to chewing. "I guess if you got the money to spend, you can accomplish about anything. Seems like a waste, though, to go to all that trouble and expense on top of what he's already paying our agency to nab his man for him."

"Like I said, his personal beef with Mackenzie must be pretty big," Blassingame allowed. "Kind of ironic, too, when you stop and consider that most of the money Leclerc is spending so freely comes from marrying the daughter of the wealthy man Mackenzie is wanted for killing. Reckon maybe he's trying to make a good impression on his bride by pulling out all stops to ensure her daddy's murderer is brought to justice."

"Spending a gal's own money to try and impress her . . . there's a novel twist," Muncie said wryly.

"If you ask me," Running Horse said, "it's just more proof of how crazy you white people can be. Especially rich white people. My people, a buck impresses a maiden by how strong he is and what a good hunter. Then he asks for her hand and, if her father is agreeable, the maiden brings into the marriage ponies and blankets and a plot of land for growing grain and vegetables. That is considered sufficient wealth for anyone."

"Then why ain't you on a rez somewhere, hunting and fishing to provide for some maiden with a bunch of ponies and a vegetable garden?" Muncie asked.

"Simple," replied Running Horse, tossing a gnawed-clean bone into the fire. "It is because I have been corrupted by too much exposure to white-eyed devils like you two."

"Yeah? Well, you've taken to it right nice, I'll give you that," drawled Muncie with a faint grin.

"Maybe so. But not so much that I don't still miss my own wikiup and my woman warming the bed inside it. Which brings me to the conclusion," said Running Horse, "that it is time for me to return to those things."

"What do you mean by that?" Blassingame wanted to know.

Running Horse made a catchall gesture with one hand. "I mean this . . . whatever it has turned into. You don't need me to track Mackenzie now that he's traveling with a cattle drive. And I don't need to waste my time or the agency's money by spending the next four or five weeks following along, pointing out cow droppings. I'll leave that to you and Muncie. I'm going home. I trust you to figure up the pay I've got coming when you get back to Denver. You know where to send it and you know where to get hold of me when you've got more work, something that requires some real tracking skill."

That was Running Horse's way. Quick, direct, simple. Blassingame knew better than to try to argue with him, especially when he had no valid counterpoints. He admitted as much, saying, "You understand you're welcome to stick through to finish off the job, Albert. But if it suits you to do otherwise . . ."

"It does. And you, in turn, understand I am not ducking out on an obligation. I simply am not needed for the rest of this so I choose to be elsewhere."

Blassingame nodded. "Duly noted."

"As for me," Muncie said somewhat wistfully, "I can't say I'm going to miss your sour disposition or the uninspiring grunts you add to our conversations. But I sure am going to miss your trail cooking. You ain't ever experienced being on the receiving end of what comes out of a frying pan when Quinn is the one swinging it over a fire. But until next time, I wish you safe travel home, you red rascal."

Running Horse responded with something roughly resembling a smile.

"Reckon you'll be leaving right away, then?" Blassingame asked.

"Still half a day's light left. No reason to waste it waiting around."

Muncie groaned. "That's fine for you, Albert. But don't go putting no ideas in his head. And that means you, Quinn. If Running Horse is leaving and you and me are going to be plodding after some slow-moving cattle drive, ain't no reason we can't spend a night in town first. Right? Treat ourselves to a barber shave and haircut, maybe a bath, a night's sleep in a real bed, a big breakfast before we hit the trail again. There wouldn't be nothing wrong with that, would there? Come on, Quinn, that ain't too much to ask and you know it."

* * *

"A detective, you say? Here in Harcourt City?"

"That's right. Showed up yesterday. Asked questions all around, then sent a wire from the telegraph office. This morning, he was back again to pick up a return message. Here's one of the business cards he's been passing around. Says his name is Blassingame, of the High Grade Detective Agency out of Denver."

Oscar Harcourt reached out and took the card Sheriff Brimball handed across his wide desk. He barely glanced at it, then lifted his gaze and said, "The High Grade Agency is top notch. I've used them myself a time or two, though I never encountered this Blassingame operative. You say his inquiries were strictly about that drifter Mackenzie?"

Brimball's head bobbed. "Uh-huh. When he checked in with me, I told him yeah, a fella by that name and description had passed through here a while back. Then I added how Mackenzie had got in a couple saloon scrapes during the short time he was here, so I ran him out of town. I was hoping that would be enough to send the detective on his way, too." The sheriff paused, tossed off a shrug. "Reckon he had to have heard from some others about Mackenzie joining the Standing L cattle drive, but he didn't show no particular interest in that."

Harcourt's eyes returned to the business card and he gazed at it thoughtfully for a long count.

Brimball frowned and began to look somewhat uneasy. "That detective can't have got too far by now. If you want, I can ride out and catch up with him. Pump him for more information about what his interest in Mackenzie is, if you think it might be important."

Harcourt didn't reply right away. Only after turning the card over in his fingers a couple of times and then tapping it, edge down, on his desktop, did he say, "No, I don't think that will be necessary, Miles. Let him go. I can't imagine why his interest in Mackenzie—or what trouble Mackenzie might be in—would be of any concern to me. In fact, if that detective is out to nab his quarry on some criminal charge and it results in the removal of Mackenzie from the cattle drive, thereby causing some disruption to the Lewises' undertaking, that might actually work to my benefit."

"If you say so," the sheriff allowed, his frown deepening. "Though I ain't so sure I follow why."

"All in good time, Miles." Harcourt gave the business card another tap on the desktop and one side of his mouth lifted in a guarded smile. "In a day or so, I plan to be leaving town. I may be gone as long as a month, maybe a bit more. I'll keep in touch by telegram and will be counting on you and Lawyer Croft to look after my affairs while I'm away. When I return, I'll enlighten you on some business ventures that I expect will have turned out very favorably for me by then. And, as always, good fortune for me means good fortune for Harcourt City. Right?"

Looking both surprised and a bit bewildered by the announcement, Brimball said again, "If you say so."

Chapter 25

After thumbing back the brim of his hat with his left hand and using the already soaked bandana in his right to mop away the beads of perspiration dotting his forehead, Rafe Tevis settled the hat back in place and said with a sheepish grin, "It is truly a blasted shame how soft a body can let hisself get. I've been riding a cushioned desk chair and making sure I found a spot of shade during the hottest part of most days for so long that a few hours out in the open is pure boiling me. And this saddle ain't suiting my backside near as good as that desk chair, neither."

Riding beside him, the gait of their horses matching the plodding progress of the bawling, dust-enshrouded Standing L cattle herd they were moving along with, Marcus Lewis replied, "Not to come across like I'm in a hurry to get rid of you, Sheriff, and certainly not to sound ungrateful for all your help, but maybe it's time for you to turn back. There's no guarantee, I understand, but if Hiram Walters hasn't tried anything by now, then don't you reckon that's a pretty good sign he probably ain't going to?"

"I'd sure like to think that," Tevis said. "We've been past the boundaries of his spread for some time now. And as far as boundaries or guarantees, either one, there was never much guarantee my being here would make much difference anyway, considering we've been outside my official jurisdiction longer than we've been beyond his spread. Still, if he *was* going to try and cause any trouble, I've been figuring it would most likely be before your herd was off his property. On the other hand, you could wonder if maybe that ain't the way he'd *expect* us to figure."

"I suppose we could ponder about forty different notions on how Walters might figure or what he might do," Marcus said. "But until he makes some kind of move, all my outfit *really* can do is stay alert for the possibility. Which, I'd say, is lessening. But unless you want to stick around and finish the drive with us, you're almost certain to be facing some kind of backlash from him once you return to Keylock."

Tevis puffed out his cheeks and exhaled a breath. "No need to remind me. I've been doing that to myself for the past couple of days."

A couple of days was how much time had passed since the tense confrontation that night at the Standing L campsite when all sides concerned with the Tobe Walters shooting—the Standing L crew, the Bar W outfit, and Sheriff Tevis caught smack in the middle—had stood nose to nose, with only one slap of leather separating the tension from a blaze of gunfire.

Walters and the Bar W had backed down at that juncture, leaving Tobe in the custody of Doc Cunningham, to be taken into town and kept there for further treatment and observation.

Ned and Ox had finished repairing the chuckwagon harness and breaking in a suitable new team. With that taken care of, Mac and Becky had made a trip into Keylock, under the watchful eye of Tevis, to purchase replacement supplies.

While they were doing that, Marcus, Eamon, Ox, and Ned had moved the herd across the stream and held them there, on a patch of fresh graze, waiting. Now, on the second day since the shooting, they'd gotten a pre-dawn start and were pushing hard to put the Keylock area and any more trouble behind them.

Tevis had ridden out early to join them, acting as a guide to get them across the narrowest stretch of the Bar W spread as quickly as possible and to be on hand in case Hiram Walters—conspicuously absent since that night at the Standing L camp—tried to bother them before they got clear of the region.

"Are you sorry you done it? Stepped in and took our side?" Marcus asked the lawman now.

"I don't see it as taking any particular 'side.' I see it as simply making the fair and proper judgment on a thing," Tevis replied. He frowned thoughtfully for a moment, then added, "If I'm sorry about anything, I reckon it's that I let Tobe Walters get away with his shenanigans those other times when I should have drawn some kind of harder line then and there. Yeah, I can make the excuse that once the gals involved withdrew their charges there wasn't no more I could do. But I knew why they changed their tunes, knew Hiram had got to 'em with a payoff, maybe even some kind of threat if they didn't cooperate. I didn't push it, I just let it settle back down each time and told myself that Hiram would somehow get a handle on his kid and it wouldn't happen no more."

"I got a hunch Walters might've been telling himself the same thing," said Marcus. "I ain't making excuses for him, not by a long shot. But I've seen that kind of thing before. It's hard for a body to admit that someone of their own blood, be it son or brother or what have you, is flawed at their core. Be even harder for a powerful, influential hombre like Hiram Walters."

"Powerful and influential," Tevis echoed hollowly. "Add intimidating and you got the whole of what I allowed to work against me." He paused, gazing out over the slowly streaming cattle, taking time before he said more. Then: "Much as I hate to admit it, each of those times I failed to come down harder on Tobe, what I was really failing was to go up against Hiram. And failing my badge in the process."

"So what changed? Why take a stand like you did the other night at our camp?" asked Marcus. "And what kind of reaction are you likely to get from Walters once we've moved on?"

Tevis locked eyes with him and his tone became very earnest. "It started with seeing Tobe lying there shot and seeing the hurt and defiance on your sister's face. Then when Hiram started getting more demanding and threatening, the rest of it rushed in and hit me all the harder. Things stood on the brink of gunfire breaking out and men who were mostly decent were at risk of getting shot, maybe killed, all on account of some spoiled pup whose

reins I should have jerked short a long time earlier. I knew
that no matter what else happens, even if Hiram tries to
see that my badge gets yanked like he threatened, I could-
n't just step aside and let him and his rotten kid have their
way again."

"Pretty gutsy play, I got to hand it to you," said Marcus, matching the sheriff's earnestness.

The sheriff grunted. "Maybe. But about halfway through,
I gotta tell you, I wasn't feeling so confident. It was your
man, stepping forward ice cold and swearing to make
Tobe the first one dead if Hiram pushed it any farther,
that really broke the back of the Bar W threat."

"Yeah, that was our Mac. Reckon his display of iciness
made all of us sit up and take pretty sharp notice," admitted Marcus. "He's kinda full of surprises . . . and a heck
of a good cook to boot."

"I don't know about his cooking, but having him on
hand the other night sure paid off. No doubt about that."

"I'm glad you think that way. But it still makes me feel
kinda lousy now, us pushing on and leaving you here to
face on your own whatever's in store for you after you
stood up for us like you did."

"You got a herd to deliver and a ranch to save. And a
good crew of folks depending on that happening," Tevis
told him. "Staying here babysitting me ain't gonna accomplish any of that. Besides, if Hiram decides to wield
his influence and *does* end up costing me my badge, you
hanging around ain't likely to make no difference to any
of that. And if enough ungrateful cusses swing to his way
of thinking, they can have this piece of star-shaped tin
and the thankless duties that go with it." The sheriff cocked
one eyebrow and formed a crooked smile underneath it.
"Comes to that, maybe I'll take my cash-out pay, use it

for a grubstake and head for those gold fields up at Rattle-snake Creek. Could be the next time you see me I'll be in line for an overpriced cut of this beef you're pushing that way."

"You end up there and I'm still around, I'll see to it you get the biggest and best T-bone available. And it won't cost you a cent."

"I'll not only hold you to it, but I'll make sure I'm powerful hungry if and when I show up!"

The two men grinned somewhat wistfully over what they both knew wasn't likely to ever happen.

Then Tevis said, "Well, one thing is for sure, and that's what you said about it being time for me to head back. Nothing for it but to return and find out how things are going to go."

"Sometimes backing down a bully and showing him for what he is can have a lasting effect, leaves things the better for it," suggested Marcus.

"We'll have to see about that," Tevis replied, not look-ing particularly hopeful. "But here's something more for you to know, before I forget. As I was getting ready to ride out this morning, Doc Cunningham told me he was sending word out to the Bar W that Tobe was well enough to go home. I gave him an added message to send out, let-ting Hiram know that I'd wired ahead to the U.S. Marshal in Lewistown, informing him you'd be passing his way and to be on the lookout you made it okay. Sort of insur-ance, you might say, to warn Hiram or any of the Bar W boys in case they get it in their heads to wait until you're farther down the trail before trying any funny business."

Marcus nodded. "Appreciate that. Sort of helps cover us, but it don't necessarily do you any good."

"Comes down to it, I don't think Hiram's got it in him to actually do me any physical harm," Tevis said. "He might try to go after my badge out of spite. But what the hell, that might be doing me a favor. On the other hand, Hiram might well find out that the things Tobe has been allowed to get away with haven't set so well with a lot of folks around these parts. And if he makes too much noise about this latest incident, it could backfire on him and call attention to things he'd rather see put to rest."

After a moment's more consideration, all Marcus could say was, "Well, I hope it works out for the best all the way around, Sheriff. And on behalf of me and my outfit, you got our gratitude for all you've done for us."

"In a way, I owe you some gratitude, too, for prodding me into doing better by this badge I wear," Tevis told him. "If Hiram don't wangle getting it taken away from me, I'll continue doing right by it."

"I got faith you will."

"I appreciate that. Here's wishing you good luck the rest of the way with your drive. And be sure to check in with that marshal in Lewistown so he gets back to me and I'll know you made it at least that far."

Marcus said he would and, with that, the two men parted ways. Tevis wheeled his mount and heeled it in the direction of Keylock; Marcus gigged a little closer in to the flow of cattle and then matched his horse's gait once more to their steady, plodding progress.

Chapter 26

Two more days passed before the Standing L crew began relaxing their guard as far as concern over some kind of retaliation from Hiram Walters. During that time, for the sake of keeping their full force as tightly grouped as possible, Mac and the chuckwagon had moved along *with* the herd as opposed to the normal practice of rolling farther ahead.

This meant the noon meal was a quick, abbreviated matter of coffee, biscuits, and jerky, and then a delay in supper being prepared and served once the drive halted for the night, but the reason for this was understood and accepted by all.

On the morning of the third day, as breakfast was finishing up and it was time to start the herd moving again, Mac, Marcus, and Ned held a brief consultation over the final dregs from the coffeepot, divided equally into their cups. They agreed that today Mac would return to standard procedure and resume traveling ahead of the herd, scouting and marking trail as he went.

The terrain was starting to grow more rugged as they passed nearer the Snowy Mountain range off to the east and drew closer to the Big Belt range ahead and to the west. Good water and graze for bedding the herd at night might be sparser and harder to find in the coming days until they passed through Judith Gap and moved into the Judith Basin not far from their destination.

With these things in mind, Mac struck out that morning and began distancing himself and the chuckwagon from the slower-moving herd. After a handful of troublesome spells, brought on primarily due to nerves and ignorance of the new duties being required of them, but also to a bout or two of plain orneriness, the team commandeered out of the remuda was working fairly smoothly, for the most part getting along and each getting the hang of what they needed to do.

Mac was glad he'd had a chance to iron out these rough spots while moving at a slower pace with the herd, while the land was still relatively flat and grassy and Ned was on hand to help him jerk the critters back in line. When the going ahead got even more rugged, he'd need a team he could count on, not one that would balk or fight against his commands.

As the sun climbed higher in a sky sliced by horizontal fingers of soot-colored clouds, Mac rolled on and the herd fell farther back in his wake. It wasn't long before Mac was reminded how much he enjoyed periodic stretches of solitude.

Not to say that he didn't like the company of everyone associated with the Standing L outfit, just as he had the previous cattle drive crews he'd ridden with. And before he'd been forced to take flight as a fugitive, he'd been regularly active in New Orleans social settings.

But that very circumstance—fleeing, going on the run, learning to be constantly cautious and to fully trust no one but himself—had necessitated adopting the life of a loner, especially during the early days and months. That made being a chuckwagon cook almost a perfect job for him. He had long stretches throughout most days to be off on his own, then a few hours of companionship and camaraderie come night.

The only downside, in this instance, was that it meant less chance to be around Becky. The days they'd been stalled at the campsite where the chuckwagon got stolen and then the following period where the chuckwagon had traveled close even after the herd began moving again had provided better opportunities in that regard. The only problem was the fact that Becky had become notably moody and withdrawn following her near-attack by Tobe Walters.

Everybody noticed it, though none more than Mac. The others speculated she must have been unsettled by the experience, perhaps even made to feel shamed. The things Tobe had said he intended to do to her, coupled with the filthy accusations spouted by his father against Becky and Tobe's other victims who preceded her, might account for such a reaction. Marcus, who knew Becky best, suggested they just allow her a little time and room and she would return to herself okay.

Only Mac had a hunch there might be something more to it. And that something more, to his misery, he had reason to fear might be him.

* * *

It had come out the day he and Becky made the trip into Keylock, aboard the refurbished chuckwagon and its still very green, rambunctious team, to stock replacement supplies for what was stolen. All during the ride in, Becky had seemed pensive, unusually quiet. Mac had chalked it up to her probably being nervous about trouble possibly flaring up as a result of the tense situation with the Bar W. When nothing happened and they were on their way back to camp without incident, though, she had remained unchanged.

Until, not too far out of town, Becky had said, "Last night in camp, after Hiram Walters and all his men showed up and things reached the point where it looked like Walters might actually order his men to go against the sheriff and take the law into their own hands . . . you were the one who prevented that from happening."

"I don't know about that," Mac had countered, actually blushing a little and feeling embarrassed because he thought she was going to heap praise on him. "The sheriff was doing a pretty good job of—"

"No," Becky cut him off. "No, Walters was getting ready to roll right over the sheriff. Everybody could see that. It was you, Mac. You were the one who shut it all down when you said you'd put a bullet in Tobe's head if any of the Bar W men made the wrong move."

"The main thing is that, for whatever reason, nobody shot anybody," Mac told her. "But the thing now, with so many still on short fuses, is that we get on down the trail before any of those fuses get relit."

But Becky remained focused on what had happened,

not what might lie ahead. "Would you have really done it?" she asked. "Were you truly prepared to pull the trigger on Tobe the way you threatened?"

Mac had frowned at the intensity of her questioning. He took a minute to think about his answer, then said, "The whole idea of me making the threat was to *stop* any trigger pulling. If it hadn't worked, if Hiram or any of his men had called my bluff and gone for their guns anyway . . . I don't know what would have happened. If shooting had broken out in close quarters like we were, I expect quite a few of us might have taken bullets."

"But would you have put your first one in Tobe? With him lying there, unconscious, would you have shot him in cold blood?"

The tone in Becky's voice had made the question sting like an accusation. Mac snapped a somewhat caustic response. "What is this, Becky? You almost sound like you're feeling sorry for that varmint!"

Her expression turning deeply anguished, Becky said, "It's not that at all. I have nothing but loathing for Tobe Walters. Nobody knows better than me what he's like. But I'm talking about you, Mac. The look on your face, the coldness in your voice when you stood there on the edge of the shadows and said those words . . . I don't know how else to say it, but it was frightening. It was like you were somebody else, somebody I didn't know and . . . and wouldn't want to."

That had stung even more. All Mac could say was, "I'm the same person I've always been, Becky. The only person I know how to be. And that's somebody who certainly never wants to seem frightening to you."

"I know that. It's not what I want either." Becky shook her head, her pale hair sparkling in the morning sunlight as it swept back and forth across her shoulders. "And I'm not saying that's how it is. It's just that the events of yesterday and last night all turned so violent and ugly. I shot at a man, at *two* men. No matter what else they were, they were still men. I can't stop thinking, what if I'd hit one of them? Or worse yet, *killed* one of them?"

"You were defending yourself. What else were you supposed to do?"

Becky shook her head again. "I don't know the answer to that. I don't know the answer to anything. I just know that the anger and hate kept escalating until it seemed like it was going to explode. But then it didn't. It didn't because you stood over an unconscious man and threatened to put a bullet in his head . . . and I can't get that image or those words out of my head, Mac."

It wasn't until they'd rolled on in silence for a ways before Mac spoke again. "I don't know what to say. I'm sorry you feel that way, that it bothered you so much. But I won't say I'm sorry for what I did. I believe it was justified in that situation."

"I'm not asking you to apologize. I'm not even saying you were wrong and I have any right to feel this way," Becky told him. "All I'm doing is trying to explain how I feel, how troubling it all was, even including some of my own actions."

Mac didn't know what to say to that, so he'd said nothing.

After a time, Becky spoke again. "When you stood up for me in the Irish Jig and when you and Ox fought off Jerry Lee and those others on the trail out to the ranch, I called your actions swashbuckling. There was an air of excitement and danger about you then, yet somehow it wasn't so . . . dark, is the only word that comes to mind now. I want to see you that way again, the first way. But, after last night, I'm finding it hard to. Just give me a little time to sort some things out in my head, can you?"

Mac met the imploring look she cast upon him and then replied, "I'll give you everything I can, Becky. But you need to understand this: I've known violence in my time. Some of it pretty harsh. And it's taught me that, in order to survive, a man sometimes has to be as harsh—or harsher—in return. That's a part of me now, and I don't know that I can change it."

And that's how they'd left it. The subsequent days had passed with Becky remaining quiet and somewhat with-drawn—to everyone, for the most part, but especially to Mac, or so it seemed to him.

Maybe that was another reason that made getting out alone again this morning feel especially good. Being in closer proximity to Becky, under the current circumstances, had actually been a kind of torment. In almost constant sight of her but meeting averted eyes and only a few mur-mured words in return was alternately frustrating and cause for gut-grinding bouts of anger.

Yeah, blast it, his action that night may have been hard and cold—yet it very likely had prevented something far worse. Nor did it help that, unless Mac's imagination was running away with him, Becky's responses to Eamon's ongoing attention since then seemed nearly as chummy as ever, in spite of her "unsettled" condition.

And overriding it all, of course, was the constant and bitter realization deep inside Mac that none of it really mattered. It *couldn't*. Not for the first time, he was being a fool for pretending otherwise and for allowing his emotions to lead him even a few steps down such a hopeless path. A path upon which there was no room for romance or love or any enticement for a decent woman to walk it with him.

Not as long as I'm a wanted fugitive on the run from a murder charge.

Mac rocked his head back on his shoulders and then turned his face slowly from side to side, sweeping his gaze over the vastness that stretched in every direction.

"What the hell," he muttered through a wry smile. "Just you and me, Big Empty. Maybe that's how it's meant to be."

Chapter 27

The days rolled by without further incident. Just the steady, plodding, grinding, dusty push of the cattle, angling ever north and a bit west over the Montana landscape. They skirted close to the high, majestic peaks of the Snowys off to their right, moved on toward the rise of the Big Belts in the distance ahead on their left. Graze for the cattle remained plentiful, though the grass was a shorter, coarser variety, and Mac had little or no trouble finding suitable watering stops. The nights grew noticeably colder, the days sometimes cloudy but fair and clear of rain.

They were more than two weeks gone from the Standing L home spread now, and except for the time they'd been stalled around Keylock, Marcus calculated they had been achieving a very satisfactory average of over seventeen miles a day.

When they passed near the town of Lewistown, Marcus had kept his promise to Rafe Tevis and rode in long enough to check with the U.S. Marshal there, letting him know they'd encountered no additional trouble from Hiram Walters or any Bar W riders. In return, the marshal had this message from Sheriff Tevis: "Things are a little tense around here. But so far, so good."

That was a relief to Marcus and also to the rest of the Standing L crew when he returned and shared it with them.

Near the close of the seventeenth day, Mac parked and blocked the chuckwagon about halfway up a long, gradual slope off to one side of a wide, shallow, spring-fed pool with an apron of rich green grass spread before it. Here the outfit would make night camp and bed down the herd, coming up about an hour behind him.

After loosening his team of horses, Mac went to work building a fire ring and stoking a bed of crackling flames inside it. As the fire popped and licked hotter, he first set a pot of coffee to brewing and then dropped down the rear flap of the wagon and propped it into a table upon which he spread his other pans and bowls and began preparing supper. The air was already beginning to cool as the bottom edge of the sun dropped behind the horizon, signaling another chilly night.

As Mac was working his biscuit dough, looking up now and then to admire the beauty of the colorful hues thrown by the sinking sun, he noticed four riders approaching from the west. They were spread out abreast of one another in a fairly tight pattern, coming at a steady but unhurried pace. They appeared to be armed but gave off no particular sense of trouble—other than it being uncommon to run into anybody out here so far away from everything.

Over the past few days, the drive had encountered a handful of other travelers—or, more accurately put, such travelers had *passed by.* Because those they'd seen were on their way to the gold strike at Rattlesnake Creek and had no time to tarry with a slow-moving cattle drive. A few times these gold hunters had stopped to chat briefly; other times they had simply hurried past, with not even a wave.

But the four now in sight were coming *from* the direction of the gold strike, not going toward it, and clearly were of some different stripe. Just to be safe, Mac adjusted the half-apron he wore down a little lower around his middle so that the Smith & Wesson in his waistband was more readily accessible.

Additionally, wiping his hands on the apron, he walked leisurely around to the front of the wagon, lifted the Winchester Yellowboy from its boot, and carried the rifle back to the rear. There, he leaned it up against the hinge where the drop-down table was fastened to the back of the wagon bed, then returned to working his biscuit dough. As the four riders drew nearer, though he still sensed no tangible threat from them, Mac glanced over his shoulder and felt faintly relieved to be able to see the dust haze of the approaching herd not too far back.

"Hello, the wagon!" called one of the riders as all four reined to a slow walk once they were within a few yards of Mac.

Mac looked up and gave an amiable nod, saying, "Evening to you, gents."

The rider who'd called out, a lean hombre of average height, thirtyish, heavily whiskered with pale blue eyes set too close on either side of a long, bony nose, spoke again. "That's a mighty admirable-looking rig you got there. You appear well set up for the cattle herd I see advancing off yonder."

Mac grinned. "Reckon I better be well set up. Punchers coming in for supper can get awfully cantankerous if they don't get their grub plenty quick."

Bony Nose grinned, too. "Guess we know a little something about that. When I say 'we,' I mean me and my brother here." He jabbed a thumb to indicate the rider on his left, another lanky sort though a bit thicker through the shoulders, a couple years younger, but with the same pinched face, prominent nose, and too-close eyes. Continuing, the speaker added, "Same holds true for our pals as well, though never on any of the same outfits."

The "pals" Bony Nose referred to were the men to his right. As a pair, they were physically something of a contrast to the brothers, both being taller and stockier in build. The nearest to Bony Nose was thick bodied and hard looking, with a bull neck and wiry rust-colored hair poking out around his ears from under the brim of his hat. The man next to him was the largest of the four, looking to top out at about six-four, wide shouldered but soft looking around the middle, with a ruddy face bracketed by thick gray sideburns.

Each of the men packed sidearms—Bony Nose's worn for the cross draw on his left side, the others all holstered on their right hips—and each had either a Winchester or a Henry rifle booted alongside their saddles. Yet there wasn't about them, as far as Mac could sense, an air of gunmen. As a lot, however, they appeared worn and weary, men definitely down on their luck, maybe close to the edge of desperation.

Responding to Bony Nose's comment, Mac now said, "So you've all wrangled cattle at one time or another, that what you're saying?"

Bony Nose sighed a bit forlornly. "For a fact. By the way, I'm Ward Ivers. My brother, he's Boyd. And over here is Red Haney and Able Craddock." Haney, not surprisingly, was the fellow with the wiry rust-colored hair, Craddock the large man on the end.

"I'm Mackenzie—make it Mac," Mac said in return. "You don't mind my saying, you fellas look pretty tuckered. I got a pot of coffee over here that oughta be about ready. Care to light down and have some?"

"Mister, them are golden words and we surely will take you up on the offer," Ward Ivers declared, as those to either side of him were already swinging down from their saddles.

"The smell of that coffee starting to bubble has been torturing me since about fifty yards back," added Craddock with a lopsided smile. "If you *hadn't* made that offer, friend, I was near ready to get down on my knees and beg."

In short order, the four new arrivals all had cups of steaming coffee in hand and were gulping the scalding contents even as they praised Mac for how good it was. In the midst of their talk, the faint bawl of cattle started to carry on the air as the approaching herd drew closer.

Mac kept working on the supper he was preparing. Once he had fresh biscuits baking in the Dutch oven, he began laying out thick slices of bacon in an oversized frying pan.

Hovering close, Ward Ivers said, "You were quick enough to spot our tuckered-out condition, friend. Maybe you're too polite to say more, but I ain't too proud to admit that we're wrung pretty dry on more counts than just being tuckered. You see, we're returning from trying our luck at the Rattlesnake Creek gold strike. Reckon it don't take no genius to calculate that if our luck had been *good*, we wouldn't be leaving there, right?"

"Not unless you were loaded down with gold nuggets and on your way to have a high time in some big city," Mac replied.

Standing nearby, Boyd Ivers gave a disgusted grunt. "Let me tell you, that is a *long* way from the case."

"We had it all planned, we put together what we thought was a plenty solid grubstake," Ward explained, sighing. "But, man, was we ever wrong. We dug and dug and brought up nothing but dirt and more dirt. And our grubstake, once we discovered the prices everywhere was jacked higher than a sky pilot's aim, petered out mighty fast. So there we were, flat busted, our pockets as empty as all those holes we dug and our bellies catching up. So all we could do was sell our equipment for enough money to put together some traveling supplies and head for home."

"Where'd that be?" Mac asked.

"Nebraska and Kansas. There's ranches through there where they know us, where we've worked before. We reckon we can catch on again with one of those outfits, start to get back on our feet."

"Sounds reasonable, I guess. Long ways to go, though," said Mac. "If you ain't in too big a hurry, might you be interested in suppering with our outfit tonight? Maybe breakfast in the morning before you're on your way?"

Ward's eyebrows lifted. "There's them golden words

again. Mac, we would be more than interested. We'd be so plumb grateful, you wouldn't believe."

"We ain't a big outfit, nothing fancy," Mac said with a shrug. "Bacon, beans, biscuits. Our trail boss is a reasonable fella. I'm sure he won't mind sharing some, you hombres being so down on your luck and all. If that works for you, go ahead and strip your saddles and bedrolls, turn your horses loose. You can see there's plenty of good graze and water right down the slope."

A quarter mile away, atop a brushy ridge crested by a sawtooth line of weathered rocks, Ray Muncie said, "You sure it's them?"

"Not a whisker of doubt in my mind," replied Quinn Blassingame, lowering the pair of field glasses he'd been holding to his eyes and leaving them to hang from a leather thong around his neck. Reaching up with one hand and squaring his hat back in place, the detective added, "These lenses are top of the line but I could spot those ugly, pinched faces of Ward and Boyd Ivers even through a dirty windowpane. Half a dozen years back, I spent ten weeks tracking their mangy hides all across northern Kansas. I was ready to nail them, too, if the blasted agency hadn't yanked me off the case and put me instead on the kidnapping of that senator's conniving brat of a daughter."

"I know about that. The senator's daughter thing, I mean," said Muncie, settling deeper back in the rocks as Blassingame did the same. "But what became of the Iverses between then and now? I remember hearing their names tossed around a time or two, but it's been a while."

Blassingame grunted. "They were smart enough to pull in their horns when they felt things tightening on them all through Kansas. They made tracks for somewhere, nobody seems to know exactly where. Best bet, I always believed, was they went up into Canada. But other than guesses and rumors as to their whereabouts, nobody was ever certain what happened to 'em—until now."

"What about those other two with 'em?"

"One of 'em, the big fella, I don't know. Not by sight anyway. His name might mean something if I heard it." Blassingame's mouth pulled into a grimace. "The remaining one, though, I recognize all too well. Never had a personal run-in with him, but I've seen that likeness on plenty of Wanted sheets. Red Haney. Used to raise hell in the North Platte, Nebraska, area."

Muncie gave a low whistle. "Red Haney. Oh yeah, I've heard of him. Pretty nasty from all reports."

"About as nasty as they come."

"Reckon him and the Iverses riding together now is a pretty good sign none of 'em took a turn down the straight and narrow while they was away," Muncie concluded.

"Putting your money down on that, I advise, would be a real safe bet," said Blassingame. "They might have been laying low wherever they were, living off their illegal gains. But I always figured, providing they were still alive, they'd be popping up again like a neck boil that never got the pus all the way squoze out."

"Before they disappeared, what kind of stuff were they doing in Kansas and Nebraska or wherever?"

"The usual. Robberies—banks, trains, stagecoaches.

Never reluctant to throw some killing into the mix. And they did their share of rustling, too."

"Interesting. And now here they are, out in the middle of where a cattle herd just happens to be coming along. You don't think that's just a coincidence, do you?"

Blassingame pinched his brows together in thought. "Not hardly. Be more certain if there was more than just four of them and if they were showing up coming from *behind* the herd. Then I'd call it a cinch they had some wide-looping in mind. But this looks like something a little different. Almost like an accidental run-in."

"Maybe they got more men holding back," Muncie said. "But, even if they don't, now that the Iverses and their pards have filled their nostrils with the smell of beef available for the grabbing, you think they're cured enough of their past bad habits to pass up making a try?"

"Be mighty tough to swallow," Blassingame admitted. "Too tough for us not to keep our eyes peeled sharp and be ready to make a move if it comes to that."

Muncie cocked an eyebrow. "Making a move how? You saying we might end up *helping* Mackenzie in some way?"

"Help get him into the hands of the Frenchman, yeah. That's our job, remember?" Blassingame scowled. "I'm not forgetting Mackenzie's wanted for murder. Nobody's saying we help him go free. But that don't mean we stand by and let him fall prey to a pack of opportunistic cattle rustlers, either. Especially not when the Iverses and Haney are part of that pack and, unless I'm mistaken—which I'm not—they still have some fat rewards riding on their heads."

Muncie pursed his lips and didn't say anything for a

minute. Then, rising up far enough to crane his neck and gaze again at the distant campsite caught in the stabbing rays of the setting sun, he said, "Well then. If we intend to keep a sharp eye on the situation out there and be ready to take action if we need to, we'd better hitch around as soon as it's dark enough and get in a little better position, don't you reckon?"

Chapter 28

Almost as soon as he'd invited the four strangers to stay for supper, Mac started second guessing his display of hospitality. It was true they had a worn-down, busted-luck look about them that matched their tale of misfortune. That was what had brought out the sympathy in him to begin with.

It didn't take long, though, to note that the four also had some pretty hard edges. They were polite enough, laying it on thick with expressions of gratitude, never coarse or profane in their speech, even displaying reasonable manners when they sat down to chow, but at the same time, there was an undeniable hint of flintiness behind their eyes and a sense of barely tamed rawness just under their beat-down, sorry-looking exteriors.

When Marcus showed up, he was agreeable to having

the men in camp and sharing a couple meals with them, as Mac had expected. During supper, the other members of the Standing L outfit were also mostly welcoming and friendly. Understandably, Becky was somewhat guarded and reserved, never straying far from the side of her brother.

Conversation as they all ate around the campfire included a retelling of the newcomers' recent experience at Rattlesnake Creek. It was Ward Ivers who did most of the talking for his bunch, though his brother and Craddock joined in some. Haney spoke hardly at all, just sat listening and watching, showing no outward response to any of the exchanges.

When the subject matter moved around to the Standing L cattle drive and the reasoning behind it, Marcus and the rest of the outfit were glad to hear Ward tell them that they'd be received at the gold camp with wild excitement.

"Oh yeah," he said, "you folks showing up with them beeves are going to be most near as welcome as somebody hitting another vein of the yellow stuff! The place is starting to take on the look and feel of sort of a town, see, and some of the more organized types have formed themselves a town council—or miner's council, I guess they call it—to try and keep order over everything.

"They laid down some rules and the council makes decisions on disputes, aiming to prevent every little argument from turning into a gunfight or knifing or such, and one of the other things they did, just before we left, was start to build some holding pens for herds of cattle they hoped would be showing up before long. I'll tell you, them miners are so sick of beans and salt pork that the chance for some fresh beef will be so appealing to them, there's no telling how high they'd pay to chomp into a juicy steak!"

"Boy, that sounds good to us," said Marcus, beaming at the report. "That's exactly the kind of reaction we've been hoping for."

"Once you get there, you'll see I'm telling you straight," Ward assured him.

Boyd's head bobbed in agreement. "My brother's right, and that's for certain. You folks are playing it plumb smart with your idea of pushing up these cattle. That's downright enterprising and practical and it's gonna pay off big for you. Us, we went at it with shiny dreams in our eyes and shovels on our shoulders and, well, it didn't work out. But my hat's off to you for playing a lot smarter hand."

Not long after supper was done, bedrolls started being spread and weary bodies got ready to stretch out and grab some shut-eye before another hard day on the trail. Ox was on tap for the first round of nighthawk duty, so he soon faded off to saddle a horse and begin circling and soothing the herd where they were bunched on the grassy apron downslope.

The Ivers group took their bedrolls off toward one edge of the main camp, acknowledging and allowing their hosts the privacy they were due.

With most everyone bedded down and a stillness settling over the scene, Marcus came over and stood close to Mac as he was buttoning up the chuckwagon for the night. Speaking quietly, the Standing L boss said, "You altogether comfortable with this bunch we allowed to break bread with us, Mac?"

Mac made a sour face in the murky light provided by the dying campfire. "Not as much as I was when I first extended the invitation. The run-down look of 'em and their tale of woe hit a sympathetic nerve . . . at first. The longer I'm around 'em, though, the less sympathy I tend to feel. I ain't saying they didn't have some tough luck or that their story ain't true, mind you. It's just that, well, there's a kind of roughness about 'em that makes a body start to think they maybe ain't so deserving of too much sympathy after all. They might have had a hard break up at Rattlesnake Creek, but I got a hunch they're the type might have dished out a few hard breaks to others in their time."

"Yeah, I get the same feeling," Marcus allowed.

"Sorry I got took in so easily by 'em."

"Don't blame yourself alone. I was all for being hospitable to them, same as you. But like you said, that was at first." Marcus's expression turned somber. "Could be we're being overly suspicious. Even if they're men with a hard past, they might still appreciate our sharing and just move on without any trouble."

Mac didn't look very convinced. "Could be. But now that they're in the barnyard, thanks mostly to me, I think it's a good idea to keep an extra close count of our chickens while they're around. Speaking for myself, I plan on sleeping with one eye open all night."

"I agree. I've spoken to Ned and Eamon, too," Marcus said. "They were already thinking in the same direction as you and me. Sounds like all of us will be sleeping with one eye open in the hours ahead."

"Best we can do." Mac glanced upward at the star-shot sky. "That makes this one night I want to see get over with as quick as possible."

Despite their concerns, the night passed without incident.

At breakfast, the Iverses and their companions were once again grateful for being invited to join in. When the meal was finished, it was time for the Standing L crew to get the herd moving again and for their guests to be on their separate way.

With Marcus's agreement, Mac handed Ward Ivers a sack containing a measure of coffee beans, flour, some leftover biscuits, and a generous cut of bacon to help stretch their own meager provisions. As before, seemingly sincere appreciation was shown for the gesture.

As the four men went riding off toward the south, Marcus and Eamon stood alongside the chuckwagon with Mac and watched them fade into a haze of dust.

"I consider myself neither an unsociable nor inhospitable man," said Eamon. "But I can't help thinking that we're somehow better off being shed the company of those four."

"You'll get no argument out of me," Marcus said.

"The thing now," added Mac, "is to stay on the lookout and hope we never see them again. Because if we do, then it can mean just one thing—their only reason for coming back would be to come for the herd."

Before any of them could say more, Becky came trotting up, already mounted on her favorite horse from the remuda. "Are you three going to stand around jawing all morning, or are we going to start covering some miles?" she asked with mock severity.

Her brother smiled, glad to see some signs of sternness lifting from her following the incidents at Keylock. "How do you know this 'jawing' isn't very serious planning for what lies ahead?"

"Because I've been around long enough to know just plain jawing when I see it," Becky replied. Then she added, "And it's only because I'm a lady that I don't call it by a different, even more accurate name."

All three men grinned knowingly.

Twisting in her saddle, Becky gazed off at the dust raised by their departing recent visitors. "Besides," she said, "I like the thought of getting a move on if for no other reason than putting as much distance as we can between us and those four. I don't know about the rest of you, but there was something about them that made me uneasy the whole while they were in our camp."

"Yeah, it seems we all developed that feeling to one degree or another," admitted Marcus.

Becky turned back. "Then why did we welcome them in the first place?" she asked somewhat tartly.

Maybe it was only his imagination but, when she said those words, Mac felt like her eyes lingered for an accusatory extra second on just him.

Marcus said, "It's a common thing, when travelers run into each other out in the open like this, for one side to invite the other into their camp. That's especially true if one of them appears to be down on their luck. Hindsight always makes things a mite clearer . . . but the trouble is, it also always shows up a mite late."

"Well, what's done is done," Becky allowed. "They're gone now. That's the main thing."

"Let's hope so," said Marcus. "But just to stay on the cautious side . . . Mac, you keep your wagon with the herd today, like before. In fact, roll along at point. Becky, you stay up near the wagon. Eamon and Ox can work the middle of the herd, I'll hang back on drag with Ned, to provide some extra lookout behind. That's the way we'll work it. Let's get a move on."

Chapter 29

From another rocky patch of high ground some distance to the east, Blassingame and Muncie were continuing to monitor events in the Standing L camp. They'd kept watch through the night and into this morning, seeing the Ivers bunch ride away following breakfast and now looking on as the Standing L cowboys took their positions and got the herd moving again.

Clutching the field glasses he'd been the last to look through but was no longer using, Muncie turned to his partner and said, "So what's our move now? The Iverses and their pals have taken their leave without making any trouble. You think they're gone for good, or do you figure it's only temporary and we can expect to see them swing around again?"

Blassingame took a long time to answer, his expression locked in thought, his eyes narrowed slightly as he watched the cattle herd flowing away. Then: "It troubles me some, not knowing where Ward and Boyd have been or what they've been up to these past few years. But no matter, the feeling in my gut and everything I *do* know about them from before makes it almost impossible to believe that they or anybody riding with 'em would pass up a chance at that herd."

"You figure they had it planned all along and camped with that outfit just to get a better lay of things?"

Blassingame ran some knuckles along his jawline. "That goes back to the trouble of not knowing what the rascals were up to before this. It could be the way you say. But looking on, seeing how they acted and moved while in the camp, I somehow get the feeling they happened on that herd by accident. Not that it makes much difference. Now that they *are* on to 'em, I stick with believing they won't pass up the chance to try and take the critters for their own."

"And you still figure we ought to take a hand in stopping them?"

"I don't give a hang about stopping them from taking the cattle," Blassingame explained. "But if doing that means shooting up the Standing L outfit—which would include our boy Mackenzie—then that's the part we need to prevent. Leclerc is coming all the way here to be in on personally apprehending Mackenzie, remember? If all we have is a dead body to hand over to him, I doubt he'd be very happy. For that, he could have saved himself a lot of trouble and extra expense by staying home, settled for receiving a report or having the ears or whatever delivered to him."

"If the law or any of the bounty hunters who've been chasing Mackenzie up to now had caught up with him,"

Muncie pointed out, "Frenchie would have *had* to settle for something like that."

"Only none of that happened. What did," countered Blassingame, "was us getting a line on the fugitive under these current circumstances and thereby giving 'Frenchie' what he apparently sees as a special opportunity for himself. If we have to kill Mackenzie in self-defense or to keep him from getting away altogether or something like that, we'll do it. Otherwise, we do what the client is paying for, even if it means taking some extra measures to keep that blasted chuckwagon cook alive long enough so Leclerc can get his firsthand vengeance."

"You're the senior man on this job. Whatever you say," said Muncie. "But that brings me right back to my original question: How do we play it from here? Do we stick with the cattle drive in order to try and be in position to help them if and when the rustlers make their try? Or do we go after the Iverses and put 'em out of business before they even make their move?"

Blassingame frowned. "I kinda like the sound of the latter. But pulling off such a stunt ain't hardly as easy as just saying it. Riding down on 'em at four-to-two odds obviously wouldn't be in our favor. And trying to smooth 'em by riding in close, friendly-like at first, don't hardly wash, not figuring one of the Iverses is too apt to recognize me."

"What does that leave then?"

"For starters, I figure we'd better make sure those Iverses are thinking the way we *figure* they're thinking," said Blassingame. "Much as it would surprise me, not to mention personally pain me to lose a chance at those bounties again, it's possible they may keep riding instead of wheeling around and heading back to rustle those Standing L beeves. If that were the case, it would simplify things a great deal."

"Excuse me if I don't hold my breath waiting for it to work out that way," muttered Muncie.

"If and when we're convinced they're after the herd," Blassingame went on, "then we'd have to decide on how best to try and protect Mackenzie."

"How about simply going to the Standing L outfit, identifying ourselves, and warning 'em about the Iverses?" Muncie suggested.

Blassingame made a face. "There are times, Ray, when your sense of humor can be amusing. But right now is hardly—"

"No, I'm serious," Muncie cut him off. "It just came to me, hear me out. I'm not saying we identify ourselves as detectives hunting Mackenzie. He's got to know he ain't the only rascal in the West with men on his trail. So we act like we got no interest in him but say we're out to get the Iverses, that's how we caught up with 'em just in time to see they're fixing to hit the Standing L herd. With no chance to go for the law or any other kind of backup, we'd be warning the Standing L crew themselves and offering to throw in with 'em against the owlhoots for our mutual benefit. That puts us right in the thick of things, see? We'll be on hand to keep Mackenzie safe and still get a chance at the Iverses' bounty to boot. It could work, I tell you. Come on, Quinn, at least give it some thought."

Blassingame stared at his partner for a long moment, his expression revealing nothing. Then, slowly, one half of his mouth curved up in a grin before he finally said, "I swear, Muncie, I don't know where you've been keeping it all this time, but I think you just had a stroke of brilliance."

"You mean it?"

Blassingame's brow puckered. "I'm not sure yet. I'm still a little stunned, so don't hold me to it. But no matter how or where it came from, it's a clever idea and I'm all for going with it. After, that is, we do like I said before and take the time to make sure the Iverses aren't showing signs of swinging back." The detective paused, set his jaw, then added, "Also, after we take time to do one other thing. With the cattle drive going off in one direction and the owlhoots in another, we deserve ourselves some hot fresh coffee to warm our innards against last night's left-over chill. You got any objection to that?"

"No, sir, I don't. Matter of fact," Muncie said, "the notion of taking pause for some coffee, especially first thing in the morning, has always struck me as a kinda brilliant idea all on its own."

"Let's not overdo it with throwing the word *brilliant* back and forth at one another."

"Whatever you say. Just don't change your mind about the coffee."

Chapter 30

Two miles south of where he and his men had camped with the Standing L outfit, Ward Ivers signaled a halt. The others reined in their mounts and pulled up on either side of him. The morning had dawned bright but with a thin layer of overcast that was now starting to thicken out of the west and bring with it increasing gusts of a chilly wind.

"What are we stopping for?" asked Boyd Ivers, raising his voice to be heard over a low moan from one such gust.

"Need to palaver," Ward said.

"Palaver about what?" Craddock asked.

It was Red Haney, speaking for practically the first time that morning, who replied, "The cattle."

Craddock frowned. "What cattle? The ones we just left, you mean?"

"Do you see any other cattle around?" Ward asked with a roll of his eyes.

"Well, no. But I still don't—"

"Oh, come on, man," Ward cut him off. "I know we wasn't able to talk much back there in that camp, what with those punchers clustered around so close and all. But I am going to be powerful surprised—and maybe even a little disappointed—if it turns out I was the only one who took a good look around and saw the prime pickings that was flung down before us like an invite to a free church supper."

"I saw it," said Boyd. "Them critters had my mouth watering like they was already cooked up and served on a platter with taters and greens."

Haney just grunted.

Craddock was still frowning. "You talking about eating 'em? Those folks done served us . . ." The big man stopped and his eyebrows suddenly lifted. "Wait a minute. You saying for us to make a try at *taking* that herd?"

"You get any slower on the uptake of a thing, Able," Boyd told him, "the rest of us are going to have to start walking backward for any chance to keep up with you."

"Yeah, I'm talking about making a try for that herd," Ward said. Then, scowling, he added, "No, not just trying, blast it—*taking* it! With a sweetheart of a setup like that laid out before us, we'd be fools not to."

"Okay, okay. Y'all are catching me by surprise, that's all," Craddock responded with a little bite to his voice. "Didn't we come down out of Canada only a few months back saying how we was gonna go straight this time around? Find a way to make do without ending up with lawdog posses and bounty hunters and the like chasing after us all over again?"

"Yeah, and how did going straight work out for us, Able?" sneered Boyd. "We put everything we had into trying to make an honest go of it up there at Rattlesnake Creek. We didn't jump nobody else's claim nor drygulch anybody or none of that. We just blew our savings and broke our backs scrounging in the rocky ground like gophers or badgers or something, and what did it get us? It got us the sorry state we're in here and now, mooching meals and spare coffee beans off of a pack of cow pushers derned near as desperate as us."

"They may be desperate," said Ward, "but they got a dream. A dream and a smart idea for achieving it. What I'm saying is that we make that achievement ours. We take their cattle and their idea and make 'em ours. And this time when we get to Rattlesnake Creek we won't be poking and hoping to dig pay dirt out of the ground. Based on what we already know is there waiting—the hunger for beef and the price those with dust will be willing to spend for it—our pay dirt will be guaranteed!"

"Dang, I like the sound of that!" Boyd crowed.

Haney nodded. "Me too. I ain't crazy about going back to pushing cows. But it's a fairly short trip, and like you said, the payday is a sure thing."

"Ain't nothing a sure thing, not yet," said Ward sternly. "First, we've got to handle those Standing L cowboys and get control of the herd. Then the rest will click into place. And that can even mean taking another stab at going straight afterwards, Able. This time maybe some of the smartness from Marcus Lewis will have rubbed off on us and we'll get better results."

Craddock looked uncomfortable. "But only afterwards. Those Standing L folks was awful nice to us,

Ward. And when you say 'handle' 'em . . . we'll have to kill 'em, won't we?"

Ward gave him a hard stare. "You know the answer to that, Able. Yeah, there was some nice folks in that outfit. There's a lot of gentle, brainless cows in their herd, too, ain't that right? And what are those kind folks fixing to do to *them*? That's the way it goes. The weak and gentle—and yes, sometimes even *the nice*—have to fall prey to the needs of the strong.

"We have to kill everybody in that outfit not just to take their herd but also if we want to go forward from this without immediately calling any hounds onto our trail. We rig up a phony bill of sale for the cattle, get rid of anybody who can argue otherwise, that gives us a good shot at coming out of the whole thing clean, leastways in the eyes of others."

"That would mean the girl, too," Craddock murmured, not quite to himself.

To which Haney was quick to say, "You leave the girl to me. I'll treat her real special."

"Now hold on a minute!" protested Boyd. "A good-looking gal like that, you can't claim her all to yourself."

Haney's mouth curved in a grim smile. "No problem. I'm a patient and ungreedy man, I don't need her all to myself. I just want her last."

"All right, enough of that talk," declared Ward. A heightened gust of wind blew up suddenly, whipping stinging grains of sand against the four men and their horses. Wincing, Ward then added, "Enough talk of any kind out here in the open like this. We've settled that we're going after those cattle, right? Let's find some shelter out of these blustery conditions. We'll make use of

those coffee beans and the rest we just came in posses-
sion of, wait out the day. Then, toward evening, we'll ride
hard to catch up with that outfit again . . . and use the
cover of dark to conduct our business."

Some time later, cautiously following the trail of the
four men, Blassingame and Muncie spotted where they
had made camp in a V-shaped notch at the base of a low
butte. Circling around to the back side of the butte and
finding a niche of their own that provided a block against
the biting gusts, the two detectives dismounted and
crouched for a discussion.

"Well, I guess this pretty much removes any doubt,"
said Muncie. "They're laying up, waiting for night most
likely, and then they'll be going back to hit the Standing L herd."

"Most reasonable way to read it," agreed Blassingame.
"The only other possibility might be that they're just
wanting to get out of the wind for a while. But it ain't really blowing that hard and they haven't traveled far
enough away from camp to be battered too bad by it. No
matter their other shortcomings, these men are a hardier
bunch than that. No, they're stopped, waiting and resting
up for some dirty business later on."

"Too bad Running Horse lit out on us," Muncie grunted.
"That slippery redskin could have skinnied around this
pile of rocks—on the sides, maybe from above even—
and got close enough to that camp on the other side to
overhear exactly what they're planning. Then he'd come
back and lay it out for us, plain as could be."

"That would be an advantage he'd give us, sure
enough," said Blassingame. "But he ain't here, so no use

wasting wishes. Besides, I reckon it's plain enough, with or without him, what those owlhoots have in mind."

"Yeah. We got no call to blame Running Horse for not being here." Muncie sighed. "But you know what I do begrudge him? He's somewhere in his wikiup right about now, maybe ain't even hauled himself out of bed yet, with that big-rumped wife of his warming his belly, while I'm squatting out here in these rocks with a cold wind whistling. *That* I do begrudge him!"

Blassingame grinned. "Just keep thinking about how you're going to be collecting a share of the bounty on Haney and those Iverses and he ain't. That may not warm your belly, but it will at least line your wallet some."

"That's a nice thought," allowed Muncie. "But where I need lining right now is the seat of my britches that have been wore too thin from too much saddle time."

"In that case," said Blassingame, straightening up, "the best thing is to plant that worn-thin part of your britches back *on* a saddle and let the heat of the horse underneath warm you through. Come on, let's go catch up with that Standing L herd again and put your cleverly brilliant plan to work getting ready for these skunks when they take their own turn at showing up again later on."

Chapter 31

The overcast sky seemed to droop steadily lower and darker as the day wore on. The clouds congealed ever thicker until they formed into lumpy, black-edged heaps that gave the sense of gazing up at the underside of charred campfire remains.

The gloominess this brought to midday, aided by a cold wind that had become a low, constant moan passing over the land, was well matched to the mood of those now grouped in the Standing L's noon camp.

"Your credentials are impressive and you tell a convincing tale," Marcus Lewis stated, eyeing the two detectives squatted before him. Along with the rest of the Standing L crew, they were gathered close beside the chuckwagon that had been parked and braked in a position aimed to serve as a buffer against the wind. The flames of a nearby small cook fire over which coffee and hot beans had been prepared fluttered and snapped under the smoke-blackened pots.

"Our own encounter with the men you describe," Marcus continued, "had already left us with plenty of reservations about what they might have in mind after they left us. I guess you've confirmed that their intentions are about the worst they could be."

"They're a bad bunch, no doubt about it. And I fear you and your herd are too much of a temptation for them to pass up," Blassingame said solemnly. Then, that much being nothing but the hard truth, he layered on some of the fabrication he and Muncie had concocted. "We trailed them this far, but now that we've caught up, we figure it's too risky for just the two of us to try and take them immediately. Before we'd have a chance to bring in any backup, though, it's become clear they're going to hit you. Tonight, by every indication. That's why we figure you and your crew—if you're willing—can be our backup, and the other way around. We help you keep from getting rustled, you help us cut those villains down and see justice served."

"Sounds reasonable enough, but only up to a point," spoke up Eamon. "You seem to be suggesting that we wait for them to make their try on the herd and then take a stand against them. Why wait? Why not ride out right now, in a force greater than two, and get the confrontation over with?"

Muncie shook his head. "Never work. Men like the Iverses and Haney are too savvy. They've been dodging posses of veteran manhunters their whole adult lives. They'd see us coming and scatter to the four winds. We'd never catch a one of 'em. They'd eventually regroup and your outfit would be left spending your days and sleepless nights looking over your shoulder, waiting for them to try again. Only this time they'd be forewarned, knowing that you knew they were out there. So, considering how much farther you've got to go, they'd hold off until your nerves were raw and your senses dulled from lack of sleep . . . and then they'd pick a time to hit even quicker and harder than before."

"You gentlemen paint an awfully bleak picture," said Becky.

"But accurate," responded Blassingame. "What Muncie says is true, but so is the reverse of it for the rustlers. Being only four in number, they aren't likely to strike in a straightforward manner: simply sweep down on the drive, overpower your crew, and take control of the herd. That would expose them to too much risk from your guns."

"Damn right it would!" declared Eamon.

Blassingame continued, "That's why Muncie and I figure they'll hit you tonight. Try to catch you in your bedrolls, kill you in your sleep, then take over the drive from there. What we're offering is an alternative, the chance to save your herd and stay alive in the bargain. But if you'd rather handle it on your own, we can always ride off and bide our time. Make preparations to take those owlhoots another day. Once they commence driving the herd the rest of the way on to Rattlesnake Creek, we'll have plenty of opportunity to recruit backup and make our move farther up the trail."

"You're mighty quick to count us out, don't you think? Count on us having no chance against those skunks on our own?" challenged Marcus.

Blassingame shrugged. "Meant no offense. Maybe you do have a chance on your own, especially now that you've been warned. Bound to be costly, though, at best. How much can you afford to wager, Mr. Lewis? How many men can you afford to lose?"

Everything went quiet for several seconds except for the low moan of the wind and the crackle of the flames under the pots.

Until Mac said, "The detectives are right, Marcus. Our best bet is to throw in with them. Sucker those rustling snakes in tonight, and catch 'em by surprise when they make their play. It won't be without risk, even then, but it will give us the most control over the situation we're likely to get."

"For what it's worth, I vote with Mac and the detectives," spoke up Ned Baker. "It's gonna be a mean, nasty night well suited for what those wide-looping rascals have in mind. I speculate right about now they're out there feeling cocky and full of themselves, licking their chops at figuring to catch us all flat-footed and dumb, not suspecting a thing. Won't be a better time to catch *them* not suspecting what we'll have waiting instead."

"I like the sound of what Ned and Mac are saying," added Ox.

Marcus's face tightened in thought. His jaw muscles visibly bulged and relaxed. He locked eyes with his sister for a moment and then swept his gaze over the others.

"I'll go along with anything except trying to run away from it," Eamon proclaimed abruptly.

"Nobody's running away from anything," Marcus responded. His gaze came to rest on Blassingame and Muncie. "You got anything in particular in mind for how to best get ready for 'em?"

Blassingame nodded. "A few thoughts. For starters, though they won't make any serious moves until dark, they're apt to ease back close before then in order to

234 *William W. Johnstone*

scope things out once more, make sure nothing's changed. Means they can't catch sight of me or Muncie." He glanced over at Mac. "You got room to hide us behind your driver's box for a while?"

"Be cramped, but we can make it work," Mac replied.

"That's the way we'll do it then, until night camp and the arrival of darkness," said Blassingame. "In the meantime, we can turn our horses loose into your remuda. They'll never notice that."

"And once we make night camp?" prodded Marcus.

Blassingame smiled thinly. "That's where we finish setting the stage . . . the one we're inviting them to step out onto and discover the play being performed is different than the one they expect."

"You have a colorful way of putting things," remarked Becky, arching one of her brows.

Mac's brows went into motion, too, pinching tight together, as he said, "Colorful words or not, the opening act of the play is likely gonna take place out in the wings. Seems to me the varmints would want to eliminate our nighthawk first, make sure he can't give warning in case he spots the killers moving in on the camp. They've seen we only put out one nighthawk at a time. We've got to protect whoever that is tonight and turn the attempt on him into our own warning that the rest are getting ready to strike."

Blassingame eyed him. "You sound as if you've had some experience with this sort of thing."

"Ain't my first cattle drive, if that's what you mean," Mac told him. "The thing now is for us to get moving again. In case they come around early to do some checking, like you said, we don't want anything to look out of the ordinary or suspicious. Then, between here and night camp, you and your partner, and all the rest of us, too, need to do some hard thinking on how we're going to protect our nighthawk. We can put decoy bedrolls in the main camp and set our own ambush for the killers who'll come gunning there. But whoever's nighthawking will be out alone, exposed like a sitting duck."

Mac was keenly aware of the fact that in addition to pursuit from legal authorities he was under equal or perhaps even greater threat from the army of manhunters hungry for the pay Pierre Leclerc was offering to track him down. Hungry for the money and willing to be more ruthless than the law in their efforts to claim it. For these reasons, when Blassingame and Muncie showed up flashing their credentials, Mac's initial reactions were suspicion and alarm.

In his early days as a fugitive, he probably would have immediately taken flight. But in this instance, a number of things—his curiosity, the obligation he felt to Marcus and the rest of the Standing L outfit, maybe just plain stubbornness about not jumping like a scared rabbit at every hint of trouble—made him stick around at least long enough to hear what this pair had on their minds. When all was said and done, he was glad he did.

Although for the most part accepting the detectives' background story, Mac did so with a touch of suspicion and a healthy dose of caution. There was always the chance it was a ruse from the start, or even if their reasons for showing up to begin with were true, the possibility still existed that one or both of the men, after spending time in close proximity, might recognize Mac from the widely circulated Wanted papers on him.

But if it came to that, Mac told himself as the chuck-wagon rolled on into the gloomy afternoon, then he'd have to deal with it if and when necessary. The first and most urgent order of business now was preparing for the part of the detectives' claims that seemed beyond doubt—how the Ivers bunch was planning to make a try for the herd.

Preventing them from succeeding and getting members of the Standing L crew through such an encounter unscathed weighed heavily on Mac's mind. If he hadn't welcomed those four pieces of trash into their camp in the first place, he couldn't help thinking, maybe they wouldn't have been so tempted by what they saw. And the risk to Becky from such curs sent a twist of anxiety stabbing deeper through Mac than any fear of capture ever could.

If it cost him his freedom—or even his life—he would make certain she came to no harm.

Chapter 32

Everything was set, everybody was ready. As ready as their planning and nerves would allow.

What came next—and when—was up to Craddock, Haney, and the Ivers brothers.

The wind that had built from morning gusts to a cold, steady moan all through the afternoon had not diminished with the coming of night. It continued to prowl through the darkness, rustling the tall grass and tossing stinging grains of dust, keeping the cattle edgy and on the prod even after they were bedded down at the end of another long day. It was almost as if they, too, knew there was trouble riding on that restless wind.

"Easy, cattle . . . Just enjoy the sweet graze and rest your weary bones," cooed Mac as he slowly roamed the perimeter of the herd. On previous drives he had learned to appreciate the calming effect that singing could have on proddy critters and had himself warbled a few cowboy tunes on previous turns as a nighthawk—though more than one fellow cowboy had suggested his off-key squawking might do more harm than good.

But tonight he refrained from singing for reasons other than his dubious talent for it. The wind and the uneasy shuffling and bawling of the cows were already blurring other night sounds sufficiently. Mac didn't need to add to it.

Still anticipating that the rustlers' first move would be to try to take out the Standing L nighthawk—the role he had insisted on taking himself—Mac wanted every possible chance to be able to sense and deal with such an attempt. In addition to relying on just his senses and reaction time, there were other measures specially designed and put in place for this particular turn at nighthawk duty, all aimed to give him more of an edge.

The anchor of these special measures, dreamed up and constructed by Ned and Ox, was basically a scarecrow figure propped securely on the back of Mac's paint horse. It consisted of a four-foot-high "T" made of lashed-together tree branches, secured to and thrusting up from the saddle horn, then draped in a long slicker and topped off with a hat. In the dark, even at a relatively close distance, it looked convincingly like a man on horseback.

In conjunction with this, providing a presence and a voice for the scarecrow, Mac was walking alongside his horse. He stayed even with the animal's thick chest, matching the stride of its front legs, always keeping to the inside with the herd at his back. This made him effectively invisible to anyone approaching from outside the herd.

It was a somewhat elaborate ruse, but everyone agreed

it had a reasonable chance to succeed and was certainly worth trying for the sake of protecting whoever rode out as their nighthawk. The only disagreement came when deciding who that should be.

Mac had argued that he was the fastest draw and surest shot of their group, giving him the best chance to return fire successfully if anybody tried to bushwhack him.

And so, here he was. Slowly circling the herd, plodding along on shank's mare, trying to sooth a tangle of nervous cattle on one side of him while fighting to keep his own nerves steeled against thoughts of intended death coming for him from somewhere out of the blackness on all other sides.

But helping to counter all that were brighter thoughts of the others back at camp, safely hidden out on the perimeter in that same blackness, their bedrolls on full display around the dying fire but plumped up with only brush and wadded blankets, more lifeless targets for the rest of the thieving, murder-minded scum who would be striking there.

Yeah, Becky might be a little cold and uncomfortable for the moment, but when it was all over, she would still be safe and alive. She had to be.

Despite all the planning and anticipation, when the attack came it was unexpected. Unexpected in its nature. Because it came not as a gunshot flashing in the dark—but rather in the form of a man rushing suddenly forward out of the inky blackness and lunging to drag the "rider" off Mac's paint horse!

The lashed-together branches crackled and broke apart as powerful arms closed around them and yanked them from their perch. The empty slicker fluttered wildly in the wind and the hat went flying. The attacker, meeting neither the weight nor the resistance he expected, staggered back with nothing but an armful of broken sticks, nearly losing his balance.

Mac came quickly around from the opposite side of his horse, the Smith & Wesson drawn and thrust forward menacingly. "Looking for somebody?" he said through gritted teeth.

With his eyes long since adjusted to the darkness, Mac could make out a burly form poised in the act of getting rebalanced. The man's facial features were lost in murkiness, but Mac had no doubt he was facing Red Haney. And the knife he was clutching in one hand, its long blade giving off a dull glint even in the minimal light, left no doubt how he'd intended to make his kill.

"Nobody important," Haney growled in response. "Just some unlucky fool on his way to becoming coyote food."

Whether the big man didn't see Mac's gun clearly in the darkness or he thought he could move faster than Mac could react, there was no way of knowing. Whatever the case, he once again made a forward rush, the knife held down low and slightly to one side, razored edge turned up, positioned to rip and disembowel with a sweeping upward stroke.

Mac fired two rounds as fast as he could cock and squeeze. Haney jerked from each impact, his steps faltering, but kept coming. He'd nearly closed the gap between them completely when Mac fired a third time at point-blank range, his muzzle jammed into the soft pad of flesh under Haney's jaw. The .44 slug went up through the brain and crown of the skull, exiting in a spray of gore and gray matter. Haney's head snapped back. His forward momentum stopped, and his body went rigid. He slowly tipped away and then crashed heavily to the ground. His dead fingers stayed closed around the knife handle.

Any sense of relief or satisfaction Mac might have felt in that moment was immediately interrupted by two things: First, coming almost instantly on the heels of the shots he'd poured into Haney was an explosion of more gunfire from over at the campsite. That was expected— the Iverses and Craddock opening up on the decoy bedrolls and then getting caught in a reverse ambush staged by the detectives and the Standing L crew. Mac was prepared to jump in the saddle and go join the retaliation.

But then the second interruption, an even bigger and wholly unexpected one, cut loose.

The cattle herd, proddy and uneasy from the dust and wind all day and the tensions crowding the night, reacted the worst way possible to the outburst of gunfire. They spooked. A few broke at first, then more. Then all at once the whole mass was off and running blindly in a full-out stampede!

Mac had all he could do to gain the saddle of his paint and wheel them both clear of the wall of bawling, crowding, slamming cattle and their thundering, pounding hooves. Up a slope and onto safety atop the rocky crest of a ridge he heeled the paint. Reining up, he scanned frantically below.

In the darkness, the boiling cloud of dust churned by the stampede showed as a paler haze against the deeper darkness, swallowing all signs of individual animals as the swirling haze veered to the north and east. Thankfully, this swung them away from the campsite, where everyone there, on foot and caught by surprise, would have had little or no chance to escape being trampled.

As this thought crossed Mac's mind, he became aware

of, above the rumble of hundreds of hammering hooves, the ongoing crack and roar of continued shooting from the direction of the camp. He wanted desperately to get over there, but was temporarily cut off by the stampede. All he could do was wait and listen until the last of the fleeing cattle had passed from below him.

By that time, which couldn't have been more than the matter of a minute or so but seemed like an hour, the gunfire was sputtering to an end. As soon as he could, Mac gigged the paint back down the slope and anxiously urged him toward the camp.

Chapter 33

As revealed in the flickering light thrown by the fire that had been built back up, events at the camp had not gone entirely well.

The three rustlers who'd come gunning were all dead as a result of the trap awaiting them. Their bodies lay sprawled in bullet-riddled heaps on the edge of the surrounding shadows. The empty decoy bedrolls they had opened up on were also bullet riddled, some of their black-rimmed holes still giving off faint wafts of smoke that immediately danced away in the wind. These parts of the plan had gone as hoped.

But unfortunately, not all of the rustlers' gunfire had gone into empty bedrolls. As a result, Detective Ray Muncie also lay dead, his blanket-shrouded body now laid out alongside the chuckwagon. A single bullet to the temple had claimed his life.

Near the fire, a folded blanket underneath him, Marcus Lewis was leaned back partly on his elbows and partly against his sister, who knelt close in support. Marcus's right leg was extended and propped up on a saddle. The pant leg had been cut away to reveal a blood-streaked thigh and the gaping bullet hole from which the blood was oozing.

Bent intently over this, beads of sweat standing out on his forehead even in the chill wind, Ned Baker was probing at the wound with a knife tip and a pair of long tweezers. Marcus, his teeth clenched in a grimace and beads of sweat also dotting his face, was doing his best to hold back grunts of pain as the old cowboy continued to dig. The others stood looking on, their own expressions grimly concerned.

At last rocking back on his heels, Ned wagged his head in defeat. Sleeving sweat from his brow, he said, "Bullet's in there too deep. Lodged in that big ol' thigh bone, I expect. I ain't got the skills or tools to get it out."

"So what does that mean?" Becky asked.

"It means we need to get your brother to somebody who can do what I can't, before infection starts to set in," Ned replied somberly.

"But the cattle. We can't forget about them. Somebody's got to—" Marcus started to say.

Mac cut him short. "Nobody's forgetting about the herd. But first things first. Where are those maps you brought along? We've got to figure out where the closest town is that might have a doctor."

"The maps are in my saddlebags," Marcus said. He took a long pull from the whiskey bottle somebody had planted in his fist before Ned had started in on his wound. Lowering the bottle, he added, "Those maps are a mite sketchy, remember. Last time I looked, I don't recall them showing a town of any size being anywhere close."

"I think you might be wrong about that," spoke up Blassingame, who had been looking on silently for the most part, his gaze frequently drifting off to rest on the shrouded form of his dead partner. Continuing, he said, "The agency is pretty good about providing us field operators with regularly updated maps. I'll double-check the ones I'm currently carrying, but if I remember right, I think there's a fair-sized town called Moccasin not too far to the east. Hopefully, it's big enough to have some kind of doctor."

"If that's the case, it would be mighty welcome news," stated Eamon.

"We need to make preparations for getting my brother there with all haste," said Becky. Looking pleadingly at Ned, she asked, "Can you get his bleeding stopped in the meantime?"

Ned nodded. "Believe so. Somebody step over here and keep pressure on this while I make up a poultice. Then I'll pack it and bind it tight. If we load him in the wagon to move him and keep his leg propped up, it should hold pretty good."

Ox silently moved up and took over applying pressure to the wound while Ned went to make a poultice and Blassingame went to fetch his maps.

"I'll clear out some room in the back of the chuck-wagon," announced Mac. "Then I'll bring the team off the picket line and get them hitched up so we can roll out at first light."

"Now just a blamed minute!" exclaimed Marcus after another jolt of whiskey. "I appreciate all this attention to me, but we've got a herd of cattle scattering themselves from Hell to breakfast somewhere out there in the dark. We didn't drive them all this way and trade lead to save them from a pack of rustling varmints just to let 'em run off into the wind! What about them?"

"Nobody intends to lose your herd, Marcus," Mac told him. "They won't run forever, especially not after being tired from a long day of bucking this wind. And once they slow down, it won't be long before they start thinking about the nearest water—which is that creek running right over there. They'll be scattered, yeah, but not so far we won't be able to round 'em back up."

"Mac is right," Ox said. "That herd still belongs to the Standing L—we just need to remind them critters of it."

Marcus grinned weakly. "Sure. You bet we will."

"We'll remind 'em first, you can join in on it later," said Mac. "While Ned and Becky and that detective are getting you to a doctor, me and Ox and Eamon will hang back and round up the herd. We three won't be enough to start up the drive again, but we can hold 'em right here until you get back."

"You hear that, Marcus?" Becky made her tone bright, encouraging, as she gripped her brother's shoulders. "You can count on the men coming through. This will all end up being just a delay, and once your leg starts to heal, everything will be the same as before."

No sooner were the words out of Becky's mouth than the cheerfulness suddenly fell from her expression and her shoulders slumped. Her eyes darted first to the shrouded form of Muncie and then swept slowly over the grotesquely twisted shapes of the fallen rustlers.

"Oh, God," she murmured, barely above a whisper. "How could I say everything will be the same after all this death, this killing. . . . Some who died may have been low, evil even, but they were still men . . . and poor Mr. Muncie, surely he didn't deserve . . ."

As her words trailed off, Marcus reached up with one hand and placed it over one of hers still resting on his shoulder. "Hey, take it easy, Sis. We all know you didn't mean anything disrespectful by what you said. As far as those three pieces of scum—four, counting the one Mac took care of—they only got what they deserved. And remember, too, they came meaning to do the same or worse to us."

"But still. Mr. Muncie . . ."

Blassingame came striding back at that point, saying in a somber tone, "Ray Muncie was a friend and a good partner. I appreciate your words of regret, Miss Lewis, as I know he would have. But Ray understood and accepted the risks that came with doing this job that he chose. Moreover, I believe he would have found a certain satisfaction in how this turned out—the villains dispatched and, even at the cost of his own life, no undeserving innocents losing theirs."

"Speaking for myself," remarked Eamon, "I don't know about the 'innocent' part. But I do know how important it was that you and Muncie came 'round to give us warning about this gang of cutthroat rustlers setting their sights on us. For that, I will long carry a deep gratitude and a sadness for what it cost."

Blassingame gave a curt nod. "Duly noted. But the thing now is to make sure there's no added cost. Namely, seeing to it Mr. Lewis's leg is properly treated before it worsens." He held up some folded papers he gripped in one hand. "I've checked my maps, and I was right—the town of Moccasin, which is indicated as decent sized, appears to be less than a day's ride to the east."

"Wonderful. You hear that, Marcus?" said Becky.

Before Marcus could reply, Blassingame spoke again. "I overheard what Mackenzie said about using the wagon to take you in. May I request also finding room in the wagon for Muncie? I kinda hate the thought of just draping him over the back of a horse."

"Naturally we'll accommodate that," said Marcus.

"What about the bodies of the rustlers?" Mac asked. "You said they all had bounties on them, right? Dead or alive?"

Blassingame's mouth pulled into a tight, straight line. "For the Iverses and Haney, yes. I'm not sure about the one called Craddock."

Mac made a face. "I don't know how much you're gonna find left of Haney. Part of the stampede passed over where he fell."

"Come light, I'll have to see if there's enough to identify," Blassingame replied. He glanced uneasily in Becky's direction. "I don't mean to sound cold or indelicate, ma'am, but delivering human vermin sometimes belly down across a saddle is part of my job, same as it was Muncie's. For their kind, I don't mind hauling 'em in that way. And I fully realize no amount of money is worth Ray's death, or can change that fact. But he has a sister in Omaha, his only kin as far as I know, who I'm sure could use his share of these bounties and whatever pay he has coming from the agency. I intend to see she gets it. If there's a telegraph office in Moccasin, I'll wire her and see if she has any particular wishes as to his burial. That's the best I can do for her . . . or Ray."

The man's voice nearly cracked under the weight of the deep, sincere sadness in his words.

"I understand. You have to do what you must," Becky said quietly. "As do we all."

Chapter 34

The new day dawned bright and clear. The cloud cover had broken apart and passed on shortly before dawn, taking the raw wind with it.

Since no one in the camp had slept during the remainder of the night, first light found everything in readiness for the departure of those who would be leaving to find the town of Moccasin. The only remaining chore was for Mac to lead Blassingame in search of Red Haney's remains. When found, they turned out not to be battered beyond recognition so with Mac's help the detective went ahead and loaded up the fourth rustler with the others.

Once this was taken care of, the procession headed out. Ned driving the chuckwagon, Becky on the seat beside him; Marcus and the shrouded body of Ray Muncie sharing space in the wagon bed; Blassingame riding alongside, leading a tethered line of corpse-laden horses.

As they rode off into the rising sun, Mac, Eamon, and Ox stood watching them go for as long as it took to finish drinking the pot of coffee brewed from the provisions left behind.

"Sure hope that town ain't too far, and they find a doctor when they get there," Ox said into the stillness.

"I think we can count on them making the town in pretty good time," replied Eamon. "That Blassingame fellow is pretty sharp. If he says his map shows a place called Moccasin, I trust it will be there."

"I agree," said Mac. "But what they find when they show up . . . I'll go along with Ox and add my share of hoping for the best."

Eamon made a face. "Aye. That hole in Marcus's leg is a nasty one. If somebody don't get that slug out of the bone, he'll likely never walk right again even if he manages to hold off infection."

"Let's not talk like that." Ox scowled. "And even if Marcus does end up with a limp, he'll still be as good or better a man than most you can find."

"You'll get no argument out of me on that," Mac allowed. "But, limp or not, it's for certain he's going to come back here expecting to find his cattle herd waiting for him. So, I reckon we ought to commence chasing those critters down, don't you think?"

Eamon heaved an exaggerated sigh. "Aye. Since I highly doubt they're going to roam back on their own just because they miss us, I'm afraid there's no other way."

With that, putting aside their coffee cups and hoisting their saddles instead, the three men headed to select mounts from the picketed horses.

* * *

Jerry Lee Lawton had no sooner lowered the spyglass he'd been peering through than the others crowding up behind him in the stand of white birch trees began peppering him with questions.

"Well, what did you see?"

"What's going on in that camp?"

"What in blazes are they up to that caused their cattle to stampede off like they done?"

Jerry Lee made a chopping motion with one hand, cutting off the voices. "Quit your jabbering for a minute and give me a chance to talk. I'll tell you what I was able to make out." He handed the glass to Floyd Sleet. "Here, you keep an eye on 'em while I'm talking. See if you spot anything different."

Sleet edged up beside one of the trees, put the glass to his eye and adjusted the focus as he aimed it in the direction of the Standing L camp off to the east of their location.

"Keep back in the shade of those leaves so the sun don't reflect off that lens," Jerry Lee warned him. Then he turned back to the others, resituating himself against a grassy hump and using the heel of one hand to rub the eye that had had the spyglass pressed to it before saying, "Near as I can figure, they got hit by rustlers last night. That explains all the shooting we heard and also what set their herd off on a stampede."

"You mean a pack of wide-loopers got the cattle?" Roy Orton said.

"That ain't what I said," Jerry Lee answered. "From what I can see, nobody's got the cattle. They're stampeded, remember? To the east somewhere."

"What about the rustlers?"

"They don't appear to have made out too well. Right at

the moment," Jerry Lee said, "their bodies are being hauled off, belly down over the backs of four horses. I make 'em as those same four hard-looking characters we spotted sharing the Standing L's camp the night before last. They must have liked what they saw and decided to try and claim it for themselves."

"I read it the same," agreed Sleet, continuing to peer through the glass. "But who's the hombre leading that string of horses carrying off the dead?"

"Ain't quite figured that part out." Jerry Lee frowned. "Near as I can figure, he must have showed up some time in advance of the rustling attempt. Maybe he brought warning. I think he might have had a partner, too, on account of I caught a glimpse of 'em loading somebody in the back of that wagon Ned's drivin' off with Becky Lewis. Two somebodies, actually. One of 'em was Marcus Lewis, looks to have taken a bullet. Couldn't make out the other, but whoever it is, has to fit in as a stranger because you can see the rest—Mackenzie, Farrell, and big ol' Ox—staying behind."

"Where'd they all come from?" grumbled 'Bama Wilkes. "Gettin' awful crowded for being out here in the middle of nowhere, ain't it?"

"Just goes to show how there's nothing like a gold strike to pull in scoundrels and lowlifes of every stripe to an area," proclaimed Edsel Purdy, totally oblivious to the irony of the statement in view of his present company.

"Wait a minute. You say Ned and the gal are heading out somewhere in the chuckwagon?" said Orton. "What's that all about?"

"I told you that part of their cargo is Marcus Lewis and it looks like he took a bullet," Jerry Lee came back. "Reckon the same is true for the stranger they're hauling with him. So my guess is they must be aiming to try and find a doctor."

"Good luck with finding a doctor anywhere out here," snorted 'Bama. "They're better off setting their hopes on running across an Injun medicine man, and even that would be if they're lucky."

"Not necessarily," said Sleet over his shoulder. "By my recollection, there's a town not too far from here. Don't remember the name of the place, maybe it didn't even have one back then, but when I passed this way a few years gone, there was a settlement building up there. It might be decent sized by now."

"I never knew that," muttered 'Bama.

"So where does all this leave us, Jerry Lee?" Purdy wanted to know. "We gonna go ahead and take over the herd now?"

Sleet lowered the spyglass and twisted around. "Oh, no. We ain't fixing to do that, are we? You said if we ended up pushing those cows at all it wouldn't be but for a day or two. We're still a good seventeen, eighteen days short of Rattlesnake Creek."

"Calm down. Did you hear me say anything about doing any cow wrangling yet?" Jerry scowled at Sleet. "But if I *did* make that call, would you really have room to complain? How easy have all of us had it up until now? Over two weeks of nothing but shadowing that bunch over yonder and the only effort besides sitting a saddle has been ransacking their chuckwagon one night."

"You don't have to tell me," said 'Bama with a scowl of his own. "I'm getting doggone bored from doing nothing but warming a saddle. When *are* we gonna see some action and commence harassing that outfit some more?"

"Well, it's too bad about your boredom," Jerry Lee

told him, "but you're gonna have to suffer through another stretch of it. Because it appears to me that the job of harassing and slowing down the Standing L drive has been taken care of for us."

"What's that supposed to mean?"

"You got mud in your ears, 'Bama?" growled Sleet. "Didn't you just hear the situation explained to you? The rustling attempt, the stampeding of their herd, their boss man wounded and carted off to find a doctor . . . Wouldn't you call that a pretty thorough job of knocking that outfit's schedule out of whack? It's bound to cost 'em three, four days, maybe more before they're ready to get the drive moving again. Add that to the time we already cost 'em back down the trail when we wrecked their chuckwagon and they got otherwise tangled up around Keylock, it amounts to slowing 'em just about the amount Harcourt wanted."

"Sleet's right," Jerry Lee said. "Ain't to say Harcourt won't have more for us to do once we get to Rattlesnake Creek. But between now and then, it appears to me we stick to doing nothing more than what we been doing. When we *do* get closer, I'll ride ahead and meet up with him. Update him on how things stand and see what he's got in mind for us from there."

"Don't worry, 'Bama," said Sleet with a wry grin. "Maybe another pack of rustlers will show up and we can see some action by helping to drive 'em off. Now that the Standing L outfit is slowed down enough to suit Harcourt, it's still them—and only them—he's got plans for on the other end. We've got to make sure they make it to him."

"Very funny, Sleet," grumbled 'Bama. "Way this is going, I might not make it to Rattlesnake Creek. I might get

bored to death! Either that, or I'll go plumb out of my
mind listening to the click of Purdy dry firing that stupid
gun he keeps practicing his left-handed draw with every
spare minute and every stinkin' night we're in camp!"

Purdy gave him a look. "Maybe you want I should put
a live round under the hammer and then see how much
bellyaching you want to do about my practicing."

"All right, you two!" Jerry Lee snapped. "'Bama, if
you can't do the job you signed on for then go ahead and
leave. When Harcourt hears you quit in the middle of
things, he can decide how much pay, if any, he figures
you got coming. And Edsel, if you ever hope to get back
on the good side of Harcourt, then all that infernal practicing you've been doing better count for something if
you have to face Mackenzie again."

"You betcha it will," Purdy declared.

Sullenly, 'Bama said, "Okay, okay. I'll bide my time
until we get to Rattlesnake Creek. But, once there, I aim
to bust out and raise me some hell, one way or 'nother."

With that bit of minor pawing settled, at least for the
time being, Sleet turned to Jerry Lee and said, "Got me a
notion of my own that might be worthwhile, if you'd care
to listen."

Jerry Lee nodded. "Spit it out."

"Seems to me we got it scoped out pretty clear as far as
what all happened in that camp last night," Sleet responded. "But there's still a few gaps we're filling in with
guesswork. Mainly, who those rustlers were and how the
other two strangers—the one leading the horses loaded
with dead men and the other one in the wagon with
Lewis—fit in. We could probably fill in those gaps for
certain if one of us rode on into that town where the
wagon is headed and picked up on the talk that's bound to

spread once they roll in and have to do some explaining about their dead and wounded."

It didn't take Jerry Lee long to make up his mind. "Sleet, that is a right good idea. Why leave anything to guesswork when we can find out for sure, right?"

"I'll do it," 'Bama was quick to volunteer. "I'll make that ride into town and suck up all the talk there is worth hearing!"

"No good," Jerry Lee said, quick and flat. "Too much risk you might be recognized."

"By who?" 'Bama challenged. "The only one of that bunch who ever laid eyes on me is that Mackenzie fella, and he's part of the crew staying behind. None of those others would recognize me if I marched right up and asked for a match to light my quirley!"

"Mackenzie might have described you well enough for them to take notice. That's too much of a chance to take, especially when we got somebody who can go in with no risk at all." Jerry Lee tipped his head toward Sleet. "Floyd here came up with the idea, I say it's only fitting he gets the chance to carry it out. Much as we'd all like a trip into town, me, Roy, or Edsel sure can't go—we'd get recognized in a heartbeat. There's enough chance of the same for you, too, 'Bama. So Sleet's the one who goes."

"I'll head out right away, then," said Sleet. "I'll swing wide and beat that wagon in. That way, it won't look as fishy as it might if I came in right on their tail. I'll find me a pack of talkative old codgers like usually hang out in a saloon or café, then settle in and listen for when they start jabbering the latest news."

"Sounds good," Jerry Lee allowed. "Just see to it that if it's a saloon you settle in you're there to soak up talk and not too much booze."

Chapter 35

Two days passed.

In that time, Mac, Eamon, and Ox succeeded in rounding up the stampeded cattle and returning them to graze where they'd originally bolted from, still close to the campsite where the others would be returning.

Returning, provided they'd found a town and all had gone well there. But the more time dragged on without any sign of them, the more anxious and fidgety the waiting men became.

Finally, near noon on the third day, after they had decided that the passage of one more night would warrant drawing straws to determine who would go in search of some answers, the lumbering, clanking chuckwagon hove into sight.

As the wagon drew nearer, Ned and Becky were plainly visible on the seat. Then, when it was closer still, Marcus leaned forward from farther back in the wagon and thrust his face into view also. The fact he was grinning was the signal that everything appeared to be okay.

The afternoon was spent with each side relating their experiences during the time apart. The town of Moccasin had been found without difficulty, and fortunately, a doctor was also found there. He successfully got the bullet out of Marcus's leg. The delay in allowing him to depart afterward had been due to the medic wanting to make sure there would be no additional bleeding and to also monitor for any signs of possible infection.

During all this, Blassingame had made arrangements for collecting the bounties owed on the quarry he'd brought in, and also sending word to Muncie's sister about the passing of her brother. In return, she had wired back a request for Blassingame—considering the remoteness of Moccasin and the distance between it and Omaha—to please oversee a proper burial of Muncie there in Montana. Blassingame had complied with her wishes, and before leaving, Ned and Becky had attended the funeral service. Blassingame then remained behind to finish conducting some business and to await word from the agency on his next assignment.

For their part, Mac, Eamon, and Ox reported on successfully rounding up the scattered cattle and getting them brought back to the current location. By their count, only about ten critters were lost to the ordeal, fallen and trampled in the thick of the stampede.

That evening, in the midst of restocking and rearranging the chuckwagon after the removals and adjustments necessary for hauling Marcus and Muncie to town, for supper Mac cooked thick, juicy steaks harvested from one of the fallen animals and served with seasoned greens he had gathered the previous day. During the meal, the group planned their continuation of the drive, starting first thing in the morning. Marcus's injured leg made it impossible for him to sit a saddle all day, so it was decided he would take over driving the chuckwagon and Mac would have to assume wrangling duties in his place.

"That's okay with me, as long as it don't mean Marcus takes over the cooking just because he's driving the wagon," spoke up Ox. "No offense, boss, but times when you fixed lunch back at the ranch . . . well, Mac's got a way with a frying pan and such that plumb has me spoiled. I've already been fretting what I'll do if he moves on after this drive is over. I might resort to crying myself to sleep at night if that day ever comes."

Ned grunted. "You go to blubbering in the bunkhouse when it comes time for me to catch some shut-eye, you better figure on dragging your pillow and blankets out to the livery barn."

"Much as I'd hate to be the cause of any trouble like that, I can't speak for the future, Ox," said Mac, grinning. "But for the time being, rest easy. I plan on still doing the cooking for the rest of this drive."

"It sounds like I might need to consider taking some lessons," remarked Becky. "Because, in case everybody forgot and at the risk of giving a certain party the night frets, I happen to have cooked a fair number of meals back at the ranch and sort of expected to be filling that role again when we return home."

Ox's mouth dropped open and he blushed furiously. "Holy mackerel, Miss Becky," he said. "I never thought . . . that is, I never meant . . ."

"Son," advised Ned, "you better just be quiet and quit while you're ahead. Elsewise, you're fixin' to end up sleeping in the livery barn and eatin' nothing but your own sorry cookin' to boot."

In the near distance, in the birch grove that had become their own campsite, Jerry Lee and his gang continued watching the goings-on over at the Standing L camp. Sleet had rejoined his cohorts the previous day, returning with a report of his findings in the town of Moccasin. What he came back with boiled down to a verification of all the things they had figured from their observations that first morning following the rustling attempt and stampede.

For what it was worth, he was also able to provide the identities of the deceased rustlers as well as the other two strangers, the High Grade detectives who'd been on the trail of the Iverses, one of whom died in the ensuing conflict.

"Like 'Bama said before," Jerry Lee commented, "there was a while there when things was awful crowded out here in the middle of nowhere."

"But when all was said and done," pointed out Orton, "the crowd did a pretty good job of thinning its own self out and now we're right back where we started."

"We're even better off than when we started," said Jerry Lee. "Less'n you're like 'Bama and are worried about being too bored, we got nothing but gravy the rest of the way to Rattlesnake Creek. With this outfit already slowed down sufficient, we can just follow along and not lift a finger until we find out what Harcourt's got in mind for them later on."

"Unless somebody else comes along and tries to make trouble for 'em. Then we might have to step in and lend a hand. Right?" There was no missing the hopefulness in 'Bama's tone.

"You can wish for that if it makes you feel better," allowed Jerry Lee. "If I know Harcourt, he's got in mind some hard business for us to dish out before this is over. Until then, I can be patient and just keep watching and waiting."

In the town of Moccasin, Quinn Blassingame was also faced with the prospect of waiting. Minus the watching. It had long been understood that in order for Pierre Leclerc to be present for Mackenzie's apprehension, as he was insisting, someone would have to first meet him at his Great Falls destination and then guide him the rest of the way for the confrontation with the fugitive at Rattlesnake Creek. Blassingame and Muncie had been figuring all along that, when the time was right, one of them would branch off to go fetch their client while the other stuck with following the cattle drive Mackenzie was part of.

Only now, with Muncie dead and Running Horse having departed earlier, Blassingame suddenly found himself on his own. Without time to solicit fresh backup from the agency, he didn't see where he had much choice but to go meet up with Leclerc and hasten him to Rattlesnake Creek ahead of the cattle drive's arrival.

He fully realized he was taking a risk by abandoning the direct surveillance of Mackenzie, but it was one he calculated as being reasonably safe. He'd spent enough time with the Standing L crew to recognize their dependence on Mackenzie and, in turn, his close bond with them. Especially now, with Marcus's wound limiting his participation, Blassingame couldn't picture anything that would cause Mackenzie not to stick around until the drive was completed.

Leclerc was very much the pompous, demanding sort, so Blassingame expected taking this chance was likely to meet with the man's disapproval. On the other hand, not having anyone there to guide him after he arrived in Great Falls would no doubt result in the same. So the best Blassingame could do was play it the way he thought would work out most favorably. And considering how this job had already cost him a friend and partner, he was hardly in a mood—if Leclerc got too mouthy—to put up with very much pomposity.

With all of this settled in his mind and a freshly provisioned pack horse following along on a tether, Blassingame rode out of Moccasin late in the afternoon, bound for Great Falls.

Chapter 36

Thirty-eight days after starting out from their ranch, members of the Standing L crew finally came in sight of the settlement that had sprung up around the Rattlesnake Creek gold strike.

The collection of tents, shacks, and a handful of fairly substantial-looking frame structures straddled the stream after which it was named. The creek itself was a twisting waterway running through the heart of a narrow, shallow valley bracketed by jagged, moderately tall peaks studded with mostly pine growth. The approach to the valley was a long, grassy slope descending through stands of birch, elm, and many varieties of pine trees.

On the crest of the slope, gazing down into the valley, Marcus Lewis set the brake of the chuckwagon and signaled a halt to those bringing up the herd behind him. It was late in the day, the cattle were tired. They gratefully ceased plodding onward and wasted no time fanning out and milling, some pausing to graze on the tall grass spread across the flat area above the incline.

With the animals settling in, the cowboys working farther back rode forward, reining up on either side of the wagon to get their first look at the valley and the town down on its floor.

"Well, everybody," said Marcus, leaning back on the wagon seat, unable to keep a satisfied smile from tugging at his mouth, "there it is. Rattlesnake Creek. We made it."

"More importantly," added Becky, "we made it intact, all of us and almost all of the herd we started out with, except for the handful we lost to the stampede."

"Aye. Lots of good beef for lots of hungry bellies, and fat purses ready to pay for a taste," declared Eamon.

"The only thing left now," said Ned, "is getting the beef down there and making the sale. If there was a morsel of truth in anything that Ivers fella told us, they've built some holding pens somewhere—though I can't say as I can see any from here—in hopes of cattle being brought in."

Marcus shifted his weight on the wagon seat and extended his wounded leg out straighter inside the driver's box. The leg was healing well but was still bandage wrapped over its thigh, the pant leg slit and then pinned loosely together to accommodate the added bulk.

"Holding pens or not, there's bound to be buyers for what we've got to offer. That's the main thing." Marcus paused and his expression became somewhat less assured. "Though getting the best price, I've got to admit, is where I might be a little lacking. I've never been very good at haggling. The times we've sold cattle back home, the price had usually been set and everybody around got about the same."

"The way that town has grown up," said Mac, "there's bound to be some businessmen there who've acquired wealth, and I don't mean by digging it out of the ground themselves. Your market is going to be them. They'll be looking to buy, butcher, and then resell in restaurants and such."

Marcus regarded him. "You've had experience dealing with their kind?"

"Only a bit around the edges. I was always just a hired hand, remember," Mac told him. "But I saw enough to get the general idea. You'll want to get the money boys bidding against one another and you'll be wanting to sell in lots. At least fifty or a hundred head, maybe the whole works at once if you get a price that suits you."

Becky said, "It sounds like what Mac is suggesting is that some of us go into town, announce we've got our herd nearby, and give the bidders some time to step forward with their best offers."

"That's the idea," agreed Mac. "Whoever goes in— and it obviously should include Becky and Marcus— could look things over, measure the mood, see if they're really ready with holding pens and whatnot, then start sorting through interested buyers."

"A trip into town," said Eamon. "Now there's something *I* am ready for. With all due respect, mates, I have greatly enjoyed this fine outdoors adventure and the camaraderie and all, but it proved to me once and for certain that I am most certainly a city lad. Even a rowdy boomtown will do for starters. Smoky saloons, muddy streets, rude people crowded too closely together . . . all too true.

But also, ceilings and roofs over your head, a chair to sit on and a table in front of you when you take a meal, and a soft bed when you lay down at night. That's what I'm talking about!"

"Talk all you want," replied Ned, wagging his head. "But it ain't a sales pitch that works on this child. I enjoy a trip to town once in a while, same as anybody. But as a steady diet? No, thank you."

"All this talk about a steady diet and a table for taking meals . . . Only thing that matters much to me, no matter the surroundings, is good grub, and plenty of it," declared Ox. "Though, now that you mention it, smoky saloons and being crowded in with rude people ain't nothing I reckon I miss."

Mac grinned. "Is that a roundabout hint for me to get some supper going, Ox?"

The big man blinked innocently and said, "Well, now that you mention it . . ."

"Hey now. I thought we was going into town," said Eamon.

"'We'?" echoed Becky.

Eamon frowned. "Well, *somebody* doggone it. We didn't come all this way to stand on a hill and just look at Rattlesnake Creek, did we?"

"It's kinda late in the day," said Marcus. "One more night ain't going to make that much difference. I kinda figured we'd wait and go in fresh in the morning."

"And I'm not going into town, even a rowdy boomtown, all sweaty and dusty from herding cattle all day," proclaimed Becky. "I fully intend to heat some water after supper, then get properly washed and changed into some clean clothes beforehand."

Eamon looked dismayed to the point of being in pain.

Mac said, "Holding off until morning ain't a bad idea. Probably don't want to wait much longer than that, though. Elsewise somebody's apt to spot us up here with this herd of cows and then a swarm of beef-hungry rowdies would pounce on us like flies on honey. Wouldn't hardly be ideal conditions for trying to strike your best deal."

Now it was Marcus who frowned. "Yeah, I see what you mean. We want to be negotiating with businessmen looking to buy in quantity, like you said before, not a pack of overeager individuals only in a hurry to slap a slab of beefsteak on a plate with some beans."

"A little reconnoitering might be in order," Mac suggested.

"What do you mean?"

"Well, Eamon is awful anxious to breathe in some smoky air and stomp the dust off his boots on a boardwalk," Mac pointed out. "And Lord knows he's capable of striking up a conversation with a post and learning information from it before he's done. What if he was to mosey on down into that town for a while and do some mingling? Strike up some of those conversations he's famous for and find out some names of the kind of businessmen you're looking to meet, ones who'd be interested in buying your beef, who maybe have something to do with the holding pens if they exist. That kind of thing. He could bring that information back and you'd be that much farther along when you go in in the morning looking to make your best deal."

"Uh-huh. I see where something like that could be worthwhile," Marcus mused. "It would be useful information and it would speed along the actual negotiating when we got down to it."

"Give me a couple hours down there among those rock choppers," boasted Eamon, "and I'll know more about the powers that be in their town than they know themselves."

"Just as long as you take in more than you give out," advised Becky. "And by 'take in,' I mean information—not anything you can get out of a bottle or a beer keg."

"I'm wounded," said Eamon with mock severity. "If I am sent on a mission to serve the good of our undertaking, I shall not falter in my duty."

Becky shot a look at Mac before responding, "Now that the seed has been planted, I don't see any way to stop it from taking root. Go ahead, if you think it might help."

From off to one side, Ox said, "But you're not going, are you, Mac? You're still staying here and fixing supper, right?"

Chapter 37

With supper over and everything cleaned and put away, Mac had poured himself a cup of coffee and was squatted on his heels, leisurely sipping from it.

For the moment, he had the campsite pretty much to himself. Eamon was off to town; Ned and Ox were out circling the herd, making sure they were calm and gathered in reasonably tight; Marcus, the limitations and discomfort from his leg leaving him exhausted at the end of each day, was propped against a saddle on the other side of the fire, dozing; and Becky was cleansing herself in the privacy of a tentlike spread of canvas the men had rigged up for her in a nearby cluster of pine trees.

The night was calm and clear, as the days and nights had been for the past two weeks and more, ever since the rustling attempt. In fact, other than shortening some of their days out of deference to Marcus's injury, things in general had been calm and without a hitch.

Reflecting on this, Mac grinned wryly to himself as he thought about some of the old veterans he'd worked cattle drives with in the past who grew anxious when things went smoothly for too long a stretch. And the fact he was again thinking about such, he realized, must mean that at least a little bit of that superstition had rubbed off on him. But with their destination now firmly in sight, practically underfoot, the need for fretting about something going wrong seemed safely past.

Considering the completion of the drive naturally led Mac's thoughts drifting on to what lay in store for him next. Drifting. That, as it long had been, seemed to be the answer. The lure of California was still there. Not just as an actual geographic spot, but equally as a state of mind. A place he would *feel* as much as one he could plant his feet on. A place where he'd have the sense of at last being far enough away from New Orleans to no longer have to worry about the tentacles of the trouble there reaching out to threaten or ensnare him.

Mac had thought he'd nearly reached that peace of mind here in Montana. But the jolt of apprehension that shot through him when Blassingame and Muncie showed up, announcing they were detectives, had proven otherwise. His awareness of being a fugitive on the run was still there, just under the surface, only a misspoken word or a glance over the shoulder away from sending him into flight if he heard or saw the mere hint of something askance.

He wanted to be shed of that. Reach a place where he could finally, truly relax and not feel like he was balanced on a razor's edge.

Mac's unexpected reverie was broken first by the scent of fresh soap mixed with the subtlest hint of perfume carrying on the still air. This was quickly followed by a faint rustle of movement. Lifting his head and looking around, he saw Becky emerging from her tent and moving toward him. Her pale hair was streaming long and loose down over her shoulders and for the first time in weeks she had traded her split riding skirt for a flowing dress. Passing from the silvery wash of moon- and starlight into the golden glow of the campfire she was a vision that would make any man's heart skip a beat.

Mac rose to a standing position.

As she passed by her dozing brother, a fond smile touched Becky's lips and then she said quietly to Mac, "He tries to hide it, but that leg still bothers him quite a bit and his refusal to use the crutch Ned fashioned for him wears him out more than necessary."

"He's a proud man. But also tough," said Mac. "The need to push himself so hard is about over now, though. So that leg can finish healing the rest of the way."

"I hope so. But knowing him, he'll push for getting back home as soon as possible."

"I expect you're right," Mac said. "If for no other reason than the lack of appeal in hanging around a boisterous boomtown. Especially exposing you to very much of it."

"Why? Haven't I proven my own measure of toughness?" Becky challenged. Then, moving closer to Mac, she added, "Don't I look suitable enough for the likes of Rattlesnake Creek?"

"No, you don't. You look *too good* for the likes of the rowdy bunch down there," Mac told her.

Becky's eyebrows lifted. "I have to admit I've heard more eloquent compliments. But I'll take that as one all the same."

Mac wasn't in the mood for coyness. He said, "You know how good you look to me, Becky. You don't need it put in fancy words."

His directness caused Becky to avert her gaze for a moment. Then, bringing it back again, she replied, "The coolness that's been between us these past few weeks . . . the chill that I caused to be there . . . I wasn't sure how you felt."

"It wasn't me who had a change in outlook," Mac reminded her. "Like you said, you put the chill there. I was just honoring your wishes."

Becky moved closer to him. "I know. And I appreciate that. Not that I'd expect you to be anything less than honorable."

"Honorable but still frightening?"

Becky paused, flinching slightly at the question. "That was . . . an unfortunate choice of words. That whole experience back at Keylock was unsettling and I was left feeling the need to lash out at somebody. For reasons I still don't understand I chose you. Probably the person who least deserved it. I've been wanting to talk to you about the things I said that day, but somehow there never seemed to be the right time. Plus, it's not easy to admit when you've been wrong and hurtful to someone you care about."

"You said you needed time to sort things out," Mac said. "I wish you'd given me some kind of sign that you were beginning to."

"That night we all set the ambush for those rustlers, and were waiting for them to strike . . . and you were out on your own as our nighthawk . . . I realized then how wrong I was. Realized that the hardness in you was at times necessary. Knew, in fact, that in that moment we were all counting on that part of you to help pull us through."

"Making sure you came through all right was the main thing on my mind."

Becky's nostrils flared. "You know, you could have pressed the matter, shown your own feelings a little bit, too. You didn't have to be so doggone standoffish. You could have *helped* me find the right time for this instead of leaving me to feel like I had to come begging your forgiveness."

"I didn't realize there was anything to forgive. Well, except for the way you started friendlying up to Eamon more and more while you were continuing to give me the cold shoulder." Mac frowned. "I sure didn't see no encouraging signs in that!"

"Eamon?" Becky echoed. "Of course I was friendly with Eamon. We *are* friends, have been for . . . You mean you were really jealous of me and Eamon?"

"Don't go putting words in my mouth. I never said anything about being jealous," insisted Mac. "But he's dang sure interested in you, and don't tell me you're not aware of it."

"Eamon's interested in every pretty girl he meets. There's no news in that. And yes, he's made it clear, without ever being out of line, that interest includes me. But I've never encouraged it. And I was certainly never 'friendlying up' to him just to bother you."

"Well, there were times it sure looked that way."

As if on cue, from down in the valley there suddenly could be heard the crackle of gunfire and faint whoops of exuberance from within the cluster of twinkling lights that marked the Rattlesnake Creek settlement.

Becky rolled her eyes. "Speaking of Eamon, you don't suppose he's down there in the thick of that, do you?"

Mac grinned. "Anything's possible when it comes to Eamon. He had a mighty strong hankering to breathe in some smoky saloon air, remember. But no, seriously, he went with the best intentions of learning some things for the good of the drive. I've no doubt he chose a saloon or two to find part of those answers, but knowing what's at stake he'd keep himself in line. Which ain't the same as saying he won't cut loose good and loud after the business is done, mind you."

Over on the other side of the fire, Marcus snorted and stirred a bit as if the faint noise from the town had disturbed his slumber.

Becky stepped closer still and placed her palms on Mac's chest. "There's too much unsaid between us, Mac. Promise me that as soon as the cattle sale is complete and things settle down a bit, we'll find time to be alone somewhere so we can . . . talk. Without being hurried or interrupted. I think it's time to decide how things stand between us."

Mac put his hands over hers. "I agree. I want to find that out as bad as anybody."

Before anything more could be said, Marcus stirred again and this time came awake. He pushed himself to a sitting position and immediately reached for his leg.

Becky stepped away from Mac and turned to her brother, saying, "It's about time you woke up, sleepyhead."

Marcus looked around. "What time . . . How long was I out?"

"Not that long, really. I'm just teasing you," Becky told him. "It's good for you to rest whenever you can."

"Oh, don't you worry. When this thing is over, I'm going to give lessons on how to do nothing but rest," Marcus said.

"I'll believe that when I see it. But, in the meantime, speaking of 'getting this thing over with,' there's still some hot water left in my tent if you've a mind to shave and get yourself spruced up a bit." Becky paused to let the suggestion sink in, then added, "After all, if you want to come across as a big cattleman out to make the slickest deal you can tomorrow, having raggedy whiskers and sweat and grime around your ears won't exactly help sell the image."

"You'll be there beside me. And if looks are important to making our best deal," Marcus said, smiling, "then you're pretty enough for the both of us."

Becky smiled in response. "My, my. The gallantry is mighty thick in the air tonight. First, I get a compliment of sorts out of Mac. And now more of the same from you."

"Too bad Eamon isn't back yet," said Marcus. "He'd be sure to join in as well. And, with that silver tongue of his—"

Marcus stopped abruptly and cocked his head, listening. Mac and Becky heard it, too. All eyes swung in the direction of the darkness a short distance beyond the camp, where the ground began to drop away into the long slope leading down into the valley. Someone was coming up the incline and not trying to hide the sound of their advance.

Marcus grinned crookedly. "Speak of the devil. Unless I'm mistaken, that will be our wandering lad returning now."

"Hello, the camp!" called out a voice moments later.

But it wasn't Eamon's voice at all. It was the well-modulated tone of a woman.

Chapter 38

"Eamon and I had time for a rather lengthy chat before the trouble started, so I feel I know all of you already. Unfortunately, the same cannot be said in reverse—as you know nothing of me."

"You're a friend of Eamon's, that makes a pretty fair start," replied Marcus. "And the fact you say he's in some kind of trouble means we don't need much more of an introduction right now."

This exchange was taking place between Marcus and the woman who had hailed the camp only a short time earlier. Once invited on in, she was revealed in the light of the campfire to be a striking, raven-haired beauty clad in black leather riding breeches, a black silk blouse, and a flat-crowned black Stetson worn at a rakish angle on piled hair. In keeping with what was clearly a favored color scheme, she rode in astride a sleek black gelding.

Accompanying her was a plump, gray-mustached, somewhat elderly man wearing a wrinkled business suit and riding a steeldust mare.

Once the pair were dismounted, the woman had introduced herself as Arabella Winthrop and identified her companion as Howard Schumacher. She'd then wasted little time adding, "I am an old—though I shudder at any direct association to the word—friend of Eamon Farrell's. He told me where I could find you. He asked me to get word to you that he has met with some misfortune down in the town."

That was all that was needed to be said in order to claim the full attention of Marcus, Becky, and Mac. As it happened, Ned and Ox were just coming in from their check of the herd so they, too, overheard the words and quickly drew closer to get more of the story.

"What sort of trouble—or misfortune, as you call it—is Eamon in?" Mac wanted to know.

"It all stems from an encounter with a recent and not altogether welcome addition to our bursting little community—him and an even more recently arrived cohort of his," answered the dark-haired beauty, speaking precise words in a clipped British accent. "Eamon said you would recognize their names and understand readily enough the problem that arose from his running into them."

"And those names would be?"

"Oscar Harcourt is the scoundrel who has been here for too long now—his new friend is an even more uncouth sort whom I only heard referred to as Jerry Lee."

"Harcourt?! Jerry Lee?!"

The names were repeated in surprised tones by more than one voice.

Arabella arched a single finely penciled brow. "I see the names are indeed familiar."

"You'll have to pardon our sort of rattled response," Marcus said. "You see, we left from near Harcourt City, off to the southeast, about five weeks ago. When we rode out, Oscar Harcourt was pretty much the he-goose of the town and a big chunk of the surrounding area, and Jerry Lee Lawton was a gunman he regularly employed to help make sure things went his way. Now you're telling us both of them are here at Rattlesnake Creek?"

"Rattlesnake Gulch is the name now applied to our town," advised Schumacher, who up until then had barely spoken.

"And a more dismal choice is hard to imagine," Arabella interjected with clear disdain.

"Nevertheless, it got the majority of votes," the plump man declared. Then, clearing his throat, he went on, "Now, as far as this Harcourt, yes, we've become aware of his background and the weight he carried back where you come from. And I can understand how his being here now comes as a surprise to all of you. What shouldn't come as a surprise, I expect, is the fact that he has been very quick to apply the same heavy-handed tactics here in Rattlesnake Gulch that no doubt controlled the town already named after him."

"And even before this Jerry Lee showed up," Arabella added, "he was equally quick to find some local trouble-makers to support what little influence his money could not buy."

"Influence and power, that's what Oscar Harcourt is all about," said Marcus through clenched teeth. "He's already got a whole town and all the wealth any ten men would ever want. But it's not enough. He'll always be reaching for more."

"That certainly describes what he's been doing ever since arriving in Rattlesnake Gulch—reaching and grabbing, with both hands," confirmed Schumacher.

"Okay. That's interesting and it fits with what we already know about Harcourt and those he gathers 'round him," said Mac. "But it still doesn't answer exactly how running into him and Jerry Lee got Eamon in trouble."

"Based on what was basically a spontaneous eruption when they all laid eyes on one another," replied Arabella, "I assumed that would be explanation enough. A brawl ensued and Eamon and Jerry Lee ended up in jail, charged with disturbing the peace. Harcourt posted bail for Jerry Lee immediately. I offered to do the same for Eamon, but he refused. He instead sent me to notify those of you here what had occurred."

"What sort of law do you have down there?" asked Becky. "A little while ago, we could hear whooping and shooting clear up here. No offense, but I took it to be what I expected was common for a boomtown."

"Unfortunately, that sort of thing is not *un*-common," said Arabella.

Schumacher was quick to amend. "But we're trying hard to change that. That's why we recently appointed Rattlesnake Gulch's first marshal, none other than William Calder."

"Blazing Bill Calder?" echoed Ox, his eyes brightening with excitement.

"I thought he was dead," said Ned.

"That's nearly true of his eyesight, and certainly accurate for his liver," Arabella remarked caustically. "But there's enough shell of a man left for the fools who act as our town council to have pinned a badge on what amounts to a staggering reputation that hasn't all the way collapsed yet."

"That's unfair, Arabella," Schumacher protested. "Calder has helped tame things down. Call it just his reputation if you like, but it's still been beneficial."

But the dark-haired beauty was clearly unconvinced. "To drunks and starry-eyed fools who can't see the difference maybe. But it's just a matter of time before the image fades even for them."

"Be that as it may," said Marcus, "it still leaves us needing to go down there and get Eamon out of the hoosegow before Harcourt figures out a way to make even more trouble for him."

"I'll get some more horses saddled up," Ox announced eagerly.

"Hold it," Mac halted him. Then, turning to Arabella, he said, "If you and Eamon talked, he must have told you about the cattle we just drove in, right?"

"Of course."

"So, since Harcourt and Jerry Lee are present in Rattlesnake Gulch and have had their run-in with Eamon, they've got to know the herd is here, too. Did that get generally revealed as part of the dustup?"

"You bet it did," confirmed Schumacher. "Hadn't been for Calder threatening to bust heads or cut loose with his six-shooter, that beef-hungry crowd in The Lady A might have broke into a riot over the news of your herd finally getting here. Well, the conditions Harcourt had already put in place regarding the cattle pens probably helped put a crimp on things, too."

"What conditions? What does Harcourt have to do with Rattlesnake Gulch's cattle pens?" Marcus demanded.

"He owns them. He bought them," Arabella explained, "right along with the attached slaughterhouse and all the other businesses he's been acquiring ever since he showed up."

"He didn't call you by name, but he told everybody there was at least one herd on its way," Schumacher said. Then, his expression souring, he added, "Because he came from cattle country, he sold everybody on the notion that if he ran the pens and the slaughterhouse he had the experience to make sure beef came in at a fair price, that it was sound stock, and would get distributed without price gouging on account of the gold money in town. Next, once he had control, he announced the pens and slaughterhouse would be closed until he could bring in a qualified beef inspector—a veterinarian—to make sure any arriving cattle were disease free and fit for buying and selling."

"That announcement, very coincidentally, was made just two days ago," said Arabella. "He allegedly has sent for a beef inspector out of Helena, but without a clear estimate of when he might arrive."

"That scheming scoundrel! He's trying to strangle us from selling at a decent price!" exclaimed Marcus, slamming his right fist into the palm of his left hand. "He made sure he got here ahead of us. And he must have had Jerry Lee dogging our progress, keeping pace, so he'd know exactly the right time to make his announcement and close the holding pens."

"But we can still sell the cattle without him and his stupid pens, can't we?" said Becky. "If there are men hungry for beef who have money to pay, why can't we sell directly to them?"

Marcus shook his head. "That would be piecemeal—one or two, maybe half a dozen cows at a time. The pricing would be all over the place. It would take days, maybe weeks, and we'd come out far shorter than what we've been aiming for."

"Marcus is right," said Mac. "In addition to everything he said, once word spreads that we've got a herd of cows stalled here, going nowhere, rustlers and poachers will come flocking and nibbling the edges like vultures on a carcass. We'd have to be on guard every minute, night and day, and for every one or two cows sold there'd be the risk of another lost to theft."

"That's where I may be of some value," said Schumacher. "I came with Lady Arabella partly to provide her an escort, but also as a representative of some other businessmen in town and—strictly unofficially—as a member of the town council."

"Okay. What does that mean to our predicament?" asked Marcus.

Schumacher frowned. "Now that it's become clear that Harcourt is primarily about power and control—after fooling too many, including me, I regret to admit, into believing he was willing to invest money in our town for the sake of giving it a sound foundation to grow and last—some of us who haven't sold our business interests to him want to band together in an effort to hold him at bay before he's gone too far to be stopped."

"I don't see how—" Marcus tried to say.

Arabella cut him off. "What Howard is trying to say is that he has maintained ownership of the town's largest general mercantile, our most popular restaurant is still in the hands of the couple who started it and haven't yet succumbed to Harcourt's repeated offers to buy them out, and the same is true for me and my Lady A saloon. We represent the three most prominent businesses not yet under Harcourt's thumb, but there are several others, smaller ones—ones he hasn't deemed worthy of going after—we believe would join with us also."

"Join with you in what?"

"In buying your cattle, your beef," said Schumacher. "Preventing Harcourt from, in your own words, strangling you from making a decent sale and at the same time holding out on our beef-starved residents unless some of them resort to trying to steal what they can't get otherwise."

"Harcourt would like that," Marcus said bitterly. "Hell, he's probably planning on it, maybe even encouraging it. If we're getting stolen blind and maybe even threatened while waiting for that beef inspector to show, I bet Harcourt figures he might get away with offering us an undercut price that I'd take out of desperation."

"If this drive doesn't make money, we'll have nothing to go back to," said Becky. "Without a strong profit, we can't restock, can't keep the ranch afloat."

"And that low-down skunk will swoop down and lay claim to the whole Standing L," muttered the usually soft spoken, unemotional Ned, his teeth bared in a silent snarl.

"Give us time. A day, two at the outside," Schumacher pleaded. "We have men all through the area, hunters and trappers, who certainly know how to skin and butcher with or without a slaughterhouse. If we can line up a few of them and then spread word that we have access to your cattle in order to get a commitment from patrons—diners at the restaurant, processed meat from my store, even a lunch and supper grill set up at The Lady A, maybe other outlets—then we could pool our money to make you a fair offer for your cattle and have reasonable assurance of earning it back."

Marcus exchanged looks with his sister. Then he cut his gaze back to Schumacher and Arabella. "You're as aware as anybody that we don't have anything better staring us in the face. We planned on holding our cattle here overnight anyway. Come tomorrow, as word of our situation spreads and Harcourt has more time to scheme against us . . . Well, as soon as you can put something together, we'll be waiting to hear your offer. Hopefully, it's something that can work out all the way around."

"But there's an important thing for everybody to be sure and keep in mind," Mac stated somberly. "Harcourt ain't gonna take lightly this kind of conniving against him. You say he's already used some local toughs and now he has Jerry Lee and most likely his other pals from back in Harcourt City on hand. Any combination of that bunch can be plenty dangerous."

Arabella regarded him. "You're the one called Mac, aren't you?"

"That's right."

"Eamon asked for you specifically. He said you're the one who could be counted on to—and I quote—'have the sand' to stand up against whatever Harcourt tries to dish out. He said to tell you to come with guns loaded and eyes in the back of your head."

Marcus's eyes flashed. "Damn right Mac is going in loaded for bear. And the rest of us will be going with him, the same way."

Mac responded with a hard shake of his head. "That's no good, Marcus. That could be playing right into Harcourt's hands, don't you see? You've got to think about the herd."

"They'll be all right for the night," Marcus said. "They're weary, they've got graze and water. They're not going to wander any—"

"Not on their own maybe," Mac cut him off. "But if Harcourt sees we're all in town and we get tied up for any amount of time with the marshal, wouldn't that give him a prime chance to send Jerry Lee and his pack of mongrels up here to raise hell? Maybe stampede the whole bunch, maybe just run a few off or even shoot up a handful to send a message. Who'd be here to stop 'em? And what proof would there be who was behind it?"

Marcus scowled fiercely. "That's exactly the kind of stunt that scum would pull, ain't it?"

"Mac's right," said Becky. "Eamon asked for him, he's the one who should go. The rest of us need to stay behind and guard the herd."

"With one exception," Mac said.

All eyes swung to him.

Mac explained, "In case there's still the chance of trouble, maybe flying lead, up here tonight, I think Becky might be better off down in the town with me and Eamon, if we're able to spring him. Provided she's willing, that is, and unless Miss Arabella and Mr. Schumacher recommend otherwise."

"Certainly not," Arabella answered with a charming smile. "I've managed to survive in the dubious environs of Rattlesnake Gulch for several months now. I think we can help Miss Lewis navigate its various menaces without undue harm. What you bring upon yourself, Mr. Mackenzie, will be of your own doing."

Chapter 39

"I don't think this is such a good idea, fellas. Not a good idea at all," wailed Roy Orton. "Especially not for me or you, Edsel. You know how important it is for us to keep out of Harcourt's sight until the time is right. We do something to mess that up, it could mean—"

Edsel Purdy cut him short, saying, "Then the idea is to *not* let Harcourt catch sight of us, right? Where we're headed and what we're fixing to do ain't like we're looking to draw an audience, are we?"

"Maybe not necessarily. But if it came to that, it wouldn't bother me none," said 'Bama Wilkes. "I been so long without female attention that once I pick me out one of those sportin' gals and we set the price, I'll be ready to go right on the spot. Anybody happens to be lookin' on, maybe they'd learn something."

Orton made a face. "You mean you'd really go at it, even with somebody watching?"

"Why not?" 'Bama said, chuckling at the other's expression. "Kind of place we're goin', ain't like it'd be anything anybody hadn't seen before—and if it was, then they wouldn't know what they was looking at anyway."

"Speaking of where we're going," said Purdy, "since none of us has ever been to this town before, how are we gonna know to find what we're looking for? Keeping in mind, like Roy said, we need to stay clear of Harcourt. And Jerry Lee, too, as far as that goes."

"Just leave it to me," 'Bama boasted. He reined up his horse and pointed. "See those bigger, more solid-looking buildings over at the south end of the main street? A couple of 'em are clearly popular saloons, looks like there's a hotel and a restaurant in there, too. That's where the money crowd who've already hit it big will be. That's got to mean Harcourt, too. Right? So we stay clear of that part of town and we'll stay clear of him."

"But what about the sporting gals? Ain't the saloons where they'll be?" Purdy asked.

"Of course. The big money kind. But down yonder"— 'Bama swung one arm and pointed again, indicating a stretch of the deeply rutted street that ran to the north and was lined by a handful of shabbier-looking structures and an assortment of tents, some of them patched and sadly sagging—"there's where we'll find some who'll suit us just fine."

The three men sat their horses on the western edge of Rattlesnake Gulch, the spot they'd arrived at upon riding in from their camp in the hills a ways farther out. It was dark, but flickering torches mounted on poles at various intervals along the town's central street provided pools of illumination. Lighting from inside the saloons and the hotel at the more prominent end of the street poured out additional bright splashes but down toward the shabbier structures things turned progressively murkier.

Orton and Purdy both frowned as they gazed where 'Bama was pointing.

"Looks like a place suited just fine for getting your throat slit, too, if you ask me," grumbled Orton. "Maybe I'm beginning to understand better now why Sleet stayed back at camp."

"Sleet stayed in camp because he's turning into an old woman, same way it sounds like you're on the brink of," said 'Bama. "He knows boomtowns just like I do. He knows how the sportin' gals flock in in all sizes, shapes, colors, and prices. How anybody can hang back in that blasted camp after all these weeks of bein' in camps all along the trail and pass up a short trip to sample some belly warmin' from a gal, it purely baffles me."

"Pass me that jug of who-hit-John," Purdy said, abruptly thrusting out his hand. After 'Bama filled it with a badly depleted bottle of whiskey and he'd tipped it high, draining it even more, Purdy then asked, "Are we gonna sit here all night talking about what Sleet is passing up while we're passing up the same thing ourselves?"

'Bama emitted a nasty chuckle. "Talkin' about it gettin' that ol' stallion in you hankerin' a little stronger, is it?"

"I got me a lot of hankering," replied Purdy, his expression taking on a brittleness. "I want a woman, yeah. And then, after waiting all this time and all these miles, and knowing now that the time is close for me to finally even the score, I got a hankering for the chance to face that quick-triggered Mackenzie again."

'Bama chuckled some more. "And you figure that left-hand draw you been practicin' to the point of drivin' everybody crazy is gonna get the job done, eh?"

Purdy gave him a hard look. "You saying it ain't?"

"Ain't sayin' no such thing, pal." But the smirk never completely left 'Bama's face. "What I'm doin' is agreein' with you. Let's get on down the street and pick us out some sportin' gals."

At which point Orton, happening to glance toward the south end of the street, suddenly blurted out, "Oh shoot."

A sign painted on a wooden board nailed to a post read: RATTLESNAKE GULCH—POPULATION . . . The original lettering had been neatly printed, as had the initial count of citizens that followed. But then that first number had been x-ed out and replaced by a higher one, soon followed by another x-ing out and a revised number written in, then another and another until, after about half a dozen crossing-outs and revisions, someone had finally just scrawled GROWING in bright red letters to signify the Gulch's booming census.

"As you can see, simplicity and practicality are liberally applied here in our burgeoning metropolis," Arabella commented dryly as she, Becky, Mac, and Schumacher rode past the sign and proceeded on into town.

At this hour, there wasn't a lot of activity on the Gulch's main street stretching out before them. The same wasn't true, however, for the businesses—especially two large, wood frame buildings easily identifiable as saloons with splashes of light, music, laughter, and the steady buzz of voices pouring out of each—lining either side. Beyond the saloons there was a hotel and a restaurant, their windows brightly lit and revealing people moving about within. Farther down were a bank and some other businesses, all closed for the night, and farther yet there could be seen rows of less substantial structures and eventually numerous tents of various sizes.

Many of these had light and noise spilling out of them, too, and Mac guessed them to be gaming parlors, cheap shot-and-beer joints, flophouses, and no doubt cribs for working gals to ply their trade—all aimed at harder-strapped and less discriminating customers.

"Over here is my place," said Arabella, steering her gelding toward the left side of the street where one of the saloons stood. Its banner, spread high and wide over the front door, proclaimed it to be THE LADY A. At a slight angle across the street, its competition had a similar banner, identifying it as THE GOLDEN WHEEL.

Raising her voice to be heard above the music and voices spilling out from The Lady A, Arabella said, "I have private quarters in the back that, I assure you, are much more peaceful. My suggestion, Miss Lewis, is for you to wait there with me while Mr. Mackenzie goes on to conduct his business regarding Eamon. The jail is a ways farther in that direction"—she gestured toward the shabbier end of the town—"and I'd recommend against accompanying him there unless you absolutely insist. If he's able to get Eamon released, the two of them can re-join us here. Eamon will know where."

Becky looked questioningly at Mac.

"Sounds like a good idea," he told her.

"We can leave our horses here," said Arabella, stepping smoothly down from the saddle and wrapping her horse's reins around the hitch rail in front of her saloon.

"I have a private livery barn out back. Eamon's horse is already there. I'll have someone come out and take these on back also."

The others dismounted as well.

"How far down will I find the jail?" Mac asked.

"It's on this side of the street, down in that shadowy area just before all the tents start in." Schumacher pointed. "It's an old ore shack, one of the Gulch's original buildings. Some of the townsmen converted the inside, bolted up a big iron grate at the back to make a cell area, put in a desk and a stove and a cot up front for the marshal."

"Will I find the marshal down there now?"

Schumacher frowned. "Could be. But then again, he goes on patrols. He could be anywhere this time of the evening."

Arabella gave a decidedly unladylike snort. "The only thing certain about our marshal at this time of the evening, wherever you find him, is that he will be drunk."

Mac heaved a sigh. "I guess all I can do is start with the jail. He's got to be somewhere."

"Howard," said Arabella, "why don't you take a quick peek inside The Golden Wheel? See if Marshal Calder might be earning his keep by being involved in a card game there. I'll do likewise at my place. That's probably wiser for right now over Mr. Mackenzie checking himself. Especially The Golden Wheel." She paused, cutting her smoldering eyes back and forth between Mac and Becky before adding, "In case we failed to mention it, Harcourt owns the Wheel now. It was one of his first acquisitions upon arriving here—*after* he tried buying me out first, I might add. At least he showed that much good taste."

Schumacher started across the street, then stopped and looked back, asking, "What do I do if the marshal is in there?"

"Just come back and let us know," Arabella told him. "We'll decide from there."

While Schumacher proceeded on across the street and Arabella went to look in The Lady A, Becky stepped close to Mac and gazed up at him with a worried expression. "I suddenly don't have a good feeling about any of this. This place is wild and unpredictable. We're putting our trust in people we don't even really know."

"We know Eamon is in some kind of trouble," Mac told her. "If he wasn't, he'd have made it back to the camp by now."

That's when a loud, sharp voice called from out in the street, slicing through the noise spilling out of the saloons.

"Mackenzie! Turn around and look, you yellow dog. Don't worry, I ain't gonna shoot you. Not yet!"

Chapter 40

Slowly, Mac turned and swung his gaze toward where the voice had come from. Out of the corner of his mouth, he said to Becky, "Move. Step away from here."

He sensed rather than saw her edge back because his eyes were now locked on the figure standing in the middle of the street, about twenty feet down in the direction of the shabbier buildings and tents. It was Edsel Purdy, his shiny new Colt .45 now holstered butt-forward for the cross draw with his left hand, just as it had been the last time Mac had seen Purdy back in the Irish Jig Saloon. The surly man's right hand, encased in a black leather glove, hung at his side, its first and second fingers thrusting down straight and stiff.

"That's right, it's me," said Purdy, a corner of his mouth peeled back in a smirk. "And it's right, too, that

I've come gunning for you. But I ain't popping up out of hiding, like you done, to get the job done. I'm standing right here in the middle of the street, face-on."

"I don't know what you're trying to prove, Purdy," Mac responded. "I got no quarrel with you."

"Well, I got one with you!" Purdy held up his gloved right hand and flexed the thumb and fingers that worked, all but the two that remained straight and unmoving. "I got a hand that's gonna be crippled for life, thanks to you. That makes for a *big* quarrel, mister, and one you owe a serious payment on."

Purdy stood in plain sight, bold and demanding in the light from one of the street lamp torches as well as from the glow pouring out of the wide front windows of the hotel on Mac's side of the street. But over on the other side of the street, just within the murky shadows there, stood two other figures. One of them Mac had no trouble recognizing as, not surprisingly, Roy Orton.

The other took him a moment longer to place. It was the amiable stranger calling himself Joshua Jones who had coldcocked him from behind and went on to steal the outfit's chuckwagon weeks ago on the trail.

"I see you got plenty of other debt collectors to back you up," Mac grated, a cold anger starting to build in him.

"Don't worry about them. They know their place. This is strictly between you and me," Purdy said. "Now step away from those horses and move out where I can see you plain."

As he edged out toward the middle of the street, Mac became aware of changes occurring around them. The pitch of the voices in the saloons had suddenly changed and the music from both had faded. There was the scrape of bootheels and the muted shuffle of bodies crowding into doorways to see what was going on.

Mac registered all that but didn't dare look around. Keeping his eyes locked on Purdy, he said, "I pull a trigger on you again, mister, the bullet will be aimed to do a lot more damage than to just your hand."

"Big talk. Bring it on," Purdy sneered. "You get off a trigger pull at all, it ain't gonna matter because it'll only be a death twitch with my slug already in you."

That was it. There was no more to say. Mac planted his feet and braced himself. He'd never been in a gunfight like this before. Part of him wished somebody would step forward, say or do something to stop it. But another part of him, icy cold and down deep, just wanted to get it over with and was prepared to do whatever it took to be the one left still standing.

When Purdy's left hand jerked into motion, reaching over for the .45 on his right hip, it almost seemed like slow motion to Mac. In the same instant, he felt the Smith & Wesson filling his own hand, saw his arm swing out and extend forward in a blur. Then the Model 3 was bucking, spitting smoke and flame.

Mac's bullet hit slightly above the center of Purdy's heart. He staggered half a step backward from the punch of the .44 slug and appeared to teeter like that for a long second. His hand remained clamped on his Colt, not quite clear of its holster. Then his knees sagged ever so slightly before, abruptly, he toppled straight back and dropped flat on his back in the dusty street.

There was a moment where everything froze silent and motionless.

Then, all at once, voices started chattering excitedly

from both of the saloons, accompanied by the stomp of feet as patrons crowded to get outside for a closer look, and even the music started playing again.

It was activity apart from that, though, that seized the attention of Mac. On the far side of the street, Roy Orton suddenly pulled deeper into the shadows, looking frightened, as if he expected to get the next bullet. But the other man over there with him—the hombre who'd called himself Joshua Jones before he'd tried to bash in Mac's brain—was reacting quite the opposite. His Frontier Colt was already drawn and gripped in one fist. He stepped forward with it aimed straight at Mac.

Mac had no chance to get set for returning fire. All he could do was try to make himself less of a target—which he did by immediately pitching to the ground and going into a roll. Jones's gun barked once, twice, and the slugs tore up the dirt inches away from the scrambling Mac.

Now the saloon chatter suddenly changed in pitch again. A couple of hoarse voices hollered, "Watch out!" and the tramp of feet signaled a desperate stampede by the observers to get back inside.

Mac squirmed onto his belly and twisted around so that he was facing in Jones's direction, hoping for the chance to get off a shot of his own before a bullet caught up with his maneuvering. A third attempt from Jones blistered the air only inches above Mac's head and smacked into the boardwalk in front of the hotel behind him.

And then the roar of a different gun filled the street. Two rapid-fire reports pounded the air and sent bullets sizzling through it—again above Mac's head, but this time much higher up. On the other side of the street, the man known to Mac as Joshua Jones took the one-two punch of lead and was knocked to the ground, dead.

Everything went silent again.

After first looking to make sure no further threat loomed from across the street and being satisfied that Roy Orton had disappeared, Mac pushed to his feet. Still gripping the Smith & Wesson, he took a step away from the hotel, craning his neck to look up at its row of second-floor windows. In one of them he found what he was looking for—the answer to who had done the shooting that cut down his second assailant.

Looking back down at him, his expression blank, was none other than Quinn Blassingame!

Mac was so stunned by this that he failed to pay proper attention to the mass of people now boiling out of the saloons and starting to fill the street around him. Until one of them, a stringy-haired vision stinking of cigar smoke and whiskey whom Mac caught only a glimpse of, stepped up close beside him and proclaimed, "That's enough killing in my town, bub!"

With that, the barrel of a Colt Peacemaker slammed down on the back of Mac's head and he pitched to the ground again, this time unconscious.

Chapter 41

There was a time when some mentioned the name William "Blazing Bill" Calder in conversations that included the likes of Hickock, Earp, Masterson, and so forth—"town tamers" who had cleaned up the rowdiest hellholes on the frontier and brought law and order, after a fashion, to the West. Most of Calder's notoriety came from a single incident in the town of Ogallala, Nebraska—itself dubbed "the Gomorrah of the plains"—when Blazing Bill shot it out with all four members of the McClatchy gang and was the only one left standing when the smoke cleared.

Trouble was, Ogallala was the last of the rowdy cow towns, the end of the Texas trail, and the springing up of new railheads everywhere a body looked brought a close to the days of the great cattle drives. Calder's exploits got him a handful of mentions in some bigger newspapers and a couple of eastern magazines, even three or four dime novels written about him, but his fame and glory never spread very far beyond Nebraska and parts of Colorado and Wyoming and didn't last all that long even there.

Calder's life became a series of entanglements with bad luck, bad whiskey, bad women, and ill-chosen pursuits . . . until the Blazing Bill who sat behind the marshal's desk in the drafty jail building of Rattlesnake Gulch this night was a drunken, shrunken shell of the former ring-tailed terror he once had been.

"The years have not been kind to me, old friend," he was saying as he squinted through the smoke that curled up from a cigar clamped between his teeth. Bracketing the mouth that held the cigar were the limp, stringy hairs of a drooping mustache and bracketing the pale, deeply seamed face that held the mustache were long, stringy strands of hair shot with streaks of gray. "I am in poor health, poor humor, and poor condition. Yet I continue to . . . strive. Strive to bring law and order to this godless place while at the same time struggling to regain . . . something. Some measure of dignity restored to what I've let myself become."

Although there were others in the room, Calder was aiming these remarks almost entirely at one man—Quinn Blassingame, who sat in a straight-backed wooden chair pulled up in front of the marshal's desk. Blassingame had been listening without expression or comment until, at last, the marshal seemed to have run out of excuses and explanations.

"You know what, Bill?" the detective said.

"I know a lot of things," Calder grumbled. "What do you mean?"

"I mean that I think you're plumb full of hogwash," came the response. "You're not striving to bring law and order to this dump of a town any more than you're struggling to restore your dignity. All you're really doing is looking for a corner of Nowhere where they'll put up with you long enough for you to shrivel up and finish killing yourself the rest of the way with cheap cigars and rotgut whiskey. And the spiel you just pitched to me was a play for sympathy that I'm fresh out of."

Calder's whiskey-dulled eyes narrowed and a weak fire flickered in them. "Damn you. There's less than a handful of men on the face of the earth I'd let talk to me like that and live."

"That might have been true at one time. But look in a mirror, Bill." Blassingame shook his head sadly. "You've let yourself go. You're only a couple years older than I am, but you look like you got twenty on me. And if you weren't hiding behind your reputation and your bluster, two-thirds of the men in this town could whip you to a frazzle before that palsied hand of yours was able to close on the grips of your gun."

"Let's see 'em try it!"

"Oh, somebody will. Soon enough." Blassingame continued to shake his head. "Or is that what you're angling for? Pushing the limit of your luck until somebody puts you out of your misery like that backshooter did Hickock over in Deadwood?"

Calder snorted out a cloud of cigar smoke. "The limit of my luck. I ran that out a long time ago. Except for the bad kind. Every hand I turn over I expect to be aces and eights."

"If you really want to try and change that, then start by keeping the cork in the bottle and making smarter decisions. Like about who you slap behind the bars of this rat trap you're running here," Blassingame told him.

"You talking about those pups I got back there now?" Calder suddenly cut his eyes over to the other persons present in the room, Becky Lewis and Arabella Winthrop. "Did you two put him up to this? Trying to wheedle your way by using an old friend against me?"

"Bill," Blassingame said wearily. "Nobody is putting me up to anything. I've been trying to tell you, I shot one of those men out in the street a little while ago. The fella you clobbered over the head and dragged in here only shot the first one. And he did that in self-defense, in a fair fight. The second varmint was trying to bushwhack him, so I joined in and cut him down before he could succeed."

"You weren't even out in the street!" Calder protested.

"I was in the hotel, up in my room on the second floor. I saw the shoot-out from my window and that's where I shot the bushwhacker from. Before I could fight my way down through the crowd and all the excitement, you'd already pistol-whipped Mackenzie and dragged him here to put him behind bars."

"That pistol whipping is a little trick I learned from Earp," Calder said, his thoughts seeming to stray. "You know he hardly ever shot anybody, except for that whole business at the O.K. Corral? He brought a whole bunch of troublesome situations to a halt just by unleathering his long-barreled sixer and bashing some ranny over the skull with it. Soon as I heard of that method, I liked it. If I want to cut down on shoot-outs in my town, then that means I ought to hold off on being trigger happy my own self, you see what I mean?"

"I guess it's all right when you can get away with it,"

Blassingame allowed. "But sometimes, like tonight, when the other fella is bound and determined to throw lead, you choosing to just swing your pistol instead of shooting back seems a mite impractical."

His thoughts apparently still meandering on a course of their own, Calder said, "When did you get in town, Quinn?"

"This afternoon. When I heard you were marshal here in Rattlesnake Gulch, I was planning on looking you up but just hadn't had time before now."

"But you managed to find time to shoot somebody down in the street. That what you're telling me?" Calder's question suddenly had a sharp, shrewd edge to it.

Blassingame leaned back in his chair and sighed. "I told you how things went, Bill. I told you the truth. If you figure you've got reason for holding Mackenzie behind bars, then I guess you need to do the same to me."

Calder glared at him. "You don't think I'd do it, do you?"

"Frankly, I'm not sure what you're capable of. I would have thought I knew at one time, but now I'm not so sure."

The two men held each other's eyes for a long moment.

Then, abruptly, the marshal slapped both palms down hard on the desk and declared, "Oh, hell, Quinn! You know I can't throw an old pard in the clink. If you say those two strangers laying dead out there in the street got what they had coming to 'em in a fair fight, then that's good enough for me." He pulled open a drawer, withdrew a ring of keys, tossed them over to Becky. "Here. You do the honors. Go ahead and release old Busted Head. But warn him if he comes out here snorting with any bad intentions for how he was treated, I'll do it all over again and next time won't be so quick to find his key."

As Becky rose from her chair, jangling the keys, Arabella stood up also. "What about the other prisoner—the one you arrested for brawling in my place earlier?" she wanted to know.

Calder waved a hand. "Go ahead, let him out, too. I'm feeling generous, we'll call it time served."

After the women had disappeared through the door of the flimsy partition that separated the office area from the cell block, Calder turned back to Blassingame. Resting his elbows on the desktop, he puffed some cigar smoke and said, "You seem to have a particular interest in those folks who, I understand, have a cattle herd waiting outside of town. That what brings you to Rattlesnake Gulch?"

"Not directly, no," Blassingame replied. "Though I did have some dealings with their outfit farther back on the trail."

"That's an answer without really being one. What *does* bring you to town, then?"

"I'm on a job for the agency."

"You still with High Grade, eh?" Calder sighed out some more smoke. "Too bad I didn't stick with 'em when I had the chance. And I know, before you say it, there was another case where me not keeping the cork in the bottle worked against me."

Blassingame just looked at him.

"And I suppose asking the nature of the job you're on will just get me the old 'privileged and confidential,' right?"

"If you already know the answer, then why bother asking?" said Blassingame. Then, hitching forward in his chair, he went on. "Look, Bill, there's things at work here that get kind of complicated. But trust me on this much: No matter what else, the Lewises—the gal Becky and her brother, who you haven't met yet—are good people. I got reason to believe, though, that the same can't be said for this Harcourt hombre, who I understand has quickly bought his way into casting a mighty big shadow here-abouts. However some of the complications I mentioned turn out, I hope there's enough of the old Blazing Bill left in you to be clearheaded when it comes to sorting out the wolves from the sheep."

Calder's shaggy eyebrows pulled together. "If you want to help me be clearheaded, Quinn, how about not talking in riddles?"

The door to the cell block opened and Becky, Arabella, Mac, and Eamon came out.

Blassingame stood up. "It's getting late. I'm glad we could get this straightened out. Now, I have my own af-fairs that I need to return to."

"Hold on a minute," said Mac. "I think there's—"

Blassingame cut him off. "Not now, kid. Maybe later." He started for the door, then paused and looked back over his shoulder. "See you around, Bill. Think about what I said."

Chapter 42

"What part of me telling you to get rid of those incompetent fools Purdy and Orton didn't you understand? How could I have made myself any plainer?"

Jerry Lee Lawton slowly pulled the palm of one hand down over his face and groaned inwardly as Oscar Harcourt's words lashed him. When Harcourt's rant finally started to taper off, Jerry Lee said, "Look, it was plain what you said. What you wanted. And I went to Roy and Edsel with that message, I truly did. But you also said you wanted the Standing L outfit to be harassed on their drive, and with them heading out right away, I had to move kinda quick to put a crew together to go after 'em. So that's when I thought—"

"Thought?" Harcourt interrupted. "Don't insult me with the use of that word! If you'd been *thinking*, you would have stuck to following my orders and cut all ties with that pair. Had you done that, then Purdy wouldn't have shown up out in the street a little while ago to get killed and complicate everything I've been working to set in place here in Rattlesnake Gulch!"

"I know, I know. I see that now." Jerry Lee made an imploring gesture with both hands. "I don't know what got into the blasted fool, coming into town like he done. Him and the others were all supposed to wait in our camp outside of town until I got back with word on how you wanted to play it now that the herd is here."

"So far," Harcourt snapped, "things have hardly gone how I intended for them to play out. It started with that hotheaded Eamon Farrell showing up unexpectedly at The Lady A while you and I were paying a visit and has only gotten worse from there."

"At least it got Farrell slapped in the hoosegow. And now the same for Mackenzie," Jerry Lee pointed out. "Have you managed to get the local law in your pocket?"

Harcourt frowned. "No. Before now, the drunken old sot didn't seem worth the bother."

"Blazing Bill Calder? I would have thought—"

"There you go with that word again. Just be quiet for a minute and let *me* do some thinking." Harcourt paced across the thick carpeting of the well-appointed room that served as a parlor for the second-floor apartment over The Golden Wheel saloon he had recently acquired. He paused at the window and glared down at the street, once again empty following the turmoil of the shooting.

Jerry Lee stood fidgeting, waiting for Harcourt to speak again. While still smarting from the tongue lashing he'd received, at the same time he understood the anger behind it. He felt plenty mad himself at those fools Purdy and Wilkes. What in blazes had they been thinking? And why hadn't Orton or Sleet done something to stop them? There wasn't much he could do in the way of taking out his anger on a couple of dead men, but he was fixing to give the other two a chewing out when he got back to camp!

Finally turning from the window, Harcourt said, "Nothing has changed as far as having the Standing L herd stalled where it is. Everything I had in place to cause that still holds. But what we've got to do now is make sure public sentiment from a bunch of beef-starved rock choppers doesn't turn on me while I'm sweating out Marcus Lewis."

"How are we gonna do that?"

"We're going to do what you suggested a minute ago. We're going to turn to the law."

"Huh?"

"One way to keep everybody from getting sore at me is to make 'em even madder at somebody else," Harcourt explained. "So we're going to arrange that. I'd already made use of a few local petty criminals before you and your crew showed up. They're anxious to earn more of the money I'm willing to spread around, so I'll provide them the chance to do just that.

"You give me directions to where you're camped, then go back and wait there with however many men you have left until I send some reinforcements out. Then, as soon as you can, I want you to hit the Standing L herd. Raise hell, make like you're trying to steal a bunch of their cattle, maybe even run some off to make it look good. Shoot a few if you have to. Hell, shoot a Standing L rider, too, if you get the chance . . . but not Lewis or his sister."

Jerry Lee nodded. "I'll do whatever you say, but—"

"Don't you see? In the meantime, I'll be talking it up

all around town, working everybody into a panic," Harcourt said excitedly. "I'll convince 'em that if the herd stays stalled like it is, all that good beef may get wasted by being stolen away. I'll explain again how I can't take the risk of buying 'em at the top dollar Lewis is expecting without having them properly inspected. But then, out of compassion for the community possibly getting robbed of having any beef at all, what I *will* take a risk on is holding 'em in the safety of my pens at a lower price, until the meat inspector arrives to clear them."

"At which point," Jerry Lee said, catching on, "you'll turn around and sell the 'cleared' beef at prime prices!"

"Not only that," Harcourt added, "but the longer Lewis holds off accepting my offer, the more it takes the pressure off me and puts it on him. And while all that's taking place, any interference from the law will be avoided by Marshal Calder distracted into leading a posse out chasing rustlers."

Jerry Lee's face pulled into a frown. "I don't like the sound of me and the boys having Blazing Bill on our tails."

Harcourt chuffed a laugh. "You're reacting to the legend of what *used* to be. Trust me, the Blazing Bill of today is nothing but a wheezing old rumpot who couldn't track muddy footprints across a freshly whitewashed floor unless, maybe, they were leading to a whiskey barrel."

Jerry Lee cocked one eyebrow. "If you say so."

"I do," Harcourt told him. "Now tell me the directions to your camp and then head back and wait. I'll have some fresh men out there tomorrow at the latest, maybe even tonight."

* * *

Not far away, in the best suite available at the Montana House, another intense discussion related to the recent shooting—or, more specifically, to one of its participants—was being held.

Pierre Leclerc, tall and aristocratic in bearing, clean shaven and nattily clad even after days of travel over rugged country, stood ramrod straight in the center of the room, hands clasped at the small of his back.

Off to one side, sprawled loosely in a cushioned chair near the fireplace, was a blockily built man whose hawk-like, unshaven face and ill-tended, coarsely woven attire made him a sharp contrast in appearance. Standing directly before Leclerc, not too far inside the door, was Quinn Blassingame, his weathered, world-weary face and clean but comfortably broken-in trail clothes placing him square in the middle of the contrasts.

"I appreciate you not letting Mackenzie be shot down by the hand of another," Leclerc was saying. "But I am not quite so clear on why you found it necessary to facilitate his release from jail in the aftermath."

"Because he didn't belong there, not for the charges against him," Blassingame responded flatly. "He killed a man in self-defense, a fair fight. He got wrongly tossed behind bars by a drunken old marshal seeking another taste of power and glory from days long gone by. He's so muddleheaded he thought Mackenzie killed *both* men who died down there in the street."

"And you," said the man in the chair, "knowing that you were responsible for plugging one of them, and being so noble and all, just couldn't let that stand. Is that it?"

"I wanted to see the record set straight, that's all. The marshal's an old friend of mine," Blassingame explained.

"I didn't want to see him stick his foot any deeper in the bucket than he already had."

"My, you *are* a noble sort, ain't you?" said the man in the chair.

"That's enough, Driscoll." Leclerc gave the command quietly, never taking his eyes off Blassingame. Then, continuing to address the detective, he said, "I have no quarrel with your motives. I do, however, question the advisability of revealing yourself once again to Mackenzie after your past encounter on the trail. Might that not risk raising suspicion in him, given he would have had every logical reason to expect your paths wouldn't cross again? He already knew you were a detective, after all, and he has long been keenly aware of the extent and expense I've gone to sending manhunters after him."

Blassingame frowned. "And you think spotting me a second time might be enough to make him bolt?"

"He's proven a very cautious and elusive devil in the past," Leclerc stated. "That is exactly how and why he's been able to avoid capture for so long."

"Even so," Blassingame replied, "I already took steps to explain my presence here as being sent by my agency on a new assignment. I think that will be enough to offset any worries by Mackenzie. Especially since my shot saved his hide and then me speaking up afterward got him turned loose from behind bars. If I was out to nab him for the warrants against him, why wouldn't I make my claim right there in front of the marshal and make it easy on myself with him already in custody?"

Leclerc arched an eyebrow. "Frankly, I have been wondering the same thing. Why, when you knew Mackenzie had been arrested, did you not seek my counsel before arranging his release? How could you know I wouldn't have wanted to go to the jail with you and take the opportunity to present my charges against him there?"

"It was my clear understanding that you wanted to be the one to personally *apprehend* Mackenzie—not just assume custody of him after he was caught," said Blassingame. "If all you wanted was to see him already in irons, you could have saved yourself a hell of a lot of trouble and expense traveling all this way. I could have delivered him to you in New Orleans or met you somewhere in between at a place far more easily accessible for you."

Now Leclerc smiled. "I'm glad to hear your understanding is absolutely correct, Mr. Blassingame. As long as your confidence is equally accurate that Mackenzie has not been given cause to take flight, then everything remains satisfactory. I will not much longer be denied the day I have awaited for so long. The day I can look into Mackenzie's eyes and see his fear and despair at knowing he has not only been cornered at last, but by my hand. The only thing that could make it sweeter is if he attempts something desperate enough to make cutting him down on the spot necessary."

"Whoa. Now wait a minute," said Blassingame. "I don't run men down to hand them over for assassination. The warrants me and my agency are acting on are to see him presented for proper legal disposition."

"But of course," Leclerc assured him. "I was merely indulging myself in a fantasy, a bit of wishful thinking, no? If you recall, I said *if* Mackenzie attempts something desperate. I fully expect he is too much of a coward to do so, but in the event he should . . ."

Blassingame's eyes cut to Driscoll, still draped in his chair by the fireplace. "I see. In such an event, your 'bodyguard' would be only too glad to play out your fantasy, is that it?"

Leclerc's expression hardened and he was quick to respond, "I assure you, sir, that if Mackenzie should give me cause, I am quite capable of taking measures of my own against him. I am exceedingly proficient with a saber and a crack shot with a pistol, and have emerged the victor in duels utilizing both. Mr. Driscoll accompanies me as a safeguard against villains who might attack me in stealth or in excessive number."

"Rest easy, Mr. Detective," said Driscoll, rising from his chair. "Now that you've done your job of sniffing out Mackenzie, you don't have to worry about getting your hands dirty if it comes to any rough stuff."

"For your information," Blassingame grated, "while you've been slouching around trying to look menacing, I already handled some rough stuff in order to make sure a pack of two-bit rustlers didn't spoil Mackenzie showing up here in one piece. Part of that included getting my hands dirty burying a partner and friend . . . so show a little respect, and watch what comes out of that mouth of yours!"

Driscoll immediately bridled. "Maybe you'd like to try and—"

"Stop the nonsense!" demanded Leclerc. "Am I paying either of you to stand here thumping your chests and growling at one another? I think not. There is one matter and one matter only that interests me enough to make being in this hovel at all bearable. That is the apprehension—*my* apprehension—of Dewey Mackenzie! So where and how soon can this be accomplished? Those are the only points of discussion I want to hear."

Blassingame and Driscoll continued glaring at one another for a couple of seconds before easing up.

Then Driscoll said, "Seems to me we ought to go ahead and get it over with, the sooner the better. If he's still in town, now that he's out of jail, wouldn't it be best to brace him here rather than when he's back with his cattle drive outfit? Those cowboy types who ride for a brand tend to stick together pretty tight. We try to pluck Mackenzie out of their midst, I'm thinking we'd have the whole bunch fighting us to hold on to him."

"I have to agree with that much," Blassingame allowed grudgingly.

"My impression, since the drive has now arrived," Leclerc countered, "was that the cattle would be sold off and then the members of the crew would typically celebrate in the town's local saloons, drinking great quantities of alcohol and cavorting with loose women. I had imagined those would be favorable conditions under which to confront Mackenzie."

"Well, under normal circumstances," said Driscoll, "that would be pretty good thinking, Mr. Leclerc. Trouble is, from the talk I've heard going around, that herd ain't gonna be brung into town right away. There's some kind of dispute about the cattle buy being held up until a meat inspector gets here to declare the animals are fit and healthy. That being the case, the outfit will be holding 'em out of town until something is settled."

"That's the same thing Becky Lewis was telling me on the way to the jail," Blassingame confirmed. "If it's true and the herd stays stalled up on that hill south of town, then the Standing L riders will tighten up like a brick wall and trying to draw Mackenzie out will be like trying to pry loose one of the bricks."

"That is not acceptable!" Leclerc said. "I have no intention of lingering indefinitely in this place while such trifles are sorted out. What of it, Blassingame? Upon being released from jail, did Mackenzie return immediately to where the herd is being held?"

The detective shrugged. "I don't know. My guess is, as late as it's getting, they would have made for camp right away. But there was another woman with Becky who'd taken an interest in the matter—a local gal, owner of one of the saloons. They might've lingered with her for a time."

"You must find out immediately," Leclerc insisted. "Determine their whereabouts and report back to me with all haste."

Chapter 43

In fact, Mac, Becky, and Eamon *had* gone to Arabella's apartment behind the saloon after leaving the jail. The two women insisted Mac and Eamon needed some attention for the battering they'd undergone that was left untended during their time behind bars.

With the aid of an elderly Oriental maid, Arabella saw to it that basins of warm, sudsy water; cleansing cloths; and dressing material were quickly provided and arrayed on her dining room table.

Because he'd been in a brawl *and* had been bashed over the head by Marshal Calder, Eamon had more cuts and bruises needing treatment. Mac suffered only a single blow from Calder's pistol barrel.

"I guess me and my stupid temper is the cause of all this," Eamon lamented as Arabella gently sponged dried blood from a cut on his forehead. "When my eyes fell on that blasted Harcourt and his pet weasel Jerry Lee, I lost my head and immediately tore into them. I ended up tangling mostly with Jerry Lee because Harcourt ducked and hid under a table. I was just getting ready to drag him out, after putting Jerry Lee down, when that blasted marshal came up behind me and laid his pistol across the back of my head. Next thing I knew, I was waking up in that jail cell with my head pounding like somebody was dancing an Irish jig inside it."

"I've had my skull cracked so many times in the past month or so that my head don't feel right if it *ain't* pounding from getting freshly whacked," Mac said.

"You're going to have so much scar tissue back here pretty soon," said Becky, dabbing at the blood-matted hair around the most recent gash on Mac's crown, "that no hair is going to be able to grow. You'll be bald before your time."

"Many more whacks, I'm likely to be so brain addled I probably won't even notice," Mac replied.

"Well, while your brain is still unaddled," said Eamon, "could you fill me in on what in blazes Jerry Lee and Harcourt are doing here in Rattlesnake Gulch? And that detective we left back at Moccasin, too."

"I know about Blassingame—he got sent here on a new job. He told Arabella and me about it on the way to the jail," said Becky. "After he finished his business in Moccasin, seeing to the burial of Muncie and all, he got a wire from his agency sending him after another fugitive, someone who was reported to be on his way here to the gold fields."

"I guess that explains him," said Mac, scowling, "but it don't end there, not with Harcourt or Jerry Lee, either. I had the chance to tell you I killed Edsel Purdy when he forced me into a shoot-out, right? That's what landed me in jail. But there was a second hombre backing him up—the one Blassingame saved me from with a shot from his hotel window. What I haven't told you yet is who that second varmint was. None other than the sucker-punching cur who gave me that other rap on the head when he and his pards stole our chuckwagon."

Eamon and Becky both reacted with surprised looks.

Becky said, "Are you sure?"

"I haven't been hit that many times yet," Mac answered. "And I dang sure ain't likely to forget the mug of anybody who made that much of a fool out of me."

Eamon took a minute to quickly relate to Arabella the event being referred to. When he was finished, he turned back to Mac and said, "So that polecat—you said he called himself Joshua, as I recall—was somehow in cahoots with Jerry Lee and his pals?"

Mac shrugged. "I don't see no other way to explain it. He was there with Purdy. Orton was there, too, but he took off when the shooting broke out."

"But what were they up to?" Becky asked. "Why, after they trashed our chuckwagon, didn't we see hide nor hair more of them until we arrived here?"

"I can only guess," said Mac. "But since we already figured Jerry Lee was dogging us, I gotta believe now they were sent to do more than just follow the drive. Like cause us trouble in different ways, slow us down, so that Harcourt could have time to make it here and put things in place to queer the sale of the herd at the hoped-for price. That done, he could play his angle to try and buy the cattle cheap, all in a roundabout way to gain the Standing L ranch."

"Only, other than that business with the chuckwagon,

Jerry Lee's bunch didn't do any more bothering or slow-ing us down," pointed out Becky. But then, frowning, she added, "Or do you think they also had something to do with those rustlers who hit us?"

"Doesn't seem to be any connection there. I think the Ivers bunch was strictly the pack of thieves they appeared to be," Mac said. "But what they did worked in favor of Jerry Lee's crew all the same. Think how long it took us to retrieve and repair the stolen wagon, plus the extra time we spent around Keylock dealing with Tobe's shoot-ing and the Bar W outfit, and then the days it cost us after the rustlers made their try. Add it all up, it totals to more than a week knocked off the herd's progress. Time for Harcourt to be doing the buying and finagling he's done here in Rattlesnake Gulch. It meant Jerry Lee's bunch didn't *have* to do any more to slow us down."

Eamon's brow puckered. "I guess that's all possible. But, man, it seems like an awful complicated way to go about it. With his money and disregard for doing things on the square, why wouldn't Harcourt just hire his own gang of rustlers—headed by Jerry Lee or whoever—to simply *take* the herd? It would have got him to the same place in the end, wouldn't it?"

"Maybe," Mac said. "But Harcourt's way isn't so much direct conflict as it is leveraging and pressuring behind the scenes, behind a mask of doing legitimate business. You saw that with the way he went after your place back in Harcourt City. So simply stealing the cattle and ruining Marcus and Becky as a way to get their ranch don't fit his methods, not if he can work it another way. Plus, remem-bering what Marcus pointed out about Harcourt's craving for influence and power and considering what we've heard about how he's been buying up places all around

Rattlesnake Gulch, maybe his appetite grew even bigger once he got here. Reckon Miss Arabella can comment on that, seeing how she's been here watching him go after things."

Eamon smiled. "I'm sure our hostess will be willing to help however she can, but things might go better if you address her properly, Mac. She is, after all, *Lady* Arabella Winthrop of royal English heritage."

"Of course I know she's a lady," said Mac, not quite getting it at first. Then: "Wait a minute, you mean she's truly . . ."

"Truly," confirmed Arabella, joining Eamon's somewhat teasing smile. "My late husband, Heathcote, was indeed the slightly tarnished heir and lord of Kraftstone Manor in the jolly old homeland. It is an altogether dreary place on an even drearier slice of rainy coastland, destined to soon erode into the sea. Heathcote, I fear, fit in rather well, but nevertheless he *was* a titled lord and I but a cobbler's daughter, so I accepted his proposal of marriage.

"Once we were wed, I tried to breathe some life into him by convincing him to embark on a trip to America, where the result was tragically the opposite: He caught a fever and died. Since his marriage to me was scandalously disapproved by his family, they were in no hurry for me to return and I was in no hurry to go. So I shipped them Heathcote's body for burial in the family plot and I remained here to seek grand adventures on my own. And many an adventure I've had, though how grand is a relative matter. I don't make the 'Lady' thing as big an issue as some, but I haven't altogether ditched it, either. When I'm feeling low, it brightens me to think that my in-laws across the pond remain anguished by the fact that I continue to have every right to use it."

By the time Lady Arabella had finished, Becky's mouth hung in awe. "That's an absolutely fascinating tale," she said. "You've lived in England and crossed the ocean. I've never been out of Montana."

"Remember what I said, dear. Almost everything in life is relative," Lady Arabella told her. "Had I remained at Kraftstone Manor and read of things out here in the West, I'm sure that would have sounded fascinating to me. And as a matter of fact, having experienced both, I can assure you that your Montana—maybe not Rattlesnake Gulch specifically—holds up very well."

"But the thing is," said Mac, aiming to pull the conversation back on course, "Rattlesnake Gulch and the shenanigans going on in it are where we're at and what we need to figure out how to deal with."

"Which brings us back," replied Lady Arabella, arching one finely penciled brow, "to the unpleasant subject of Oscar Harcourt and any pertinent observations I might have about his actions since his arrival here. Unfortunately, I can't think of anything to add beyond what Howard Schumacher and I initially shared with you. Within a day of his arrival here, Harcourt began buying businesses and is pressing to acquire still more, including mine and Howard's and the others we mentioned. From that, it seems one would have to reach the conclusion that his plans are even bigger than merely trying to tie up the beef rights here and gaining your ranch back near Harcourt City."

"That could be," Mac said, his jaw set tight. "But we can only fight one fight at a time. And the first one has to be protecting the herd and making a sale that saves the Standing L."

"Who's Howard Schumacher?" Eamon wanted to know.

Mac gave him a quick rundown on the general store proprietor and the plan he was trying to put together with other businessmen who weren't yet under the thumb of Harcourt.

"If he can pull that off," Mac concluded, "then we've still got a good chance to see things work out in Becky and Marcus's favor. Hopefully, Schumacher will have some positive feedback by tomorrow. But in the meantime, like I said, we've got to protect the herd from any stunts Jerry Lee and his crew might try to pull on Harcourt's behalf, and maybe from some other scavengers who might come around as word spreads about the herd being stalled just outside of town."

"That means we ought to get back to camp to provide Marcus and Ned and Ox some added firepower," said Eamon.

"Just when we get you patched up from one round of mischief, you're bound to race off and go looking for more?" Lady Arabella questioned.

"Not look for it, but ready to meet it if it comes hunting us," Eamon responded.

"You'll be dragging Becky into that possibility as well?" This time the lady's question had a sharper bite to it.

"I belong there," Becky was quick to say.

"It's an unnecessary risk for you," Lady Arabella insisted. "You're welcome to stay here. At least for tonight. Hopefully, by tomorrow, Howard will have some good news and everything will change accordingly."

"She's right, Becky," Mac said. "Out there tonight is no place for you. Not when you've got a better, safer option. With any luck, nothing will happen. But in case it does . . . please."

"The Standing L is half mine. Those are my cattle. If somebody has to fight for them, it should include me," said Becky.

"Your brother's already got a bullet hole in him," Eamon told her. "If the both of you should go down, what of the Standing L in that case? Who'll fight for it then?"

Becky pressed her lips tightly together and nobody said anything for several seconds. Then, abruptly, she lifted the towel she'd been using to pat dry the back of Mac's head where she'd cleaned his gash, and tossed it on the table. Very softly, she said, "Go then, before I change my mind."

Chapter 44

Following directions from Lady Arabella, Mac and Eamon had no trouble finding their way back to the private livery barn behind The Lady A, where their horses had been stabled. Judging from the sounds drifting out into the night, there was still a good deal of activity taking place inside the saloon, though perhaps tapering down some as the hour grew later.

"Did you get your lungs sufficiently filled with saloon smoke before you got interrupted by Harcourt and Jerry Lee?" Mac asked, making small talk as they followed a path through a grove of trees back toward the barn.

Lighting their way with a lantern held at arm's length ahead of them, Eamon replied, "Not entirely. But encountering Lady Arabella and breathing in her intoxicating perfume instead was a welcome replacement . . . until those scoundrels interrupted that, too."

"Uh-huh. You and Lady Arabella go back quite a ways together, do you? Or is that prying too much?"

Eamon's grin flashed in the weak light. "It's prying, yeah. But I won't deny it. Moreover, it goes to a time that was quite special. Special enough, I find myself reflecting now, that I regret more than ever my part in allowing it to come to an end."

Mac had a hunch that asking more, unless Eamon went ahead on his own, *would* be prying too much. So, since they'd reached the barn anyway, he said nothing further.

Swinging out the wide double doors that opened to the barn bay, they were met with the heady smell of horses and fresh-cut hay and musty straw. Mac heard the familiar chuff of his paint. As Eamon found a nail sticking out from a support beam on which to hang the lantern he'd carried out, Mac found another lantern already mounted on a post that he struck a match to. The barn became bathed in illumination, showing a row of three stalls on either side.

The men started for the stalls, meaning to go bring out their mounts. They made it only a couple steps, however, before a voice calling from the doorway now at their backs stopped them in their tracks.

"Freeze right there where we can see you plain! Hold your arms out wide and keep your hands away from those guns."

Thinking they were probably being accosted by an employee of the saloon who mistook them for horse thieves, Eamon was quick to try to explain. "You're making a mistake, friend. Lady Arabella knows we're here, it was she who—"

"Silence! I care nothing for your pathetic excuses or

explanations. And the mistake is yours—*friend*—for the poor choice in associates you have made."

This came from a different voice than the first. There was an unmistakably imperious tone to it and . . . something more. An accent that Mac couldn't quite place, but felt he should. And on top of that, a vague familiarity that . . .

Mac's heart suddenly became a ball of stone, a boulder, crashing down to the pit of his stomach. That voice—from long ago and far away—was seared so deep by hatred and the smoldering desire for revenge that he couldn't be wrong. It was impossible yet he had no doubt. And inside him, there was an instant rage of conflicting emotion—part of him *wanting* it to be who he was convinced it was, part of him dreading such a harsh reality.

In response to the tenseness that gripped Mac's shoulders, the way his torso went straight and rigid, the voice continued, "Indeed it is so, Dewey Mackenzie. Your worst nightmare, my supreme delight. At last, you murderous wretch, your evasion of justice is over and it comes at my very own hand! All of your former fiancé Evangeline's tortured nights, haunted by the thought of you still on the loose and unpunished, will come to an end and it will only deepen her gratitude and affection for me!"

Mac couldn't hold back. He spun around to face the treacherous piece of scum he had been hating and running from for all these months. The act immediately caused the two men standing on either side of Pierre Leclerc to raise their arms and aim pistols at him, the snap of hammers being cocked seeming almost as loud in the quiet barn as if they'd pulled their triggers.

Eamon half turned with Mac and clutched him by one

arm. "Easy, boy! Try not to be in too big a hurry to get us both shot, eh?"

Mac's glare burned into Leclerc, planted boldly in the doorway between his two hired guns. He looked exactly the way Mac had last seen him—cocky, a disdainful glint in his eye. Exactly the way he had looked in a hundred dreams that had come to Mac in the middle of sweat-drenched nights, dreams that ended with that cocky look disappearing in a smear of bloody vengeance.

Oh, how Mac ached to make those dreams come true right there on the spot. But he didn't dare try, of course. Not just because those drawn guns would cut him down before he ever laid a hand on Leclerc, but also due to the risk it would bring to Eamon.

It wasn't until Mac managed to bring his rage and wildly vengeful thoughts somewhat under control that he took a closer look at Leclerc's gunmen. One of them he had never seen before. But the other . . .

"You!" The single word rasped from Mac's throat.

Quinn Blassingame, his jaw set tight, his expression grim, met Mac's eyes. "Sorry, kid. Just doing my job," he said in a flat tone.

"What the hell's going on?" Eamon suddenly blurted. "What's this crazy talk about murder and justice? And what 'job' gives you call to put us under your gun, Blassingame?"

"If you wish for any chance to walk away from this matter unharmed," responded Leclerc, "my advice for you is to stay perfectly quiet and do nothing to displease me."

"You got no quarrel with that man, Leclerc," said Blassingame. "He's part of the same cattle drive, true enough, but he doesn't know anything about Mackenzie's past trouble or the charges against him."

"How can you be so certain what he is or isn't aware of?"

"I spent time with them. I think I have a pretty good idea what—"

"I'm not interested in speculation, Mr. Blassingame," Leclerc cut him off. "Unless you have facts to offer, I am perfectly capable of forming my own opinions. You've done a good job up until now, don't ruin it by overstepping your bounds."

Blassingame's mouth pulled into a grimace, but he held his tongue.

"Very well," declared Leclerc. "You have one more task to perform, then we can consider this matter satisfactorily and officially concluded."

"What task is that?" Blassingame wanted to know.

"I should think it obvious. The town marshal you mentioned earlier—the 'rumpot,' I believe you called him? I feel it only fitting and proper to include him in serving the Wanted papers on our Mr. Mackenzie. A drunkard though he may be, the marshal can be our legal authority for witnessing this apprehension now that I have fulfilled my desire to successfully capture the fugitive."

"Why not just take the prisoner to the jail? That's where we'll likely find the marshal anyway."

"Why not simply do as I say instead of questioning everything?" Leclerc snapped. "I'd rather not go parading through the streets of this miserable eyesore brandishing guns, thank you, without the marshal accompanying us. Mackenzie may have accomplices lurking about who'd like nothing better than to attack us from the mouth of some dark alley."

Blassingame started to make another protest, but then held it in check and said instead, "All right, if that's how you want it. But keep a sharp eye on the prisoner. Like you keep reminding me, he's proven plenty tricky in the past."

"Don't you worry about it, Mr. Detective," said the hawk-faced Driscoll. "He ain't pulling no tricks, not when I'm the one who's got him covered."

In concert with that, Leclerc reached inside the lapel of his finely tailored suit jacket and withdrew a short-barreled, nickel-plated revolver. He pointed the shiny weapon with predictable flourish as he announced, "Nor am I unprepared, if need be, to assist in ensuring Mackenzie's captivity is maintained. Now, if you please, go fetch that marshal, Blassingame."

A moment later Blassingame had turned from the doorway and disappeared into the murkiness outside.

Leclerc stood gazing at Mac, his mouth curved into a wide, smug smile above the gaping muzzle of his pistol. "So, at long last, the moment has arrived. We face each other once again, Mackenzie. I must say, the interim has not treated you well. You are weathered and worn by the elements, weary looking from running like the frightened rabbit you have been all this time. Fleeing from the legion of dogs I have relentlessly sent after you."

"You may be right," Mac allowed. "But you haven't changed much at all. You still look exactly like the piece of slime I remember."

Leclerc's smile widened. "Yes, you always had a mouth on you, didn't you? All mouth, no brains. Had it been otherwise, all of this could have been avoided. If you'd been smart enough to recognize your place, accept you were never good enough for a woman of Evangeline's stature, none of this would have been necessary."

Mac felt the rage inside him coming to a fresh boil. "Necessary? What was it about my love for Evangeline—

and hers for me, until you poisoned her mind against me—that made it necessary for you to savagely murder her father and then frame me for the killing? Leading up to that, you'd challenged me to a duel, remember? You, the renowned duelist who'd already emerged the victor seven times, against me, the inexperienced bumpkin who was certain to go down as your eighth victim. Why wouldn't that have been good enough? Why make Evangeline suffer the torment of losing her father in such a horrific way and at the same time ruin what little I ever had—my good name—and put me through the living hell of a fugitive's life?"

Leclerc's mouth stretched wider, baring his teeth in a silent snarl and then emitting a short burst of disgust. "You simpleminded, unimaginative fool! Yes, I could have easily bested you in a duel. But what would that have gained me? The gratitude of banker Holdstock, to be sure, for removing you as the pesky, unsuitable lout his daughter had become infatuated with. But I was already in his favor as a suitable replacement so what more would such added gratitude accomplish? Oh, no doubt it would have been sincere and long lasting because the hearty old rascal himself showed every sign of being long lasting . . . which was part of the problem. The even greater problem was the fact that, even if I'd bested you on a field of honor, in Evangeline's eyes you would have been elevated to tragic hero status and I would have been relegated to the cad who put you there.

"So, you see, in order to gain all I was after with any expediency I had to resort to bolder measures. Measures calculated to still eliminate you while at the same time shortening father Holdstock's longevity and, in the process, endearing myself to Evangeline as the strong shoulder she could rely on at such grievous times and into the future." Leclerc paused to heave a somewhat fatalistic sigh before continuing. "I must say, it all succeeded quite well . . . with the exception of you not being eliminated by hanging for murder, as I'd envisioned, but rather escaping to a seemingly endless series of remote locations. As long as you were alive, I had to face the possibility you might return and somehow, some way find the means to ruin all I had so carefully set in place."

"You just admitted to murder in front of witnesses," said Mac through gritted teeth. "But you're not done yet, are you? You have no intention of keeping me alive until Blassingame gets back with the marshal. You mean right here and now to permanently eliminate any possibility of me ever tripping you up, no doubt claiming I tried a desperate escape and you had no choice but to shoot me down, is that it?"

"My, my. You're showing a flash of intelligence after all, Mackenzie," taunted Leclerc. "Unfortunately for you, it is too little too late. And unfortunately for your friend beside you, he must suffer for that tardy display as well . . . due to him being a witness to my admission, as you so astutely pointed out."

"What about your pal beside you," said Mac. "Doesn't that put him in the same boat?"

Leclerc chuckled. "Rest assured, I pay Mr. Driscoll well not to remember certain things he hears, sees, or participates in. Also, I know particulars from his past—things that would be very detrimental for him should they be revealed, which they will be if he ever allows anything to happen to me—that make him very loyal and trustworthy."

"I say that's enough talk," snarled Driscoll. "Apologize

to your friend for dragging him into this with you, Mackenzie, and then get ready to be thankful that your days of running are finally over with. . . ."

On the heels of those words came the rustle of sudden movement directly behind where Leclerc and Driscoll stood—the rustle accompanied by the squawk of metal hinges and the rushing sound of heavy objects moving rapidly through the air. Before the two gunmen could react in one way or another—either to fire on the targets in front of them or turn to whatever was happening behind—both of the tall double doors that had been standing open all this while came swinging inward with the force of having been whipped by a fierce wind. The sheets of side-by-side thick planks slammed into Leclerc and Driscoll, jolting them off balance, sending them staggering forward as they finally began triggering their guns.

The moment's hesitation by their captors, coupled with their aim being jostled when hit by the swinging doors, provided Mac and Eamon a chance to throw themselves out of the way of the sizzling lead that cut the air all around them. Both men hit the ground and went rolling frantically in opposite directions.

Crashing guns and angry curses filled the air, mixing with the shriek of frightened horses. Powdersmoke and kicked-up dust boiled in the pulsing gold light thrown by the lanterns.

Mac rolled until he bumped up against a stack of bloated feed sacks, all the while clawing to free the Smith & Wesson from his waistband. An instant after he bumped to a stop, a bullet whacked into the side of a stall less than a foot from his shoulder and a heartbeat later another one punched into a grain sack just inches over his head, the ruptured burlap releasing a stream of oats to pour down on him.

Across the way, Mac saw the flash and heard the roar of Eamon getting off a shot.

"Kill the lanterns!" Driscoll shouted from up near the front.

But it was too late. As he was reaching to follow his own advice, two long tongues of red-yellow flame licked out of the gap between the double doors that were starting to swing open again. The bullets hammered into Driscoll, lifting him up on his toes and causing a great shudder to pass through him. As he was starting to topple back, two more blasts pounded him and drove him the rest of the way down hard.

With the Smith & Wesson now filling his hand, Mac raked his gaze over the scene, looking for Leclerc. And then, in a moment of clarity between swirling clouds of dust and smoke, like the answer to a prayer, there he was. His face was smudged with dirt and twisted by fear and anguish at everything suddenly going so wrong.

"Here!" Mac shouted, wanting to make sure the French bastard saw who it was who was going to kill him.

When the dirty weasel's eyes darted to him, Mac was smiling as his finger stroked the trigger and the revolver bucked in his hand. A thumb-sized, red-rimmed dot appeared in the middle of Leclerc's forehead. His head snapped back and his body quickly followed, falling away and dropping with a flat, limp finality.

In the sudden silence, Mac swept his gaze again.

Eamon was across from him, on his knees, apparently unharmed.

In the widening gap between the double doors at the front, a stringy-haired, wild-eyed Marshal Calder—Blazing Bill—stood poised with a smoking Frontier Colt in each hand.

Stepping up beside him, also with a drawn Colt in hand, was Quinn Blassingame.

Chapter 45

The sound of the shooting naturally drew a crowd from inside the saloon, Becky and Lady Arabella included.

Marshal Calder took charge and did a good job of getting the situation under control in short order, even though he used a healthy dose of fabrication to do so.

"Two assassins clear up from New Orleans have been fatally dealt with," he claimed to those clustered out in front of the livery barn. "An old friend of mine, Quinn Blassingame of the High Grade Detective Agency out of Denver, has been on their trail for a long time. He tracked them here, where he enlisted my help to apprehend them. Unfortunately for them, they decided not to go easy. They made a fight of it, and they lost.

"That's all there is to say for right now, until we get some more details ironed out. So you folks go on about your business. Better yet, considering the hour, get on home to your beds. There'll be more to tell you come tomorrow."

With the crowd dispersed and kept that way by a burly bouncer from The Lady A stationed outside on orders from the marshal to bust heads if he had to, the doors to the livery were again closed and a smaller group gathered inside, consisting of Calder, Mac, Eamon, Blassingame, Becky, and Lady Arabella. They settled into a discussion of the true facts.

"Here's what was at the center of it all," said Blassingame as he handed around one of the Wanted posters on Mac. "Sorry to let out your secret, Mackenzie, but it doesn't matter anymore now. The real truth behind all the lies claimed there—the fact that the actual murderer was Leclerc himself and the rest was all an elaborate frame to get you hanged and him elevated through marriage into the Holdstock banking fortune—got revealed by Leclerc himself in front of three witnesses. Considering what happened to him just seconds later, you could almost call it a deathbed confession. And that's enough to get you cleared in any court in the land, even down in New Orleans."

Becky lifted her eyes from the paper and cast them softly on Mac. "Oh, Mac," she said. "Being under the weight of these awful lies for all this time, never being able to stay in one place for too long, never knowing who you could trust . . . It must have been so dreadful for you."

"The hardest part was not being able to open up to folks I *did* want to spend time with and put my trust in," Mac told her.

"Unfortunately, I was almost a prime example of why you had to hold back your trust," Blassingame said. "It's obvious, I guess, that it was you, not the Ivers gang, Muncie and I were after when we showed up back on the trail. But we were under orders to hold off on doing anything until we got here, where Leclerc, our client, would be waiting to be in on apprehending you personally. In order to satisfy that requirement we had to keep you from any harm at the hands of the Iverses . . . not realizing we were saving you for intended assassination."

"How did you figure out that's what the Frenchman had in mind?" Eamon asked.

Blassingame grunted. "The more time I spent with him in person, the more of a bad feeling I got about him. And that lowlife gunman Driscoll he was dragging around with him pretty much sealed the deal. I didn't know *exactly* what the two of them had in mind, but I had a strong hunch that a fair trial for Mackenzie wasn't any part of it."

"Yeah, and I almost got the same treatment they had in mind for Mac." Eamon aimed a sour expression at Mac and added with mock seriousness, "Thanks a lot, by the way, for causing me to get about ten years scared off my life. From here on, *I'm* going to be somebody who won't be so quick to make new friends."

Mac grinned and then said to Blassingame, "So, after Leclerc sent you to fetch the marshal, how did you get back here so quickly with him? And what made you wait outside the door, just listening?"

"Yeah, listening until blasted near too late!" lamented Eamon.

"I didn't have far to go when I left here to fetch Bill. I already had him waiting outside," Blassingame explained. "When Leclerc sent me earlier to find out where you'd gone after getting out of jail, I quickly determined you were here at Lady Arabella's. That's when I looked up the marshal, told him my suspicions, and asked him to shadow me without being seen until we found out where things would lead once I returned to the Frenchman."

"Well, I guess it's clear enough now where and how everything ended up," said Calder, his mouth twisting grimly as his gaze swept over the sprawled forms of Leclerc and Driscoll.

"Indeed it is," agreed Lady Arabella. Then, arching one brow somewhat skeptically, she added, "I can't say I'm particularly pleased with turning my livery barn into a shooting gallery, but at the same time I can't argue with the results."

"Yeah, and something *I* can't argue with," said Calder, "is what Quinn reminded me of earlier today when he told me that sometimes whopping polecats with a gun barrel ain't always sufficient. Hell, we swatted these two skunks with *barn doors* and still had to end up shooting 'em. I guess what works for Earp don't necessarily work for everybody."

"Never mind about Earp or Hickock or Masterson or any of the rest," Blassingame said. "You're Blazing Bill. That's good enough all on its own."

When the others echoed this sentiment, even Lady Arabella, the old marshal beamed appreciatively.

In the midst of this, the door opened a crack and the bouncer stationed outside stuck his head in to say, "Pardon me, Lady Arabella, but there's a fella out here—Howard Schumacher—who claims it's real important he talks to you."

"By all means, let him in."

Moments later, plump, rumpled, and very anxious seeming Schumacher was ushered in. But after his gaze had swept the room, lingering first on the dead bodies and then on Blassingame, he seemed suddenly hesitant to get into whatever had brought him.

Sensing this, Lady Arabella urged him, "You can feel free to talk in front of everyone here, Howard. Get on with it."

Schumacher cleared his throat, still looking a bit reluctant. Then: "I just got back from the north end of town, visiting a couple of the gaming operators there to see if I could get some backing for our plan. While I was doing that, I caught wind of something that's bound to mean trouble." He paused to again glance at the bodies of Leclerc and Driscoll before adding, "Well, more trouble, I guess I should say."

"More trouble how? Get to the point, man," said Calder.

Schumacher's brow puckered. "It's Harcourt. He's really stirring things up. Word is spreading through the shanty businesses that he's looking to hire men for gun work. Ten to a dozen, and he's paying top dollar. I couldn't get any clear details beyond that, but the word is spreading fast and men are stepping forward even faster."

"He's planning to hit the herd," responded Eamon. "That's got to be it!"

"Seems like an awfully desperate move for him to make," said Mac, grimacing. "But you're right, I can't think what else it could mean."

"Somebody's got to warn my brother! And Ned and Ox," Becky said.

"That's what we were on our way to do," Mac reminded her. "And now it's more important than ever that we get to 'em!"

As he and Eamon wheeled simultaneously, heading for the stalls that held their horses, Lady Arabella said,

"But just two more of you won't be enough to stand up to a dozen hired guns, no matter how much warning you have."

"I can fix it so there's more than just two," Calder declared. "I *am* the marshal around here, remember. I'll whip up a posse as soon as I can call together some of the men I just got done chasing home."

"I'll be the first one signing up to ride with you," said Blassingame.

"You do that, and much obliged to the both of you," Mac called over his shoulder as he continued to lead his paint from its stall. On the other side, Eamon was doing the same with his horse. "But you'll have to excuse us for not waiting."

"Understood," Calder told him. "You go ahead, we'll be there shortly. Come on, Quinn, let's start rounding up some boys!" As the two men crowded out the door, the old marshal hollered back, "Just make sure you don't shoot when you see us coming!"

Chapter 46

"What a couple of slackers!" exclaimed Marcus Lewis. "Is that all you accomplished the whole time you were gone? A couple of shoot-outs, a hitch in jail, dodging a trumped-up murder charge . . . what did you do then? Take a nap on some couch in that saloon lady's fancy apartment?"

"How do you know Lady Arabella has a fancy apartment?" Eamon asked with a sly grin.

"Because I had a good look at *her*, that's how," replied Marcus. "I speculate nothing about that gal is *un*-fancy."

"Matter of fact, you'd be right," Eamon told him. "But you ought to be ashamed, doing that kind of speculating about a lady. And if she ever heard you call her 'a gal,' your speculating days might be over permanent-like."

Talk of the lovely Lady Arabella had the other men gathered around the campfire grinning, too.

Until Mac said, "What I speculate, now that we've filled you in on all that took place while we were in Rattlesnake Gulch, is that we'd better start making ready for the visitors we figure are gonna be headed our way. And I don't mean the marshal and his posse."

"You really think there's a chance Harcourt can scare up enough men for a raid that fast?" asked Ox.

"Maybe, maybe not." Mac wagged his head. "I don't know when he started putting out the call or how fast he got his dozen takers. It wasn't all that long ago that Schumacher got wind of it, but it may have already been spreading for a while by then."

"Mac's right. Safest way is to make ready as quick and thorough as we can," said Ned.

"How we gonna do that? Set up a dummy camp again?" asked Marcus.

Mac looked thoughtful for a minute, then answered, "Reckon that would be best. Be most thorough, like Ned said. But if Harcourt's sending a dozen men, probably headed by Jerry Lee and maybe Orton, then it could be they'll go straight for the herd and not bother with whoever's in the camp unless somebody comes out to try and stop 'em."

"You figure they're aiming to *take* the herd?" said Marcus. "That would be mighty bold and at the same time kinda stupid, wouldn't it? What would they do with 'em? Where would they take 'em to sell or get any benefit?"

"I got no answer for that. That part's a puzzle," admitted Mac.

"Well, Harcourt ain't sending a dozen or so hired guns to shoo the flies off their backs, that's for certain," stated Eamon.

"Could be he's figuring to just hoorah the herd . . . and us," suggested Ned. "Maybe set 'em off on another stampede, maybe shoot a few, maybe pick off a couple of us in the process."

"What would be the sense in that?" said Marcus.

"Make it harder—and less desirable—for you to hang on to 'em. Make you more willing to sell at a cut-rate price rather than risk losing the whole works, including some of our crew." Mac's eyes narrowed. "I think Ned may have hit on the answer."

Fifteen minutes later they had the fire choked to a few meager flames, as if it had died down on its own, and there were five empty but plumped-up bedrolls arranged around the edges of the weak light circle it gave off. The men were gathered at one end of the chuckwagon, discussing how best to position themselves in anticipation of the raiders they believed would be showing up at some point, when they heard the low rumble of horses ascending the slope that led down to Rattlesnake Gulch.

"That should be the posse coming, but everybody spread out just in case," Mac told the others.

Moments later, a familiar voice called, "Hello, the camp! This is Marshal Calder with the posse I promised I'd be bringing."

"Come ahead, and welcome," Mac returned.

In the spray of moonlight and starlight that added a faint wash of illumination along with that of the low fire, a cluster of riders came up onto the flat above the slope and into the camp. Calder and Blassingame were in the lead, another eleven well-armed men behind them.

As he scanned the way the camp was set up, with the low fire and the rigged bedrolls, a corner of Blassingame's mouth tugged back wryly and he said, "This looks familiar."

"When a plan works, a body is inclined to stick with it," said Mac. "What we're chewing over now, without knowing when or from where those polecats will be coming, is how to place ourselves in order to be best suited for turning them back. You fellas showing up gives us a heap more options."

"And we think we brought an option of our own," said Calder.

"How so?"

"What if you knew where those raiders were forming up? Might the notion appeal to you to head out and pay them a visit instead of waiting for them to pay a visit here?"

"You're blasted right it would!" blurted Eamon.

"The marshal can be a hot-tempered and stubborn man," explained Blassingame. "First, he decided it plumb ticked him off to have Harcourt pulling the kind of shenanigans he was up to. Then it occurred to him that the pistol-whipping habit he'd gotten so fond of wasn't worthy of being cast aside after all."

"You're blasted right it wasn't," Calder declared. "And once I'd laid the barrel of my Colt alongside Harcourt's head a couple of times, he was quick to see the error of his ways and real eager to make amends by telling me where he'd sent all those hired guns to meet up with Jerry Lee and from there make their raid on your cattle."

"You mean you know where they're camped?" said Mac.

"That's what I said, didn't I? I recognized the exact

spot from the directions that skunk gave me," Calder replied. "It's a box canyon only a couple miles west of town. Would you like me to show you?"

Mac looked around at Marcus and the others. The eager expressions on their faces gave him all the answer he needed. "What are we waiting for?"

Chapter 47

"You ask me, these hombres Harcourt sent out make for a pretty sorry lot," Floyd Sleet was lamenting. "Bein' sided by a pack of scruffy half drunks don't exactly make me feel comfortable going into a shooting situation."

Jerry Lee frowned at him. "We're going to hoorah a bunch of cows, pop off some rounds to scatter 'em, maybe knock down a dozen or so . . . how is that a shooting situation? The cows gonna return fire?"

"And what's the Standing L crew gonna be doing while we're raising hell with their cattle? They ain't gonna come out to do some shooting back?"

"By the time they get untangled from their bedrolls it'll be too late," Jerry Lee said. "Their cattle will be scattering to Hell and gone. That'll be their main concern.

And what if they do come a-shootin'? We got 'em out-numbered about three to one."

"One is all it takes if it's a bullet with your name on it," spoke up Roy Orton. "And if that Mackenzie is part of the lead throwing, that counts for a lot. Already this night I seen him cut down Edsel clean as a whistle."

"Yeah, and what was Edsel doing? He was drunk enough to think he'd got fast with his left hand," Jerry Lee sneered. "He wasn't, nohow. But if he'd still had his right, it would've been a different story."

"Either way, he's dead, and so is 'Bama. And they wasn't no couple of scruffy no-accounts," pointed out Sleet.

Jerry Lee threw up his hands. "So what do you want me to do? Go back to Harcourt and tell him you two are out unless he brings in the Prussian army or some such to back our play?"

The three were standing slightly apart from a large campfire around which a dozen men Harcourt had sent from town were gathered. They were all stoked with the promise of action and a good payday and were jabbering too boisterously amongst themselves to overhear any of what Jerry Lee, Sleet, and Orton were discussing. Plus, to help keep themselves stoked, there were three or four bottles of whiskey being passed around.

"I ain't asking for no army," Sleet said in protest to Jerry Lee's sarcasm, "but that don't mean I want to settle for no drunken mob, either. Can you at least get those bottles of hooch away from them and pour some coffee down their gullets instead? If we're gonna hold off riding out until just before daybreak, maybe by then a few of them will be able to sit their saddles straight."

Jerry Lee scowled at Sleet for a long moment. Then, after glancing over at the rowdy crowd of hired guns, he said through gritted teeth, "You're right about that much. Roy, get a big pot of coffee brewing, you hear."

Turning back to those around the campfire, Jerry Lee raised his voice to be heard above their row. "Listen up, you pack of roughnecks! Now that you're here, it's me you're taking orders from. And my order for here and now is to get rid of those whiskey bottles! There's gun work coming up in a couple hours, just before daybreak, and I want clear heads for that. Afterward, you can drink yourselves blind and I'll provide the first bottle. But that's *afterward*, you got it?"

The pack of gunmen went quiet and their murky faces swiveled to aim displeased frowns at Jerry Lee.

Jerry Lee weathered the hard looks and returned as good as he got. "Sorry, but that's the way it's got to be. Now, that's Roy Orton over there putting together the makings for a pot of coffee. If you're thirsty, once it's boiled up I suggest some of you gulp down plenty of that. If that ain't good enough, you're free to leave."

There was some foot shuffling and a few grumbles from the pack but, one by one, the whiskey bottles were put away and nobody made any move to leave.

But then, coming from the darkness on the perimeter of the camp, a new voice suddenly rang out. "Hold off on that coffee—ain't no sense wasting it! And every one of you skunks make like fence posts and plant yourselves real still! This is Marshal William Calder and I got forty deputies surrounding your camp with shoot-to-kill orders on anybody who don't do exactly as I say!"

To give emphasis to the marshal's words there came

the unmistakable ratcheting of several rifle hammers being thumbed back to full cock.

The men around the fire froze and their eyes went wide and glisteningly bright in the flickering illumination.

Until Jerry Lee, his voice quavering slightly, responded, "You're the marshal of Rattlesnake Gulch. You got no jurisdiction clear out here."

"I say otherwise! And so do the forty guns leveled on your bunch!"

"You're bluffing! You ain't got no forty guns!" Jerry Lee challenged.

Calder's voice was hard as steel, replying, "There's one sure way to find out, though you won't be around for the final tally on account of I got my sights set square on you for the first bullet if there's any trouble."

"Why draw down on us at all?" demanded Sleet. "We ain't doing anything wrong."

"Not yet, you ain't. I aim to keep it that way. Now start shucking those gun belts, and don't make no sudden movements getting the job done!"

A tense silence clamped down over the scene.

From where he crouched in thick, shadowy under-brush just outside the reach of the campfire's light, Yellow-boy held at the ready, Mac sensed that the men out in the clearing were on the brink of giving in, surrendering without trying to make a futile fight of it.

But then one man, one stupid fool, faceless within the mass, broke. "Nossir! I ain't throwing down my irons for nobody! Somebody kill the fire!"

Just that fast, in the matter of a single second, the rest broke, too. One or two did take time to make hurried attempts at kicking dirt over the fire, but most immediately wheeled and rushed toward where the horses were picketed. As they ran, they pulled handguns and began firing blindly, indiscriminately into the darkness surrounding the camp.

Anticipating that if anybody in the bunch tried to bolt they would go for the horses, the strongest concentration of deputies were assembled on the rim of the camp just ahead of the picketed animals. This included Mac, Eamon, Calder, and Blassingame. As the wave of gunmen rushed toward them, throwing a wild hail of lead as they came, the waiting line of men met them with a punishing volley. Mac saw his target stagger and fall, as well as others on either side of him. But more kept coming, and even as he levered a fresh round to fire again, Mac was uncomfortably aware of bullets slapping and cracking through the leaves all around him.

Powdersmoke rolled thick and the throbbing wash of campfire light quickly diffused into a mustard-colored haze filled with shadowy, jerky shapes and repeated flashes of fresh gunfire. The roar of the guns and the shrieks of the picketed horses filled the night.

Mac fired again, unsure if he'd hit anybody this time or not. Off to his right he heard a sudden loud grunt that made him fear one of his comrades had been struck. As he turned his head to look, someone came barreling out of the haze and rammed into him full force, knocking him onto his back and landing on top of him. Having lost his grip on his rifle, Mac instead clutched his assailant, grinding out a curse through clenched teeth, and rolled to one side so that they fell into a flailing, struggling tangle.

Whoever his opponent was didn't lack for either size or strength, and he clearly knew a few tricks about rugged infighting. Mac took a hard elbow smash to the side of his head and a knee driven into his stomach before he managed to get one arm free enough to throw a return punch.

It was a good one, though, a solid right landing on the hinge of the other man's jaw. It seemed to briefly stun him, cause him to sag against Mac for just a fraction of a second. Which gave Mac both time and an opening to jerk his head forward and slam his forehead against the other's face as hard as he could. In the different cattle outfits he'd ridden with, Mac had been involved in his share of scuffles, enough to learn a few infighting tricks of his own.

The head smash he landed knocked his opponent away, broke apart their entanglement. But Mac didn't let the other man get very far. He scrambled after what was only a shadowy shape and threw himself on it, instantly raining down punches and kicks, giving the polecat no chance to raise his hands either in defense or to strike back.

As he was doing his best to pound the man into the dirt—all the rage and frustration pent up in him from all he'd been put through as an unjustly accused fugitive suddenly finding a release—Mac was vaguely aware of the shooting elsewhere around the camp starting to sputter and lessen, and then abruptly end.

Until the next thing he knew, Eamon was grabbing his arms and pulling him back, shouting, "That's enough, Mac! Enough! You've beaten him and the rest of it is over, too. Take it easy, man!"

Mac sagged back, collapsing into Eamon's arms, feeling totally spent for a moment. But the gravity of the situation made him quickly pull away and shove to his feet.

His gaze swept the scene, straining to penetrate the swirling clouds of smoke and dust in order to comprehend it all. There was a cluster of hazy forms in the middle of the camp standing very still, with hands raised to shoulder height and several rifle-wielding shapes encircling them. On the ground lay other shapes, motionless.

"How is our side?" asked Mac. "Did any of ours get hurt?"

Eamon said, "A few scrapes and bullet burns, nothing worse that I know about . . . except for one."

Mac remembered the grunt he'd heard that made him think someone near him had been hit. "Who?" he demanded.

"Over here." Eamon gestured, his expression grim.

It only took a couple steps for them to reach where somebody lay on the ground with three others kneeling close around him. One of the three was Ned Baker, bent over the wounded man—William Calder. The marshal's head was resting in Blassingame's lap, his shirtfront pulled open to reveal, just above the beltline, a still-seeping bullet hole that Ned was intently trying to stanch.

Calder appeared conscious and alert, though his lips were peeled back in a painful grimace. "Gut-shot by some stumbling sonofapup banging away blindly in the dark . . . Can you beat that luck?" He groaned.

"Just lie still and stay quiet," Blassingame told him. "You haven't turned over your aces and eights yet."

"Just give me time, the cards are falling slow is all. You think I ain't been around enough bullet wounds in my time not to know the real deal? That blasted Hickock . . . at least he had the luck to take his bullet where it was quick and final."

His voice thickening, Blassingame said, "But he took it in the back holding nothing but a handful of paste boards. You took yours in the front with Colts filling your fists."

A shudder passed through Calder and then he managed a somewhat ghastly smile. "That's right, old friend. See to it they remember it that way, you hear? Blazing Bill to the end!"

A moment later, his chin dropped forward onto his chest and he was gone.

Chapter 48

They buried William Calder two days later. There was a large turnout, including a heartfelt eulogy spoken by Quinn Blassingame.

In the interim, much else happened in and around Rattlesnake Gulch.

Of the men who gathered to cause trouble for the Standing L cattle herd, four were killed in the shoot-out and three received minor wounds. Roy Orton was one of those killed. Of the survivors, all were run out of town with the exception of Jerry Lee, who was jailed awaiting formal charges pending the arrival of a U.S. Marshal who had been summoned from Great Falls. Jerry Lee's claims, when addressing the group in their camp, of "gun work" and "it's me you're taking orders from" and raising hell had been overheard by all of the deputized posse, making them strong witnesses against him.

Jerry Lee, on the other hand, even though he was a known accomplice of Harcourt and it had been widely circulated that Harcourt would be bankrolling the gang, refused to name the powerful businessman as having anything to do with the plans against the Standing L herd. Jerry Lee insisted it was all his idea. With no hard evidence against him, Harcourt promised Jerry Lee he would provide him the best lawyers available and then promptly made tracks back for Harcourt City.

With Harcourt's departure, the Rattlesnake Gulch town council promptly declared temporary custody of all his recent business acquisitions until such time as more binding legal arrangements could be made. The first action taken after that was to reopen the cattle pens and slaughterhouse and to get the Standing L cattle herd finally brought in.

The backers Schumacher had put together were waiting to buy the lot at forty dollars a head and the residents with beef-starved bellies and fat pokes began instantly clamoring for the butchering to begin so they could see some results on their dinner plates.

In the lull that came following the funeral, a somewhat subdued yet still intense meeting took place in Lady Arabella's finely appointed parlor. Present were Marcus and Becky Lewis, Mac, Eamon, Blassingame, and of course the lady herself.

"Looking at all of you gathered here," Lady Arabella said, "it's hard to believe the short time any of you have been present in our town and yet the impact you've had in that brief period."

"Some impacts can be good, some bad," said Eamon. "How would you rate ours?"

The dark-haired beauty shook her head. "Oh, no.

You're not going to trap me into making that assessment. For one thing, it's hard to tell what the lasting effects will be."

"Measuring lasting effects on a boomtown can get mighty tricky," Blassingame said. "If the gold runs out in the surrounding hills, like it can in a heartbeat, just the way it has in countless other places, then all this will be soon gone and barely a memory."

Lady Arabella arched a brow. "There's a cheery thought."

"Well then, let's concentrate on some lasting effects from all of this that *are* cheery," said Becky. "We can start with the exoneration of Mac for that awful crime he was framed for and has been running from far too long. With the aid of Mr. Blassingame that can all be erased. Isn't that wonderful?"

"Sounds pretty good to me," Mac said.

"Let's just remember that it's likely to take a while for all of that to play out," Blassingame said. "I can begin sending wires and start calling in some of those dodgers as soon as I get somewhere there's a telegraph office. But to settle it completely, I can't see no way around a trip down to New Orleans in order to present testimony there. For which I'm willing to accompany Mac and stand by his side when the time comes."

"Well, that can't happen anytime soon," Eamon pointed out. "You're going to have your hands full with your job as the new marshal of Rattlesnake Gulch."

Blassingame held up one hand, palm out. "Whoa. I agreed to act only as the *temporary* lawman hereabouts. Once the U.S. Marshal shows up and the city fathers get around to appointing a new full-time town marshal, I'm done." Then, after a moment's pause, he cocked his head to one side and added, "On the other hand, when word gets back to the agency how I was in on the shooting of my latest client and then took this part-time position . . . well, I may *need* a new full-time job."

"Seems to me, there's a lot of folks suddenly taking on new jobs," said Marcus. He locked his gaze on Eamon. "I understand you're going to take over running The Golden Wheel for a while."

Eamon nodded calmly. "That's right. I convinced Schumacher and the council that, leastways until things get settled with Harcourt, I'm the right man for the job."

"Putting him directly in competition with me, I might point out," Lady Arabella remarked.

"Aw, you can take it. Competition brings out the best in everybody," Eamon said. "Besides, it wouldn't be the first time we were in competition with each other . . . and we survived that okay, didn't we?"

"We survived, let's leave it at that."

Eamon looked around at the others and gave a quick summary by way of explanation. "We once ran opposing roulette wheels on a Mississippi riverboat. Don't feel too sorry for her. Any time she was the one running her own wheel, how much attention do you think anybody paid me? I could have been spinning big winners every turn and more bettors still would have flocked to her."

"I guess that means, however things turn out with ownership of The Golden Wheel, you won't be returning with us. That what I'm hearing?" asked Marcus.

Eamon's expression turned serious. "Afraid so, friend. Accompanying you on the drive was an undertaking and an adventure I'll long remember and never regret. But it made it clear to me, as I indicated a short time back, that cigar smoke, whiskey fumes, sawdust on the floor . . . that's the world I prefer to inhabit."

Marcus wagged his head. "I'll never understand it. But to each his own, as the saying goes, and whatever you do from here on will never erase our obligation for your help in getting us this far."

"I appreciate that. I truly do," Eamon responded.

Everybody was quiet for a long moment.

Until Mac spoke. "I guess now is as good a time as any," he said, "for me to announce my own intentions from here. You see, much as I appreciate everything Mr. Blassingame is offering to do on my behalf—and I hope he follows through with as much as he can—there ain't no way I'm going back to New Orleans. There's nothing there I care about anymore and the pool of corrupt poison that I know remains ain't worth wading into, not even armed with the truth and a prime witness."

Blassingame frowned. "But if you don't go back, I doubt the charges against you will ever be completely lifted. No matter how much I spread the real story."

"I understand. And in no way do I want you to think I don't appreciate the help you're offering." Mac looked down at the floor, making eye contact with nobody. He sighed. "But going back flat ain't gonna happen. In fact, once things are put to rest here, my plan going forward is the same it's been for some time. I'm continuing on to California."

"You mean you're not coming back with us, either?" Marcus's question came with a pained expression.

Mac finally lifted his face. "Afraid not, Marcus. It ain't the right thing for me."

Then, reluctantly, he shifted his eyes to Becky. She was watching him with a wide, imploring gaze. Quietly, she said, "But I thought . . ."

"So did I, Becky. For a while." Mac shook his head

slowly. "But it wouldn't work. I've been thinking hard on it and there ain't no getting around the fact I still got too much wild left in me. Even if I ain't on the run. Just like Eamon craves saloon smoke and sawdust on the floor and the rest, the wide outdoors has got the same kind of hold on me. And the lure of California . . . I'll never be able to settle down until I make it there. Right or wrong, smart or dumb, it's under my skin and I can't fight it."

An awkward silence fell over the room.

It didn't last long, though, before Becky stood up and said to her brother, "I believe it's time for those of us who *are* going back to the ranch to start making preparations for getting started."

Marcus rose also, pushing himself up with the aid of the crutch Ned had fashioned for him. "Reckon so. Although I gotta say, there's one part of getting back I ain't particularly anxious for . . . and that's the fact Harcourt will still be there, probably planning ways to give us more grief."

"Not necessarily," Blassingame said. "Once the U.S. Marshal gets here and hears everything we've got to tell him, I have a pretty good hunch he'll be paying some mighty close attention to Harcourt even once he gets back where he's the big he-goose. Harcourt might find out that, under that kind of scrutiny, he don't honk near as loud as he thinks he does."

"That'd be a welcome thing," Marcus allowed.

The Lewises went ahead and took their leave.

Not long after they were gone, Lady Arabella looked around the room and settled her smoldering gaze on Mac. "If nobody else will say it, I will. You just broke that young girl's heart."

"I don't think so. Not really," Mac disagreed. "She

may think we go together like . . . like biscuits and gravy, but she's wrong. I did what's best for her. She'll realize that soon enough."

"What about you? Was it also the best thing for you?"

Mac didn't answer right away. Then: "I don't know. Reckon I'll find out the answer to that, along with a lot of other things, when I make it to California."

Mac said his good-byes and left shortly after that. He stood on the boardwalk out front of The Lady A, considering. Then, before he changed his mind, he went to look up Ned and Ox to say his good-byes to them. That done, he bought some provisions from Schumacher's store before retrieving and saddling his paint.

There was still enough afternoon left to cover several miles . . . on his way to the ocean.

Keep reading for a taste of the next Johnstone adventure!

**National Bestselling Authors
William W. Johnstone
and J.A. Johnstone**

**LAST STAGE TO EL PASO
A Red Ryan Western**

**Riding shotgun, Red Ryan leads a doomed stagecoach
of the damned on the longest, deadliest journey of his
life . . .**

According to local legend, the stagecoach known as the
Gray Ghost is either haunted, cursed, or just plain
unlucky. Each of its last three drivers came to a violent,
bloody end. And now it's Red Ryan's turn to guard five
foolhardy passengers on the stage's next—and possibly
last—trip to El Paso. The travelers are a small troup of
performers with dark histories of their own: a song-and-
dance man with a drinking problem, a juggler with a
secret, a knife thrower with a past, a singer, and a beautiful fan dancer who's on the run from a one-eyed,
vengeance-seeking outlaw . . .

Red's not the superstitious type. But with Apaches on the
warpath with bloodlust—and a one-eyed cutthroat killer
on his trail—this 400-mile journey is like something
straight out of his worst nightmare. And all the roads lead
straight to hell . . .

**Look for LAST STAGE TO EL PASO,
on sale now!**

Chapter 1

In the late summer of 1889, a six-horse team brought the Abbot and Morrison mail stage safely home to San Angelo . . . with two dead men in the box.

"How many does that make?" Captain Anton Decker said.

Long John Abbot looked miserable. Stunned. His bearded face ashen. "Six," he said. He shook his head. "I can't believe Phineas Doyle and Dewey Wilcox are dead. Just like that . . . dead."

"Believe it, they're all shot to pieces," Major Lewis Kane, the 10th Cavalry doctor, said. Gray-haired with a deeply lined face, he didn't appear too old to be a doctor but was well past his prime as an army officer. He climbed down from the box, shook his head, and added, "There's nothing I can do for them. They look like they've been dead for several hours."

Captain Decker, at twenty-seven, the youngest company commander in Fort Concho, was somewhat less than sympathetic. He badly wanted a name as an Indian fighter, but the Plains tribes were subdued and there was little glamour in fighting Apaches. "I'll report the incident to Colonel Grierson but I'm sure he'll agree that this is a civilian matter," he said.

"The army could help me round up the road agents that are responsible for my six dead," Abbot said.

"As I said, I believe it's a strictly civilian matter," Decker said. "Perhaps if your stages were carrying army payrolls we would've taken an interest, but since they were not, it's unlikely Colonel Grierson will become involved, especially after the 10th Cavalry moved out and left us so undermanned."

"I'll talk to the county sheriff," Abbot said. "But he won't do anything."

"Try him. He might round up a posse or something."

Abbot laid bleak eyes on the soldier. "He'll sit in his chair with his feet on his desk, drink coffee, and give me sympathy, not a posse."

"That's just too bad," Decker said. He saluted smartly. "Your obedient servant, Mr. Abbot. Now, see to your dead."

"Two more, Long John," said Max Brewster, a small man dressed in buckskins, dwarfed by Abbot's six foot six and maybe a little more height. "On the El Paso run like the other four."

Brewster had once been a first-rate whip until the rheumatisms in both hands done for him. Now he wore a plug hat and his stained and ragged buckskins and helped around the Abbot and Morrison stage depot. He favored a pipe that belched smoke that smelled bad.

"Phineas Doyle dead, murdered," Abbot said, shaking his head. "He was the best whip in Texas, bar none."

"And afore him, it was me," Brewster said. "Least-wise, that's what folks said."

"I ain't gonna dispute that, Max," Abbot said. He was a slightly round-shouldered man wearing a sweat-stained hat, a white collarless shirt, narrow suspenders, and black pants tucked into mule-ear boots. A man who had never carried a gun, he now had a Remington tucked into his waistband, a sure sign that the death of his men had shaken him to the core.

"A gray stage," Max Brewster said after a while. He shook his head. "Now, that's unlucky. The Indians say like black, gray is no color at all and it can betoken loss and sadness. There are some Arapaho, and Utes as well, who would rather freeze to death than use a gray army blanket. It disturbs the hell out of them."

"So, what are the other drivers saying?" Abbot said.

"I just left the Alamo saloon and it's all folks are talking about," Brewster said. "They're saying three drivers and three messengers shot dead and not a bullet hole to be found anywhere in the stage is mighty strange. I reckon that's why they're calling the coach the Gray Ghost. Some say it's haunted and it was the restless spirit of Phineas Doyle that drove it back here to the depot."

"That's foolish talk," Abbot said. "It's a coach like any other."

"No, sir, it's a coach like no other," Brewster said. "It's a death trap, just ask Frank Gordon and Mack Blair, Steve

Tanner and Lone Wolf Ellis Bryant, and now Phineas Doyle and Dewey Wilcox."

"They're all dead," Abbot said, irritated. "I can't ask them anything."

"And they're all dead because of the Gray Ghost," Brewster said. "Long John, it was your last stage to El Paso. You ain't never gonna find another driver or shot-gun guard to work for you."

Abbot watched as the undertaker and his assistant lowered the bodies from the seat of the coach, bloody corpses with blue faces, open eyes staring into nothingness. Phineas Doyle's gray beard was stained with blood and there was a wound that looked like a blossoming rose smack in the middle of Dewey Wilcox's forehead.

The undertaker, a sprightly skeleton dressed in a broadcloth suit with narrow pants and a black top hat tied around with a wide taffeta ribbon, the ends hanging over his skinny shoulders, laid the corpses on a flat wagon and then said, his voice like a creaky gate, "Same as the other four deceased, Mr. Abbot?"

"Yeah, Silas, board coffins but clean them fellers up nice for viewing," Abbot said. "The womenfolk like that."

"I'll take care of it," Silas Woods said. His eyes moved from Long John to the stage. "Gray," he said. "Now, that's unusual, a gray stage."

"I know," Abbot said.

"Gray as graveyard mist," the undertaker said. "Why gray?"

"A canceled order," Abbot said. "I was told it was originally destined for a count in Transylvania, a country in eastern Europe somewhere. The coach is worth eighteen hundred dollars and I got it for fourteen hundred."

"You didn't get yourself a bargain," Woods said. He shook his head. "No, sir."

Abbot watched the undertaker's wagon leave, drawn by a black mule. His great beak of a nose under arched black eyebrows gave Long John the look of a perpetually surprised owl. He turned and said to Brewster, "If I can't find a driver, I'm out twelve hundred dollars and out of business." He thought for a moment and said, "What about Buttons Muldoon?"

"He's working for Abe Patterson," Brewster said. "Muldoon's messenger is a young feller by the name of Red Ryan who's right handy with a gun and they say fear doesn't enter into his thinking. But I don't think those two will switch, and even if they did, they won't come cheap."

"All I can afford is cheap, the cheaper the better," Abbot said.

Brewster gave the man a long, speculative look and then said, "By the way, Abe Patterson is in town. He's over to his depot."

"What's that to me?" Abbot said.

Brewster smiled. "Long John, Patterson is made of money. Some folks say he's so rich he's got a half interest in the whole of creation."

"Made of money, huh?" Abbot said.

"Got a big, turreted mansion house up San Angelo way and a young, high-yeller wife to go along with it. A lively-stepping filly like that costs a man plenty and ol' Abe sure spends plenty on her."

Long John brightened. "Here . . . Max . . . you've given me an idea."

"I figured as much," Brewster said.

"Sure, Patterson is made of money. Like you said, everybody knows that. Hell, I can probably unload the stage. Abe won't pass up a bargain like that."

"How much, Long John?"

"How much what?"

"How much are you willing to take for the Gray Ghost?"

"I think maybe a thousand."

"Think again," Brewster said. "How much?"

"Nine hundred?" Abbot said, his face framing a question.

"Seven hundred and fifty and let him talk you down to seven hundred," Brewster said. "Abe will dicker and he's good at it."

"That's half what I paid for it," Abbot said. A thin whine.

Brewster smiled. "As the starving man said, *Half a pie is better than no pie at all*."

Abbot thought that through and said finally, "You think Abe will go for it?"

"Damn right he will," Brewster said. "A sharp business-man like Abe Patterson won't pass up a new Concord stage for seven hundred dollars."

"Maybe he doesn't know it's a bad luck coach," Abbot said.

"Long John, the whole town knows, and you can bet so does Abe," Brewster said. "But he ain't the supersti-tious type and to him a bargain, even if it's on the creepy side, is still a bargain."

"I could go into another business with seven hundred dollars," Abbot said. "I always figured I could prosper in hardware."

"There you go, Long John, selling pots and pans is just

the thing for a man like you. Help you make your mark in the world."

"Right, I'll go do a little hoss trading with Abe."

"Good luck, and don't let him get you under seven hundred, mind," Brewster said.

Long John Abbot poured another splash of whiskey into Abe Patterson's glass. "Abe, seven-fifty, and I can go no lower than that without starving my wife and children," he said. "Have a cigar."

Abe Patterson took a cigar from the proffered box and said, "I hope the cigar is better than your whiskey. And that wouldn't be difficult."

"Two-cent Cubans," Abbot said. "Top-notch." He passed on commenting on the busthead that he bought by the jug.

Patterson took his time lighting his cigar and behind a curtain of blue smoke said, "I'm thinking about it, Long John. Giving it my most serious consideration."

"Red leather seating, Abe," Abbot said. "Now, that's class. I mean, that's big city."

"What about the sign on the doors?" Patterson said. "Some kind of fancy letter *D*."

"Ah, the coach was a canceled order from some count in Transylvania . . ."

"Where?"

"Transylvania. It's a country in eastern Europe. I guess the gent's name began with a *D*."

"Davy? Donny? Deacon?"

"Something like that, I guess," Abbot said. "Them foreigners have strange notions and stranger names."

"Seven hundred," Patterson said. "I will go no higher.

Hard times, Long John, with the railroads expanding an' all, laying rails all over the place and taking a big chunk of my business. I just don't have as much capital to invest as I once did."

Abbot pretended to consider Abe's offer for a moment and then jumped to his feet.

"Done and done," he said. He extended his hand to Patterson, a feisty little banty rooster a foot smaller than himself. Abe took Abbot's hand and said, "Have some of your men push or pull the thing to my depot as soon as the blood is washed off the driver's seat. Then come over yourself and I'll pay you."

"I'm glad you don't believe all that loose talk about the stage being haunted and all," Abbot said.

Abe Patterson smiled. "If I did, I'd tell you to hitch up a team and have Phineas Doyle drive it over."

Chapter 2

"Phineas Doyle drove the stage back to the depot even though he was as dead as mutton," Patrick "Buttons" Muldoon said, his blue eyes as round as coins. "His ghost was standing over his shot-up body, the ribbons in his hands. Ol' Max Brewster says he seen that with his own two eyes and he says the coach was almost invisible, like a gray, graveyard mist."

"I don't believe it," Abe Patterson said.

"And Max says that letter *D* on the doors stands for death," Red Ryan said. "He says it must be a stage that carried the souls of the deceased and that's why Long John Abbot got it cheap."

"I don't believe it," Abe Patterson said.

"And, boss, you got it even cheaper, mind," Buttons said. He was dressed in a blue sailor coat decorated with two rows of silver buttons that gave him his name. He and Red Ryan had just arrived at the depot after a short mail run to Abilene and were mostly dust-free. "Boss, they call the stage the Gray Ghost and they say it's cursed," Buttons continued. "It's already been the death of six men and me and Red would make it eight."

"I don't believe it," Abe Patterson said.

Red Ryan said, "Max Brewster says that over to the Alamo saloon, Lonesome Edna Vincent, she's the red-head with the big . . ."

"I know who she is, and whatever she said, I don't believe it," Abe Patterson said.

"You haven't heard what I have to say yet," Red said. "Well, anyway, Max says that Edna says that she was asleep in her cot the very night the stage was delivered to Long John Abbot's depot. Then, when all the clocks in town chimed at the same time, saying that it was two in the morning, a loud and terrible scream woke her."

"I don't believe it," Abe Patterson said.

"Then Max says that Edna says she got up and looked out the window and then she heard the howls and wails of the damned coming from a gray coach. Max says that Edna says that the stage was rocking back and forth and seemed to be covered by an unholy blue fire. Max says that Edna says she got the fear of God in her and didn't get another wink of sleep all night."

Buttons said, arranging his features into an expression that passed for sincerity, "So, boss, after all them scary ha'ants you can savvy why me and Red can't drive the Gray Ghost. And now let us both thankee most whole-heartedly for your kindness, consideration, and under-standing."

"I don't believe it," Abe Patterson said. "I don't be-lieve that two grown men would set store by such nonsense. Road agents and maybe Apaches done for Long John's men, not a curse."

"But, boss . . ." Buttons said.

Patterson held up a silencing hand. "No buts. Here's the situation. You already know, or maybe you don't, that the Apaches are out, a dozen renegades riding with the four half-breed Griffin brothers."

"I heard them Griffin breeds were hung by vigilantes up in the New Mexico Territory," Buttons said. "Didn't you hear that, Red?"

Red shook his head. "No, I can't say as I did. But folks don't tell me much."

"Seems that you heard wrong, Mr. Muldoon," Abe said. "A Texas Ranger by the name of Tom Wilson told me that five days ago the Griffins and the Apaches with them attacked a ranch house to the east of here, killed three men, and ran off with a couple of women. Wilson said he doubts that the women are still alive, but if they are, by now they'll be wishing they wasn't." Abe consulted his gold watch, snapped it shut, and said, "Ranger Wilson had more to tell. He told me no later than this morning that Powell left Fort Worth four days ago. Remember him? The local lawman wired that Powell has took to wearing an eye patch, and he swears that him and his boys are headed south."

"Or so the lawman says. Nobody's heard of Luke Powell in years," Red said.

Buttons said, "Who is he? I never heard of him until now. Maybe I was at sea at that time."

Red said, "It was before my time as a messenger, when I was still cowboying for Charlie Goodnight's JA Ranch up in the Panhandle, that Powell worked his protection racket, guaranteeing owners that their stages wouldn't be robbed if they paid up. He made some good money at it, too. But the last I heard he was an expensive hired assassin who squeezed cash or property from the marks to spare their lives. That way he got paid at both ends. But he suddenly dropped out of sight two or three years ago. Some say he fled abroad to escape the law, some say he found religion, so who knows what happened to him."

Abe waved his cigar and blue smoke curled in the air. "Maybe Luke Powell has returned to his old ways and he and his boys killed Doyle and Wilcox last night or this morning . . . or the Apaches did. The Apaches would do it for fun and Powell out of spite because the Abbot stage carries mail and never a strongbox. Well, I should say that it did carry mail. Long John told me he's quit the business and he's transferring the mail and his passengers to me."

"Powell was never known to be a road agent," Red said. "It's not his style."

Buttons snorted his disbelief. "Of course it wasn't Powell or Indians or anybody else. Everybody knows it was the Gray Ghost its own self that done for them six fellers."

"Mr. Muldoon, I don't wish to hear that again," Patterson said, frowning. "The coach is now with the Abe Patterson and Son Stage and Express Company and you will kindly refer to it as Number Seven. Do I make myself clear?"

"Why us?" Red Ryan said. "Boss, you've got other drivers and messengers."

"None of them as reliable as you and Mr. Muldoon," Patterson said. "That's the fact of the matter."

"And suppose we refuse?" Buttons said. His chin was set and stubborn and the buttons on his coat shone like newly minted silver dollars.

"Ah, if you refuse to work?" Abe rubbed his chin. Suddenly his eyes had all the warmth of shotgun muzzles. "Hmm . . . well, in that case, you'll be dismissed instanter. And you'll never work for an employer more caring of his men than me. That is, if you can find another situation in these hard times."

Abe Patterson saw Buttons's crestfallen look and his face softened a little. "Here, have a drink." He opened a desk drawer and produced a bottle of Old Crow and three glasses. He poured the whiskey and said, "I know how you men feel, and I don't have a heart of stone. Your maidenly fears have not gone unheeded, and that's why I've chosen an easy run just for you . . . five theater performers to Houston, passengers as genteel and gracious as they come. Drink up, boys."

"I'll be driving the Gray . . ."

"Careful, Mr. Muldoon. I don't want to hear that name ever again, remember?"

"Driving ol' Number Seven," Buttons said, his face glum.

"Yes, and she's a beauty, ain't she?" Patterson said, beaming. "Red leather upholstery and curtains, special-order thoroughbraces so it feels like you're riding on a cloud. She's a work of art, by God, and once you get used to her ways, you lucky boys will love her."

Despite the warm caress of the whiskey, Buttons was still in a funk. "Three hundred and fifty miles of nothing but grass," he said, "on a route I've traveled only a couple of times afore, plus Apaches, the Griffin brothers, and road agents takes a heap of loving."

"And that's exactly why I kept the Houston run for you and Mr. Ryan," Patterson said. "The Apaches and the Griffin boys are raising hell to the west of us so you'll be well away from those savages. And Luke Powell need not concern us. The Ranger said he stays close to towns, especially Fort Smith and New Orleans, where there's whiskey and whores and pilgrims to be fleeced. I can't see him crossing an empty prairie, even to get his revenge on Miss Erica Hall." Abe spread his hands. "I'll tell you about her later. Now, Mr. Muldoon, don't complain. It will be an easy run. The way is smooth and the weather is fair. It will be like taking a bunch of flowers to your favorite maiden aunt for her birthday." He smiled. "And you boys can see paddle steamers in the Houston canal. Now, that's worth the trip, don't you think?"

"If we get there alive," Buttons said. "If ol' Number Seven doesn't decide to do for us like it did to them others."

"Well"—Abe's smile was as sincere as the grin on a Louisiana alligator—"it's come down to this . . . You boys have a choice to make and I can only hope it's the right one."

"And that is?" Buttons said.

"Get on the stage or get fired. Think it over."

"We've thought it over," Red Ryan said.

"And?" Patterson said.

"We'll ride the stage," Red said.

Buttons looked at him aghast. "Are you out of your mind?" he said.

"Study on it," Red said. "Summer's almost over and winter will come down fast. We got a cozy enough berth here in San Angelo and don't need to be spending December with empty bellies riding the grub line."

"And here's a kicker, a real humdinger as they say up Montana way. A twenty-dollar bonus for each of you after you deliver your passengers safely to the Diamond music hall in Houston, where they expect to be hired in a heartbeat, and I reckon they will," Abe said. "So there it is, gentlemen, an extra double eagle each for a nice, easy drive in the late summer sun. Even if you were my own sons, my own flesh and blood, I couldn't say any fairer than that."

"We'll take it," Red said. "When do we start?"

Abe glared at Buttons. "You don't look too sure, Mr. Muldoon."

"All right, I'll drive the gray stage," Buttons said. "I'm not a one to believe in ghosts and ha'ants an' stuff, but the first time it comes up with something spooky, I'll mount the passengers on the backs of the team and leave Number Seven right where it's at."

"It won't come to that pass," Abe said. "Trust me, you'll have a safe journey, I guarantee it. Now, let me read you the passenger list I got from Long John Abbot. Remember, these are all theater performers, what they call vaudeville artistes, so needless to say there will be no cussing, tobacco spitting, or crude jokes when you're around those nice people. Do I make myself clear?"

Red nodded, and Abe took that as a yes from both of the men. He balanced a pair of pince-nez spectacles at the end of his nose and read from a scrap of paper.

"As I said, all this is from Long John," Abe said. "He said the artistes came from Fort Worth to San Angelo on two different C. Bain and Company stages, and that Erica Hall is the main attraction. She's a fan dancer from England and by all accounts is a lovely lass."

"What's a fan dancer?" Buttons said. He was surly. He guessed fan dancing was another of those fancy, big-city notions that were steadily eating away at the already shaky foundations of the western frontier.

"According to Long John, Miss Hall dances naked around the stage with two Chinese fans, but she uses the fans to cleverly cover up her lady bits so nobody ever gets a glimpse," Abe said. He saw the puzzled expressions on Buttons's and Red's faces, shrugged, and said, "That's what Long John told me. I've more to say about her, but I'll leave that till later. The other woman is a singer, goes by the name of Rosie Lee. Then there's the Great Stefano, a knife thrower, Paul Bone, a song and dance man, and Dean Rice, a juggler." Abe took off his spectacles and laid them on his desk. "All in all, an interesting group of people."

"Boss, you said there's more to tell about the dancer gal," Buttons said. "Does she ever drop them fans?"

"I don't know," Abe said. "Maybe at the end of her turn."

"I'd sure like to see that," Buttons said. "I reckon I've never seen the like before."

"Maybe she'll dance for you on the trail," Abe said. "Stranger things have happened."

"Hee-haw! Now, wouldn't that be something," Buttons said.

"Boss, what else were you aiming to tell us about her?" Red said. Something deep inside of him feared that this was news he really didn't want to hear. And he was right.

Abe Patterson thought for a while and then said, "All right, you boys are boogered enough and I figured I wouldn't tell you, but now I've studied on the right and wrong of the thing, my conscience won't allow it. One thing about Abe Patterson, he's always fair."

"Now you got me worried, boss," Red said. "Wring it

out. Tell it slow and easy so we understand. Me and Buttons don't want any head scratching."

"Well, see, this is how it is, plain and simple," Abe said. "You know I told you that Luke Powell left Fort Worth with just one eye."

"Yeah, we know," Red said. "He's got a patch over it."

"Well, it seems that Miss Erica Hall made him that way," Abe said.

"What way?" Buttons said.

"The one-eyed way," Abe said. "Rosie Lee told Long John Abbot that Miss Hall took out one of Luke's eyes in Fort Smith with a hot curling iron. It was a quarrel over Luke cheating her out of some money and it turned violent. Rosie said it was Luke's shooting eye that got poked and he ran out of the hotel screaming in search of a doctor. Well, sir, Miss Hall packed a bag and wisely skedaddled on a C. Bain and Company stage that was just pulling out of town headed for San Angelo. Later Powell came back looking for her with a knife in his hand and only one eye in his head only to find that the bird had flown. Four days afterward, the other artistes talked with a driver who remembered the beautiful lady who boarded his stage at the last minute and the next day they fled in another C. Bain stage to San Angelo with all the luggage, most of it Miss Hall's."

"Luggage? Seems to me all she needed to pack was two fans," Buttons said. "Me and Red ain't boogered none by that story. It don't scare Red and me any."

"You ain't boogered because that ain't the scary part," Abe said. "The scary part is that chances are Luke Powell also talked to the same stage driver and by now he could know where Miss Hall is at. He's left Fort Worth, and

Rosie Lee says he vowed to take both Miss Hall's eyes and kill all he finds with her."

"All he finds with her . . . You mean, like me and Buttons?" Red said.

"That's what he means, all right," Buttons said. "And kill all he finds with her . . . It ain't a friendly thing to say."

"I told you, and now I'll tell you again," Abe Patterson said, "Powell will stay close to settlements. You won't see hide nor hair of him between here and Houston, trust me on that. And besides, Houston has an excellent police force. I'm told twenty-two stalwart officers stand ready to uphold the law and protect the innocent." Abe sighed and rose to his feet. "See, you boys got nothing to worry about. Now, if you will excuse me, I got to talk to the bank about a business loan." He shook his head. "Hard times coming down, boys, hard times."